A VICIOUS GAME

MELISSA BLAIR

UNION SQUARE & CO.
NEW YORK

UNION
SQUARE
& CO.
NEW YORK

ISBN 978-1-4549-4791-2 (paperback)
ISBN 978-1-4549-4792-9 (e-book)

Library of Congress Cataloging-in-Publication Data

Names: Blair, Melissa, 1995- author.
Title: A vicious game / by Melissa Blair.
Description: New York, NY : Union Square & Co., 2024. | Series: The Halfling saga | Summary: "With her enemies closing in, Keera and her fellow rebels must rally after a devastating defeat, but her discovery of new powers gives them a fighting chance"—Provided by publisher.
Identifiers: LCCN 2023033050 (print) | LCCN 2023033051 (ebook) | ISBN 9781454947912 (trade paperback) | ISBN 9781454947929 (epub)
Subjects: BISAC: FICTION / Fantasy / Romance | FICTION / Romance / LGBTQ+ / General | LCGFT: Fantasy fiction. | Romance fiction. | Queer fiction. | Novels.
Classification: LCC PR9199.4.B557 V53 2024 (print) | LCC PR9199.4.B557 (ebook) | DDC 813/.6—dc23/eng/20220322
LC record available at https://lccn.loc.gov/2023033050
LC ebook record available at https://lccn.loc.gov/2023033051

Union Square & Co. books may be purchased in bulk for business, educational, or promotional use. For more information, please contact your local bookseller or the Hachette Book Group's Special Markets department at special.markets@hbgusa.com.

Printed in China

4 6 8 10 9 7 5 3

unionsquareandco.com

Cover design by Gina Bonanno
Map art by Karin Wittig
Interior design by Colleen Sheehan and Jordan Wannemacher

To anyone who has ever been strong
enough to try again

Content Warning

This book is a fantasy romance that explores themes of alcoholism, addiction, relapse, colonialism, depression, and systemic violence. While it is not the focus of this book or depicted graphically on the page some content may be triggering for readers who have experienced self-harm, assault, domestic violence, depression, war, or suicidal ideation. It also contains on page sexual content.

Elverath

The Treaty of the Faeland
Aralinth
Caerth
Cereliath
The Dark Wood
The Burning Mountains
The Poison Fields
The Pool of Elvera
Myrelinth
Silstra
The Cliffs of Elandorr
Wolford
The Singing Wood
Belmoor
Volcar
The Barren Lands
The Frostlands
Exiles Rest

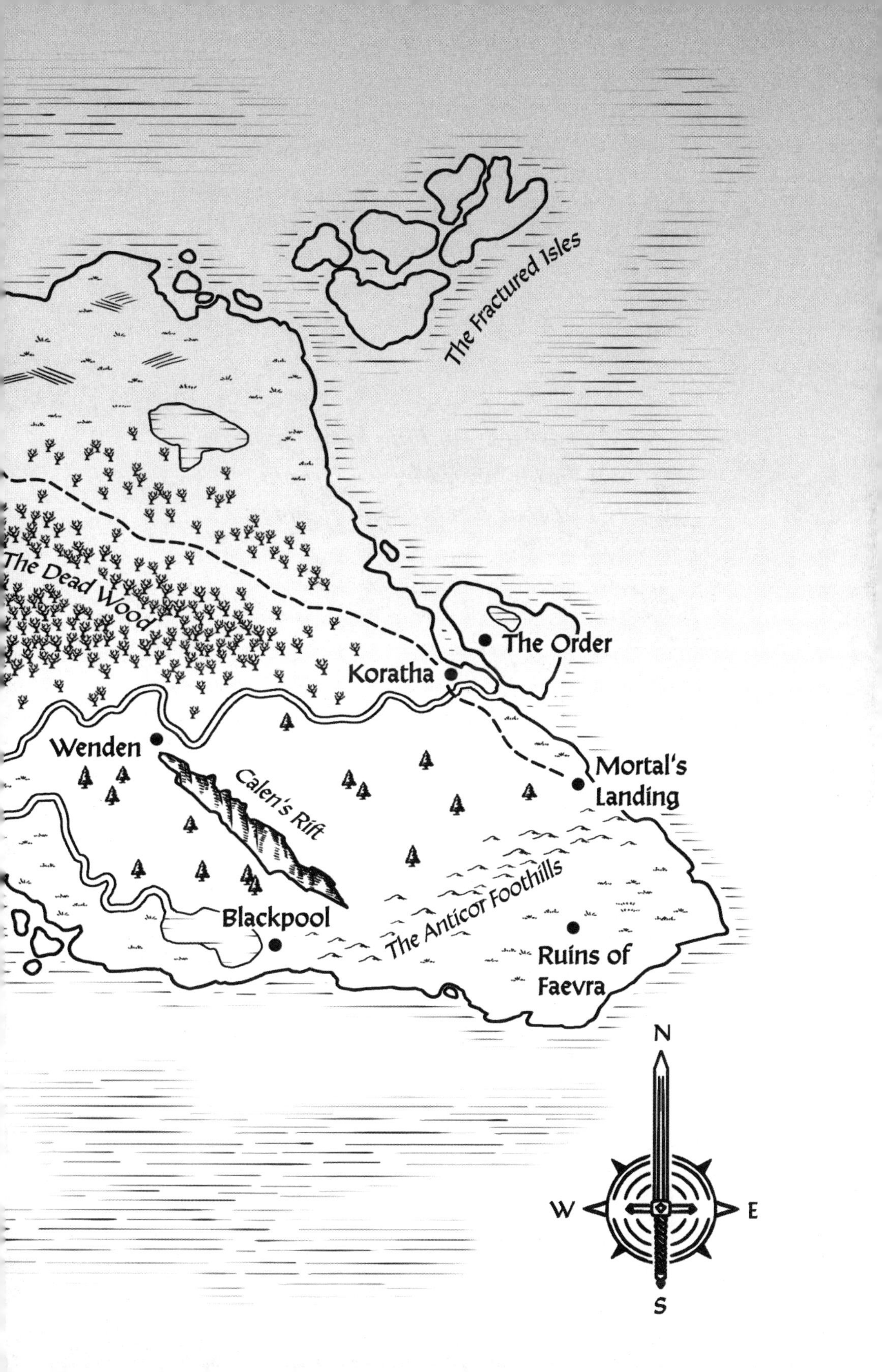
The Fractured Isles
The Dead Wood
The Order
Koratha
Wenden
Calen's Rift
Mortal's
Landing
The Anticor Foothills
Blackpool
Ruins of
Faevra
N
W
E
S

My past was nothing but a game,
A pawn moved by the Crown,
But that pawn began to play

CHAPTER ONE

A COLD WAVE CRASHED over me and drowned out my dreamless sleep. Unfortunately, it wasn't the first time I'd been woken up, in a stable, by having a bucket of water poured on my head. "Do you have a death wish?" I seethed through my teeth as I reached for the dagger at my hip, but it wasn't there.

Gerarda Vallaqar peered down at me with pure revulsion etched into her round cheeks and flat nose. If I didn't feel like there was an ax sticking out of my skull, I might've found it unsettling. Gerarda was short for a Halfling; she hadn't inherited any Elvish height from her immortal ancestors and was only as tall as a small Mortal woman. It might have been the first time she'd ever looked down at me in her entire life.

From her smug grin, I could tell she was enjoying it.

"This is pathetic, Keera." She waved her hand over the stall that had been my bed for the night. I was propped against a watering trough with a saddle blanket strewn over my legs. There was no horse in the stall with me but the scent of its shit lingered on my clothes.

I rubbed my temples, which did nothing to quell the headache. There was only one thing that could. "You speak as if I *meant* to spend the night in the stables."

Gerarda folded her arms over her chest. There was no longer any hint of a grin on her face. Only a stern expression that she'd learned from Hildegard, our mentor when we had trained together at the Order. I flinched and looked away. I didn't need any more reminders that Hildegard was dead. Or that her death had been my fault.

"That only makes it more pathetic," Gerarda mumbled. "You drank yourself into such a stupor that you couldn't find your way back to your room?"

Every muscle in my stomach screamed as I pulled myself into an upright position. I patted the ground, feeling for my wineskin. "I knew where my burl was. It didn't move." Even the sound of my own voice rattled the ache in my skull. It wasn't finding my burl that had been the problem, it was my inability to get up the Myram tree without falling to my death. If anything, I had been responsible. Not that Gerarda would give me the credit.

My fingers rubbed against something soft. I pulled the cork free from the skin and hung it over my mouth. A few droplets of rich Elvish wine splattered against my tongue and the burning in my throat eased a little. I let the wineskin drop to the floor of the stall and pulled myself up onto my feet. I slipped and whacked my entire body into the wall of roots.

Gerarda took a quick step backward. She made no move to help.

I closed my eyes and ignored the pain radiating from my ribs. They weren't broken and the bruise would be mended by my healing gift before it had time to fully ink my skin. “If I’m such a disappointment, why are you here?”

Gerarda glanced down the aisle between the two rows of stables to where the root-packed ceiling gave way to the outside air. “The Shadow is digging a hole around the Myram with his pacing.” Gerarda shrugged. “He may be too cowardly to say that you’re a pathetic excuse for a savior, but I’m not. Your sorrows are not bigger than this war, Keera. Even if you’ve given up.”

I scoffed and slammed my hands on the top of the stable door. It rattled hard enough to shake the others in a series of metal clanks that echoed down the corridor. “Given up? We *lost*, Gerarda. I may be a drunk, but I am not a fool. I attended the same meetings as you.”

Gerarda’s black eyes narrowed. “So you *choose* to do nothing while our sisters are left at the mercy of Damien? Left to be farmed for their blood until they’re too weak to breathe?”

My shoulders sunk to the ground. Gerarda spoke as if being haunted by what had happened to the Shades wasn’t the very reason I needed to pull myself into that familiar oblivion each night. “The Shades haven’t been spotted since Damien crowned himself king.” Two moons had passed since then. I didn’t say the rest aloud. If Gerarda had any hope that the Shades were still alive, I would not be the one to take it from her. Even when I knew there was no hope to be found.

Their helpless screams rung in my ears. I shivered at the memory. My throat dried as I swallowed down the truth. Gerarda would come to accept their deaths in her own time. I didn’t need to give her the details.

She folded her arms. I could have recited the script of her argument before her lips even opened. I thought it was best if we skipped to the end. “What is there left to do?” I threw my arms into the air. “Damien has raised an army larger than this continent has ever seen and adds more swords to it still. The Light Fae are gone. They are *never* coming back, and neither is their magic. The Shades are—" I stopped myself and kicked the door of the stable. A strong gust of wind blew down the corridor hard enough that Gerarda had to grab a root to stay upright.

I took a deep breath and tried to get my newfound powers under control. "Any mission to free the Shades would only end with more lives lost. Don't blame me for stating a truth you refuse to name."

Gerarda stretched up on the tips of her toes but she still didn't reach my chin. There was nothing but cold disgust on her face as she glowered at me. "Are you calling me a coward?"

I shook my head, already exhausted from the argument. "We can't rescue the Shades with a team of two, Gerarda. So who would you ask? Who would you call to sacrifice themselves for a fruitless mission purely to assuage your guilt?"

She pursed her brown lips as she fell back on her feet.

I didn't give her time to answer; my words were hot steam that I needed off my tongue. "I hope you never need to become as practiced at measuring the weight of people's lives as I have, but I didn't just *give up*. The numbers are against us. We have no great army and our swords and arrows can't match the weapons Damien has created. The best we can hope for is that he doesn't try to take the Faeland to prove himself a better conqueror than his father. We must try to find a way to be content spending our days here."

And forgetting what happens at night. I pulled a small vial of spare wine from my pocket and drank it in a single swallow.

Gerarda's teeth snapped together. "But we have *magic*."

"Barely." My eyes crossed as they adjusted to the sunlight peering in from the outer meadow.

Gerarda raised a pointed brow. The movement was so quick and precise it reminded me of the throwing knives she'd always carried with her as the Dagger. They weren't with her now. Perhaps she'd left them behind along with her title when we fled the capital. She jutted her head to the side. "We have a dozen magic wielders."

Of course Gerarda was arrogant enough to count all the Fae when Feron had yet to decide to join the rebellion.

It took every ounce of will I had not to grab her by the arms and shake her. "We have *eleven*. And that's including me and a Dark Fae who can barely control our powers, let alone use them." I couldn't bring myself to say Riven's name. Even knowing that he was outside somewhere in the city waiting for me made me feel sick enough to want to drown myself in the watering trough.

Gerarda lifted her hands in exasperation and yanked open the stable door. I didn't know if she was letting me out or preparing to fight me inside. "You haven't even attempted to train your powers!"

"I hardly see how that concerns you."

Gerarda pulsed her fist over and over again, refusing to get out of my way. "Once the seals are broken, magic will be returned to its full strength. A dozen—"

I raised a brow.

Gerarda rolled her eyes. "*Eleven* wielders will be more than enough to halt Damien's plans. Enough to protect the Halflings we left behind."

I didn't hold in my laugh, though the sting of pain in Gerarda's eyes cut it short. "You and Vrail have been working on the seals for weeks. It's time for you to accept that we missed our shot at bringing the magic back."

I had been so close. When I found that Elder birch in the Rift, I thought it had been the final step to bring the Light Fae home.

My mother's kin.

My kin.

But they were gone. All that remained was their magic, which they had locked away in different parts of Elverath to keep Aemon from using it to kill the rest of the Fae. It had worked, but at great cost to this land and its people.

All that magic could've been unlocked with one single pierce of my bloodstone dagger through Aemon's heart. But Damien had gotten there first and now the magic was out of reach.

Gerarda blinked up at me like I was a violet moon. "You truly have given up."

My throat seared but I didn't bother answering her question. No one knew the exact locations of the seals. Vrail had come to the same conclusion I had that day in the Rift with my mother. Five groups of Light Fae sacrificed themselves to create five siphons that drained the mainland of all its magic. But magic couldn't be destroyed, only stored. The Light Fae had used water as a barrier to protect each siphon and the seal that kept the magic stored within it, but there were countless islands where each could be. Vrail had yet to find one of them, let alone discover if the seal could even be broken after Aemon's death. I stepped around her and into the aisle between the stalls. Killian's horse poked his head over his pen, his glassy, bored eyes staring at us.

Gerarda followed me out of the stables, right on my heels. I sighed and stopped mid-stride. She spun in front of me, her hair fanning out in a black wave before settling along her jaw. "Hildegard died believing you had a plan."

My breath caught with such force it was as if the air had turned to water and filled my lungs. Gerarda's eyes were sharp and piercing like a blade pressed to my throat, daring me to breathe again. I refused to recoil. "I *had* a plan. It failed."

Gerarda lifted her chin. "Then help us craft a new one. You're meant to save us—"

The wind outside whipped violently at the ground as I stepped toward Gerarda. "And I failed at that too." Hot air burned through my nostrils like fire smoke as I tried to rein in my gusts. "I never claimed that title. No matter what my mother wanted, what Hildegard wanted, whatever plans this *guild* of yours had for me."

Gerarda's jaw tightened, but her lips stayed shut.

"Perhaps the true mistake was you all putting your trust in me. Where I go, death follows." The heaviness of those words was almost enough to knock me to the ground, but I did not drop my gaze from Gerarda's face, even as my magic flicked black hair across her freckled cheeks.

She glanced down at the strands and I could hear her thought as plainly as if she had voiced it. *Imagine what you could train this to do to him.*

A small part of me—the trained soldier who still yearned to protect her kin—shuffled in the depths of my despair. But I knew the truth. I had seen it. The skin along my arm itched from it.

Magic or no, the Crown could not be defeated.

Damien had proven himself to be more bloodthirsty than his father. It wasn't enough for him to rule over Halflings, he had begun to use their blood to make magical weapons that would wreak havoc on anyone who thought to oppose him. And the weapons he didn't need, he sold to the highest bidder. And those bidders had paid for an army so large there was no chance we could take them, even if every soul in the Faeland joined the fight.

All we could do was survive and I wouldn't be judged on how I planned on doing so.

"I thought you were better," Gerarda whispered, more to herself than to me.

I plucked a piece of grass from the tangle of my braid and let it drift to the ground, my gusts finally settling. I thought of all those

Shades who had never made it off that island. Whose last days had been spent in cruel misery at Damien's command. My throat seared as I thought of the young initiates I had helped train. Their lives had been ended before they'd had the chance to begin.

My fists shook beside me as I met Gerarda's gaze once more. "I don't have anything to be better for anymore."

I thought Gerarda had been exaggerating, but Riven had left a flattened, brown line around the Myram tree. He spotted me the moment I stepped into the clearing and halted. I dropped my gaze back to the brown ring, so I didn't have to see the wave of disappointment that crashed across Riven's face.

I shielded my eyes with my hands as I looked up to where the tall groves swung against the sky. The suns had already reached midday.

I spotted two familiar figures walking along one of the bridges of twisted branches just above our heads. Vrail was chattering away while Syrra stared down at me. This had become our routine. I pretended she wasn't perched above me like a bird and she kept her mouth shut.

"If you're wanting to lecture me, Gerarda already did." I dropped my hands and continued toward one of the five branches that curved down from the top of the Myram and sunk into the hidden city below. I wanted to swipe a casket of wine from the cellars while I still had enough wits to carry it up to my burl by faelight.

Riven did not take a step toward me, he just stopped. I could feel the grass around him relax. Sweat hung from his thick brow, down to his neck. His long mane of raven silk was tied back, though not in its usual half braid, like he hadn't found the time to weave it. "We need to talk." He flexed his jaw. There was no warmth in his face, none of the usual kindness that he always reserved for me. Instead, his expression was one of pure resolve.

I had become another thing for him to fight.

"No, we don't." I kept walking, but my throat tightened until my breath was nothing more than a wheeze. I had been avoiding Riven for weeks and being the kind Fae he was, he kept his distance, though his burl was lit each night.

That was part of the reason I was finding other places to sleep in the little spurts I allowed myself. I didn't need the constant reminder of his goodness in the face of my emptiness.

"Keera." He took a step toward me as his shadows circled around my ankles.

I ignored them and kept walking.

Riven only quickened his pace. "There are things you need to know." His words were strained and breathy.

"I'm not interested in hearing them." I had missed the last three meetings with the other rebels. I had no energy left for planning and plotting. My jaw flexed as I stepped by him, pointedly avoiding his pleading gaze.

Riven grabbed my arm.

"Don't." I spun around to face him and a gust of wind shot from my hand. It collided with Riven's chest and threw him onto his back. I stared at my open hand but I didn't apologize.

When Riven's surprise settled, he looked up at me with the worst expression of all.

Pity.

"Keera—"

I closed my eyes. "I don't want to hear whatever you have to tell me, Riven. I don't have enough strength for hope and I don't have enough wine for any more disappointment. When you need someone dead, come find me."

Riven stood and his shadows flared out in every direction along the ground. The usually soft curves had turned sharp as they always did when he was angry. Riven's face was hard as he stared at me. My breath hitched and for the briefest moment I thought Riven might move to strike. Not to maim, but to spar. I readied myself for a battle but Riven didn't budge.

Instead, his shoulders collapsed and he rubbed his brow. "I don't know how to help you, *diizra*."

My heart twinged at his special name for me, but it was nothing compared to the burning in my throat or the hollow ache in my core. The fresh screams that fueled my nightmares echoed through the grove for only my ears to hear.

I turned away from him, knowing there was nothing Riven could do to quiet them. "I don't want you to help me."

I don't want help at all.

CHAPTER TWO

I DIDN'T BOTHER SHOWERING before I made my way to the kitchens. Stinking of horse and shit only gave others more of a reason to keep their distance. I stalked down the spiral staircase of one of the Myram's branches and descended into the city of faelight below. I crossed the grand hall with its root-packed ceiling echoing my footsteps from thirteen stories above. Lunch had already been served so the hall was quiet. The children were playing out in the sunlight while their parents finished their duties. The only ones still there were the older Elverin seated along the shallow pool cooling their calves.

Their boisterous chatting echoed through the circular hall but they went silent as soon as I entered. I clenched my jaw and ignored their stares. Part of me longed for the days when my presence was met with fear and caution instead of pity and disgust.

Familiar voices sounded from the kitchens, and my stomach dropped. I hadn't expected to encounter anyone in the kitchen so far from supper. I softened my steps and slipped into the storeroom across the hall. A small faelight floated by my shoulder, illuminating the jars of nuts and crates of fresh berries and dried meat. The caskets of wine that usually covered the floor were gone.

My heartbeat quickened as I rummaged through the shelves looking for anything that resembled wine. All I found were two glass bottles, dusty and forgotten on a bottom shelf. There was a small *pop* as I pulled a cork of one bottle free and sipped the liquid inside. I spat the oil from my mouth and wiped the rest off my lips with my sleeve.

I grabbed the other bottle, but it was empty.

My skin rippled with heat as the onslaught of rage focused my vision. I grabbed the empty bottle by its neck and stalked into the kitchens. Lash'raelth was standing by one of the giant hearths at the middle of the room. His violet eyes were full of laughter as he towered over Pirmiith, who sat across the stone counter next to Nikolai.

"What did you do with it?" I bellowed, ignoring the way they all flinched at the desperate rasp of my voice.

"Do with what?" Pirmiith asked, tucking one of his tiny braids behind his ear in a transparent attempt of ignorance. My eyes narrowed. Whatever loyalty I had for the Elf who had saved my life from the Unnamed Ones had disappeared.

Just like my wine.

I stalked toward him like a hungry bear. "You know *exactly* what I am talking about."

Lash stepped around the counter, placing himself between me and the others. The fire in the hearth roared brighter, the dancing flames reflecting dangerously in his purple eyes. A reminder that Lash would use his powers if needed.

Nikolai smoothed the nonexistent wrinkles on his silk jacket. He raised a manicured brow as he finally looked at me, peering out from behind his Fae guard. "Pirmiith didn't hide the wine. I did." He tucked his head back behind Lash, tugging at his hair. "And you will find everyone intends to follow my lead."

I tilted my chin up at the mountain of a Fae. I could force the truth from Nikolai if needed but Lash was another matter. "Where is it?" I shouted, flinging the empty wine bottle in my hand across the room.

The glass shattered against the wall and someone gasped. It wasn't a scream or anything close to a word, but I recognized the tone of her breath all the same. My body froze, arm still extended like the hand of a compass pointing directly at Gwyn.

Her head was pinned against the table, shielded by her arms and mane of red curls, both now covered in bits of glass. They fell to the floor as she stood and were ground to dust as she stared at me with nothing but vitriol in her eyes.

My throat tightened until it hurt to breathe. "Gwyn. I didn't know you were there," I mumbled, fully aware of how pathetic I sounded. "I didn't mean to scare you."

Gwyn's lip curled back as she shook the rest of the glass over of her shoulders. There was no hint of the young girl who had once hovered around my chambers for hours. Damien had taken so much more than her childhood when he had sliced into her. Her smile had yet to be seen in the Faeland, and no one here had heard Gwyn speak, let alone laugh. I worried that wouldn't change no matter how many moons passed.

Gwyn grabbed the book she had been reading from the table and signed something at the others with the slow movements of unpracticed fingers. Nikolai nodded glumly and she started out the door.

I gritted my teeth and turned back to Nikolai. "Where is the wine?"

Lash shook his head in disbelief and threw a tray of pastries into the oven. Pirmiith wisely turned around, knowing the conversation no longer concerned him.

"Are you going to throw something at my head next?" Nikolai crossed his arms.

Guilt flared across my face like one of Lash's fire tendrils. I dropped my gaze to the floor and stormed out of the room.

I didn't turn around as he called after me. I didn't look as the Elverin in the hall whispered as I stalked toward the faelight.

Every ounce of energy I had was being spent on keeping my newfound powers controlled. My muscles ached from the tension as I climbed onto a large ball of covered faelight and was carried to the highest burls in Myrelinth.

My vision blurred from the pain and nausea as I stepped through the door. The full force of my cravings had returned as soon as that first bottle had touched my lips six weeks earlier. I had been so naïve to think I could control them. So desperate to think that I could keep the cost hidden from anyone but me.

I rummaged through my clothes with shaky hands, feeling for the soft skin on my leather pouch. I found it under a soiled tunic. I threw the shirt over my shoulder and onto the floor with the rest of my unwashed clothes and unused blades. It took three tries to untie the drawstrings and dump the contents onto my lap.

A flash of gold sent a shiver along my unmarked skin. But this was not a craving that could be settled with my mage pen. I picked up the vial of black liquid—the same elixir that Hildegard had given me to help with the cravings—and unstoppered the top.

The scent of *winvra* relaxed my shoulders. I had never needed more than a few drops to lessen the cravings before, but that wasn't all I needed. Guilt had already exhausted my body and I needed to sleep.

But to sleep, I needed oblivion.

I brought the vial to my lips and swallowed what was left of Hildegard's gift.

The memory of that first night haunted me as I fell asleep. It replayed in my mind like I was living through it for the very first time:

I tumbled onto a field of grass with no recollection of where I'd fallen from. I groaned with the little bit of air left in my lungs but there was no pain. No broken bones or split skin from the fall.

I stared down at my sleeve; the top of the jagged scar along my forearm was peeking out over the cuff. The sudden urge to pull it back into place overtook me and I tugged the linen before I gathered my bearings.

I never walked into a field. I had just been underground dropping Gwyn off at the infirmary in Myrelinth. The healers had swarmed around her the moment I lay her on the cot.

Riven had been there and told me to lie down too, but I couldn't keep my eyes off Gwyn. She had taken ill again as we passed the boundary into the *Faelinth* and nothing I did seemed to help. I needed to know she was okay. I needed to know that I hadn't hurt her by using my healing gift to stitch her belly back together.

Riven pulled me into his chest. "You brought her here alive, *diizra*," he whispered so quietly only I could hear him. "You don't need to worry now. She's safe and she will stay that way."

Somehow his words penetrated my fear enough for the exhaustion to blanket me. My brows creased along the grass, trying to place the rest of the memories, the journey to the field, but there were none.

Moments before Riven had lifted me into his arms to carry me to his burl, but then I had tumbled out of them into a field I didn't recognize.

A soft breeze blew hair across my face, but it carried no scent. No hint of birch or florals, no spray of sea in the air. I shifted against the soft earth and strained to hear something out in the distance. No crashing waves, no birdsong or carriage wheels. It was as if the field existed in a world of its very own.

Something shifted behind me, loud as thunder in the eerie silence.

My chest tightened. The hair on the back of my neck raised as I pulled myself off the ground and slowly turned. Damien stood tall with his hands tucked behind his back. He was not dressed in his usual undone tunic, but instead in new finery: his shirt was pressed and buttoned to its high collar, as black as the night sky, paired with a jacket of interlocking buttons that formed a jagged, inky pattern down the length of him. The only color on his person was the jade eye patch he wore to cover what Gwyn had done to him.

I lurched back at the sight of him, reaching for weapons that were not hanging from my hips. Damien's eye flared. A deep crease appeared between his brow and patch for the briefest moment, but then it was gone.

"Where have you taken me?" I hissed, fear and anger igniting in my chest.

Damien waved his hand over a patch of grass and a gold throne appeared out of nothing. He sat down, his back perfectly straight instead of slumped over the armrest the way he used to as crown prince. Perhaps that had all been part of his ruse.

"I haven't taken you anywhere." Damien's cold gaze sliced right through me, accentuated by the short cut of his hair. This was not the rowdy prince in front of me, but the king. Someone entirely new. My muscles tightened sensing something else in his stare. It was stern and hard in a way the prince's had never been. But I could recognize the contempt he had for me in the slight curl of his lip. And below his hatred and disdain, there was the calculating observer that Damien had spent years hiding away. Now that I knew it was there, Damien couldn't mask that side of him any longer.

A chill ran down my spine. For the first time, I could see the resemblance between Damien and his brother, Killian. A new wave of fear crashed over me. This was not the aloof prince who spent his time entertaining gentlefolk in his bedchambers and drinking until dawn, this was a patient, strategic mind that had spent decades crafting his plot to seize the crown.

"You have magic?" I asked, pointing to the throne.

Damien gave a stoic nod. "Of a kind."

Confusion stirred inside me, thoughts whirling in my mind, too fast and too many to catch. My hand rose, feeling my upper arm where Damien had plunged his needle into it before ordering his guards to take me from the throne room, and the whirlwind stopped. "The injection . . ."

"Another experiment of mine," Damien answered with no expression and a hard edge to his voice. Both his hands were wrapped tightly around the ends of his armrests. "There is much to be learned from the arts of Fae."

I blinked. Damien had found a way to cultivate enough magic to mimic the Fae gifts. He had been using that knowledge to fuel his newfound weapons economy, but it was clear he had other inventions he'd been keeping just for himself. I cleared my throat, already knowing what magical gift Damien had gotten inspiration from. "Mindwalking."

Damien nodded, his back even straighter. "What better way to forge a connection between two minds." He drummed his fingers along the armrest and bit the inside of his cheek. The hollow under his eye patch darkened.

Nausea gurgled in my stomach. "You experimented on me?"

Damien's jaw pulsed. "That seems apparent."

"Why?" The question was off my tongue before I could think the better of it.

Damien's mouth was a straight line, but there was a ghost of his wicked grin in his eye. "Insurance."

I straightened my back, sensing the threat but not knowing what form it would take. "You wanted a way to search through my memories?" I lifted my hands uselessly. Whatever this place was, I doubted I could hurt Damien here.

"No." The first smirk appeared on his lips. "I wanted to show you mine."

I swallowed down the bile in my throat at the thought of everything Damien might delight in showing me. "Your speech was enough. I don't need to see how you hung Curringham and Tarvelle. Or what you—"

Damien lifted his chin in victory. "How I killed your chambermaid?"

My breath caught. Both at the idea of seeing Gwyn being cut open by Damien's own hand, from his own mind, but also because Damien had revealed so much in five simple words.

He didn't know Gwyn had survived.

I feigned a flinch, pretending the thought of Gwyn's death was too much to bear. Damien's thin lip twitched upward.

"Perhaps another time." Damien tilted his head and I knew he was imagining the pleasure of giving me such pain.

"Then what did you bring me here for?"

Damien stared at me for several long moments, trapping me in his unblinking gaze. When he decided to answer, his tone was hard. "I wanted to show you the consequences of your actions."

I scoffed, crossing my arms.

Damien's eye patch shifted as he raised his brows. "Don't you recognize this place?"

I shrugged, refusing to answer him.

"It is a bit unfinished"—Damien raised his hand and the edge of the small field began to expand—"but I'm surprised you don't recognize it. It is home after all."

A strong gust of sea spray filled the air as the Order took shape in front of us. The three towers held us in their shadows, each topped with a giant piece of gemstone, identical to the palace of Koratha visible along the horizon.

The wind carried more than brine on its gusts. Guttural screams pierced the air, echoing out into the sea where they were consumed by the hungry waves. My bones froze, chilling my blood as Damien's cruel smile finally appeared.

"I hadn't planned on killing them so quickly," Damien whispered, suddenly standing behind me. His ungloved hand trailed down my back, feeling the jagged scars he had cut into it. "But someone needed to suffer for the Blade's treason, and you left them completely unprotected."

A high-pitched wail echoed through the corridors. The sound hit me like I had dragged a blade across each one of their throats myself, their blood splattering my face.

Damien pushed me between the shoulder blades. "It's time to see what happens when the Blade tries to cut the Crown."

I took one step and fell to the ground. "No."

I hated how defeated I sounded. I looked up at Damien expecting to see anger at being refused, but his good eye only flickered with delight.

He lifted his hand and the earth beneath me shifted to cold stone tile smeared with amber blood. "There's no escape from this, Keera," he whispered before the screams started again.

I woke with a skull-splitting headache that left me vomiting on the floor. The bile was black just like the elixir I swallowed. I hadn't fallen into a dream, but the effects of downing the *winvra* elixir were not worth it. My entire body ached, much worse than before, spurred by my misuse of the liquid. There was only one thing that could make me feel better and keep the dreams away.

My throat seared as I stretched along the mattress. The suns had already set and the city was quiet once more. I pulled myself to the edge of the bed and stared at the empty vial and scattered wineskins on the floor. Even without the dreams, I could still hear the Shades' screams as Damien forced his new Arsenal to line them up one by one. He had made sure I'd witnessed every death, again and again.

I had tried limiting my sleep. In those first few weeks, I'd haunted the empty groves each night like a ghost, needing to stay in motion to keep the pull of sleep off my shoulders. But no matter how brief, no matter what time, when I finally succumbed, Damien would find me in my dreams and turned them into nightmares.

Worse than nightmares, into his memories. They were the proof that I had spent my life trying to protect the Shades and I had failed.

I lasted three weeks before I had my first taste of wine. It seemed to quiet the dreams. I had spent decades keeping my dreams of Brenna at bay with each sip and knew it would do the same once more. Desperate to sever the connection Damien had with my mind, it had become my only choice. I had already failed so many people, failing myself barely took any effort at all.

CHAPTER THREE

"DAMN YOU, NIKOLAI!" I yelled, shooting a bag of flour across the floor. It dusted the kitchen in beige powder. My footprints trailed after me as I opened the bottom cupboards looking for a spare bottle of wine or ale. My entire body ached with fatigue, but I couldn't fall asleep without something to keep the dreams away.

I had already checked the lower storerooms. They had been completely emptied. I suspected Lash and Nikolai had put all of it in the main pantry behind the kitchen but it was sealed with a rock too heavy and thick for me to move. My thighs burned from trying, even though I knew three of the strongest Elverin could not move the stone. Lash had used his touch of earth gift to seal it by magic.

My nostrils flared against the door. Breaking the seal that the Light Fae had cast to temper my *Valitherian* gifts had not only increased my healing powers but had given me some control over the wind too. I glanced down at my hip, where the scar of the seal was still carved into my skin. Perhaps I had also been given the gift of earth but it had yet to show itself?

I slowed my breathing and imagined roots climbing along the gray stone, clasping the boulder within their web before rolling the door back far enough for me to slip in. I focused on the warmth in my body and tried to extend that warmth to the boulder but nothing happened.

The door stayed shut.

I grabbed the nearest object off the counter and chucked it at the stone. The clay vase shattered against the rock. Its tiny pieces scattered along the floor, leaving long wispy trails in the flour.

"Rough night?" Killian asked from the entrance of the kitchen. He was leaning against the door, the perfect tableau of nonchalance, but his thumb was almost raw from where he had picked the cuticles around his nail.

"I can't sleep." I bit my tongue to keep any other truths from escaping. I was too restless and it was too loose.

Killian frowned. He had not cut his hair since that day in the capital. His blond curls hung low across his brow until his ink-stained palm pushed them back. In that first week, he had tried many times to talk about what had happened. Not just Hildegard's death, but what Damien had revealed about my Trials. My body tensed at the thought of it, stiffening my loose tongue. I couldn't tell Killian anything about that night and bring those memories to the front of my mind. What if Damien found out? If he gained access to my memories and discovered the truth, there would be no stopping his rampage. Damien had already proven how far he was willing to go when he felt bested.

"Nikolai stationed people at every nearby portal if you're thinking of raiding someone else's kitchen." There was a touch of humor in Killian's words, but it was false and hollow. He wore the same expression that everyone else in Myrelinth wore around me now. A vile combination of pity and disappointment.

I gnawed on my cheek. "How many guards?"

Killian frowned even more deeply. "We're your *family*, Keera. We will play the role of jailers if we must, but we would all prefer that you try to follow Nikolai's regimen. There are other ways we can help you—"

"I don't want your help!" I screamed so loudly my voice cracked.

Killian grabbed my arm and jerked me back to face him. "Even if you are right and all is lost. Is this how you would want Hildegard to remember you? Is this how you honor her death? With disdain and hopelessness?"

I wrenched my arm free and balled my hands into fists. I had no qualms about punching Killian in the jaw again. "Hildegard no longer has expectations for me. They died the day your brother slit her throat."

I waited for Killian to flinch or back away. He had told me how guilty he felt for his legacy, that he thought himself responsible for his father's actions. I knew that extended to his brother's now that the crown sat upon Damien's head. I had selected my words with purpose, sharpening them to fine points, before I shot them his way. But if they had pierced him as I'd hoped, Killian didn't show it.

His face softened with his shoulders as he looked at me. "And what about Brenna?" His eyes fluttered to my forearm. He had gone months pretending he had never seen my scars, but his gaze betrayed him now.

A cold wave crashed through me as I remembered the way Killian had looked at me that day. The disgust in his face as Damien told him what I'd done. But there was none of that now, as if I had imagined it entirely. Killian's brow was furrowed with the weight of his worry for me; his hand hung in the air halfway between our bodies, the beacon of a friend reaching out in the dark, ready to lead me to the light.

But I didn't want to be led out of the depths of my shadows. The fire that had once filled my chest had gone out and not even Killian's most desperate hopes could relight it. And with Damien able to access my mind, everyone was safer if I succumbed to my old vices.

Killian turned his hand so the pale palm faced upward. "Keera, please. Let me help you."

Tears welled along his bottom lashes, but Killian stood strong. He gazed down at his hand and I knew there was nothing I could say to dissuade him. He would keep reaching out, just as Riven kept his light on. Just as Syrra stood watch over me. And Nikolai took my wine. No matter what I said, they would be within my reach the moment I needed them.

Unless I showed them I was beyond reaching.

I laced my fingers through Killian's hand and stepped toward him. He smiled with relief as he looked down at our joined hands. I took another step and pushed Killian into the earth-packed wall behind him. Nikolai would have complained about the stains to his fine clothes, but Killian's black cloak had seen worse.

His throat bobbed as my other hand slid up his thigh to his hip, trailing over the brown hilt of the dagger hanging there. "Keera, don't," Killian whispered, half in disbelief, half in a desperate plea.

I let my fingers linger over the hilt as I leaned closer to him, pinning him against the wall. It would be so easy to pierce the blade through his chest, but I couldn't add Killian's name to my list. I only carved the names of people I couldn't save, the lives I had no choice but to take.

There was another way I could lose the goodwill of everyone; it wasn't violent but just as devastating. I lifted the hand from his blade and trailed it up Killian's chest. His frame was so much smaller than Riven's—he was more fragile than his Fae half-brother. I felt his heart hammer in his chest as my hand gripped his jaw and my forearm pressed into him.

He opened his mouth to say something, another plea, but I didn't hear it. I leaned into him and pressed my lips to his. I waited for the revulsion. For Killian to push me away and yell at me for toying with him, but he didn't.

Instead, his hands gripped my waist, wanting and hungry. He nipped at my lips, like they were wine and he was the one who had ransacked the kitchens looking for it. His bites were desperate and yearning, his breath filled my body with warmth, the burning kind that you only noticed after being too cold.

He pulled me tighter to his chest, flattening the smallest of spaces between our bodies, but that was still not enough for him. His hand trailed up my back, tangling in my braid as it found my neck and then my hair. Killian's hand closed, tugging at my roots until I moaned.

The sound broke the spell over him. Killian's hands froze on my head and waist. He released my lower lip from his teeth and a piercing pain shot down my spine. It was as if a thousand arrows had flown into my back, paralyzing me for just a moment but causing so much anguish that a breath felt like an eternity.

I saw the same pain pulse through Killian. His knees buckled against the wall and he choked as if a large force had punched the air from his guts. He looked up at me, sweaty and out of breath. "Be as self-destructive as you want, Keera. I still won't leave you. And neither will Riven."

Guilt stormed inside me. Even my magic had known I had taken this too far. Already sharp like knives, it threatened to strike if I reached out to Killian again.

I stepped back. I turned down the corridor and left Killian where he'd collapsed against the wall so he didn't see the way my kiss-bruised lips quivered at the mention of Riven's name. It didn't matter if Killian remained by my side, my pain and my guilt would swallow me whole and everyone who stood too close.

I deliberately avoided looking at Riven's burl as I crossed the tangled bridge of branches to my own. My shoulders already buckled under the weight of what I had done. I didn't need to see the way the light shone from his bed, a beacon for me to find in any darkness.

I pulled off my clothes and doused myself in the shower. I didn't care that I had already washed away the scent of the stables from my hair, I could still feel Killian's touch on my skin. It ached like a fresh scar, a mark of my betrayal. I stood under the spout until the last of its warmth drained away.

The burning in my throat flared with every breath. Almost as unbearable as the wave of pain I had felt down in the kitchens. Whatever new power of mine had been awakened, I did not want to feel it again.

I rummaged through the piles of dirty clothes in my room, searching for the small bit of relief I had left.

I found it under a disheveled tunic that was now more brown than white. The thin gold tube that had only met the worst versions of me. I uncapped the mage pen and lifted my nightgown to bare my left leg.

Hildegard's death had left a gaping hole too big for the tiny script I'd used along my arms and torso. I held the mage pen to my skin and retraced the lines the blade had already cut several times before. Carving her name into myself once was not enough. It had been my taunts that had set Damien on the hunt, that had cost Hildegard her life. But it was not just her life that I'd taken, I'd taken the mentor of every Shade. The one person we all relied on, the one we looked to.

I watched my skin stitch itself back together, smooth except for the thick lines that marked the letters of Hildegard's name. Whatever magic the mage pen's blade was made with was enough to stifle my healing abilities just enough to scar. I traced the name once more with my finger before collapsing onto the bed.

My hand fell between the pillows and hit something hard. I turned and saw the notebook that Dynara had given me. I opened it to the front page. There was no note waiting for me. I bit my lip, using every ounce of my concentration to count the days. It was almost a fortnight since she had last made contact.

I stretched for the pen sitting next to the bed and wrote her a single line.

I hope you are still among the living. K.

Dynara's message inked the page almost immediately.

I hope you are still among the living too. D.

I huffed into the notebook as I scrawled my next line.

If I weren't, who would be writing this message?

Her reply didn't come as quickly as the last. My chest tightened in anticipation.

If I had lost all the courtesans to Damien, I would not be living. Breathing and living are not the same.

I hadn't said the words aloud, but I had written them to Dynara after that first dream. She was the only soul I had told. She didn't know the specifics, but she knew enough. Tears welled at the corners of my eyes. Dynara was a half a continent away, risking herself at every moment in the House of Harvest, yet still I felt like she understood me more than anyone else. Perhaps the distance made it easier to tell her the truth. I couldn't see the pity on her face while she sat in her room in Cereliath. Perhaps I would be more useful there—surely Dynara had a few lords for me to kill.

You don't need to let the pain go completely. Just give yourself enough room to do more than breathe, Dynara wrote, as if reading my mind.

Do you need any help bringing the Halflings across the border? Damien had sent several battalions to Cereliath to guard the remaining orchards the moment he'd hung Curringham and Tarvelle outside the throne room. The House of Harvest was no longer under the control of House Curringham since there was no House Curringham left. It had been wiped from existence; not even the third cousins had been spared in Damien's strike.

The atmosphere in Cereliath was tense, which only made Dynara's plans more difficult to carry out.

No. There won't be any soldiers left to chase us when I'm done here.

The thought of Dynara battling with Damien's sellswords set my throat ablaze. I didn't want to picture all the ways her plan could fail. I couldn't lose more Halflings, and I certainly couldn't lose another friend.

I scribbled the only thing that I knew would shift the conversation to less violent ends. *I kissed Killian.*

Dynara took an excruciatingly long time to write thirteen words. *You thought being utterly selfish and a fool would make you feel better?*

My breath shook as I inked the truth onto the page. *I thought it would make this easier.*

Her next line appeared much more quickly than the first. *Are you pushing everyone away because you want to be alone or out of habit?*

I didn't fill my glass pen with any more ink. I didn't know the answer to that question.

After several long moments, Dynara had discerned the truth for herself. *It is not your job to protect us from whatever truth you're keeping. It might feel sharp and heavy in your hand, but it is not a blade you have to cut with. It can just be. With love, D.*

Thick tears fell down my cheeks as the weight of that loneliness pinned me to the mattress. I wanted nothing more than to run away to Aralinth and spend the next week dancing with Dynara at my side. But she hadn't given up. That flame of hope still flared in her chest. Mine was hollow and empty, unable to hold even the ghosts of my hope or the sting of my loneliness. I closed my eyes, too exhausted to fight off sleep any longer, and knew that I wouldn't be alone soon enough.

CHAPTER FOUR

I WOKE UP ON THE FLOOR of the throne room. The marble tiles were cold against my arms and back. I sat up, realizing that I was wearing one of the dresses that were fashionable at court. The plunging back revealed the full length of the scars I kept hidden. My stomach knotted with relief when I saw all my names were covered by the sleeves of the dress.

Damien didn't need to know how far back my treason went.

I looked up from where I stood at the center of the room. It was empty. The walls were brighter than they ever had been in real life. The white stone and birch door were pristine, unmarked by time or dust. It made my skin ripple.

The doors leading to the royal chambers behind the throne opened and Damien walked through. I couldn't see the hallway behind him, only blackness. Whatever control Damien had over my mind it seemed he could only construct one room at a time.

He was dressed in a dark green jacket and navy boots that made his remaining eye sparkle with the light of the springtime suns. Anyone else would have found him handsome, even with the jade leather patch over his missing eye, but all I could see was the touch of death hidden in his sharp cheeks and the kiss of violence hanging from his lips.

"I finally got you into one of those dresses." There wasn't a hint of pleasure in his tone as Damien slowly lowered himself into his seat. The wide buttons of his vest kept his back perfectly straight. His eyes traced the outline of my shoulder. "*Turn.*" The cold command echoed along the stone pillars.

Part of me wanted to ignore him. To press my back into one of the columns and refuse to move until I woke. But resisting was what Damien wanted. It is what he enjoyed, slowly breaking me down until he knew there was no way for me to put the fragments back together.

I pulled the soft waves Damien had given me over my shoulder and turned. His breath hitched as he witnessed the scars he'd cut into my flesh for the first time. I peered up at him over my shoulder. His throat bobbed as he leaned back into the chair, his hand curving around the end of the armrest so hard I thought the gilded wood would crack.

"Marvelous," Damien whispered, licking his lip. "I'm glad to see my masterpiece healed so well."

My jaw flexed. I hated seeing the satisfaction on his face. I couldn't bear to give him any more of it. "It didn't," I lied, without thinking.

Damien tilted his head like a hawk.

I turned back to face him, suddenly deciding to test something. "This is a dream—your dream. You're only seeing what you want to see. I carved over your scars years ago. There's nothing left of the design." I'd thought about doing it so many times that the words didn't even taste like a lie as I said them.

Damien's eye narrowed. "Then I will make you wear that dress for me in person."

My stomach fluttered at his reply. It wasn't a blatant rejection of my lie, which meant that Damien didn't know the rules to this place either. I would take any bit of leverage I could get. "Is that an invitation?"

Damien's face was expressionless and his tone even less lively. "We both know you can't stay in the Faeland forever, Keera."

"Is that where I am?" I exaggerated my gaze around the throne room. Even though Damien's suspicions were correct, I would never be foolish enough to corroborate them.

My eyes fell to the small dagger holstered at Damien's hip. I was unarmed, but if I could run the blade through Damien's heart, perhaps the dream would end before his torment even began.

I shifted my foot, preparing to strike but my boot slipped along the tile. I crashed to floor. Thick, hot blood soaked through my clothes and covered my face. My heart pounded against my chest as I tried to push myself up. I slipped, ramming my shoulder into the floor.

A groan escaped my lips but I refused to look up at Damien's satisfied face. I couldn't do it any longer. I kept my gaze locked on the blood-soaked tiles so I didn't have to see the Shades hanging by their feet. I planted my boot and lifted myself up, only to slip once more. This time, I landed on something soft.

Hildegard stared up at me with dead, open eyes. Her body was cold, drained of all its color just like it had the day she bled out in front of me. My stomach lurched and I fought the urge to be sick. I tried to stand but it was pointless. The sticky blood had coated every inch of the floor and my boots.

I ran my hand over Hildegard's eyes, shutting them as I shut my own. Damien sat above it all, lounging in his throne as he let this piece of his memory merge with our dream.

A sob stirred deep in my chest, but I wouldn't let it out. Instead I looked back down at Hildegard, but she was gone.

Gwyn was laying in her place. Her almost lifeless body gaping at her belly from where Damien had cut her. Where Damien had rummaged inside of her in search of Gwyn's cursed womb, only to cut the organ out for himself. She wheezed as she looked up at me, full of fear and defeat.

I was grateful I didn't have to imagine my horror. I let the memory of finding her on that day overwhelm me with regret and loss. The sob that had been building burst and Damien smiled down at me with his cruel grin, watching my pain like a playwright.

"So much blood on your hands," Damien whispered.

I stared up at him, unwilling to wail like he wanted any longer. "*You* killed them." I wouldn't deny my part in Hildegard's death or Gwyn's attack, but Damien had dealt the blows.

His hungry expression shifted to something darker. He sipped from his goblet before throwing it to the ground, face hard and emotionless. "Then perhaps it's time to revisit a death where *you* drew the blade."

The throne room disappeared in a blur of shadow before reshaping into a place I'd only set foot in once in my life. The stage was coated in dust so thick it felt like snow underfoot. The empty rows of seats had a presence about them, like the ghost of every initiate who had died in her Trials was watching me. Waiting for what came next.

I was in the room where it happened, revisiting the memory that had haunted me for decades, no matter how hard I tried to kill it with poison or lock it in the deepest trenches of myself.

This was the room where Brenna had died.

It was a small theater. Its rows of seats circled around the curved stage where I assumed Elvish musicians and fire spinners had once performed for their people. Had the room existed in the palace, Damien would have used it to entertain the royals at court, but it was left in disuse on the island of the Order.

Except for when the king called forth the Trials, when the latest group of initiates would be tested to their limits in the hope of earning a hood.

Damien stepped out onto the stage, dragging an old wooden chair behind him. He placed it in the center. The exact spot it had sat thirty years before.

Damien drummed his fingertips over the back of the chair, but it was no longer empty. My heart squeezed at the sight of her—Brenna bound to the chair with a rope so tight it had left bruises on her skin. Her blond curls were covered in her own blood, amber-stained strands stuck to her neck. Some of the blood had dried along the scars that formed faint lines across her honey eyes. They stared up at me in fear, just as they had that day.

Not fear that she was dying. Not even fear that I would kill her.

Fear that I wouldn't.

Damien paced along the back of the stage, eyes locked on the bloodstone dagger with a wooden hilt that had appeared on the table beside Brenna. He licked his lips in anticipation of rewatching his favorite play being acted out in front of him.

Damien had designed an impossible choice that could only end in bloodshed. And his thrill had come from not knowing whose blood it would be. I could still recall the satisfied grin he'd given me after I'd done it. It was the same one he wore now. He'd known he had witnessed a transformation I could never come back from. And I had stoked that ruse for three decades. I let him and his father believe in my ruthlessness because the truth would only get me killed.

Brenna had stacked the game before Damien ever made me play it.

"Do you think she forgave you before she died?" Damien asked as Brenna thrashed against the bindings. The wooden chair scraped against the stone like a cry for help no one would hear.

"No," I answered, unable to look away from Brenna for one moment. Even in her terror, even knowing what came next, my entire body yearned to touch her, to protect her. Even after thirty years. "Would you forgive someone who betrayed you so completely?"

Damien stalked across the stage and picked up the dagger. Brenna's eyes stayed focused on me, locked in the memory of what had really happened. "Life is nothing more than a vicious game." He placed the blade into my hand and curled my stiff fingers around the hilt.

I scoffed. "And your aim is to win?"

Damien tilted his head, carefully considering the question. "My aim is for everyone else to lose." His jade eye flicked to Brenna, still squirming in her chair. "You know how to end this."

Brenna rocked so violently, the chair almost tipped over. When she lifted her head back up, she had pressed her gag deeper into her mouth so I could see the faintest line of blue on the inside of her lip. Just as I had glimpsed that day.

"You promised," she rasped through the gag.

My stomach turned to stone. In anger for what I had to do and anger that once again the choice wasn't truly mine.

I tightened the grip on my dagger and plunged it into Brenna's chest once more. Just like the first time. Just like all the other dreams where Damien had forced me to do the same. Thick streams of tears poured down my face and I fell to my knees. The memory faded and all I could hear was the resonating sound of Damien's laughter before I woke.

CHAPTER FIVE

I WAS FERAL. An entire day had passed since I had woken vomiting over my bed. It had taken two showers for me to realize the sweating was not going to end. Not without a drink. My entire body shook as if I was standing naked in the snowy abyss of Exiles Rest, yet beads of sweat dripped from my nose onto my chapped lips.

The city began to quiet as the night sky darkened, and I could no longer take it. I walked past the three trays of untouched food that Nikolai had brought to my burl and stalked into the night. He might have taken the wine out of the cellars but I doubt he had taken the trouble to search every room in Myrelinth.

There wasn't a single drop of wine in the eastern wings of the lower city. I walked through each of the rooms with a tiny faelight to light my path, covering it with my brown cloak every time I heard someone draw near.

I took an alternate route past the kitchens but could still hear Nikolai and Lash cooing over each other. Knowing Nikolai, I didn't need to ask why they had sought a snack in the middle of the night.

I left them to it and slipped into the first room I came across along the curving tunnel. The only light inside came from the hearth along the back wall. The fire had mostly burned away, though a few small flames still dance along the burnt remnants of a log.

The bed was grand with a canopy of silks hanging from the four posts at each corner. On either side were piles of dusty books and scrolls. A white tunic was strewn across one of the piles with an ink stain along one sleeve.

Killian's room.

My breath hitched. I hadn't realized that the tunnel I had taken reconnected with the wing where Killian and the others slept. I knew his room was close to Feron's and Nikolai's—Vrail's was somewhere near too, but I had never been in it.

I turned to the bed. Not a single wrinkle marked the coverlet that was split down the middle with the amber leaves of an Elder birch. One side of the leaves was a dark violet, the same shade as the first streaks of night, while the other was a bright jade like morning sun along dew-covered grass.

Dusk to dawn, the hours one was meant to sleep, but it didn't look like Killian had touched the bed at all.

I glanced around the rest of the room. There was a small closet filled with black jackets and the occasional burgundy tunic. Apart from that and the books, the only other thing in the room was a cabinet.

The tall cupboards were stocked with quills and bottles of ink, nothing that would satisfy the craving at my throat. I rummaged through the bottom drawers and found more of the same. Papers and books with more sheaves stuck inside them.

I kicked the cabinet and something clinked along the floor.

A glass vial had rolled out from underneath the dark wood and sat at the edge of my boot. The top was a simple cork and the vial was filled with something other than ink. Three black *winvra* berries sat inside. The same ones that Killian had tossed to me the day we ran for our lives through the portal.

I stilled, staring at the dark berries. The elixir had stopped the dreams, at the cost of heightened pain, but the berries would be different. I wouldn't feel any pain, I wouldn't feel anything at all. I would be beyond reach, of Damien, of my grief or the ghosts that followed it. The craving in my throat cooled, as if it was considering the choice too. There was no going back if I decided to take them, but I knew even Damien's inventions could not reach me in the euphoria those black drupelets would provide.

My hand reached for the vial without my permission. I lifted it up to my face as I stood, inspecting the contents. My mouth watered at the thought of a night of peace, regardless of the cost.

Without warning, a hand broke through the darkness and snatched the vial from me. I turned, reaching for my dagger that was not on my hip, and saw Syrra throwing the berries into the hungry flames of the hearth. "Have you lost all sense?" she shouted in Elvish. Her dark eyes were frenzied in a way I had never seen them. Her nostrils flared as she looked at me, expecting a better answer than any I had to give.

My cheeks turned hot and my tongue turned sharp. "Are *you* really in a place to lecture me?" I knew I was being cruel and I didn't care.

Syrra's lip curled back and for a moment I thought she was going to strike me. "I have stayed silent these long weeks because it was not my place to dictate how you grieve. But if you insist on harming others while you mope, I will not condone it." Her fingers curled around the hilt of her curved blade.

I scoffed. "How I choose to escape will not harm anyone. Not in a way that matters."

Syrra's eyes softened but her hand did not move. "I know you do not believe that, Keera. Do you not think it will scar everyone if you make them watch you waste away any more than you already have? Do you think any of us could easily live out the rest of our days without you?"

I swallowed the thickness growing at my throat. "The time of easy days is gone, but perhaps they would be easier without me." I looked at the swirling flames so I didn't have to see Syrra's disappointment.

She took a step toward me, so delicate and quiet I couldn't hear her boots on the floor. Her hand reached out like the branches carved into her arms and brushed my cheek before lifting my chin. "Pain is like a poison. It is better leeched than swallowed." She glanced down at the fire, and I could see the strain in her neck. "Make sure whatever you swallow is worth the pain it causes."

The truth sat on my tongue, hot like a flame, but I didn't dare speak it. There was nothing Syrra could do to stop the dreams. And from her speech it was clear she knew the Shades were dead even if the others refused to accept it. Telling her wouldn't leech my pain, it would only infect her with my burden.

Sometimes secrets had to be swallowed.

She sighed and let go of my chin. "I do not know if your stubbornness is your favored trait or your undoing."

I leaned against the mantel. "Both."

Syrra's gaze lingered on the way my hand shook even as it held me up and she sighed. She pulled a small skin out of her belt pocket and tossed it at me. I knew from the hard set of her mouth that it wasn't filled with water.

"This is the only time." She walked to the door, leaving me alone once more. "And if I catch you with *winvra* again, I will have the healers put you to sleep so no one need fret over your poor choices."

My chest tightened and I hoped the fear didn't show on my face. Syrra had no idea how piercing a threat she had just thrown at me.

I nodded and she walked to the door. "When you are ready, I am here to help. I know how hard it is to stop on one's own." She pursed her lips when I didn't answer and disappeared back into the dark.

I uncorked the skin and let half the bag spill down my throat. My shivers stopped and my head cleared in the sharpest moment of relief. I tucked the rest of the wine into my satchel and started back to my room.

Vrail turned around the corner with a small pile of books in her arms. I flattened myself against the wall and tucked the faelight into my cloak, but I wasn't quick enough.

"Keera! I was hoping to speak with you today," she said, much too loudly and much too quickly for the middle of the night.

I walked past her covering my satchel with my cloak. "We can talk later."

Vrail followed me like a duckling after its mother. "We have a council meeting later this morning. I would like to brief you on everything Gerarda and I have discovered before I present it to the others—"

"I don't sit on the council anymore." I lengthened my strides. Vrail's short legs couldn't keep pace and balance the books. I recognized the one on top as the book she had stolen from the library in Koratha.

She stopped and my chest relaxed. I glanced back and saw her pull one of Nikolai's handkerchiefs from her scarlet robes and place it on the ground. She sat her pile of books on top of it and turned to me. I broke into a light run.

Vrail's short legs only hastened. "Keera, it's not worth my time presenting it if you don't agree—"

"Then I guess you're not presenting anything." I gritted my teeth, trying to hold back my annoyance. Vrail had developed a habit of cornering me in tunnels.

"I know how to break the seals!" Vrail shouted, her breathy voice echoing down the hall and into the kitchens.

I turned so slowly, Vrail gulped. "You've made no progress for weeks on even *finding* them. But suddenly you know how to break them?" I folded my arms, suffocating any flicker of hope. "My mother's instructions were *very* clear. The seals on the syphons were spelled to Aemon. And they died with him."

"That was her intention but the seals themselves have their own magic—"

"So which one?"

Vrail blinked. "Which what?"

"Which seal did you find and break?"

Vrail's leg started to bounce. "Well, I haven't yet because *I* can't—"

"Then what is the point of this conversation?" I spun around on my heel to keep going.

"But, Keera, *you* can." Vrail grabbed for my wrist but her fingers slipped upward, brushing the thick scars along my forearm. Both of us stopped breathing for a moment that seemed to stretch for hours.

Vrail's eyes slowly lowered and I felt her fingers loosen their grip. Fear ignited inside my chest like a wildfire. "I have given enough!" I screeched as I wrenched my arm free from her grasp.

A strong gust of wind blew through the corridor. Vrail flew backward in a blur. She gasped as her back collided with the wall, the sound of it echoing down the tunnel.

I stood helpless, staring at my hand as tears clouded my vision. I hadn't meant to call my magic, but I could feel it whirling inside my chest, ready to attack again.

Something dropped in the kitchens. I didn't turn. I was frozen to my spot, too scared to move in case I hurt Vrail again. "I'm sorry," I whispered. A hot stream of tears trailed down my cheek but I didn't wipe them away.

Nikolai rushed past me and ran over to Vrail. She coughed as he pulled her into his chest. "I'm okay. I'm okay," she murmured. Lash knelt beside them both and checked her for any damage. The whirling power in my chest only grew as the moments passed. I felt like my lungs were going to burst if Lash didn't say Vrail was going to be okay. Finally, he nodded.

Nikolai's head snapped up. For the first time, he looked capable of using the knife that he was holding in his hand. "What is wrong with you?"

"I didn't . . . I didn't mean to . . ."

Vrail patted Nikolai's shoulder as she stood. "I surprised her, Nik."

"And she attacked you." Nikolai seethed.

"I'm sorry." A whisper was all I could manage.

Lash turned to me and froze. Nikolai tilted his head at him but the Fae waved his hand and slowly placed himself in front of both of them.

"Lash, what—"

Lash waved Nikolai into silence, his calm voice not matching the panic in his expression. "Her eyes."

Nikolai turned to me and his arms tightened around Vrail.

Lash slowly raised his hand. "Keera, does your chest feel tight?"

I nodded. The pain had become almost unbearable.

"How tight?" It was strange for such a mountain of a person to seem so scared.

My lips quivered as I admitted the truth. "I'm about to explode."

Lash only had one word for me. "*Run*."

I didn't hesitate. I tried to keep control on my magic, but I could feel gusts of wind whipping in all directions as I sprinted down the tunnel. I needed to get out. The pressure inside my chest was peaking and when it blew, I felt as if it would take the entire city with me.

Silver light from the moon fell on my cheeks as I tasted fresh air, but I didn't stop running. I kept moving along the lake until I knew I was out of the city and out of anyone's reach.

I collapsed on the sand and I screamed until the taste of blood coated my tongue. A flock of songbirds deserted the nearby trees, sensing danger was near.

The whirling in my chest squeezed the air from my lungs and I let the power overtake me. A strong wind tugged at the trees until the branches curled to the point of snapping. A chorus of cracks filled the wood as the gusts spun around me, tangling my body in their hold.

Thin lines of breeze wrapped around my throat. I lifted my hands, trying to pull them away, but they weren't like rope. They shifted around my fingers, squeezing tighter, until my body was lifted off the ground entirely. My feet kicked uselessly as my own magic strangled me in the air.

Something moved along the lake. I tried to shout at them to leave me. That it wasn't safe. But I had no air to scream let alone speak. Tears spilled down my cheeks as I glimpsed fiery red curls. Panic pushed my heart to the brink and I knew in a few short seconds Gwyn would witness my death. Gerarda stood beside her and

I stared helplessly, pleading with my eyes to turn the girl around, but she didn't.

Gerarda pulled something out of her belt and brought it to her lips. She lifted her head to look up at where my magic had lifted me stories above the lake.

Something sharp pricked my thigh and the winds died. I dropped forty feet, free falling, before the shadows found me, wrapping around my waist. My finger trailed over the cool water of the lake as Riven pulled me back toward him. My vision blurred and I finally closed my eyes to rest.

CHAPTER SIX

I didn't need to open my eyes to know that the room was full of people. I could hear several steady heartbeats and one that was hammering in the corner of the room. My eyelids opened slightly as someone sat at the foot of my cot. Maerhal peered down at me like a cat, wide eyes and sitting on all fours. Her hands were shrouded in the shadows that covered me like a blanket as Riven spoke to someone above my head.

I blinked and Maerhal blinked back. "Her troubles wake her," she whispered. Vrail stood next to Nikolai but her face was turned to the old woman with yellow eyes on the other side of me.

Rheih Talonseer was crouched over a wooden bowl, mixing together something that smelled like rotting fish.

Maerhal plucked a flower from the table beside the bed and placed it behind my ear. She smiled widely at her son and I realized I was in her bed. We were in the small room off the infirmary where Nikolai brought his bouquet of flowers each day now that his mother had returned.

I brushed the petals with my fingers. "*Miivra gwethir*," I whispered, squeezing Maerhal's hand. It was the closest words Elvish had to "thank you." She lifted our joined hands and placed them on one knee while her chin rested on the other.

Nikolai glanced down at us with a stiff smile. I could spot the worry in his warm eyes, his arm still wrapped around Vrail protectively. She tucked her arm behind her, but not before I noticed her wrapped wrist.

My stomach clenched knowing I was responsible.

"I'm sorry," I mouthed, flicking my eyes to her wrist.

Her full cheeks bloomed red but she nodded. Her small smile was just as forgiving as it was genuine.

"And you're sure that she won't . . . *explode* again." Nikolai whispered the word as if I wouldn't hear it. He waved his arms around mimicking the whirlwind I had caused in the wood.

Rheih leveled him with a deadpan stare. "I have no power over that. That's up to her stubbornness." She slapped my shoulder with a surprising amount of strength for a Mortal her age. "The elixir has dampened her powers for a few days, but she's going to have to make the effort to train. I'm merely a Mage. I can't cure insolence." Her long pupils narrowed as she glanced down at me. "Or stupidity."

"I didn't mean for it to happen," I mumbled, pulling myself into a seated position.

Gerarda stepped out from behind Maerhal. Her lips were chapped and bleeding, but she didn't seem to care. "We all warned you that you needed to train your magic."

I winced. Riven turned toward Gerarda with a flash of violet in his eyes, the shadows along the walls darkening. "We said we would ease into that."

Gerarda shrugged. "If you didn't treat her like a child, you'd know this *is* me going easy. I would have dragged her out of bed by now. She could have killed someone."

My hands balled into fists along the coverlet and I lifted a hand to Riven's arm. "Gerarda is right."

Gerarda's jaw went slack. She turned to Rheih. "Whatever concoction you gave her. Give her all of it."

Rheih snickered and whispered something to Syrra in a dialect of Elvish I didn't understand. Syrra's eyes widened for the briefest moment before she nodded.

Maerhal wrapped her arms around her knees and leaned against Syrra, who stroked the top of her sister's head. Syrra had spent the better part of two days braiding thin vines into Maerhal's shorn hair. The result was a beautiful fountain of deep green braids that bloomed in sunlight. Though from centuries of surviving underground Maerhal's eyes were too accustomed to darkness for her to step outside until the suns had fully set.

"She thirsts like a fish," Maerhal whispered in her singsong voice.

My throat burned at her words. Even after everything that had happened, the craving was still latched onto my mind.

Rheih crossed her arms and turned to Nikolai. "It's no wonder why." The stark edge to her tone surprised me.

Nikolai tugged on the strand of his hair until it was completely straight. "I couldn't just stand by any longer. No one was doing anything."

Rheih muttered something under her breath as she threw a black leaf into her bowl and started mixing it into her paste. "Why does no one listen to a healer unless someone is bleeding?"

I glanced up at Riven but his jaw was as hard as stone and his gaze still locked on Gerarda. I turned to Syrra. "What are they on about?"

Syrra sighed. "The state you were in only made you more susceptible to burnout. Rheih thinks it's best if we ration your wine while you train your powers. Going without is obviously too dangerous." Syrra's eyes narrowed and I registered the statement for what it was. She hadn't told the others about the *winvra* but she would if I gave her any reason to.

I bit my lip, but the burning in my throat had already made the decision for me. "I will train my powers with Feron and Lash and any of the other magic wielders you think may help." I turned to Vrail and then Gerarda. "But that is all I have to offer. I cannot spend my days chasing lost dreams or this"—I raised my hand and a small gust of wind breezed through the room—"will only get worse."

Vrail opened her mouth, ready to launch into the expertly prepared argument that she had constructed while I was unconscious, but Gerarda held up her hand. Riven's eyes narrowed and the shadows around my legs tightened protectively.

"I can see that trying to persuade you will only be a waste of our time." Gerarda tucked the thin Elvish blade she had been flipping through her fingers into her weapons belt with an emphatic tug.

She left the room and Vrail chased after her. Nikolai looked down at me with a hard line across his mouth. "I'm one for dramatics, but what happened yesterday can*not* happen again, Keera."

The lack of *dear* at the end stung more than anything else. I grabbed his hand and nodded. "It never will again."

Nikolai smiled, not as widely as usual, but with the same warmth as ever. "Good." He squeezed my hand and then lifted an arm to help his mother off the bed. "We'll meet you at dinner."

Syrra followed, revealing the small bundle of limbs in the corner. Gwyn's chin was resting on her knees and her red curls were pulled back into a messy tangle behind her head. Deep purple crescents hung under her icy glare from the far corner of the room.

My heart fluttered. I reached out to her. "Gwyn . . ." I trailed off, unsure if I should offer some words of comfort or an apology. I had never realized how much of our relationship was her pulling me into conversation until she stopped speaking altogether.

All I wanted was to pull my voice out of my throat and wrap it with beautiful lace so I could watch Gwyn laugh as she opened one last gift from me. But there was no gift that could give Gwyn back her voice.

She stood and my chest flickered with hope for the briefest moment, thinking she was going to take my hand. Instead she lifted her chin to hide her trembling lip and ran out of the room.

I collapsed back onto the pillow. Riven's thumb caressed the back of my hand, but he said nothing. Somehow, he knew being comforted about my failings would only make me feel worse.

Tears pricked the corner of my eye. "It's torture to watch someone fall away and have no idea how to catch them."

Riven flinched. I turned my head and saw his violet eyes were swirling with too many emotions for me to read. He lifted a gentle hand to my brow and stroked my skin until whatever concoction Rheih had given me blanketed me once more.

Just as I was pulled back into the dreamless sea from the wine Rheih had given me, I heard Riven's whisper through the water. Distant, but clear. "It is."

CHAPTER SEVEN

I COLLAPSED ONTO A BROKEN LOG the moment Feron ended our first training session. My body ached, but not in a cold way that rattled my bones; it was warm and spent. Each breath took work but my lungs could hold more air than the day before. Though I was just as lousy of a wielder.

Riven lingered by the lake as Feron and Lash made their way back into Myrelinth. Exhaustion burned through me and I wanted nothing more than to run into the city and find Nikolai so he could give me my daily ration of wine.

I had more than earned it.

But there was a hollowness in Riven that pierced my gut to see, because I knew I'd caused it. I sat on the sand directly across from the spot along the lake where we had first talked after he returned to Myrelinth. Somehow the world was so different, colder and woven in threads of gray instead of color.

Riven paced behind me.

"When's the last time you released your magic?" I asked. Riven's shadows were oozing out of him like a black fog, casting sharp lines into the ground that slashed at the broken trees my own outburst had snapped behind him. I knew the pain of his powers was at its peak.

His jaw pulsed. "A while."

"You should do it now." I glanced back at the soft faelights that hung from the branches of the city. From this distance they were nothing but tiny orbs in the trees, like stars in the night sky that were beginning to settle above us.

"I can wait." Riven paced in front of me once more.

My back stiffened. "I trust you, Riv. You needn't worry about hurting me."

Riven ran a hand through his long, black mane, pulling his head back so I could see the tendons in his neck pulse. "That's not what I'm worried about." There was an edge to his words, like they were grating over something he didn't want to say.

My skin heated in shame. With everything that had happened after, I had forgotten about that desperate kiss. "Killian told you."

Riven halted. He blinked down at me and I could see the internal debate raging inside of him. Whether his patience had finally been ground too thin. All the things I wanted to tell him—about all the nights I hadn't come to find him even while his burl stayed lit—crashed through my mind, but I didn't know how to say them.

I didn't know where to start.

I closed my eyes and waited for Riven's fury but nothing came. I opened an eye to find Riven's brow was in his hand. "That is not what I'm worried about either, *diizra*."

The nickname felt like a red-hot knife cutting across my skin. I hated the softness in his eyes as he looked at me, perfectly gentle like he thought any sign of anger might make me break.

"It doesn't cause you worry that I *kissed* him?" I stood unable to contain the whirl of emotions inside me.

Riven's eyes narrowed but he didn't relent. "It was a mistake."

The certainty in his voice aggravated me. I didn't deserve it. I didn't deserve any of the kindness or softness he was giving me. I needed him to be angry just as I was. It was twisted and wrong, but I had filed all the broken parts of me to fine points, and I needed to know Riven was hard enough that I wouldn't cut him if he drew too near.

"You don't care that I pressed your own brother against a wall?" I scoffed. "You don't care that he kissed me back?"

Something feral flickered in Riven's gaze. The softness melted away into something less tame. "You've been wasting away in front of my eyes for *weeks* and you think I'm worried about a *kiss*?" He tossed his arm into the air and shook his head. "You think I care that you know what his lips taste like or how his hands feel on your waist?" Riven stalked toward me like a mountain cat tracking its prey. "It doesn't matter. Because we both know that when I touch you"—Riven stroked my jaw with his thumb—"that you won't remember what his touch felt like. When *I* kiss you"—Riven's fangs left a trail of goosebumps down my neck—"you won't remember his name."

I swallowed thickly as Riven's hand grabbed the back of my throat and pulled me into his chest. "And when I lick you"—Riven's other hand slipped between my thighs—"you won't remember he existed at all."

His gaze fell to my mouth and he inched forward. I closed my eyes and felt the brush of his lips for the first time in weeks. I breathed him in like my lungs were empty and he was the only thing that could sustain me.

Riven groaned into my mouth, refusing to separate even to breathe, as his hand wrapped around my waist. I caught his lip between my teeth and Riven scooped me up, wrapping my legs around him.

He carried me to the start of the tree line, shading ourselves from any beach dwellers across the lake. Not that either of us cared who saw. We were starved. Ravenous. Riven finally pulled away from my mouth to drag his teeth along my neck. I fisted my hand in his hair and moaned softly, feeling the warmth of our magic swell beneath my skin.

There was a dangerous edge to it I had never felt before. Something sharp beneath the electric charge that reminded me of a dagger held against my throat. I grabbed Riven's cheek and pulled his lips to mine once more. He tasted sweet, like nectar tea that I couldn't get enough of.

Tendrils of shadows swirled around my legs and waist, binding me against the hardness of his body. Riven slammed me against a tree and nipped at my ear. A wave of shivers ran down my spine, eliciting a gasp that made Riven only more daring.

Pinned between him and a thick trunk, he no longer needed two hands to hold me. One stroked my jaw, tilting my head up to his, as the other pressed at the throbbing spot between my thighs. He moved his hand in circular strokes and a moan escaped my lips. He pressed harder, running his thumb over my mouth as I tried to catch my breath.

He smirked with his head pressed against mine. His hand trailed to the nape of my neck and something in his eyes darkened. He tugged at the root of my hair in a way that felt achingly familiar and I groaned as his lips claimed mine.

A loud snap echoed through the woods. We both froze.

Nikolai cursed in the distance. "I feel compelled to tell you I was turning *around* when that branch decided to announce itself. With my foot."

I chuckled into Riven's chest as his hand shifted from between my thighs to my waist.

Nikolai kicked one half of the stick. "Is the moment over or should I go?"

Riven's jaw flexed. "What do you want, Nik?" It sounded like a threat.

I nipped his bottom lip and felt his fingers dig into my hip.

"It's dinnertime," Nikolai said as an explanation. "Arda told me that you had finished training. I didn't want to keep you waiting . . ."

I jolted against the tree and shimmied out of Riven's grasp. His neck flexed as he watched me adjust my tunic before stepping around the trunk. My eyes immediately fell to the wineskins in Nikolai's hands.

I swallowed, throat suddenly dry and wanting.

Nikolai took his time trailing his eyes over the disheveled state of Riven's collar and my braid with a sideways grin. Riven grunted, but didn't comment on the wine. His eyes were pained as he watched me grab at the wineskins just as I had grabbed at him. He swallowed the rejection and straightened his back. "I need to let off some of my power before we head back to the city. Can you stay?" He made a point of looking at Nikolai.

Nik's eyes widened, but he played off his shock well enough. "You know you never have to ask."

I looked up at Riven's pulsing jaw. "Do I need to stay?"

Riven's lips were nothing but a thin line as he looked at me in the same defeated way he had outside the stables. "No."

I didn't even make it back to my burl before I needed to sit from the wine. It had been hours since I ate and the use of my powers burned through all my energy.

I leaned against the tall tree that shaded Maerhal's statue. I found myself coming here often since I had returned to Myrelinth. Mostly because Maerhal's return meant that the small meadow was usually empty, but also because it reminded me of my own mother. The one I had barely gotten the chance to know.

All I had was that brief moment in the Rift where she had left me with more questions than answers. The selfish part of me wished she had been the one to return home from the dead rather than Maerhal. I was happy for Nikolai and Syrra, but there was a loneliness that came from witnessing their joy that I could never admit to. They had kin who still lived. Relatives and loved ones who had known them their entire lives.

But I was alone. A Halfling turned Light Fae, destined to either be the savior or extinction of my race.

I swallowed another swig of wine. Once I finished both skins I would be able to fall asleep without worry for who would find me there.

And then I'd do the same on the morrow. That was all I had to offer. That I would be a blade that could be used then holstered. I had broken free from the kingdom only to become exactly what Aemon made me. Gerarda had been right when she called my existence pathetic.

I took another gulp of wine and the liquid turned sour on my tongue. I closed my eyes and I saw Damien's face painted on my eyelids. I hated him. I hated the way that his cuts never seemed to truly heal—that he had found a way to use my own vices against me and that I was too weak to fight back.

CHAPTER EIGHT

I WAS TOO RESTLESS to return to my burl when I left the meadow. I kept the second wineskin slung around my shoulder and I walked aimlessly around the tunnels of the lower city, as far as possible from Riven and the burl I knew would still be lit.

I was angry. At myself. At him. At the world and the terrible choices it had given us. I didn't know if there was room inside me for anything else. Until there was, I would deal with the anger alone.

Eventually I found myself in the infirmary. I would've walked straight past if it weren't for the strange humming coming from inside. I shielded my faelight and stepped into the main room. Maerhal sat, cross-legged, on the middle of a bed. She had a book in her hands, but the cover was upside down.

Her wide, pretty eyes glanced up at me and she smiled, pointing to the chair. I pulled the wineskin onto my lap and sat. "You don't sleep?" I whispered in Elvish.

Maerhal sighed and curled one of the braided vines along her finger. “A bear rested too long must wake.”

I slumped back into the chair. After so many years trapped in that dungeon it was no wonder Maerhal’s body did not want to sleep. She had slept for years—decades—at a time in order to survive. I’d always thought of her Elvish sleep as a refuge but after weeks avoiding Damien’s visits into my dreams, I wondered if Maerhal’s dreams had become her jailers too.

I uncorked the wine and took a hefty swallow. Maerhal turned her head to look at me with the wide, unblinking eyes she shared with her son and sister.

“A river is not a wet stone,” she murmured in Elvish, switching the cross of her legs.

I scoffed and took another drink. “I am not the Blade.”

The truth of those words echoed deep inside me like a rock at the bottom of a well. I had taken that title as a way to end the Crown and protect the Shades. It seemed fitting that I should lose it the same day I failed at both those tasks.

Maerhal nodded, accepting my answer with a flip of the page. I watched her gaze shift amongst the words and noticed the way she always seemed to be half in a daze. Like she couldn’t tell if the world she was walking in was made of dream or not. Nikolai had told me that the healers didn’t think her mind would ever be the same after centuries in that hole.

My heart twinged. Maerhal had chipped away at herself as a matter of survival, letting her memories fade year after year. I knew what it was to wake up different and alone. In a world that had forgotten you.

I wanted better for her.

Something warm flowed under my skin. My healing gift pooled in my chest and then down my arm closest to Maerhal. I lifted my fingers to the bed and brushed her knee. The moment I did, the magic flowed out of me, slow and controlled like a lazy river.

Maerhal flinched at the touch but then she relaxed. Her eyes softened and for the first time when she looked at me, I knew she was seeing me for exactly who I was. She lifted her hand to my face and held my cheek. "You and I spent a long night together," she whispered in perfect Elvish. No riddle to untangle.

I kept my magic flowing over her. "Many." I swallowed knowing she had spent so many more alone than we had ever shared.

Maerhal shook her head. "Our days are too many to count by the turn of suns. We count by how tall and wide the forest grows."

She finally blinked and gave me a pointed look. "A tree does not grow in darkness."

I sighed. I was tired of growing. I was tired of standing in the same spot, unable to change anything that was happening around me. I understood why the trees of the Dead Wood had curled into themselves, withering away into blackness to protect their sisters in the neighboring woods. That was all I was trying to do, contain the pain to myself and not let it spread to the rest of the wood.

"Your mother wore that same face." Maerhal waved her hand above her head in tight delicate movements like she was painting a design into the air.

My magic stilled. "You knew my mother?"

Maerhal nodded slowly, her gaze still focused on her fingers. "I know her still."

I pursed my lips to the side and slumped back in the chair. Syrra had told Maerhal about the Light Fae and everyone else who had been lost to the Blood Wars, but some days Maerhal spoke as if the present and the past were the same. Happening all at once in a single braid of time.

I didn't have the will to tease apart the order only to watch her tangle the strands again. "My mother is gone."

Maerhal brushed her fingers along one of the open blooms glowing in the warm faelight floating above our heads. "The wind dies but surely blows again."

"My mother is not the wind," I answered, shocked by the anger in my words. "But if she were, she'd be a storm lying in wait to unleash her gales onto the realm."

A slow smile grew across Maerhal's face. She grabbed my hand and the flow of my healing gift returned. Maerhal's eyes focused on me once more as she tapped my nose. "She used to torment the older Elves with her gusts." Maerhal giggled and fell on her bed. "She'd carry their food away on the wind, letting children chase it before she brought it back to them. But her favorite thing to do was craft wings for the children of Kieran'thar and let them fly on her gusts over the sea."

Maerhal spread her wings and I knew from the joy on her face that she had been one of those children.

"My mother lived in Koratha?" I swallowed. "With you?"

Maerhal nodded, her arms still extended. "I would come and visit Syrrie as a child at *Niikir'na*. Your mother was always there with her. And when I met Nikolai's father, she would come to visit in our wood. Though Syrrie says the wood has died now." Maerhal's face fell as the ghosts of her past closed in.

I grabbed her hand, bringing her focus back to me. "Syrra knew my mother?"

Maerhal nodded and cupped my face in both her hands. "A wind may die but it will always blow again. There are many in this city who can breathe life into her gusts if you let them. To die is not to end."

I looked down at my hands. I had never considered that the gift I had been given in the Rift had come from my own mother. My vision blurred as I looked back up to Maerhal. She had stopped speaking in riddles. I let my magic flow between us once again. "Do you have any more stories?"

She nodded. "Ravaa taught me how to make purple nectar tea from *lilthira* blooms. It was Miiran's favorite; he would never stop laughing every time I made it for him." She smiled widely and I pictured the small child bouncing on Maerhal's knee in that statue, tight curls covering his eyes.

"You should make it for Nik again."

Maerhal's smile faltered. "The blooms must be picked under daylight for the nectar to be its sweetest." She pulled on the ends of her hair that still hadn't fully bloomed.

"Maybe I can find a way to bring the suns to you," I whispered, half in jest, half in wonder.

Maerhal tilted her head and squeezed my hand. "Your mother made the same for you."

I wrinkled my nose, eyes suddenly itchy. "I don't remember."

Maerhal frowned. "I am not your mother, but I know how grateful I am to my sister and Feron for loving Miiran like their own son. I think Ravaa would want the same for you." She squeezed my hand. "If you would let me."

I wiped my eyes. "You might come to regret that offer."

Maerhal laughed in her singsong way and nodded. She opened her mouth but then a figure appeared at the entrance of the tunnel.

It was the first time I'd ever seen Rheih Talonseer show the tiniest bit of surprise. Her yellow eyes immediately fell on the still full wineskin in my chair. "Didn't mean to interrupt," she said gruffly, putting down her bunch of flowers and weeds on the table in the middle of the room. She started stuffing petals and clippings into glass jars with labels too small for my eyes to read from Maerhal's bedside.

"Your burl is ready whenever you don't want unexpected visitors." Rheih raised a brow at Maerhal. I got the sense this was a nightly conversation.

Maerhal scrunched her nose like a disgruntled cat at the large faelights hovering over the Mage's shoulders. She jumped down from the bed and walked out the door, waving her hand in slow circles above her head as a farewell.

"The sunlight still hurts her eyes," Rheih explained with a shrug.

"Why are you here so late?" I glanced across the empty beds.

Rheih clucked her tongue. "It seems the other healers can't find the right mixture so I am trying."

I froze. "Is someone hurt?"

Rheih shook her head and grabbed a small marble bowl to crush three sprigs. "Killian's friend is sick. He hasn't been able to keep food down for weeks. He barely sleeps."

The blood from my face drained. I had no idea someone had been sick for that long, let alone someone close to Killian. "Who?"

Rheih shrugged. "I remember elixirs not names."

I ran through a list of faces in my mind, but I hadn't made a point to be good with names either.

"The blond one," Rheih grunted trying to open a sealed jar with her bent, spotted fingers.

I grabbed the jar from her hand. "Collin?" I asked with a resounding *pop* from the lid.

Rheih snapped her fingers for me to hand it back. "Yes. The Halfling."

"He's ill?" I placed the jar on the table. Rheih stuffed her hand inside and pulled out three jellied eggs. "How long?"

Rheih shrugged. "Long enough to call me back."

My stomach tightened. "Wouldn't it be quicker if I heal him?"

Rheih snorted. When she realized I hadn't been asking in jest she shooed me away from her table.

"Your gift is a powerful one, but often useless." Rheih took a loud sip from her tea. Her yellow eyes watched me daringly over the rim.

"Useless?" I balked. "It's saved my life. It saved Vrail and Gwyn."

Rheih rolled her eyes. "No need to squeal like a kettle. I said *often* not *always*."

I shook my head in disbelief. Rheih had a gift for getting under my skin.

She pointed to her bowl. "Do you know what any of this is?"

I crossed my arms smugly. "Fish eggs, dew root weed, red clay, and honey pool petals."

"Wrong."

I pointed at each label on her jars. "You can't possibly deny your own handwriting."

Rheih clucked her tongue again. "To you, they are ingredients because when it comes to healing you're as dull as a pair of rusted scissors."

"And to your sharp wits?"

"Medicine." Rheih waved her hand in the air like it was obvious. "Magic does you good, but it can only stitch as well as your knowledge goes."

My cheeks heated, thinking of Gwyn and what the healers had told me after we first returned. "Gwyn . . ." I trailed off not knowing how to pose the question.

Rheih squeezed my hand in a rare display of gentleness. "Do not blame yourself for that. You did what needed to be done to save her life and you succeeded."

"But had I known more, she wouldn't have been left barren?" Gwyn had been nauseous the entire journey back and grew weaker each hour. By the time I had reached the healers and Riven, she wa cold and mostly unconscious. They called for a Dark Fae with a small gift for healing. He confirmed that Damien had left Gwyn's womb disconnected from the rest of her body, but inside. So new to my gift, I had fused her wounds without it and the organ had begun to rot.

Thankfully the healers saved her in time.

Rheih stepped around the table and grabbed me by both arms. "I will only say this once because I know what it is to have a mistake weigh on you. But had I trained you, the result would've been the same. There was no saving that organ—not even with your gift—but you could have known enough to remove it first and prevented the rot. *That* is how you sharpen your gift. You need to learn all the rivers and caverns of the body, just as a healer does. Knowing the limits of your power will only sharpen them."

My breath caught in my throat but I nodded. "Could you? Teach me, I mean."

Rheih placed her hands on her hips and assessed me from boot to braid. "I'm not sure you have the stamina. This isn't swordplay."

I resisted the urge to roll my eyes. "I think I would manage."

Rheih pushed several gray hairs back into her mane of curls and nodded. "I will call you for your first lesson in a few days' time. Go get some rest." She pointed to the door and started crushing an ingredient with her other hand.

I grabbed my second wineskin and nodded in farewell. I hummed to myself down the tunnel in complete darkness, all my earlier anger having cooled to a quiet stillness that was closer to peace than anything I had felt in months.

There was a soft noise behind me, like a leaf brushing against stone. I slowed, listening for the sound again and was hit in the back of my head. I was unconscious before my body crumpled to the ground.

CHAPTER NINE

"WE SHOULD UNTIE HER HANDS before she wakes." The voice was familiar but I couldn't place it. For once, I hadn't woken to a piercing ache in my skull but instead found my mind was hazy and slow like an empty port creaking in the morning fog.

The second voice was sharp and short like a dagger. "Don't touch her. Keera will break my nose for what we did."

Gerarda.

"*You* did." The first voice again. Even with my eyes still closed I knew it was Vrail. "I had no idea you planned on *kidnapping* her!"

I peered up at them through my lashes and saw Vrail's round face was flushed and sweaty while Gerarda merely shrugged. She flipped a hiltless Elvish blade through her fingers. "If you'd known, you would have told her or that miserable gloom that follows her around."

I swallowed to clear my throat. The air tasted of brine, meaning we were near the sea. My heart quickened, thinking Gerarda had been foolish enough to bring us back to the Order in search of the Shades, but the air was also tinged with the scent of sulfur—we weren't anywhere near the capital, but somewhere on the western shores of Elverath. As far from the Shades as we could be.

I stretched my fingers through the bindings and felt the damp grass underneath me. There was no ash in the sky or snow on the ground, so wherever Gerarda had taken me was not the frigid city of Volcar, but close enough to taste the first hints of its fiery mountain.

Vrail and Gerarda were still bickering. Neither noticed when I opened my eyes fully and squinted from the rays of the suns. High above us, gulls floated in the sky like droplets of water, disappearing between wisps of cloud that stretched across the blue expanse.

I tried to sit myself up but failed. My body was heavy and my arms were bound tightly behind me at the wrists *and* the elbows.

Gerarda's dark eyes landed on me with the sharpness of a hawk and she stopped flipping her blade through her fingers. A small smile crept along her lips as I struggled against her bindings.

Always a perfectionist, I thought to myself. I shot Gerarda what I hoped was a hard enough look to force her compliance. "Untie me before I stab you."

Gerarda raised her brows at Vrail before turning back to me with a fully formed grin on her face. "I doubt you've ever escaped a kidnapping by issuing empty threats."

I ran my tongue along my fangs. I had built a reputation for never issuing a threat I didn't intend to keep. Gerarda knew that, her remark was just to irk me. "The last person who kidnapped me got punched in the jaw."

Gerarda's lips had moved beyond a grin to something more feral. "Try it."

I rolled my eyes. Vrail rocked back and forth on her feet, unsure of where to look. "Hitting someone in the back of the head is a cowardly way to overcome your target," I said.

Gerarda slipped her blade through her fingers once more. "You say cowardly, I say efficient. *A blade must be sharp and always at the ready.*" She bent down and cut through the rope along my elbows with her knife.

I groaned as the blood flow returned to my upper arms. Gerarda had tied them tighter than she needed to. "Didn't we hear the mistresses say that enough when we were initiates?"

"Apparently you needed some repetition." Gerarda left the binds along my wrists uncut so I had to struggle to loop my arms around my legs and pulled the knots free with my teeth. Vrail stepped forward to help but Gerarda shook her head.

"She won't hurt you, Vrail," I said, rubbing the red marks along my wrists. "Gerarda may rattle like a snake but she rarely bites."

Gerarda pulled back her lip to flash her fangs.

"I'm not so certain," Vrail mumbled.

I stood and was welcomed with a salty spray against my face. The mist cooled my skin and helped clear the fatigue from my mind. I peered down and saw waves taller than any dwelling in Elverath crash against the cliffs like ripples in a pond. We stood at the point where two towering cliff edges merged. As I looked into the distance, one cliff verged to the south, decorated with the descending foothills of the Burning Mountains and swirling trees that I had only ever seen in the Singing Wood. The other cliff broke to the west, climbing even higher in elevation until its peak tickled the bellies of the gulls above.

It was as if powerful magic had cut through the middle of a mountain and cast it into the sea. I had never beheld the sight before, but whispers of these cliffs had reached me even in the kingdom. The

Cliffs of Elandorr were said to be cursed by the souls of the Elves who had been lost the day their city crashed into the water and was never seen again.

"I thought this was only a story," I whispered in disbelief.

Gerarda stared out at the cliffs with the same reverence. Her voice was soft like the breeze that blew through her short hair and my messy braid. "We were told many stories as children. It will take more than one lifetime to find the seeds of truth within the soil of Aemon's lies."

I turned to her but didn't say anything. Gerarda and I had spent the entirety of our lives in opposition. Competitive initiates and then adversarial Shades. Even now, my every muscle twitched in anticipation for her strike, but how much of that was founded in truth and how much in the way Aemon had made us distrustful of those who should have been our closest allies?

The thought made my throat burn, yearning for the sweet taste of wine that would wash any other revelations from my mind completely.

I patted my pocket for the wineskin I'd been carrying when Gerarda knocked me over the head. It was gone.

"You thought it wise to kidnap me *and* take my wine?"

Gerarda didn't say anything, but walked behind us to where three horses were grazing in the meadow. She undid one of the saddle bags on the small brown mare carrying Gerarda's favored weapons. Her small hands slipped inside and reappeared carrying two wine-skins. They hung from her fists like geese held by their necks.

I swallowed against the dryness in my throat and snatched them from her. Vrail's foot tapped uncontrollably as I uncorked one of the skins and took a heavy gulp.

"That is all we have," Vrail said. Her soft jaw pulsed as she stared at me in that shy but unrelenting way only she could master. "Best ration your supply until we know how long this will take."

I took another, smaller swallow and replaced the cork. My gaze bounced between them. The only reasons I could think for the two of them to go to the trouble of kidnapping me would be to travel to the Order. Yet we were leagues from there . . . That only left one other option.

I pinched the bridge of my nose to dampen my anger. "This is about the seals?"

Vrail bit her lip guiltily, but she didn't evade my gaze.

"I already told you, I'm not going to listen—"

"The time for listening has come and gone." Gerarda held her thin blade to the belly of my wine sack. "I realize your hopes have left you and you're determined to spend your days chained to your despair. But I will not allow one of our best warriors to drink herself to ruin until I *know* the Shades are gone."

Gerarda's blade pushed a little harder against the sack. I leaned back and clenched my jaw. "You fill my cup but ask me not to drink from it?" I stepped back and my laugh seared my throat.

Gerarda lifted her chin. "Your wine eases the pain of lost hopes—I intend to reinvigorate them."

I was about to ask her how she meant to do such a thing when the breeze from the cliffs grew into a gale, blowing Gerarda's claim out to sea. The gulls that had been resting their wings suspended in the winds high above dove for the water, plummeting from their heights as the entire sky turned black.

There were no wisps of cloud or hints of the moon along the horizon. Even the suns were gone, entirely covered in shadow. The sea below us disappeared but the roaring waves echoed through the darkness, marking the passage of time as all other markers were stripped from our senses.

The blackness settled across the land as far as we could see. A tiny ball of light floated by my head and I reached for it, but could not touch it. As it slowly grew larger, I realized it was not a tiny faelight floating in front me at all but a much larger one coming closer in the distance.

Vrail ignited a faelight of her own, illuminating the open fear in her face and the resolved, hidden worry in Gerarda's. I grinned wickedly at them both. Whatever plans they had for me were moot. They had failed to outrun Riven and his shadows.

Three figures appeared on horseback. In the middle, riding a tall stallion the same color as his shadows, was Riven. Nikolai rode to the left of him while Syrra protected them from the right. All three had their eyes locked on the Dagger.

Riven leaped from his mount before his horse had come to a full stop. He slashed his arm through the air and tendrils of shadow broke from the black ground, circling around Gerarda like coiling vipers. She had a shadow snake around each limb and one that hung loosely from her throat, not tight enough to cause her harm, but enough to issue the threat it was.

Riven flashed his fangs and his chest rose in heavy breaths as he stalked closer to Gerarda. "What is the meaning of this?" His voice boomed against the darkness like a boulder crashing down a mountain.

She did not answer him or struggle against the shadows, instead she lifted her chin just as she had done to me dozens of times before, and glowered up at Riven. "You had no patience for the advice of a stranger, so the stranger took matters into her own hands."

Nikolai turned to Syrra, who tightened her grip on the reins of her horse. Riven gritted his teeth and stepped so close to Gerarda I knew he could smell the salt and flame of her skin. "Keera is a citizen of our people and a protector of this land. Kidnapping her is considered treason against the Elverin and all of Elverath."

My throat tightened. The only thing I had done that came close to deserving of those words was saving Vrail and Maerhal. And even that had been more for me than for the Elverin.

The shadow rope around Gerarda's neck tightened but she did not strain. "If this doesn't work, then tie me up in shadow and take me to wherever traitors go."

Syrra closed her eyes. It seemed Gerarda was not the only one who had grown impatient. "What are you proposing, child?"

"We think Keera can break the seals." She fought against the shadows to turn to Vrail.

Syrra assessed her student carefully. "Is this true?"

Vrail nodded several times in quick succession. "I've learned everything I can about the magic the Light Fae used. Killing Aemon would have broken all the seals simultaneously, but I believe Keera can also break each one individually."

I scoffed. "You can't even find them." Vrail and Gerarda had spent the past two months trying every possible location for the seals, but they were gone.

"I think that is part of their magic. They will only appear for the one able to break them." Vrail nodded so rapidly my own neck ached. "I tried to ascertain the magic that spelled them from the book we stole, but it took some time. Eventually I realized that the seals were spelled to that blade so Gerarda stole Keera's dagger—"

I stalked toward Gerarda. "You did what?"

"You didn't even notice." She sighed, apparently bored. "You won't get an apology from me."

The shadow along her neck tightened ever so slightly. I gave Riven a satisfied smirk but his face was stony and unyielding.

"We were wasting time searching for the seals on our own," Vrail continued, ignoring the tension between me and Gerarda. "The spell requires *zibi'fir*, which I had mistranslated thinking it meant water since *sibi'thir* is a derivative—"

"Vrail." The crease between Riven's brows deepened. "What is your point."

"I'm getting there." Vrail took a deep breath before spiraling out again. "But in that specific instance it had actually been referencing blood, which was confusing since our ancestors used the same word for both."

"We need Keera's blood to undo the seal," Gerarda interrupted bluntly.

I reared back. "Why mine?"

Vrail's leg bounced. "Because the seals were set by a Light Fae so only a Light Fae can undo them."

"My blood can break the seals?" I swallowed. "It's amber not red like my mother's kin."

Vrail bit her lip, unable to commit to the certainty.

"Yes," Gerarda answered for her without a problem.

Syrra's brow lifted by the tiniest fraction. "And the results would be the same? The siphons would stop draining magic from Elverath and the magic would be restored?"

Vrail tilted her head side to side. "That is my assumption. However, every use of magic has unpredictable outcomes. If we're correct, Keera would be breaking five times the amount of seals as the Light Fae intended. That poses its own risk."

"Something tells me Keera is unconcerned about the risks," Nikolai quipped without looking at me.

I narrowed my eyes at him and crossed my arms. "That is what you brought me here for? To break a seal?"

Vrail nodded.

My mouth twitched, unconvinced. "And you're certain the seal is here? You just admitted you cannot see it."

"She's sure enough to kidnap you and suffer the consequences," Gerarda interrupted, still refusing to take her eyes off Riven.

I thought Vrail would contradict Gerarda, let the others know the kidnapping had been left out of whatever version the Dagger had told her, but instead she gave the group one decisive nod. She pointed to the small bridge that led over the crevice in the tall cliff. A thin path trailed up the split mountain to a flat meadow at the top. "It's there."

Riven's eyes narrowed. "That doesn't answer Keera's question."

My heart tightened but Riven didn't look at me. His gaze was focused on ensuring his shadows didn't tug too tightly around Gerarda's throat.

Vrail took a deep breath before tumbling into her rapid explanation. "We know the point of origin for the original spell that created the siphons and their seals. The locations would spread out from there."

"And they couldn't be connected to the mainland," Gerarda interjected as she leaned back against a slithering shadow.

"Yes." Vrail nodded. "The likely locations were easy enough, there were only five possible places and I doubted the Light Fae would put two seals in one place. If you take the shortest line between the point of origin—the Ruins of Faevra—and the split half of the Cliffs of Elandorr, I can assume that the seal will fall along the eastern side."

"Water takes the easiest path," Nikolai whispered, staring at Vrail in proud awe.

She smirked. "And so does magic. If my estimate is correct, then it will confirm the location of all the seals."

Riven lowered his hand but his shadows were still wrapped around Gerarda. "And you thought it best to kidnap Keera instead of bringing the matter to us?"

Vrail's gaze was suddenly locked on her boot. "This . . . experiment solves all our problems. We can ascertain if my theory is correct without risking an attack from Damien or endangering the Shades. And Gerarda was sure you'd both say no."

I gritted my teeth, unable to disagree with that assessment.

Riven's violet eyes shifted to me for the merest second, softening with concern before returning to Gerarda. Every one of his muscles was flexed, holding his power in that thin, middle place between exerting his gift and maiming her.

"If Keera is the one who must do it, then she is the one who decides." Riven stood tall and his shoulders relaxed for the first time since he'd arrived. The shadows uncurled themselves from Gerarda's limbs and neck and dissipated back into the inky blackness underneath our feet.

She rubbed her wrist and gestured at the blanket of shadow that still covered the horizon. "I'd ease up on those too, Gloomy, or Damien's armada will find us before we can ascertain shit."

Nikolai let out a laugh, quickly covering it with a cough. Riven's lips did not twitch, but a single shadow coiled up Nikolai's torso and tugged on his hair hard enough to jerk his head. Nikolai swatted the tendril of darkness away. "Uncalled for."

Riven ignored him; he only had eyes for me. His violet irises brightened as the shadows faded and the skies once again filled with sunlight. For the first time in weeks, Riven looked hopeful. More than that, he had hope *for* me. I shifted in my boots but was unable to look away from him. Too many things had been outside of the tight grip I kept on them, too many things had gone wrong. But this, this I could do. Even though I didn't believe it would work, Riven did. And I could give him that.

I turned to face the towering cliff with my decision made. "Vrail, lead the way."

CHAPTER TEN

RIVEN RODE BESIDE ME as we climbed the steep mountainside of days long passed. I didn't speak because I didn't know what to say to him. He didn't speak either, once again letting me set the course between us.

Riven slowed his horse so we followed the others, riding just out of earshot from even Syrra's sharp hearing.

Riven's gaze dropped to the ground. The muscles in his neck flexed, as if trying to hold the words back before he spoke.

He grabbed a small parcel from his saddlebag, tossing it to me. I caught the leaf-bound packet with one hand and waited for Riven to explain but he only nodded for me to open it.

I unraveled the wrapping as best I could on horseback and found a leather box holding five vials. Four of them were soft pastel shades of liquids I didn't recognize, but the middle one was black and inky. Just like the *winvra* elixir Hildegard had given me to ease my pain.

I traced a gentle finger along the edge of the glass and turned to Riven. "I don't know what the others are for."

Riven relaxed into his saddle. Guilt pricked my heart. I had given him every reason to expect another fight. "They're other medicinal aids. The yellow can help with headaches and the blue will help spark your appetite again. The lavender is made from dew root and it can stop even the worst bouts of nausea."

I swallowed and looked back at him. No words climbed up my throat because there was nothing to say.

"I'm not here to judge you, Keera. And I have *never* thought you weak, even now. But your healing gift only goes so far. The *Faelinth* has many ways to help you, I just wanted you to know." One of Riven's shadows appeared from under his cloak and hung in the air between our horses. It circled once around my wrist before caressing the back of my palm.

It took a few moments before I trusted my voice enough to speak. "Thank you. That is very kind."

Riven smiled; it was still tight but there was a warmth to it too. "Whatever you need, *diizra*. Though you should know it was Syrra who put the package together."

I glanced up the hill where Syrra's dark green cloak and black waves billowed in the salty air. It shouldn't have surprised me that Syrra would be the one to bundle all the aids I would need to quit drinking again. She had overcome her own vice, and *winvra* was much more potent and much more deadly than Elven wine.

I turned back to Riven. Part of me wanted to tell him that even if I cared enough to stop, I couldn't. That every night I would be visited by Damien and taunted by whatever memory he wanted me to relive. I bit my tongue, keeping that truth deep inside myself where it could not harm anyone.

But then a thought occurred to me. "Is there an elixir that can take away my dreams?"

I could see the question settle on Riven's brow but he didn't ask it. Instead he rubbed his reins between his finger and thumb and watched as a group of gulls soared up over the cliff beside us. "I'm not sure, but that doesn't mean there isn't one. I can ask the healers what can be done as soon as we return to Myrelinth. If not, perhaps Rheih can make something."

A weight rolled off my shoulders and back down the trail as I looked at Riven. It had been a small step, a minuscule ask in comparison to everything we faced, but I couldn't ignore the way the pain at my throat seared a little less.

"You have been too kind."

Riven opened his mouth to protest, but I shook my head.

"You have been nothing but kind and patient when I have been everything but. I can't undo the things I've said or the things I've *done* . . . but I will try to be kind again. To you and the others."

The shadow around my wrist uncurled and lifted to my cheek. I felt the ghost of Riven's touch along my face, soft and quick like a summer breeze.

Riven stopped his horse and I thought he was going to say something else, but his eyes were wide and focused on the trail ahead. We had climbed to the highest point of the cliff. It towered over the sea the way mountains peered down at their valleys. Time had flattened the peak, leaving nothing but a small meadow with long blades of grass and shrubbery swaying in the wind. A large gorge split the peak from the rest of the summit, leaving only a small bridge for our horses to cross.

The others had dismounted and let their horses graze. Their eyes tracked along the ground but I knew they saw nothing but green grass covering the peak. Riven let out a tight gasp and his brows furrowed. He pointed to the ground as I finished crossing the bridge, seeing what the others could not. The untouched meadow had disappeared and instead there was a circular design cut through the grass in thick black lines as if a fire had permanently scorched the earth.

Riven dismounted his steed and walked the perimeter of the design. Still perched on my saddle, I saw that the curved lines intersecting the others grew tighter at the center of the seal. They formed a web across the ground, just like a spider's silk.

I dropped my reins and dismounted my horse. From the gasps that echoed into the wind, I knew the glamour had shattered for the others the moment I touched the ground. I stepped to the edge of the seal and knelt beside it. Nikolai started to speak, but Syrra held up her hand as I traced my finger over the circular edge.

I grazed the scorched earth, staining my fingertip black with ash. A harsh wind blew across my face and I lurched forward, scared that the gust would blow away the seal before we could decode it. But instead the seal had reignited. What had been black scorched earth was now dark red embers. As I peered closer, I saw the middle lines were not solid at all, but tightly written script.

Riven's eyes narrowed, noticing the script immediately. "Can you read this?" he asked Syrra. The Elf shook her head. Gerarda turned to Vrail who was circling around the seal caught between a walk and a run.

"I can't read it fully, but I've translated enough." She paused and stepped delicately inside the circle. We all held our breath, waiting for something to happen, but when it didn't Vrail settled her second foot in another space between the curved lines.

"*Iq'troth danzir, El'ferah kiiltho iqwe'fir,*" she whispered to herself and then again to us.

I turned to Syrra but she only shrugged. "That tongue is long forgotten. There were some speakers left when Faelin cast the second sun, but all were gone by the time I was born. I doubt even Feron could decipher the script."

"This is why you all must read more books," Vrail mumbled to herself, still studying the writing. "This word here—*iqwe' fir*—means magic. And this one I recognize as Elverath. *El' ferah*, they are different on the page but similar on the tongue."

"Very clever, Vrail," Nikolai whispered. He looked down at her like she was one of his inventions. As if he wanted to take apart her mind and put it back together again until he understood exactly how it worked.

The tops of Vrail's full cheeks flushed. "I have my moments." She pointed to the third line. "This is where it speaks of a blade marked by blood."

"Aren't all blades marked with blood eventually?" Nikolai grabbed his elbow, letting go of his stretched strand of hair.

"Drawing blood and being marked by blood are not the same," Vrail answered more to herself than to us. Her gaze was locked on my hip where my dagger was usually kept.

Syrra's brows rose. "You think Keera's blade was blood-bound?"

Vrail nodded several times. "It would explain how it made its way back to her. But I've only read about them. I've never seen a blood-bound blade in its glory."

"Have you?" Riven turned to Syrra.

Syrra shook her head. "Not one that has not been broken."

My headache scratched at the base of my skull. "Can one of you explain what she's talking about?"

Vrail straightened her back, ready to give a lesson, but it was Syrra who stepped forward to explain. "The courtyard at *Niikir'na* had a design made from the stone, it had five circular branches on it like the branches that surround the Myram tree."

I stilled. How many times had I trained in that courtyard at the Order? How many times had I walked across the stone without giving that design a second thought? I had never realized how similar it was to the Myram tree. I swallowed and ignored the urge to tell Syrra that the same symbol was carved into my back.

"Yes, it's still there," I said instead.

Syrra nodded. "Just as there are five branches of the Myram tree, there were five Elvish warriors who first built *Niikir'na*. When they were done, they sealed their own swords with each other's blood. It was said that Elverath herself blessed those blades and imbued them with special powers. They were passed to the best warriors for generations until eventually each weapon was lost or broken."

"And you think my dagger is like those blades?"

Syrra tilted her head to the side. "The others were blades of gold or bronze. One still hangs in Sil'abar, though its blade has been shattered."

"When I spoke to my mother that day . . . she said magic has a way of bringing us what we need."

Syrra smiled softly. "It is said that each of those blades chose their next wielder. Somehow they would find their way into the hands of whoever they chose. I would think your dagger chose you in the same way."

"To kill the king?" I choked on my own laugh. "It didn't stop Damien from doing it first."

Syrra's arms flexed, pulling her scars tight. "Magic can only go so far."

"I would wager my keys to the library in Volcar that this word means *to cut*." Vrail interrupted by jumping up onto her feet again. She looked at me. "Do you trust me?"

I swallowed, suddenly feeling the weight of everyone's eyes on me, and nodded.

Vrail waved her hands until Riven and Gerarda stepped back from the seal. "I need you to retrace the seal with your blade. Start with the outer circle and end in the middle."

"That's it?" I blinked back my surprise. "My mother meant for me to stab Aemon through the heart, but I could have cut through dirt instead?"

Vrail bit her cheek. "This is powerful magic, Keera. I have no way of knowing what breaking a seal of this magnitude could do to you. It took dozens of Light Fae to create and seal the siphons. And that magic cost them all their lives."

Riven hardened beside me. "You're saying Keera could die?" His shadows crept up my legs.

Vrail twisted her fingers nervously. "I'm saying we need to be prepared to help her in whatever way we can."

Riven stepped in front of me, blocking my view of the others. "You do not need to do this, *diizra*."

"Are you stopping me?" I lifted a brow up at him.

Riven closed his eyes and sighed, already knowing the point was moot. "No."

"Good." I stepped around him and looked at Vrail. "I'll do it."

She nodded and turned to Gerarda who pulled my bloodstone dagger from her satchel and handed it to me. I gripped the bone hilt tightly in my hand as I stepped to the edge of the seal.

Everyone stood a few feet back, equidistant from one another along the perimeter. I could hear the elevated heartbeats of Vrail and Riven and the slow, steady tempos of Gerarda's and Syrra's. I focused on those as I brought the point of my blade to the burning ground and cut into the earth.

Something powerful took hold of my wrist. It was as if my arm had plunged through the dirt and was being pressed by the weight of the mountain. I couldn't pull it back or let go of the blade, all I could do was step backward along the curved edge of the seal, dragging the blade across it.

As I did, the seal transformed behind my cut. The burning embers flashed bright and turned into a silver liquid that glowed with moonlight.

Gerarda nodded. "I told you."

I gritted my teeth and kept cutting. The winds blew in violent circles around us but no one moved. The pull of the seal's magic drained me of my energy with every inch. Ten times worse than any training exercise Feron had put me through. It was like I was using my healing gifts, feeling the warmth of my magic flow out of myself, but there was nothing warm about this. All I could feel was cold earth. My skin didn't even notice the warmth of the burning embers as I cut through them.

I finished the outer circle and the coldness only grew, the lock on my arm got only heavier. I slowly maneuvered myself through the seal, careful not to step on anything but the small patches of green grass through the design.

Somehow I reached the final cut, dragging the red blade back through the seven other lines I had already carved in the earth. I paused, waiting for something to happen but it didn't. The lines of silver I had left behind in the seal still shone, rippling like a pond waiting for something to dive into their depths.

The magic was waiting for something too.

"A blade marked with blood," I whispered to myself as I lifted the dagger to my palm and sliced it across my skin. Riven took a step forward as a pool of amber blood dropped onto the center of the seal. The moment it touched the silver liquid the entire seal gleamed with gold light, just like the portal at Myrelinth.

Without knowing why, I plunged my dagger through the middle of the seal again. The world went silent as I was blasted by a gale of warm air that pushed through my lungs until I thought they would burst. I fell backward onto the ground that was now covered in blooms and small shrubs of every color.

I looked up at the sky and saw that the clear blue expanse was thick with raging storm clouds. They roared overhead, swirling in a spiral of dark green. I lifted my hand out to them and a clash of lightning split the sky. My body jerked violently and everything went white.

CHAPTER ELEVEN

I OPENED MY EYES to five worried faces hovering over me. My head was in Riven's lap and I could hear the strain on his teeth from clenching his jaw as hard as he was. "What happened?"

Gerarda smirked. "You electrocuted yourself."

"I thought you were dead," Nikolai rasped. Vrail reached into Nikolai's chest pocket and handed him his own handkerchief to wipe his eyes.

Syrra crossed her arms and glanced at Riven. Both seemed unconvinced that I was unscathed.

I blinked. I remembered the crack of lightning and the smell of burnt earth. I fidgeted on the ground, expecting to ache from the blow, but I didn't. I didn't feel pain at all. My head was suddenly clear and each breath felt easier than the last. The warmth of my magic hummed under my skin, somehow more powerful than ever before.

I grabbed Riven's hand and he flinched.

"You feel it too?" I whispered as his eyes shone violet.

Riven nodded. "Your magic is stronger. Warmer."

"And yours?"

Riven's jaw pulsed and he shook his head.

I sat up and waved my hand over a patch of weeds. My gusts flattened them immediately, but the whirlwind in my chest barely roared. I flexed my fingers, knowing they were capable of so much more.

I spun around in excitement and something scorching shot down my arm. A new form of magic dancing under my skin. It felt raw and deadly.

Vrail squealed shoving Nikolai to the ground. His eyes widened in surprise as Vrail threw herself on top of him. "Not in front of Keera." Nik had the audacity to wink at me from the dirt. "She'll get jealous."

Vrail started slapping the hem of his jacket. "You're on fire, you fool."

Nikolai's eyes widened in horror as he saw the smoke. Syrra grabbed a waterskin from her saddlebag. She snatched Gerarda's blade from her hand and sliced through the leather, dousing Vrail and Nikolai with the flames.

She tossed the skin to the ground and smirked at me. "It seems Lash'raelth is no longer our only fire wielder."

It took me a moment to realize she was talking about me. "*I* did that?" I whispered, staring at my fingers. The hot liquid rumbled under my skin once more and a small flame ignited over my hand.

Vrail stood up and studied the flame. "What did you feel when the seal broke?"

"It was hard to cut, like it was draining all the energy out of me." I retraced the movements of my arm with my free hand. "But then when it finally broke, I felt a flood of power and the sky cracked."

Vrail's eyes narrowed. "You don't seem drained now."

"I feel amazing." I smiled widely. "Better than I have in months."

"But not until the seal was broken." Vrail bit her lip.

Gerarda elbowed Vrail in the arm. "What does it matter. It worked."

My chest fluttered at those words. I stared at Gerarda's smug smile. She'd been right to drag me out to the cliffs and prove me wrong. I felt my magic surge inside me and thought of just how much more it would grow with every seal we broke.

Vrail's lip twitched upward. "I just hope the seals don't take their toll."

"Everything isn't a problem for you to solve." Gerarda patted Vrail's full cheek and flipped her blade casually through the air. "This is a victory."

Riven flinched and bent over. He let out a small gasp of air that made Syrra rush to his side.

"What is it?" she whispered.

Riven clenched his teeth. "I didn't take my elixir this morning."

I was already at Riven's horse. I helped him onto the saddle before climbing up in front of him. "How bad is it?" I whispered once we had started back down the cliff.

Riven took a moment to answer. I could feel him wince against my back. "I'll be fine once we get back." I grabbed his arm with my hand and wrapped it around my waist, refusing to break contact with his skin for a single second.

Riven relaxed into my touch with a soft sigh that proved to me the pain was worse than I feared. In that moment I was grateful for the *miiskwithir* bond we shared and that my touch could ease his pain. "Is that better?"

Riven nodded against my shoulder. "Much. Thank you, *diizra*."

He didn't speak as we crossed through the portal and then rode through the Dark Wood to the next one. I heard the others keeping pace behind us, but couldn't see them in the darkness. When we reached the edge of the city, Feron and Lash were waiting for us, both of their gazes wide and unfocused as if they were witnessing a parade of ghosts.

Lash helped Riven dismount his horse and handed him a small vial of green liquid Feron had been holding in his hand. I narrowed my eyes at the vial and Feron pointed at a vine hanging from one of the nearby trees. "I sensed he needed it when you crossed into the wood."

I blinked. "I didn't know your magic could do that."

Feron stood straight, barely leaning on his cane, as he took in a deep breath. "My magic can do so much more now."

Lash waved his hand and five giant rings of fire spiraled overhead before splintering into dozens of tiny stars of flame. They danced in the air, spinning and twirling like puffed seeds as the others broke through the edge of the wood. Lash waved his hand once more and the tiny flames faded to smoke and blew away on the wind.

I turned to him. There was no sweat on his brow and no labor in his breath. His displays at the moon ceremonies were just as intricate yet took him days to recover from, but now he was barely winded. Lash cracked into a smile wider than I had ever seen. "I do not know what you did. But we felt it immediately."

Riven grabbed Feron's shoulder and they exchanged a brief look.

"It is not enough to fight Damien's armies," Feron said. "But it gives hope at what may come to be when the other seals are broken."

I nodded. The magnitude of the task ahead finally settling on my shoulders. Riven noticed and squeezed my hand. "We only have to break one seal at a time."

My chest eased. That was an easier task to manage.

I turned to Lash. "I want to increase my training. I think it's best if I do one session with Feron every day and then another just with you."

Lash's bushy brows furrowed together. "There is nothing I can teach you that Feron cannot."

I raised a brow and lifted my flame-covered hand. "There isn't?"

Lash's eyes went wide and then he broke into a devilish grin. "Shall we begin right now?"

I opened my mouth to speak but Gerarda threw her knife into the ground. "That can wait until we know how we're getting to the next seal." She grabbed her blade and stalked back to the city without waiting for any of us to follow.

My mouth went dry. The rest of the seals were all in the kingdom.

Lash's face fell to a serious mask. "Which one will you go after first?"

I sighed. I knew there was only one Gerarda would allow.

CHAPTER TWELVE

THE MEETING ROOM WAS COLDER than I remembered. The fire still burned in the hearth, long dancing flames licked the stone chimney and cast amber rays across the floor, but there was a piercing chill to the room, like a winter breeze had entered through an unseen window.

I hadn't been here in weeks. All I remembered from that last meeting was Gerarda spilling my goblet of wine across the floor and scratching the table with one of her Elvish blades. I peered down at the stone circle from where I stood in front of my regular chair.

Eight hundred fifty-two.

The number of Shades and initiates that had been left at the Order. The number I'd abandoned, just like Gerarda had told me that day. My skin itched as I looked down at the thick lines of Gerarda's perfect scrawl.

There was a hollow ache in my belly knowing we would be returning there too late to save them.

I waited in silence for the others to arrive. Nikolai and Killian walked in first, whispering and laughing almost arm in arm. They took their usual seats and Nikolai leaned over his armrest to offer me one of the rolls he had brought up from the kitchens. They were still warm to the touch.

Collin walked in next. There was no longer any disdain in his face when he looked at me, but there was none of his boldness either. After weeks of being ill, his blond hair was less vibrant and his complexion had lost its warmth, his skin sunken around his eyes and cheeks. It was as if wherever he walked he brought the gloom of an overcast sky and damp weather with him.

He took his seat without so much as a glance at Killian. He even opted for Tarvelle's old chair so he didn't have to sit next to anyone.

I would make sure to ask Rheih how her elixir was working the next time I saw her.

I felt Riven's shadows before he walked into the room. They stretched toward the table, seeking me out and curling around my legs. Riven's jaw pulsed and his brow trembled as he fought the urge to pull them back into the dark circle that shrouded his feet.

I dropped my arm and let one of the tendrils weave through my fingers. It was as warm as a summer pond. Riven's shoulders relaxed by a fraction and he took his regular seat beside me.

"Shall we begin?" Killian asked the group as Gerarda stalked in and sat beside Syrra, who had claimed her seat without making a sound.

I pointed to Vrail's empty chair.

"Vrail thought her time was better spent learning everything she could about the consequences of breaking the seals." Killian fixed the collar of his red jacket. "I will brief her later."

I shrugged. Vrail had already done the hard part of convincing me the seals were worth pursuing. Now it was time to return to her books.

I pulled a folded piece of parchment out from my vest and placed it on the table. Gerarda's eyes widened as she saw the map Riven had given me for the first time. I pulled two faelights over the crinkled paper and let the light reveal the symbols that marked each viable portal across Elverath.

I turned to Gerarda. "Would you like to brief everyone on the seals?"

She stood, sharp and straight just as she had as Dagger. "There are five seals that have been draining the magic out of the mainland." She pointed to the Cliffs of Elandorr first. "Each one is located on a part of Elverath that is separated by water. This creates a barrier that has allowed the siphons to drain the continent of its magic and contain it in each of these five locations."

She moved her hand to Volcar and then to the island in the middle of the Pool of Elvera. She frowned as her fingers lingered over the Fractured Isles but then she finally marked the last location. The Order.

Riven crossed his arms. "Those locations are not small. How can we find each seal if it's glamoured?"

Gerarda's eyes narrowed but she answered the question like a dutiful soldier. "Knowing that the seals exist should help us break any glamour once Keera gets close enough. As for precise locations, that is a challenge. But Vrail hypothesized that each seal would be located at the shortest line from where the spell was initially cast." She placed her finger over the Ruins of Faevra in the east. "Her hypothesis was correct when it came to the first seal. We suspect it will continue to be correct for the others."

I nodded. Vrail had proven herself more than enough for me to trust her best estimate.

Nikolai stuffed a loaf into his mouth. "So which seal is next?"

I knew Gerarda's answer before she even said it. "The Order."

I glanced at Riven, both of us wary of the hope in Gerarda's eyes.

Riven lifted his chin. "Even with a small team traveling by portal, Damien has too many swords at his command to make the journey a safe one."

"Whoever expects safety is a fool." Gerarda emphasized her point by tossing her blade into the air and catching it in the holster attached to her forearm. "And we won't be traveling by portal."

Riven's eyes widened.

Gerarda traced the tip of her finger along the southern shores of Elverath. "It's better to sail."

"Is it?" Riven's tone was unconvinced.

Killian stood, reaching across the table to place tiny little shields around the capital. "Damien has patrols stationed along all the major roads in the east. He has battalions in every village. In the cities, his men number in the thousands." There were so many shields on the map that it was clear none of the portals were viable.

I pointed to a blackened symbol inked beside the small illustration of the Order. "And we are certain this portal is closed."

Syrra nodded. "It was one of the first to fade."

"Nothing is ever easy." I sighed. "I agree that the sea is the safest course."

Gerarda rolled her eyes. "It's the only course. We can't shuffle hundreds of Shades through a portal."

No one in the room spoke. Gerarda's gaze shifted from face to face but her determination only grew. My heart raced against my ribs. I knew it would be kinder to tell her the truth, to let her process it on her own instead of reaching the shores full of hope only to be pierced by the arrows of eight hundred fifty-two ghosts. But I also knew Gerarda, and she wouldn't believe it until she saw it for herself.

I shook my head and turned to Nikolai. "Do we have a ship that can carry that many?"

He blinked, glancing at Riven who was equally shocked. "Yes."

"It will need some accommodations for the return journey," Gerarda interjected.

I pressed my knuckles into the table. "Can you and Gerarda handle those?" I asked Nikolai. "She knows everything that would be needed."

His brows creased but he nodded.

Syrra pointed to the sailing route Gerarda had marked. "Even with the fastest ship it will take weeks."

I straightened my stance and scanned the room. "I think we could manage the journey in one."

Gerarda's black eyes locked on Riven. "Are you sure she didn't hit her head?"

Riven grunted but turned to me. "Keera, Elvish ships are fast but even they cannot make the journey that quickly."

I couldn't help the smile that tugged along my lips. "They can't?" I slashed my hand through the room and a strong gust blew across the table, carrying the map with it until it flattened against the root-packed wall.

The wind whipping at their clothes was enough to make my point, but it wasn't enough for me. I closed my eyes, feeling the wildness of my newfound gift and pulling it taut. The gust of wind grew more powerful, but was now streamlined, creating a tiny whirlwind over the table that had captured every faelight in the room.

I lowered my hand but the swirling gust kept spinning. Syrra smiled widely at the spinning lights. "You can maintain it for the entire journey?"

I nodded. "I'll need to sleep occasionally."

Riven blinked at the whirlwind. "Breaking that seal has advanced your control too." His tone was nothing but awe.

I glanced at Riven sheepishly. "I've already shown Feron and Lash and they think I could master a steady gust in less than a week." So much of Riven's training focused on containing his powers instead of using them, I didn't think he would be the best tutor.

He smiled proudly. "You can do no better."

I sighed in relief just as Gerarda reached out to touch the whirlwind in the middle of the table with her sword. My body stiffened and the gusts unwound, tossing Gerarda's blade through the air and thrashing against the wall.

I turned to the others. "This will be dangerous. No matter how we travel, Damien's soldiers may find us before we ever make it to the Order. And if the second seal is anything like the first, his men will know when we've broken it."

Collin shifted in his seat. He kept his eyes down toward the map as he spoke. "I don't think I would make the best seafarer in my current state." He held his fist to his throat, swallowing the urge to vomit. "But I will do everything I can to help with the preparations." He glanced at me with no malice or contempt, just a tired and defeated look in his eyes.

I nodded once. "Thank you, Collin. I hope your sickness passes."

He paled and slumped back in his chair.

Riven crossed his arms and jutted his chin toward his brother. "It would be foolish for all of us to go. On the off chance Damien falls off his balcony, the heir to the throne shouldn't throw himself into the midst of battle."

Killian pulled at the collar of his jacket and nodded. "I'm sure Vrail will take my place. She's become the better swordsman anyway."

Riven chuckled under his breath and nodded.

Nikolai's head snapped up. "Five days," he said, slamming his glass pen on the table. "I can have the ship ready in five days."

I took a deep breath and stared down at the map of the entire continent. "Then we have five days to create a plan that gets us out alive."

CHAPTER THIRTEEN

I WOKE TO THE ANNOYING MELODY of birdsong and children's laughter booming from the groves below my burl. My head ached from the night before. Now that we were preparing a mission into the kingdom, I was terrified that Damien would find out the plan by pulling me into a dream and tormenting the truth from my lips.

But compromised or not, I had to go on this mission. I was the only one who could break the seals. Which is why each night before sleep I drowned out my worries and each morning I woke with a craving stroking my throat.

I peered out the window from my pillow. It was barely morning, which meant I had hours before Nikolai would replenish my rations and I could soothe the ache. The elixirs Riven had given me sat across the room, but I was too exhausted to get them. I groaned and pulled a pillow over my head to go back to sleep.

"Are you calling me a liar?" The voice was muffled through the down but I instantly recognized it as Vrail. She was shouting somewhere close by.

"You told me you'd wake her—"

"I tried, but—" I could tell from the high pitch of Vrail's voice that her cheeks were crimson with fury.

Gerarda yanked the door open. "And yet she's still in bed."

I refused to acknowledge her and hoped the problem would go away.

"You can't just walk into other people's burls!" Vrail's harsh whisper was not nearly as threatening as she wanted it to be.

I heard Gerarda's soft feet come to a stop. "I thought you said Keera had been training you?"

"She has! Well, she was . . . it's been a while since we—I've learned a lot from her!" Vrail finished with a stomp of her boot.

My stomach tightened with guilt. I hadn't given Vrail any reason to defend me. I hadn't coached her once since I rescued her from the dungeons.

"Then you should know by now that the only rule Keera abides by"—I heard the clang of something metal—"is to break the rules." I turned just in time to see the flick of Gerarda's wrist as she poured a water canister over my head.

I sat up in an instant and spat out the water at the back of my throat. I was glad that I had gone to bed in a long tunic that covered my arms even when soaked right through.

"You need to stop doing that!" I wiped the water off my face.

Gerarda raised one brow to a sharp and daring peak before tossing the rest of the vase into my face again.

I snarled at her with my fangs but Gerarda only turned on her heel back at Vrail who was standing, dumbstruck, at the end of the bed. "That is what I meant when I said do whatever needed to be done. Don't coddle her." She turned to me. "You have five minutes to dress and meet us on the bridge."

I pulled my legs over the edge of the bed and let my feet drop onto the floor. "I have the morning off from training."

Gerarda crossed her arms, still holding the bronze pot. "From your special magic training, sure. But if we're headed to the capital we need to train *all* our weapons." She flipped the small Elvish sword that Syrra had given her.

I fell back onto the bed but Gerarda grabbed my hand and pulled me back up. "I have to help Nikolai with the ship this afternoon so this is the only time that works." Gerarda took a moment to take in the state of my room. She sniffed. Loudly.

"Do you want me to cut off your nose?" I wrapped my fingers around one of my shorter knives. "Remember you don't heal as easily as me."

Gerarda smirked. "I promise I'll make it worth your while, *Keera dear*." She waved her hand in a sarcastic but accurate rendition of Nikolai's dramatic flair.

She practically skipped out of the room. Vrail turned to follow but waved her hands over the room first. "I'll come over tonight and help with . . . this."

I threw my knife at the wall and Vrail squealed her way out of my burl.

I stepped outside in the only clean clothes I had. Gerarda merely nodded her head once before jumping off the bridge to the ground below. She floated along the vine like she'd been doing it for centuries. Curving around the slick rope in lazy circles as the ground grew closer until she finally let go and landed softly on both feet.

I clenched against the smooth vine until my skin ripped, stopping only a few inches from the ground, and collapsed. My chest heaved from the exertion, but Vrail and Gerarda ignored it. They marched through the main grove toward the lake, silently checking every few minutes to ensure I was following them.

"No," I said when they stopped outside of the training field. Syrra and Riven were waiting at the center of it surrounded by a series of posts sticking out from the ground at different heights. It reminded me of the bridge to the Order. Before Damien's soldiers had blown it into nothing. I had already been too tired for basic sword work; this was going to kill me before I ever got my wine.

"You need the practice," Gerarda said, shoving into me as she walked past.

"I haven't lost my skill in two months."

Gerarda spun around on the tip of her toes with a boyish grin on her face. "That is a *lie*."

I scoffed before realizing she was serious. Riven had crossed the field and reached me in time to stop me from pouncing on the little Halfling, but Gerarda shoved his hand down. "Keera doesn't need to hold your hand to face the truth."

I straightened my back. "I have bested you as an initiate, as a Shade, and within the Arsenal." I raised my brow at Gerarda. "You want me to do the same here?"

Gerarda didn't waver. She looked up at me with narrowed eyes and issued the challenge like it had been her plan all along. "Name the skill."

"Archery," I answered without hesitation. It hadn't been my best skill at the Order, but it had always been Gerarda's worst.

"Predictable." Gerarda unbuckled her own weapons belt and placed it carefully on the ground. "But I accept." She eyed the wall of bows and arrows in the training room.

"Should we stop this?" Vrail whispered, glancing between Riven and Syrra. Riven shrugged and I could feel the weight of his gaze on my back as Gerarda and I selected our bows.

Syrra only watched us with a hint of curiosity in her dark eyes.

Gerarda and I crossed to the center of the field facing the three targets at the edge of the beach. Each one had a tiny blue dot at the center of the circle, just wide enough for the head of an arrow to slice through. I waved my arm in front of me. "I selected the skill. It's only fair that you shoot on clean targets."

I half expected Gererda to refuse the gesture on principle, but she smugly stepped past me with an arrow already nocked. She didn't stop to shoot her first shot, but aimed at the first target mid-stride, nocking the second arrow by the time the first split right through the center of the target.

She never paused. I watched her chest rise with a slow breath and then exhale. She released the second arrow in that moment between breaths, still walking across the field.

It found its mark too.

My neck tensed. Syrra's chin nodded in approval.

Gerarda flashed a grin over her shoulder as she pulled back on the final arrow and let it fly. It landed with a resounding *clunk*, embedding itself deep into the target, but ever so slightly to the left. It wasn't enough of an error to maim instead of kill, but it was just what I needed to win our bet.

My dry lips had never tasted so sweet.

I drew the string of the bow feeling the tension in my shoulders and back. I was stiff but the pressure felt good after so long without practice. I released my hold and noticed a stray hair caught along the grip. I plucked it free and let the crimson strand float away in the morning breeze.

"Do you want to call it now?" Gerarda shouted from the far end of the field.

I shot her a look and pulled an arrow from my quiver. Gerarda's smug grin fell to a straight line as I aimed my first shot. My stance was tense, every muscle in my back felt stiff as I drew the string. I closed my eyes and sighed deeply, letting the memory of each muscle take over. My body shifted into place and my eyes flashed open. I aimed the arrow at the bright red end of Gerarda's and let it fly.

The arrow slid into the target, nestled beside the other. It was so close, the stone heads screeched as they were forced to share a hole inside the linen. I couldn't keep my lip from twitching.

I lined myself with the second target and felt my body relax as I pulled back the second time. The bow felt like an extension of my arm. I aimed once more and trusted that my arrow would hit its mark.

Vrail gasped as my arrow split Gerarda's right down the middle. Syrra's smirk made my stomach flutter with pride.

Gerarda crossed her arms. "You still have one more."

I shrugged and grabbed the last arrow from my quiver. I found my spot along the line and squared my shoulders with the target. I drew back as I inhaled the fresh scent of the wood, pausing for a moment, and then releasing.

A perfect shot.

But then there was a flash of silver across the target. A throwing blade had embedded itself into the linen. My arrow, colliding with the metal, bounced off and landed in the grass.

I turned to Gerarda in disbelief. "I best you so you sabotage me?"

"You didn't best shit." Gerarda glanced at the others. "Who would you rather have protecting you on the field of battle."

I crossed my arms, expecting to hear a chorus of *Keera*s from them all, but I was only met with silence.

My neck cracked as I turned to face them. Gerarda laughed. "A shot that takes a century to load is little help in the midst of battle."

My fingers tightened into a fist around my bow. "That was not the challenge."

Gerarda narrowed her eyes. "Perhaps not. But the Keera I trained with would have made sure to outmatch me in precision *and* speed."

My stomach tightened. The part of me that hated to admit Gerarda was right, knew she was. My technical skill might not have waned in a few short weeks. But I had become blunter. Slower. My arms ached with the memory of me tumbling from that roof in Cereliath, wine sloshing in my belly as I chased a hooded Nikolai through the streets.

I may not be Blade any longer, but I was still useless dulled.

I dropped my bow onto the ground and pulled off my quiver. Gerarda's lips pursed to the side and I knew she was expecting me to walk away.

I turned to Syrra, determined not to see Gerarda's smug grin again. "What are we training first?"

CHAPTER FOURTEEN

"DON'T YOU THINK THREE on one is a little unfair?" Vrail shouted as Riven and I circled around Gerarda. I smirked and tightened my grip on my blades. We had already been training on the posts for an hour. It was time to end this and I would be more than happy if Gerarda fell first.

Vrail jumped from one of the taller posts to a longer, flatter one at the same height as Gerarda's knees.

Gerarda hopped over the swing of Vrail's sword. "Don't concern yourself with me when you should"—Gerarda somersaulted through the air, kicked off Vrail's post with both feet and landed on the post below—"worry about yourself."

Vrail's post shook wildly to the left. She tumbled off onto one of the beds of faelight Syrra had set up along the ground. Uldrath,

Pirmiith's young son, cheered from where he watched along the roof of the training room. The other children behind him giggled.

Gerarda turned her sights on me and Riven. Riven was on one of the lowest posts with swirls of shadows curling around him in all directions. Gerarda's gaze caught along the thick blade of Riven's long sword and I took the opportunity to attack.

I jumped from the highest post, swinging one blade and then the next as the children gasped. Gerarda leaped backward to the post behind her, blocking my strike with her own sword. I didn't give her any time to think before I pushed off the next piece of wood and slashed again.

We danced through the air, setting the tempo with the clashes of our blades, barely stepping on the posts as we twirled and spun. The youngest Halflings clapped each time one of us dodged a strike.

Vrail rubbed the back of her head and rolled off the faebed. "Riven has it easy," she mumbled, pointing her chin at where Riven stood in a defensive position taking even, perfect breaths.

Syrra's eyes narrowed as I sliced through the thin end of Gerarda's laces but missed her boot. "Conserving your strength is a wise strategy, especially for one as large as Riven."

Vrail crossed her arms. "Keera's tall."

Gerarda leaped over my head, twisting her torso as she swung her blade at me. The sharp edge missed my braid by the width of a hair. I snarled.

Syrra chuckled under her breath. "Keera is *niimithir vraak*."

Vrail's eyes went wide as I jabbed the sharp end of my blade into the blunt end of a post. I left it there and jumped to the lower post beside it, setting my trap.

Vrail tilted her head, trying to map out my plan of attack from the ground. "You always say the lightning-hearted make for the most fearsome warriors."

I evaded Gerarda's attack by feigning a leap to the left and hopping over her blade. I ran along the tops of the posts, climbing toward my abandoned sword. I jumped. My hand wrapped around the hilt and I spun mid-leap. My body rocketed at Gerarda's chest like a sling shot.

"The *vraak* also die the soonest," Syrra said loud enough for me to hear.

I grinned and raised my hand in victory, but a tiny blur of black pounced at my legs. I cursed, realizing I hadn't won quite yet.

Gerarda had clung to a nearby post by her fingernails. I swung at her with my remaining blade but she was already gone. I wheezed as I jumped to the center pole and watched Gerarda make her next move.

She ran along the posts in wide strides, her black cloak trailing behind her. I predicted her path and jumped, sword drawn over my head.

Gerarda dodged, sensing the attack. She threw one of her knives into the middle pole, embedding it to the hilt as I chased her through the air.

My body was on the verge of collapse. I needed to win so I could drown myself in a warm shower and the wine that was waiting in my burl. Then I would sleep for eternity.

I hopped to the next pole and then another. I was barely watching my feet as I stepped onto the third. Riven took advantage of my momentary lapse in focus and slammed the hilt of his sword into the pole with everything he had.

The rattle was enough that I slipped off the edge. The blunt end of the post rammed into my side but I clung to the top, determined not to fall.

Gerarda grinned and rolled through the air. I watched from below as a flash of silver cut through her neck and her cloak floated slowly, directly in Riven's line of sight. He pushed the cloak out of the way, but Gerarda was already there—on the post beside him. She dropped into a tight spin and landed a blow right behind his knee.

Riven fell so hard he bounced off the faebed with a heavy gasp.

I dropped to the lower post and Gerarda pounced on me. I ran along the wood, realizing too late that was exactly what Gerarda had planned. Her tiny hands clasped the hilt of the knife she had thrown into the center post, using it as an anchor as her body spun through the air and was launched directly at me.

My rage flared knowing she used my own trick against me.

I dove for the bottom pole, but Gerarda's boot collided with my stomach leaving me short. My fingers split as I grabbed for the post but all I left behind were amber streaks in the sun-baked grain.

I landed next to Riven on the faebed. He was smirking at me with a boyish glint in his eye. I shoved his shoulder, a little harder than I meant to. "You attack *me* before you attack *her*?"

His grin was devilish as he lowered his head and nipped my finger. My entire body flooded with waves of heat at the touch. "I take my chances where I can." One of Riven's shadows trailed down the open part of my collar, leaving no doubt about what other chances he'd be willing to take.

Gerarda shook her head in disgust. "You lasted longer than I thought." She gave a hard, pointed look at Riven. "Both of you."

Riven's grin fell. "Was that a compliment, *Arda*?"

"Don't call me that." Her nose wrinkled like an angry cat.

I pulled myself to the edge of the faebed and wobbled. Breaking the seal had made me stronger, but I was still not in a soldier's form. Being scared to sleep didn't help.

Gerarda picked up my fallen sword and tossed it to me. Riven caught it in a straight arm directly over my face when I didn't move to catch it. "We've trained enough."

"It's not even noon." Gerarda raised a brow at him.

Riven wrapped his arm around me. "How are you feeling?"

"Like I'm going to vomit," I admitted.

Gerarda crossed her arms. "So vomit." There wasn't an ounce of sympathy in her voice.

Riven's neck flexed. His shadows turned sharp like blades of his own. I put a hand on his chest. "It's okay," I whispered. His violet gaze shifted to me and immediately softened.

I pulled my body up on the soft ball of light, suddenly aware of how depleted I truly was. But Gerarda was staring at me with a smug look that set my blood to boil.

I grabbed my sword and stood as tall as I could on the grass.

And then I vomited on the ground.

Riven covered the field in his shadows, shielding us from everyone else as he pulled me into his lap. I wretched again and a thin blade of shadow pulled a waterskin beside us. Riven uncorked it and held it to my mouth. When I was done, he wiped the water from my lips with his thumb. "You have done more than enough today," he whispered so quietly only I could hear him.

My body jerked again, forcing me to agree. I leaned against his shoulder and felt the sunlight on my cheek once more.

"We are done for today," Riven said in a voice as hard and as cold as the tops of the Burning Mountains.

Syrra nodded and Vrail skipped toward the training room in search of her own waterskin. Something shiny peered through the laces in Gerarda's tunic. A small bead along a chain. Gerarda caught me looking and scowled, tightening the laces to hide the necklace.

"You're coddling her again." She threw her arms out in exasperation at Vrail and Syrra too. "You all are."

Riven's lip tightened against his teeth. "There is a difference between coddling and caring, *Arda*." There was no jest in how he said the nickname now. It was pure threat.

Gerarda raised a brow. "Keera has trained hundreds of initiates and led countless Shades. She did not excuse them when they vomited during training. That's when she pushed the hardest."

My stomach hardened, knowing it was true.

Riven's shadows curled around my leg that wasn't shaking and all I wanted was for them to carry me into my bed and let me sleep. "We are not pushing today."

"How can we expand our limits if we do not cross them?" Gerarda tilted her head at Syrra. The Elf swallowed thickly but did not correct her.

"Keera is not a weapon that must keep striking for the kingdom any longer." Riven towered over Gerarda, placing himself between her and me. "Out of everyone *you* should understand that."

Gerarda took a single step forward, lifting herself up on the tips of her toes until she was inches from Riven's fangs. His shadows spurled out in every direction and I was amazed that Gerarda could stay so calm in the face of a Fae so close to losing control.

"I'm treating Keera like a *soldier* because that's what she is. Leaving the Order doesn't change that and it never will." She sheathed her sword and shoved past Riven. "And, one day, she will thank me for it."

Gerarda's dark eyes fell on me, and I knew she wanted me to say something. To grab her arm and pull her out into the training field until even she couldn't stand. But I couldn't.

Gerarda swallowed her disappointment and headed for the beach. "I'll ready the ship and hope that Damien's soldiers are just as *undisciplined* with their training."

"How do you know she will thank you for it?" Riven shouted after her, there was a hard edge to his voice, not anger but something more like worry. It pulled at my chest until it hurt to breathe.

Gerarda lifted her chin, taking her time to trail her gaze over Riven. "Because I'm a soldier and it's something only soldiers can understand."

CHAPTER FIFTEEN

The suns had already set and my body protested with every step that carried me farther from my burl. I wanted to sleep, but I also wanted to see Maerhal. I'd come to enjoy our nightly chats. And the slow release of my healing gift made the new depths of my power easier to manage.

Maerhal seemed to enjoy them too.

I stepped down each of the spiral steps in slow, painful movements. My legs ached from training and now every bend felt like a challenge of its own. Eventually, I made it into the empty hall and limped across in the dim light of a small faelight that trailed behind me.

A horrible rasp echoed from the far side of the hall. I turned and saw someone slumped over a chair, retching onto the ground.

I ran as quickly as I could manage and found Collin falling out of his seat. I wrapped his arm around my shoulder. His skin was cold and sweaty and he was barely able to utter a word.

"I'll take you to Rheih," I muttered as I half dragged him down the hall to the infirmary.

His faelight joined mine and they lit our path down the winding tunnel. Maerhal covered her face, wincing from the light as I stepped through the door, but as soon as she saw Collin she ran out of the room. "I'll get her," she yelled in quick Elvish.

I laid Collin onto one of the open beds. There was a canister of water on the table. I grabbed a clean cup and filled it halfway.

Collin coughed after it touched his lips. I held him steady through the fit and then we tried again. "Thank you," he rasped after a small sip. His eyes widened as he looked at me, like he hadn't realized who had found him.

I stared at his sunken face. It had thinned to the point that his round cheeks had turned sharp and the skin under his eyes hung low and dark. The hair along the sides of his face was patchy and lifeless.

"Rheih told me your illness has not improved."

Collin moved his shoulder in an attempt to shrug. "I've always been prone to sickness." He laid back down on the bed but didn't meet my eyes.

I just held the cup of water not knowing what to say or not to say.

"I misjudged you." It was barely audible, but I could tell from the hard set of Collin's jaw that he had said the words.

I swallowed. "You judged me fairly. I would never expect anything else."

"I told the Dagger what you did to them." I froze. I didn't need to ask who Collin meant to know he was talking about his family. The family I had killed on orders from the king. "Do you want to know what she said?"

My fingers gripped the cup so tightly I thought I would dent the wood.

"She told me she would not have taken the risk." Collin's voice shook as he spoke. "That she would have come to Cereliath but only to make sure the Shades had carried out the deaths exactly as they were ordered to."

I bowed my head. "Gerarda has seen many of her trainees be punished at the hands of the king. She just wanted them to survive." My eyes stung knowing that her determination to do just that is what kept her focused and that soon it would all crumble.

Collin huffed and stayed silent for a long moment.

Where is that damned Mage? I thought to myself, glancing at the door. It felt wrong to leave Collin alone in his sickly state.

"She also said that you replenished your stores of sleeping draught more than any of the Shades. More than some units combined." Collin's honey-colored eyes were sharp and cutting as he looked at me. "She suspects that was not the first time you used it to give someone grace at the very end."

A tear rolled down my cheek as countless faces flashed across my mind, their names warming my skin underneath my tunic. "No, it wasn't," I whispered. "And it wasn't the last."

Collin watched the tear pool along my jaw and fall onto the bed. I straightened under the intensity of his gaze but did not look away.

"What you had to do was not fair." Collin took a deep breath and I held mine waiting for the final blow. "But thank you for giving them as much comfort as you could. And all the others."

I blinked in disbelief. My shoulders slumped and I let out a hard breath. "It was not enough."

Collin pulled himself farther up on the pillow. "Is that what keeps you up at all hours of the night, walking around the meadow?"

I shrugged. "In part—" I stopped, turning my body to fully face Collin. "You can only know I spend my nights there if you are also lurking in the wood."

Collin looked away. "I'm exhausted and sick, but I can't seem to find a way to sleep," he whispered just as Rheih scurried through the door, muttering angrily under her breath.

Rheih started throwing ingredients into a bowl. She shook her head when she spotted me. "I'll never finish that elixir you need if I'm constantly interrupted."

I froze. "You can make it then?"

The Mage gave a gruff nod. "Give me a few days. But it seems I've succeeded where the healers have not. Again."

She shooed me out of the room to examine Collin. My throat ached, as if my body knew that my excuse for dousing my sorrows in wine was almost over. I swallowed, knowing that I would have to fall asleep sober to test Rheih's newest concoction.

I closed my eyes, hoping her confidence was earned. I did not want to face Damien again.

Riven's hand stiffened on my shoulder as he watched the flame flicker gently in a steady wind. After three hours of practice, I could finally feel the tug of my magic inside me tightening as I used it. My gusts felt nothing like my healing gift—that was a warmth that flowed like honey out of me when I needed it—instead the wind whipped inside my chest, gaining speed until I gave it some direction.

It was like climbing on the back of a wild stallion. My power was nowhere near tamed, but I understood it in a way I hadn't before and felt like it understood me too.

Lash waved his hand over the flame and it split into three singular tendrils, one blue, one crimson, and one the color of sunset. He stood in front of me as tall as a mountain. "Blow out the center."

I focused on that whirlwind inside my chest and aimed it at the crimson flame. It flickered wildly for a moment before going completely flat.

Lash nodded. "Blue."

I directed the wind to the left and flattened that one too. Lash waved his hand once more and the two flames returned. He called them out in series, replenishing them each time I smothered the fire with my gust.

Before long, sweat had pooled along my brow, dripping down my face. Riven paced behind me, and Gerarda had gotten up from the hammock to watch.

"All three," Lash commanded.

I looked up at him and fought the urge to puke. I took a deep breath and tried to spread out the gust of wind so it flattened each flame at once. They only flickered.

"She's on the cusp of burnout." Riven stepped forward, staring at Feron to intervene.

But the Fae only raised his hand. "Rheih gave her the same elixirs you take. She has only exhausted their limits, but nowhere near the limits of her gifts." Feron's eyes were wide with wonder as he watched me. Some long-forgotten part of me thrilled at the sight of his amazement. Suddenly, I was an initiate again wanting nothing more than to please whoever trained me.

I clenched my jaw and closed my eyes until the tightness in my chest bordered on suffocating. Then I released my power at the flames. They went out immediately and the wind was strong enough to blow back Feron's twists and Lash's long cloak.

I collapsed backward. Gerarda reached out and grabbed my shoulder as Riven's shadows supported my back.

Lash murmured something to Feron in Elvish, but my heart was pounding too loudly inside my skull for me to hear. Riven glanced between them with a furrowed brow. Gerarda's eyes narrowed before looking down at me.

"Good progress." She patted my shoulder like I was one of her initiates.

I rolled my eyes. "Mocking is beneath you."

"It is." Gerarda's lips twitched to the side. "That's how you know I meant it."

I tilted my head up at her. "You're being very kind, Gerarda."

She didn't even flinch at the full use of her name. She only smiled wider. "If you had a looking glass, you would know why I couldn't be rude to you in such a state."

Riven made a guttural sound that reverberated from his chest.

Gerarda's lip curled back in disgust. "Did you just *growl*?"

I coughed to hide my laugh. "Riven's on edge." I reached out and grabbed his hand. Instantly the warmth of our bond settled between us and Riven relaxed beside me.

"Riventh, can you assist Lash in the kitchens?" Feron smiled at his nephew.

Gerarda crossed her arms and shot him a victorious look.

"And take Gerarda with you," Feron finished. They both recognized it as the dismissal it was. Lash patted my shoulder with his heavy hand once before stalking out of the clearing flanked by Riven and Gerarda on either side of him.

If it was anyone else, I would be worried.

"Your gusts are excellent." Feron relaxed back into the chair he had made for himself. "With some rest, you will be able to braid them for your journey."

I crossed my arms, I had only managed to braid a single gust. It was useful magic, once braided the gusts kept blowing until I untangled the braid, but I would never do it as easily as Feron braided roots from the earth. "That's not my definition of excellent."

"You are too hard on yourself, Keera. Even well-seasoned wielders like Lash have trouble with that exercise."

My brows lifted in disbelief.

"We cannot all be earth wielders." Feron shrugged off his jest.

I chuckled and then let a silence build between us. It wasn't awkward, but peaceful. The more time I spent with Feron the more I learned that he preferred quiet company.

"Did you know my mother?" The question surprised me as much as it surprised him.

Feron's smile was soft but sad. "Yes. I knew El'ravaasir since the day she was born. The sky cracked five times when she drew her first breath. A sign of a powerful magic wielder."

I turned my head. "There was lightning when I unlocked the first seal. It hit me."

Feron shook his head. "It came from you."

He chuckled at my stunned expression. "I do not think you have fully tapped into all your power. Your control of wind is the first sign of your mother's gift, but it is in its infancy. As you grow into it, you will be able to call storms and lightning at will."

I fluttered my hands as if they would spark right in front of me.

"I'm angry at the choice she made." My voice was barely more than a whisper.

Feron nodded. "As am I."

"You are?"

Feron drummed his fingers along his cane. "I do not know how Ravaa discovered Aemon's secret, but I struggle to accept there was not time to convene with the western Fae. So many bloodlines were lost that day. So many friends."

I sighed but there was a strange comfort in knowing that Feron had as few answers as I did. "She must have thought that it was right."

Feron chuckled. "I am certain she did. Ravaa was one of the most talented and caring Elverin I ever had the pleasure of knowing. But she was prone to rash decision-making and self-sacrifice." He gave me a pointed look. "A trait she passed down to her daughter."

"I wonder what other traits she passed on to me." Apart from our eyes and powers, I knew so little of the Fae that had been my mother. She was just a portrait painted into my memory with no context for who she was or how she lived.

"She had a lovely singing voice," Feron offered.

I barked a laugh. "Definitely not something she passed on to me."

Feron smirked. "You have the same laugh. The first time I heard it I almost fell at the sound."

My heart twinged. "She liked to laugh?"

Feron's smile was uncontainable. "Yes. She made a point to host the funniest Elverin. Though she was also prone to seasons of sadness."

"Even before Aemon came?"

He nodded. "You mother felt everything as deeply as she could. It made her a fierce leader and a loyal friend, but it also made her lonely." Feron glanced at me.

I leaned back against the bench. "I don't think that's an inheritable trait."

"Perhaps not. But Ravaa had trouble asking for help when she needed it." Feron eyed the empty wineskin that was sticking out of my bag.

Ten thousand years had drained him of his subtlety. I swallowed the thickness at my throat. "I don't need help with that."

Feron's eyes fell on me like a blacksmith's hammer. "Is there anything you do need help with?"

The fears in my gut bubbled forward. I glanced at his gold ring with the large green stone. Feron had told me of its glamour, the magic that kept others from seeing anything they might use against the wearer. If Rheih managed to find an elixir to stop the dreams, I would have to test it. I would have to make myself vulnerable enough to risk seeing Damien again. The scars on my skin prickled. Those were only some of the secrets I didn't want Damien to see. I had to protect everyone who was risking their lives to unlock the seals. I didn't need Damien glimpsing something he shouldn't if I found myself asleep and unprotected again.

Feron didn't need me to ask the question. He merely slipped the gold ring off his finger and handed it to me. "Do I get to know what you need it for?"

I blinked at the ring in my palm. "You don't need it?" I asked, evading the question. "But what about the glamour?"

Feron shrugged. "There are very few Elverin who have not yet broken through the enchantment and of those who will be shocked, I do not think they pose a threat." Feron closed my fingers around the ring. "I wear it to protect it, Keera. It is a dangerous object if left in the wrong hands."

I clenched my jaw. "I will not lose it."

"I know." Feron smiled. "And I am proud you asked."

I sighed and pulled the ring onto my middle finger. Until I had a way to completely sever the connection Damien had with my mind, I wouldn't take it off.

"Can a mindwalker only use memories? Or can they control the mind in other ways?" I bit my lip, nervous my question had given away too much.

Feron went completely still. It was a long moment before he answered. "Most mindwalkers can only sense the emotional state of others."

I tilted my head. "But you accessed my memories and showed me and Riven yours."

"Yes," Feron said more slowly than usual, "But only with the compliance of the mind's host."

"So a mindwalker couldn't do anything more than that?"

Feron's lips fell to a straight line. "If such magic was possible, it would only be done by a very powerful wielder."

My shoulders tensed. How powerful had Damien made himself with his experiment?

Feron's purple eyes narrowed. "A person only has as much power over our minds as we allow, Keera."

I leaned back in my seat and let those words sink in. I rubbed the golden ring with my thumb. I had already given Damien so much power over me. It was time I took some of it back.

CHAPTER SIXTEEN

WE FOLLOWED THE TRAIL along the Dark Wood to the north side of the lake before heading to the western shores of the Faeland. Nikolai and Vrail chatted freely in the middle of our small group as Syrra and Gerarda bookended the line, never speaking but slowly sweeping the trail as if Damien's armies were about to ambush us.

Riven and I didn't speak, but rode side by side wherever the trail allowed. There was an edge to the air we shared that reminded me of those first weeks out of Aralinth. I could feel Riven watching me, knowing there was something I wasn't telling him.

I smelled the sea before I saw it. The brine sat heavy on the air with no breeze to cast it through the tree trunks that were beginning to thin. I waved my hand and a steady gust blew from behind us as we crested over the last hill. Even though it had only been a few weeks of training, the small use of my wind gift felt as natural as walking.

Riven's shadows wafted in the breeze. A proud smile flickered on his face.

"You're a marvel, *diizra*." Riven pulled on his reins, slowing our pace. "You're learning control faster than anyone I've ever heard of. Feron is impressed."

I sighed and let the compliment fall onto the ground between us. "Not fast enough."

Riven's brow softened and a thin shadow gently caressed my cheek. "I wish I could share some of the burden your mother left for you to carry. But *whatever* happens, the outcome of this war doesn't fall just on you, Keera. Seals or no seals."

Whatever I would have said to Riven evaporated from my tongue. The forest had given way to a sandy beach. The grains were not white like they were in Koratha or even black like the pebbled beaches of Volcar. The entire beach was the color of a sunset with streaks of coral and lilac that had blended from the waves of high tide.

Syrra reached the sand first and dismounted from her saddle. I expected her to untie her saddlebags, but she knelt and tore at the laces of her boots. She peeled off her gray socks and guided her horse on bare feet.

I turned to Riven, who was smiling widely. "Look," he whispered, and nodded to where Syrra had left footprints in the sand.

Only in the places she had stepped, the grains of sand had transformed into a deep, burnt crimson. It reminded me of a trail fire burning low in the late hours of the night, still hot enough to burn a forest to the ground, but content in knowing how long it had flamed.

Nikolai and Vrail dismounted their horses and pulled off their boots. Nikolai scooped Vrail's up and carried them with his own.

A muted yellow trailed after Nikolai while Vrail left footprints in her signature scarlet red.

"Why does everyone have a different color?" I asked, pulling off my own boots.

"Everyone leaves behind a color unique to them. Though the hue may shift depending on the state someone is in while they cross." Riven pointed to the deep tone of Syrra's footprints. "Syr's are always richer when we leave on a mission and lighter when we return."

"The changes track your mood?" I understood how heavy a mission could be.

Riven's bottom lip protruded as he mulled over my question. "In part, I suppose. But it reflects the embodiment of your health as a whole. Your mind, your body, and your spirit all at once. If each are in balance, then the sand will appear as your true color."

I stilled, suddenly nervous to step onto the beach. It felt like I was putting myself on display but had no knowledge of what I looked like. I swallowed the panic and grabbed my horse's reins.

I looked down at Riven's bare feet. "Do all Dark Fae have some kind of purple?" My chest fluttered in excitement, thinking mine would be a simple silver. Nothing more to understand than the color of my eyes.

Riven's laugh was hollow. "No. It's a rare color, for Fae and Elverin alike."

Nikolai and Vrail had stopped in the sand and turned back to us. "Stop stalling and get on with it, Riven," Nikolai shouted. "Keera doesn't care about your abnormally long toes."

My head dropped to see what Nikolai was talking about, but Riven had clouded his feet in shadow.

Nik crossed his arms and I could see the arch of his brow from a beach away. "I'm not shocked," I called back. "He's abnormally long *everywhere*."

Nikolai exploded into a fit of laughter as Riven choked on air. I nudged him with a sideways grin.

"That was an unnecessary amount of information," Gerarda muttered behind me. She tucked her short boots underneath her saddlebag and stepped into the sand. Her footprints were pristine impressions of her tiny feet, each dyed a mulberry so pale it was almost gray.

Gerarda didn't look back once to see the color of the trail she'd left behind. "We need to move, Keera."

I took a deep breath and stepped onto the cool sand. It felt like any other beach I'd ever walked on. My heart twinged thinking of the day I brought the sand into my room for Gwyn to walk on since she wasn't able to pass the palace threshold. That day, her footprints would have been something bright and lively just like her laugh. My stomach tightened, wondering what color they would be now.

I took three steps along the sand and turned back. My footprints were not silver at all, but green. The springtime jade of new buds along the trees and the fresh leaves of flowers yet to bloom. It was a pretty color, but rimmed with a thick line of black that cast a gray wash over each print.

Riven's eyes were locked on the sand. His back rigid, like he had forgotten how to breathe. I waved my hand and his head snapped up, walking beside me without a word.

Syrra waited for us at the edge of the water with the others. Nikolai's eyes were wide, staring at the footprints behind us. I fought the urge to cover my own, but Nikolai's gaze was locked on Riven's.

His footprints were so dark, the deep blue tones were almost indistinguishable from the black. Nikolai met Riven's hard stare and raised his brows, having some kind of unspoken conversation. Vrail grabbed Nikolai's arm and stepped into the water. The moment they touched the sea, they both disappeared as if walking behind a veil.

Not a veil, but a glamour.

That thought was enough to break it. The glamour dissolved into tiny droplets of water that fell back into the sea, revealing the long port filled with ships of every size and shape. Some had no sails, vessels that could only be powered by Fae gifted with water magic. Others had huge sails stacked along their posts like a bouquet of flowers for several wind wielders to fill.

But we only had me.

Our ship was docked at the very end of the port. It was long and skinny and reminded me of the single-person vessels that some fishermen use. It had a short staff with two small sails hanging limply from the top. There was a small upper deck on each end with chambers underneath them.

I grabbed Syrra's arm as the others brought their bags onto the ship. I waited until they were out of earshot to ask my question.

"What do the colors mean?" I pointed to Riven's dark footprints that had set Nikolai and him on edge.

Syrra crossed her arms, the scarred branches pulling tight across her muscles. "I am not trained in such arts."

I scoffed. "I have no patience for lies. You know enough to explain it to the likes of me."

Syrra's lips pressed together, and I thought she would turn away and ignore my pestering entirely, but she cracked. "Everyone's color usually stays within the same family." She pointed to mine. "Yours will likely always be some shade of green, but hopefully they will brighten."

I flinched, sensing the worry in Syrra's words. "Why?"

"Because black is the color of treachery." Syrra shrugged. "The darker your prints, the more treacherous you've been."

I blinked. "But I've not committed any treason. I would never—"

Syrra chuckled. "I know that, child. It is most often a sign that one is being treacherous to oneself. To live deceiving yourself is a heavy burden to carry." She eyed the wineskin hanging from my horse.

I stared at Riven's footprints next to my own. There were hints of a brighter blue hiding beneath, but there was no denying that Riven's were entirely shadowed. Its depth sent a cool wave down my spine as I wondered how much pain Riven had been hiding from me. From everyone.

My footprints were only rimmed with black and my secrets ate at me with every breath. Syrra seemed to misread my silence as worry for myself. She wrapped her arm around my shoulder and squeezed gently. "Do not fret about the black. It is the gray that concerns me most but I supposed that is to be expected. This is the first time in centuries that mine haven't been and you are responsible for that."

My brows knitted together as I faced her. "How?"

Syrra smiled softly and in that moment she looked so much like her sister. "Gray is the color of grief. It can drain every ounce of pigment from you if you let it."

CHAPTER SEVENTEEN

WE LEFT OUR HORSES tied along the edge of the forest for a group of Halflings to tend to. They were only an hour behind and would camp along the beach until we returned.

I watched as Syrra and Gerarda wordlessly prepared the ship to set sail. It looked nothing like the ships docked in the royal ports of Volcar or Koratha, but Gerarda had been preparing it all week. My stomach fell when I saw she had stocked it with supplies to feed and bandage a thousand.

Nikolai cast off the last of the lines and nodded at me. "Whenever you're ready."

I let that whirling power grow in my chest and aimed my magic at the sail. A strong gust lurched us forward. I added another and then another, pulling us quietly away from the dock and out to sea. I tried to fold the gusts together in the braided sphere Feron had shown me, but the setting suns made it difficult to see where one gust ended and another began.

"I thought you had this handled," Gerarda whispered through clenched teeth. Sailing the natural way would lengthen our journey to over a month.

"I've never trained at this time of day." I shook my head and made eye contact with Riven. The shadows by his head flattened ever so softly under my gusts.

An idea sparked.

I waved my hand so only one powerful gust remained. Everyone jerked as the ship immediately slowed. "Can you add your shadows in to this stream?"

Riven nodded and strings of darkness mixed with the moving air so it looked like fog.

I smiled. "Now keep them to only that stream."

Riven nodded and I added another gust. I wrapped the two around each other twice, letting Riven gain control of his shadows before I added the third. The visibility was all I needed to weave the streams together just as Feron had taught me. It wasn't nearly as big or pretty as the tangle of roots he had shown me, but it was enough.

A never-ending gust.

I pushed it against the large sail and the ship gained a swift and silent pace. I looked back over my shoulder and saw that the mainland had already disappeared behind us.

Gerarda finally dropped her gaze from the sail. "It's holding well."

I waited for the piercing comment that usually followed any of Gerarda's compliments, but it never came. Her gaze returned to the orb of wind as if the realization that we were headed back to the Order was finally settling into her mind. Her lips pursed and in the shadow of the sail, I thought her eyes were misted, making the dark pupils almost gray.

Just like her footprints.

I opened my mouth to say something, but Gerarda cleared her throat and turned to Syrra with her arms tucked behind her back. "I'll take first sail. I prefer to navigate by night."

Syrra passed her a naval map that glowed under the dark blue sky. Just off the coast of the Faeland was a tiny dot that seemed to shine from the parchment.

Vrail appeared at my side and pointed to it. "This is one of the only maps that still tracks its own ship. Before Aemon, the Elverin made maps out of the same trees as their ships. Then they imbued the parchment with the magic of water wielders so each map could show their ship's location."

Gerarda's brows lifted in a rare moment of shock. "How many maps were made for each ship?"

Vrail clapped her hands excitedly and her talking speed went from a gentle creek to a rushing river. "Typically, five. It allowed for the captains of each vessel to have a few copies for navigation, but also allowed for others on the mainland to track where their loved ones were."

Gerarda's lip twitched as the shiny dot moved ever so slightly south along the map. "Ingenious."

"It would've been wonderful to see." Vrail sighed. "Unfortunately, most of the ships were burned when Aemon took power. And some of the surviving vessels' maps have never been found."

Nikolai stepped beside Vrail. "When the seals are broken we can build more ships."

"Perhaps." Vrail bit her bottom lip but was unable to contain the rest of her thought. "But the last of the mapmakers died in the Purges. There are some records left that document the process, but it would be hard to replicate from texts alone. And we would need a water wielder—"

Nikolai gave Vrail a playful nudge. "We can weigh the difficulties when we're back in Myrelinth. But until then we need to sleep." Her turned to me and whispered. "I left your things in your room."

My throat burned knowing exactly what he meant.

I took the opportunity to follow Vrail and Nikolai to the lower deck where we each had our own room. Riven had climbed to the top of the highest mast and was watching the horizon. It would still be another hour until the sky was dark enough for Riven to feel comfortable going to bed. His shadows were the only thing we had to mask our ship if we met any unexpected sailors.

I opened my door and collapsed onto the mattress. My body was exhausted from the day of travel and heavy use of my magic, but my mind roared like the water thrashing against the hull outside. I opened one of the wineskins Nikolai had left on the bed and swallowed.

The cravings hadn't disappeared entirely, but I couldn't deny that they had lessened. The elixirs Riven had given me were working. My headaches could be managed well enough each morning and I could keep enough food down to recuperate from training. But there was still a part of me that longed for night to come. Not because the wine let me sleep without worry that Damien would find me, but because for those precious few moments before sleep came my worries were washed away. Though the numbness always made the pain that much sharper when I woke.

My hands shook as I took another sip. I didn't know what we would find on that island. The reports from our spies in the capital said the island appeared empty apart from a few patrols of Damien's soldiers.

But they didn't concern me.

I was worried about the bodies. What had Damien done to them? Did he bury all those Shades when he was done torturing them? Or did he set them alight in a giant pyre for the entire city to see?

Bile crawled up my throat at the idea that we would find them rotting away in the hall where it had happened. I took another swig of wine. I hoped the others didn't find them first.

Part of me wanted to run out of the room and tell everyone the truth. But at least by keeping it a secret, that meant no one would do something stupid while we were so close to the capital. Riven charging into the palace in a blind rage would be exactly what Damien wanted and I would not allow it.

But I was scared to fall asleep.

I picked up the open wineskin and swallowed it all. I no longer tasted the wine and only felt the heaviness of it in my belly.

I opened the second skin and drained a good part of that as well. I laid on the pillow and watched the fine grain of the upper deck swirl. But no matter how long I laid there, sleep didn't find me.

Something cold crawled up my leg and I looked down to see one of Riven's shadows. It pressed tightly into my calf with a sharp edge that left a thin line of amber blood along my skin. I jumped out of bed and pulled my cloak around my nightgown to cover my scars, before opening the door into the lower deck.

Riven's shadows were scratching at the walls, leaving deep grooves in the wood as they slithered from under his door. I opened it and saw the large outline of his body in the bed. The only source of light was the small faelight that had followed me from my room, everything else was blanketed in shadow.

Riven was thrashing in his sleep, his brow furrowed and covered in sweat. I tripped on the edge of the carpet and fell onto the bed beside him. He bolted from the mattress and swung his arm, sending a cascade of sharp shadows at the door.

I grabbed him and let that familiar current pulse through both of us. "It's just me," I whispered, trying to call forward my healing gift. The warm magic trickled through my fingers and flowed down Riven's arm to the thick red slashes his shadows had left behind.

"Keera?" Riven's chest heaved in relief and he fell back onto the bed.

I grabbed his hand and watched his shadows disappear along the floor. "Bad dream?"

Riven's jaw pulsed and he shook his head.

I rolled my eyes and slid farther up the bed. I trailed a finger down the sharp hook of his nose and tapped the point. "You don't have to be strong all the time. No one expects that of you, Riv. Especially not me."

He moved closer to the wall and made more space for me. I didn't move, holding his gaze until he answered the question.

Riven sighed. "I'm not having nightmares, but the pain seems to be getting worse." His eyes dropped to the bed, unable to look at me.

I stilled. "How much worse?"

Riven shrugged and I shoved his shoulder.

"Bad enough that I can feel it even when I sleep." Riven swallowed.

I grabbed his hand and felt the *miiskwithir* connection once more. "Does this help?"

His lip turned up at the side. "You always help."

He wrapped his hand around my waist and pulled me against his chest. I let the cloak drop to the floor and bathed in the thrill that Riven's hungry gaze sent through me. Any hint of pain had cleared from his face as he trailed along every curve of my body, licking his lips.

His desire wrapped around me, pressing me into the mattress until my heartbeat fluttered against my chest. My worries about sleep fell away just like Riven's pain. We were no longer at sea. No longer headed directly into the enemy's territory. The world outside of the room and his bed no longer existed.

Riven pulled himself on top of me and traced the neckline of my nightgown with his lips. His fangs scratched along my skin, leaving a trail of goosebumps as he pinned my arms beside my head in an iron grip.

I writhed against them but Riven only grinned. "The more you fight, the longer I'll hold you there." I stopped immediately and Riven chuckled against my ear. "So you *can* listen."

I kneed him in the gut and used the moment of shock to flip myself on top of him. My hair spooled down one side of my face. Riven growled and grabbed the back of my neck, claiming my mouth with his own.

I let my body collapse into his touch. A soft moan grew inside my chest, ready for Riven to coax it out of me as his tongue brushed against my lip, and then he stopped.

His eyes pinched shut. "You've been drinking."

I blinked as I sat back along his hips. Part of me wanted to lie, part of me wanted to tell him why I had drowned myself in wine, but I wasn't willing to do either. I just sat there as the feral need in Riven's eyes disappeared into something colder.

My face burned at the rejection. I flipped my leg over him and climbed off the bed. "I should go."

"Keera, wait." Riven pulled himself into a sitting position.

I shook my head and made for the door. A wall of shadows pressed against it so I couldn't open it. I exhaled and turned around.

"If you want to leave, I won't stop you." Riven's voice was hoarse, like he struggled to say the words let alone mean them. "But I *want* you to stay."

I huffed a laugh. "You don't seem to want me at all."

Riven's shadows curled around my legs, dangerously close to the short hem of my nightgown. "That has never and will never be true." He tugged at my leg with the shadow, beckoning me closer. I planted myself to that spot.

Riven eased out of the bed, his head almost scraping the rafters of the upper deck as he walked over to me. "Come to bed, *diizra*." He grabbed my hand.

My throat tightened. I didn't want to go back to my room and face my nightmares alone. Riven had subdued them before, maybe he could even keep Damien at bay. I swallowed my pride. "Okay."

Riven pressed a gentle kiss to my forehead and scooped me up against his chest. He laid me down on the mattress so gently I didn't feel his arms slip out from underneath me as he climbed in beside me. I rested my head on him and let one of my fears bubble to the surface.

"I don't know if I can stop." It was as close to the full truth as I would say, but still my heart raced at admitting it. I froze, waiting for the anger to come, but Riven only stroked my hair.

"Have you been using the elixirs?"

I nodded my head against his bare chest. That familiar scent of birchwood filled my nostrils and I took a deep breath of him.

Riven leaned his cheek against my head. "Have they been working?"

I nodded again.

"I'm proud of you for taking them." Riven's hand traced circles over my arm. "Rheih thinks she should have a sample of the elixir you asked for when we return."

My lip trembled at the kindness in Riven's words. Even in the face of my deepest shame, he didn't turn from me. He didn't try to force me to do something the way I'd been forced by so many for so long. He only offered his help and his comfort and trusted that I would find my way.

My eyes welled. I didn't know how to have that much faith in myself.

"Your footprints were darker than they've been before, weren't they?" I asked, ready to take the focus off myself.

Riven's hand stilled. "How did you know?"

"Subtlety is not Nik's specialty." I laughed into his chest. "Syrra explained it. I hope you haven't been hiding your pain more than usual to spare me from it."

Riven's heartbeat slowed and his back eased into the mattress once more. "I haven't been trying to. I think it makes it easier to pretend that it isn't getting worse." Riven held me more tightly. "That I might not have as much time as I need."

I shivered. There had only been one other Dark Fae born since the magic and the Light Fae had gone. Riven had never told me what had happened to him, only that his magic had been fractured too, getting more painful until the day he died.

"Perhaps when the seals are broken, Feron and the others will find a way to help you." My words were shaky just like the hope I had for that being true.

Riven wrapped his arms around me and breathed deeply from my neck. "Then we should get some rest so you can get us to Koratha as quickly as possible."

As if sleep was at Riven's command, a wave of fatigue crashed over me and I closed my eyes, welcoming the darkness. Riven held me against him all night long in dreamless, painless slumber.

CHAPTER EIGHTEEN

WE MADE IT TO KORATHA by the sixth night. The crescent moon had risen to its peak, casting a silver streak over the rolling waves. Apart from the crashing rhythm of the sea, the world was silent. Tranquil. I didn't trust that peace. The calmer it was, the deadlier the storm, and we were sailing right toward it.

"The canoes are prepped?" Gerarda asked. I turned to the others who were also staring out at the horizon where the Order was waiting just out of view.

Nikolai nodded and tugged on his stretched coil of hair. "And the smaller rowboats."

A string of watercraft lined the ship, each tied together like the strands of a braid so we could sail the entire fleet to shore. Gerarda had insisted.

When we found no one to paddle them back to the ship, we would abandon them on the shores along with the Shades we couldn't save.

I adjusted the strap of my quiver across my chest. My throat burned with the urge to drink. Not to calm my nerves, but to calm the worry that Damien was going to peek into my mind and have his soldiers waiting to ambush us. Or that he already had.

I pulled out the lilac elixir Riven had given me instead and let the sweet liquid calm my stomach. As long as I didn't fall asleep until the mission was over, I wasn't risking anyone's life.

I checked my weapons belt for the third time. Gerarda placed a gentle hand on my wrist. "We need to leave."

I swallowed. I was stalling. I could see in the kind way Gerarda held my gaze that she thought she understood why. That no matter how much I'd barked to the contrary, she believed there was still a tiny bit of hope inside me thinking we would find the Shades alive.

My chest tightened but I didn't tell her how wrong she was.

I turned to Riven and felt the whisper of his shadows curl around my legs as I nodded. "Do it."

Riven stepped forward and raised his hands. At first, there was no change to the sky. The moon shone down on Syrra as she adjusted the sails and glowed against the others' backs as they pulled the anchor up using the large wooden wheel at the center of the ship. But then wispy strands of black blew over the moon, indistinguishable from clouds to anyone who didn't know it was magic. Riven took his time, pulling thin shadows across the crescent as slowly as a gentle wind. He didn't completely obscure the light but darkened the sea enough to hide the real magic.

Riven walked down to where the others had stopped turning the anchor wheel and climbed the mast of the ship. When he reached the small platform at the top of the post, he raised both his arms and a fog of shadow rose from the sea. Within seconds we were entirely encased in darkness.

Syrra steered the ship as I used my gusts to fill the sails just enough to move us through the water. We were as quiet as an eagle through the sky.

Riven used his vantage point to stretch the fog across the entire horizon. Anyone on lookout would misjudge where the night sky and the sea met, concealing our ship completely.

It was minutes before we reached the perimeter of the island. There was no way to sail a ship so large directly to the shore. The towering rings of jagged rocks were meant to keep the Order safe from naval attacks. But smaller vessels paddled well would get us to the shore unscathed.

Hopefully.

When we neared too close to the outer ring, Riven cooed like an owl. Syrra's teeth clamped shut in the darkness before Vrail ignited a large faelight along the deck.

Riven dropped down beside us. We worked silently to lower each of the vessels into the sea. Twenty-seven large canoes and nineteen rowboats all tied together to one larger vessel Nikolai had outfitted with a small sail. Too small a sail to tow such a load under normal conditions, but with my gusts we could maneuver the line of watercraft through the rings of rocks between our ship and the island.

Gerarda stepped into her own craft. Nikolai had made it smaller and thinner than a canoe. It had no seat, but a cushion that sat at the bottom of the shallow hull. Once she was inside, Nikolai threw his custom design over her head and then fastened the bottom of it along the tiny hole Gerarda sat in. Every part of Gerarda's body from her neck down was encased by the vessel or the black bodysuit, completely secure from the sea.

She pulled her double-sided paddle against her canoe and ducked her head. Nikolai tapped her back once and pushed her into the freezing water below with a single kick. I heard the splash as Gerarda hit the water and ran to the edge of the deck. Her vessel popped through the surface and she began paddling toward the shore of Koratha.

Syrra dropped a wide ladder made of Elvish rope over the side of the ship. "We have one hour."

Nikolai took a glass vial of black liquid from his pocket and shook it. It transformed into a bright orange color. "This will slowly darken. When it's black, time has run out and our *only* mission will be to return to the ship." He gave me a hard look.

I lifted my leg over the edge of the deck and secured my foot on the first rung of the ladder. "You're acting like I'm not the one who set that time limit."

Nikolai rolled his eyes before daintily stepping over the lower edge. "And you're acting like you don't have a habit of breaking the rules. Even ones you set for yourself."

It took everything I had not to stick my tongue out at him. We descended the rest of the way in silence. Syrra and Vrail sat at the back of the boat while Riven and Nikolai sat at the front, ready to adjust the sail as needed. I called that turbulent power forward until it whipped inside my chest and aimed it at the small sail.

The fabric bloomed within the black fog. Riven lifted the shadows off the sea and cast a faelight in front of our tiny armada to light our way. The fog still hung in thick blankets above our heads, shielding us from being seen from the high cliffs of the island.

I indicated for Nikolai to sail us a little south where I knew the first small break in the rocks would be. It was wide enough for our vessels to glide through but the tight turn to the north left two of the canoes stuck between the rocks.

"Cut them," I ordered after Vrail's attempts to shake the line loose had failed. Syrra ignited a faelight of her own and cast it along the line of canoes and row boats until the two thin vessels were visible. They had been pulled onto a jagged rock.

Syrra pulled an arrow from her quiver and aimed at the rope connecting the canoes to the main line. She released her shot and the sharp tip sliced the joining rope right through. She sat without saying a word and I filled the sails once more.

I maneuvered us through two more turns, narrowly avoiding a rowboat being forced aground along the jagged reef that surrounded the Order. We only had one more passage, but it was too small to make while towing all the vessels at once.

I lowered my hand and the sail went limp. Vrail crossed first, expertly walking along the thick towline, like it was one of the small bridges of Myrelinth, and dropped herself into a canoe. She pulled a thin blade from her belt and sliced through the guiding line. Riven went next, the shadows momentarily fading as he focused on crossing into his own canoe. He cut himself free just as Vrail did and thickened our cover once more.

Syrra had somehow already boarded her own canoe and cut herself free of the line. Nikolai and I were still towing the majority of the vessels, but now they flowed behind us in a single line. Nikolai tightened his grip on the sail rig and I used my magic one last time, gently pushing our ship along as the rocky obstacles got tighter and tighter around us.

I peered over the front of the boat as best I could and pointed to a tiny white rock sticking out of the water. "Watch the water in front of us. Some of them sit just under the surface and are sharp enough to cut through the hull even as slow as we are."

Nikolai nodded and adjusted the sails, slowing our pace even more. I glanced at the vial along his belt and saw that it had turned from brilliant orange to something more muted and flecked with brown.

"Nik, watch out!" I shouted too late. A large crack split through the air and suddenly I could feel water on my feet.

"I was trying to avoid the one over there!" Nikolai pointed to the sharp hook protruding from the water a few feet to our left. I glanced between its edge and the rock sticking through the hull of our boat. There was no angle that wouldn't have left our sailboat stranded.

"Rock with me!" I shouted, standing up and swaying side to side.

Nikolai stood but didn't match my rhythm. "Keera, there's no saving this." He shook the vial, and the brown flecks dispersed into the orange. "There's no time."

I gritted my teeth. "And there's no way for the rest of the vessels to go through unless we can free the hull from this rock. Including on our way *back*."

Nik's eyes widened and he matched my rhythm. We leaned to one side of the boat and quickly sidestepped to the other. Again, and then again until finally the hull popped over the jagged edge. "Walk on this side," I told Nik, pointing at the side that now sat closest to the water. The hull was delicately propped on top of the rock, but any added pressure to the other side could pierce it once more.

Syrra was waiting at the back of the boat. Nikolai hopped in and held his hand out to me. I took it and used it to balance myself as I ran across the edge of their canoe and jumped into Riven's.

"If we're careful, our canoes should ferry the rowboats through," Vrail said, assessing the space between the jagged rocks. "But how do we get that out of the way?"

My chest tightened, knowing there was no other way. "Quickly."

I aimed a gust of wind at the lifted side of the hull. The boat flipped through the air and shattered against the tall, jagged rocks. The noise of the crash echoed off the tall rocky pillars and bounded against the cliffs like wind through chimes.

If the watch at the Order didn't know we were here beforehand, they certainly did now. I grabbed my paddle and kneeled inside my canoe. "No use wasting time being quiet now. Reach the shore as quickly as you can."

Riven extended his fog past the shoreline until it hit the rocky cliffs of the island. It would be obvious to anyone looking down that magic wielders were close by, but it also would give us the protection we needed to dock the vessels and scale the cliffs.

By the time Syrra and Nikolai had landed at the beach, Riven and I had already begun our climb, hammering the cliff edge with anchors for the others to use behind us. A loud horn sounded in the distance and I sighed with relief. It was too far to have been blown from the Order. Gerarda's distraction had worked.

I only hoped that meant the guards of the island were looking to the mainland instead of the small squadron ascending to the east.

Riven reached the top of the cliff first while I added anchors for Vrail and Syrra. When I pulled myself over the top, Riven was casting spike after spike into the edge of the cliff. "We only have minutes. If we find anyone, we'll need as many lines of descent as possible."

My heart ached as I watched him plow another spike into the rock in one blow. I knew Riven thought the worst, but he also knew I would never forgive myself if we lost any survivors from lack of planning. It was unneeded, but touching.

"Thank you," I whispered as I unfurled a spool of rope from my back and let it drop down the cliff below. I felt it collide with the shore and then pulled it up a few inches before tying it to the spike.

The screech of a fish owl broke through the air—I spun on my knee with my bow and arrow ready. Riven's shadows curled around my fingers, keeping me from firing my shot.

In the distance, I saw Gerarda crouched beside the large lake. She had made the call. I smirked at Riven, knowing he must have suggested everyone use owl calls as their signal.

Syrra pulled herself over the cliff edge and grunted. "If I die tonight, Riventh Numenthira, I will haunt you as the owl haunts the mouse."

Nikolai wheezed his laugh as Vrail pushed him over the edge from below. "I think she would rather face ten thousand of Damien's men than fight one measly bird."

"Too young to know what those creatures are," Syrra muttered to herself. "When the magic is unsealed you will see."

We ran to the lake under the cover of Riven's shadows. Gerarda had torn off her bodysuit and was outfitted with her bow and countless blades. "I set fire to one of their ships. I was hoping to torch three more but I was almost seen."

"You're alive, that's all that matters," I said, not caring to hide my relief. "We know the island best." I pointed to Gerarda and Syrra. "Syrra, take Nikolai. Gerarda, take Vrail. Your parties will search the Order after Riven and I will run the grounds and take care of any guards we see."

Each of them nodded. Riven and I left first, curving around the northwest side of the island. There was a single sentry standing guard at the watch tower. The sound of his body falling into the sea was covered by the waves crashing along the rocks below.

Riven moved to continue along the edge of the island, but I grabbed his arm. I pointed toward the castle. "This way."

Riven's brow furrowed. "Traveling in the open field is more dangerous." His last words were slow, realizing I was well aware of the risk. He turned back toward the tower. "You don't want to cross by the tower?"

I shook my head. "I don't want to cross by the *grave* near the tower." My throat burned. I had never returned to that spot and I had no intention to.

Riven opened his mouth and I could see the question sitting on his tongue. In that moment, I knew he knew. That Killian had told him that it was *me* who stabbed a blade through Brenna's chest. His eyes softened and I didn't know if it was with pity or disappointment. There was no time to tell him the truth of it now, no time to learn what he thought of me.

He only nodded. "Lead the way."

We cut through the middle of the island. There were no other soldiers stationed at any of the watch points. I clenched my jaw. Hildegard and Gerarda had maximized the guard positions to train as many Shades as possible each night, but this few men felt neglectful.

Or like a trap.

As we neared the Order, I saw a group of soldiers standing on the terrace. They had no weapons drawn and their gazes were locked on each other and not the grounds they should be watching. I signaled to Riven and he covered the nearby windows and entryways with shadow before I shot an arrow through each man's heart.

Riven knitted his hands together and hoisted me up onto the terrace. We both dragged two men to the edge and dropped them onto the ground below, hopefully out of sight to the rest of their crew. I loaded my bow with two arrows as Riven unsheathed the long sword behind his back. His hand shook for a moment as he gripped the hilt, his magic was beginning to drain. But Riven didn't say a word. Instead, he raised a hand toward the white stone wall, turning his shadows into nothing.

We stalked along the third floor, checking rooms for guards or Shades but found no one. Riven's cheeks became more hollow with every room we checked. "Something isn't right," he whispered.

I pointed to a small hallway that led to a narrow staircase. "There are dormitories up here. But the soldiers may have turned them into barracks."

Riven's jaw pulsed as he took the lead up the staircase, flooding the narrow passage with shadow.

I pressed my hand on his back and followed him up step by step. "One more turn and then you'll reach a small landing. The door will be directly across from the last step."

Riven's shadows curled protectively around my legs. Just as I felt the flatness of the landing beneath my foot, Riven kicked open the locked door in a single blow and filled the room with darkness.

I drew my dual blades and followed Riven into the room, crouched and ready. There were no other heartbeats apart from his and mine, but there was a thick stench of shit in the air. Something about it reminded me of death.

Riven sensed something too and let his shadows fade into the walls, revealing the horror about the room. Fifteen bodies hung from the bed posts, their boots just scraping the floor underneath them.

Soldiers not Shades.

Riven grabbed one of their hands and choked. "They're still warm."

Every bit of warmth drained out of me. This *had* been a trap, but I had no idea who set it.

CHAPTER NINETEEN

THE SOUNDS OF CLASHING STEEL filled the air as I reached the lower levels of the castle. My heart pounded against my chest, unable to slow despite the way my panic wrapped around it. I stowed one of my blades and held my bow in the other hand, ready for whatever I found waiting at the end of the large stone staircase.

I had almost reached the great hall doors when the palace went silent. Finally, my heart slowed, my panic crumbling as the quiet lingered. It stretched out over the grounds until it felt like time had stopped.

I reached the top of the last staircase. Behind me was a statue of a fearsome warrior dressed in Elvish armor. In front of me was Lady Curringham protected by a guard on either side of her. It seemed the schemes of the late husband had been picked up by the wife.

The air in my lungs was so hot as I exhaled, I was sure it was smoke. The wife of the late Lord Curringham and the daughter of one of the largest trade allies to the kingdom. Now, she was trading in Halfling blood. I swallowed the vile taste in my mouth and reached for an arrow, ready to make the kill.

"Don't shoot!" Gerarda's desperate plea did not reach my ears in time, but the thin blade she had thrown at my arrow did. It fell at my feet in two even pieces, each bouncing down the steps.

The guards glanced at each other in confusion, raising their blades an inch but neither moved, unsure of who to attack.

I grabbed another arrow but Gerarda had her sword ready and a knife aimed at my throat. "Keera, I don't want to kill you, but I *will* if you don't listen to me for once in your life!" Her wide cheeks were sweaty as her chest rose and fell in a sharp rhythm. Her dark eyes held the same resignation that I knew mine had countless times. The look of someone who would strike if given any reason to.

"She's in on it." I seethed through my teeth. "Damien used her husband to stage a coup and now she's working with him to send his weapons to the other realms. Weapons he makes by *killing Shades*." I snarled down at the foreign lady. Her light brown skin was more sallow than the last time I'd seen her, and her perfectly manicured curls were tangled and unkempt behind her head, but there was no denying that she was Lady Curringham.

"Keera." Gerarda took an exaggerated deep breath, trying to calm me, as I stalked down the steps. I turned my arrow on her.

"Why would you protect her? Lady Curringham of all people." Too many possibilities were running through my mind, my entire body shook under the weight of them. "Did you *know* about this?"

I gestured to large white doors, identical to the ones that had fronted Aemon's throne room. Dark stains of amber blood were inked deep into the grain. They had turned the one place where Shades could laugh and eat freely into a place of horrors.

One of the guard's dropped his sword. "Lady . . . ?"

He never finished his thought because at just that moment, Lady Curringham pulled a gold hairpin from her curls and drew it across the man's throat in a long, ragged cut. His body hadn't even hit the floor before her pin was lodged in the other's eye. "Would one of Damien's allies do that?" she asked. There was no harshness to her consonants and no lull added to end of her question. Her foreign accent was nowhere to be found on her chapped lips.

My eyes narrowed but I refused to lower my bow. "If that's what it took to escape, that's *exactly* what Damien would do."

"This is ridiculous," Gerarda muttered under her breath. She drew a knife from her belt and tossed it at Lady Curringham's feet.

I tightened my grip on my bow but didn't release the arrow. "Friends don't arm the enemy, Gerarda."

She only rolled her eyes.

Lady Curringham's fiercely green eyes never left mine as she slowly bent over to pick up the knife. "What Ger is trying to tell you"—she pushed the mountain of curls out of her face with a feline smirk, before sliding the blade down the middle of her third finger—"is that I can't be your enemy." She raised her amber-covered hand. "Because I am one of you."

I blinked and slowly lowered my bow. Gerarda broke from her spot across the landing and charged at Lady Curringham. I thought for a second that she had changed her mind, and was going to kill her after all, but instead Gerarda kissed her.

Lady Curringham dropped the blade stained with her own blood and picked Gerarda clear off the ground, spinning the Halfling around three times.

"Why do I miss everything interesting?" Nikolai quipped from the main entrance flanked by Vrail and Syrra.

Vrail's full cheeks were red and her lips had almost disappeared into her mouth. "This is what she leaves me for? Takes off across the island without warning and no care for who sees her." Vrail folded her arms and shook her head in disgust as Gerarda's hand made its way into Lady Curringham's curls.

"I'd break protocol too if I knew someone was going to kiss me like that," Nikolai mumbled as he stared at the couple. His eyes flicked to Vrail for the briefest moment before shaking his head out of his daze. He lifted the vial—it was already a muddy brown color.

I turned to Riven who immediately cloaked the landing in darkness, getting the attention of Lady Curringham. She stared, wide-eyed, as the shadows faded into the white stone. "It's even more splendid than I'd imagined," she whispered, curling an arm over Gerarda's shoulders. There was almost as much difference in their height as between Gerarda and me.

"If you're not an enemy, then tell us how you're alive and the Shades are not, *Curringham*?" I made sure to flash my fangs when I said her name.

Gerarda had a blade pressed to my ribs before I could blink. "Her name is Elaran and she is the only reason you weren't left on this island to rot. You will treat her with respect or I will cut out your tongue."

Riven's shadows wrapped around me just as Lady Curringham placed her arm in front of Gerarda. She grabbed the knife from her hand and tossed it over her shoulder onto the floor, while smiling widely up at Riven.

I snarled and Gerarda grabbed another one of her daggers to point at me. I looked down at the thin blade and she raised her brow. It was a dare as much as it was a threat.

"Apologies, Elaran," I said through clenched teeth. Gerarda's gaze trailed over me before she nodded.

Vrail threw her arms up in exasperation. She tugged at the vial attached to Nikolai's belt, yanking him into her. "We need to break the seal. Now."

"Seal?" Elaran asked, pushing back her tremendous curls. "You didn't come for the Shades?"

The entire world stopped, even my heart froze in my chest. I stared at Elaran, unable to think, unable to breathe.

Syrra was the one to clarify. "The Shades are alive?"

Elaran glanced at Gerarda, who wiped her eye on her sleeve. "You didn't come as a rescue mission?" Her full lips hung open.

"We have a ship and the means to get you to it," Riven said. He straightened at my side as he admitted the truth. "But our reports were bleak. We anticipated the worst."

"I told you," Gerarda sneered, but it evaporated the moment her eyes landed on Elaran again.

Elaran plucked the gold hairpin from the guard's eye. "I am happy to provide you with a better report."

Gerarda held out her sleeve to her. Elaran wiped the pin clean and pulled her hair back in an effortless cascade of curls. She reached for one of the iron handles along the tall, bloodstained doors and pulled.

A vile, sweet scent filled the room. The others pulled their collars up to their noses but I still could not move. I finally scanned the room and my lip trembled to see that it was filled with bodies. Some were soldiers, unconscious or dead along the floor, but most were Shades.

The very faces I had seen drained of life in Damien's memories were wearing thick handkerchiefs tied over their noses as they gathered in small groups about the room, tending to those who were badly injured.

Oh gods. It had all been lies. I had been so quick to believe Damien. So unwilling to explore the rules of our minds' connection that I assumed it behaved the same way Feron's mindwalking magic had. I never questioned that what Damien had shown me wasn't real because I thought he could only show me pieces of his memory. Bile coated my tongue realizing Damien had constructed those dreams out of his own fantasies.

My eyes fell to the Halfling at the center of the room. I was already running to her as she pulled down her scarf. I wrapped my arms around her shoulders, neither of us caring how her chair rolled back as we embraced.

"I knew you'd come," Myrrah whispered. She patted my face and looked over her shoulder at Gerarda. "I told them so."

My chest cracked open with my voice. "I thought you were dead. All of you." Thick streams of tears poured down my face. Myrrah wiped them away.

"Not all of us." Her smile fell for a moment. "Not yet."

I pressed my head to hers. There weren't enough words in any tongue I knew to tell her how sorry I was. To tell her how much I missed her wife too. But at least I would have the chance to try.

I stood, wiping my eyes. Riven and the others were already organizing the Shades by injury. Identifying who would need help crossing the island and who was fit enough to carry others.

"How did you survive?" I pulled at her black scarf. "How did you know to attack tonight?"

Myrrah pointed her chin at Elaran who pulled a tiny faebead from between her breasts. It was bright red, the same color as the orb that Gerarda had kept around her neck.

Gerarda had the decency to look at her boots. "I didn't tell you because I thought Elaran was dead. She never made it to where we said we would meet. I went back there every day for *weeks*." My heart ached at the pain in Gerarda's voice. She had kept her grief so hidden. The burning at my throat flared. Perhaps, I'd been too preoccupied to notice.

Elaran swallowed thickly. "I overheard the soldiers talking about destroying the bridge that day and I knew what Damien was planning. I came to the island to warn everyone, but I was too late. There was nowhere for us to go when the soldiers came. I thought about using the bead so many times, but I knew that Gerrie might be stupid enough to come on her own . . ."

Gerarda huffed a laugh. "You let me think you were dead all this time for the *chance* that I might come here and hope to find you alive. You weren't even supposed to be here in the first place."

"I had no way of telling you where I was anyway." Elaran gave Gerarda a quick peck on the top of her head. "And I knew you'd be romantic enough to hope."

Gerarda's cheeks flushed but she didn't say anything more. Vrail stepped between me with Riven and Nikolai behind her. "It will be tight, but we have enough vessels to move everyone. But we need to move *quickly*." She glanced at Riven. His jaw was hard and his brow sharp enough to kill. I could see from the thick veins pumping along his neck that the pain of using his magic was draining on him. He wouldn't be able to keep the ship concealed much longer.

"Where are we going?" a soft voice asked from behind me. I turned around and saw a teenage Halfling with light brown hair braided down her back and a smear of red blood across her face. Fyrel. The young initiate I had helped with her bow training what felt like a lifetime before. She was taller now, but thinner. She had grown into her lanky limbs, but her cheeks were hollower than they should have been for one so young. Her arms were marked with circular bruises from where Damien's needles had stolen her blood.

My throat tightened as I watched her grab a blade from one of the fallen soldiers and stand ready for a fight. "We're not going to battle yet. I'm taking you home."

The room broke into a chorus of whispers. None of the girls or Shades in this room had ever known a home outside these walls. My eyes stung as I thought of the wonder that would cover their faces when they beheld Myrelinth for the first time.

The ones who could, stood as one, ready to follow my lead. I turned back toward Riven and Vrail but noticed something move in the corner of my eye. I spun around and saw one of the soldiers who had been laying along the floor stumbling toward the wide window. He pulled a torch from the wall and I aimed my arrow for his hand.

It pierced through the back of his palm. His scream filled the hall, erupting chaos as the Shades reached for anything that could be a weapon, but that was the least of our problems now. I had been so concerned with stopping the guard that I hadn't thought of why he had reached for a torch at all.

I watched in horror as it sailed through the air and landed against the tall tower of dried grass that was leaning against the Order. The grass ignited, becoming a tower of flame.

A beacon to warn Damien that the Order had been taken.

I turned back to the room. "Everyone follow Gerarda and Elaran to the east side of the island. Move as calmly and swiftly as you can."

I searched the room for Syrra and Nikolai. "Can you take Myrrah and the wounded with whatever Shades can help?" They both nodded.

Vrail stepped through the crowd toward me. "Keera, we still have to unlock the seal."

I grabbed a blade from my belt and shook my head. "I'll go on my own."

Vrail grabbed my hand. "And if this seal knocks you unconscious like last time?"

I shook my arm free as Riven appeared at my side. "I'll go with her."

"No." I looked up at him, resolute. "You need to protect the ship. And the Shades."

Riven's brow knotted together and his shadows lashed out behind him. But he didn't fight my command. He knew I wouldn't be able to concentrate unless I trusted the Shades would be protected. I had only just got them back.

"I'll wait along the grounds so I can protect all of you." His neck twitched. "But we don't have much longer."

"That settles it. I'll go with you," Vrail said with a smug tilt of her head.

Riven squeezed my hand once. "Live so you can bring your people home, *diizra*," he whispered in my ear before pressing a kiss to my temple and running out the door.

CHAPTER TWENTY

Vrail and I left the others to ferry as many of the Shades as they could to the ship. Now that Damien's beacon had been lit, the beaches along Koratha were swarming with sellswords. Vrail and I ran until our lungs burned. I tried to ignore the torches carried by the charging soldiers, but my heart pounded in my chest. Hundreds of them were rushing to the water's edge with large bows and full quivers while others ran toward catapults Damien had dug into the sand.

"Do you see it?" Vrail shouted, her voice breaking in desperation.

I hurriedly scanned the training field in front of the Order. In the dim light of the moon, I almost missed the seal. This one was not marked by ash but with water. A wide circle with the same webbed pattern inside it was painted onto the ground with turquoise dew caught along the grass. The water hung to each blade in thick drops, glimmering in the pale silver light from the stars above.

I grabbed my bone hilt and pointed to a spot at the edge of the circle. "You stand watch there. Tell me when they get close."

Vrail nodded absentmindedly, her gaze locked on one of the largest dewdrops. Gold lettering floated in and out of view, like words written on glass and then plunged into the sea. Vrail leaned closer trying to decipher the script. I groaned and reached for a pebble on the ground, chucking it at her head.

She reared back in shock, rubbing the back of her skull.

"There." I pointed to the edge of the seal. "Now." Thankfully, she did not need to be told a second time. I glanced at the beach and saw a thick line of flame marking the shoreline and the rowboats waiting along it.

We only had minutes until the sailing archers would be close enough to strike us with their arrows. And they would be nothing compared to the cascade of stone that was about to rain down on us or the ships docked along the port.

I plunged my bloodstone dagger into the edge of the seal and felt the same strong pull I'd felt at the Cliffs of Elandorr. I couldn't have let go of the hilt even if I wanted to. My entire body leaned toward the seal and my arm ached from the pressure of the magic pressing down on my blade as it cut through the earth. As I dragged the dagger through the seal, the dew formed a thin river behind my blade, not of water but a silvery liquid that glowed all on its own.

I finished the perimeter of the seal just as the first catapult launched its load into the air. I kept going as the stones plummeted to the sea, crashing loudly against the large rock wall that protected the island.

A minute later, I still had half the pattern to cut through. A loud crash of water boomed through the night. Vrail lifted her hand in victory at something along the beach. "The last two catapults are too far. Both their loads have landed short!"

"Have they loaded the first one again?" I shouted, not letting my gaze drift from the end of my blade.

Vrail danced on the tips of her toes. "The bucket's half full."

"Let's hope they fill it then," I mumbled as I traced the first of eight intersecting lines across the circle.

"They're cranking it farther back, Keera!"

I cut the second and third lines.

Vrail froze and my breath stopped. "They're about to cut the rope."

"Tell me when you see rocks in the air!" I shouted back, cutting the fourth line into the ground.

Vrail crouched at the knees, as if preparing to run, but she stood her ground. Her fingers fluttered at her sides as she watched the men surrounding the front of the first catapult, waiting for the arm to release and send a shower of death our way.

"Anything?" I started the sixth line. Only two more to go.

Vrail's answer was exasperated. "Not yet."

I finished the line. "Anything?"

"Wait for my signal, Keera!"

I cut the seventh line across. "Vrail, tell me when to—"

"Rocks in the air!" Vrail shouted, covering her head with her arms. I turned with my arm and blade still rooted into the ground and waved my free hand across the sky. A gust stronger than any I had ever made blew through the air and crashed into the flying boulders with enough force to shatter some of the smaller pieces. The large ones landed on the ground with a resounding shake a short distance from Vrail.

She uncurled her arms from around her head and blinked at me with wide eyes. Once she realized we weren't dead, her face broke into a grin. "I wish you could teach me that!"

I huffed a laugh and started cutting the last line. "Watch for the second catapult."

"They're loading it now."

Not good. If breaking this seal was anything like the last. I would be incapable of protecting Vrail. It would take everything I had to stay conscious.

The rivers of silver turned gold the moment my blade finished the last cut. I looked up at Vrail. "Run to the ship!"

"I'm not leaving you!"

"That's an order, Vrail!" I seethed through clenched teeth. She folded her arms in determination, unwilling to move. My chest ached, seeing the same stubbornness in her face that I'd had as an initiate. There wasn't enough time for me to teach her how often it was deadly.

A smug smirk tugged at Vrail's round cheeks as strings of shadow curled around her ankles and arms. Then more covered her legs and chest. The next moment, she was lifted into the air and sent flying toward the east side of the island in a harness of shadow. Her protests were blown away to sea.

Thank you, Riv, I thought as I finally released my blade and pulled it into the air. With Vrail gone, I had nothing to distract me from doing what needed to be done. I cut my hand with the bloodstone dagger and plunged it into the center of the seal.

A bright light exploded from the ground and cascaded over the sea in every direction like a wave. My back arched as the magic flowed through me. Tears welled in my eyes and I went limp. I fell forward onto the hilt of my blade, bruising my stomach.

My senses exploded. The surge of magic overwhelmed my body to the point of making the world spin. I tried to gather my bearings, but every sound, every scent, every touch, was suddenly too much. It pinned me to the ground, my heart hammering against the earth.

Somehow, I sensed the boulders. I turned on my side and saw the white rocks plummeting toward me like a barrage of arrows.

I closed my eyes and let out a shrill scream as one collided with my thigh.

Warm blood soaked through my trousers and I could feel the cold air on the jagged end of my bone. My vision blurred and I succumbed to the pain, drifting into the blackness. But something warm and gentle found me there. Riven's shadows trailed over my body, assessing the damage before he crouched over me with thick tears in his eyes.

"Keera, wake up!" His voice cracked with the force of his shout.

My eyes fluttered shut again, but I forced them to stay open. My mind cleared just enough to see his face come into focus. "My leg."

Riven choked on his breath as he assessed the damage. "I can get you to a healer."

"There's no time." I winced as I tried to look down at the break. Rheih had taught me what needed to be done to expedite my magic. "I need you to set the bone. My healing gift will make quick work of the rest."

Riven's hands trembled as he wiped his face, but then a shadow of hard resolve settled across it. "It will hurt, but I'll be quick."

I nodded and closed my eyes. Riven was kind enough to not announce himself. He pushed my femur back into place in one quick snap of his arms. I screamed so loudly the ground shook underneath us. Only when the pain faded to something that felt a little less like death did I realize there had been another barrage of boulders. The white rocks had landed too far north to hurt us.

A battle horn sounded in the distance. I recognized it as the same one Myrrah used on naval missions for the Arsenal. Damien's soldiers had already boarded their ships. If they were as armed as his beaches, every Shade's life was still at risk.

"Riven, I need you to cover those ships." I huffed a breath of pain as I slowly sat up on the ground.

Riven's jaw flexed and he shook his head. "I'll burn out if I try." His violet eyes faded as he looked at me.

I wiped my own blood from my mouth. "Then we should be grateful that we're *miiskwithir*."

I held out my hand. The second seal had reinvigorated my magic. I didn't know how deep the stores of my powers went, but I knew Riven was not at risk to deplete them.

He grasped my hand and I instantly felt the flow of warmth through my body. He was pulling at every ounce of magic I had and I gave it to him. I knew to Riven his magic was cold and sharp, always painful and never easy, but as he used his powers through our bond, it felt like sunlight and warmth blooming inside my chest.

Angry shouting filled the air as Riven covered their ships in shadow. My cheer was cut off by a yelp as my bone fused together in a final shock of pain. The magic pulsed around the break and I was imbued with a strength I was not sure I had ever felt.

Riven's brows rose as I stood, but he did not let go of my hand. I held our connection and felt something unfamiliar in my magic. It was the same newness as when I unlocked the last seal. I had suddenly sensed the flame underneath my skin, waiting for me to ignite it against the world. Now there was a coolness to my magic, a wetness I had never felt before. It bubbled inside me until I knew exactly what it was.

I squeezed Riven's hand. "If you see me burning out, tackle me."

Riven's nostrils flared but he nodded.

I let that new power swell under my skin, it churned and lapped inside my belly, thrashing for me to let it out but I didn't. I needed to release as much of it as I could at once.

Riven squeezed my hand, sensing the building attack through our bond. "On the count of three, *diizra*."

I nodded, unable to speak.

"One."

Riven dropped my hand. The thrashing in my stomach raged wildly.

"Two."

I screamed and pulled my hands toward the sky. It felt like I was lifting a thousand men under the weight of so much power.

"Three!"

Riven's shadows along the beach vanished to reveal the towering wall of water barreling toward the sellswords. The archers screamed, jumping from their boats in a futile attempt to escape. The wave crashed down to the sea once more, cresting over the ships and flooding the beach. Splintered wood was thrown into the sky in all directions as the sea settled from its meal.

I fell to my knees, exhausted.

Riven grabbed my arm and pulled me to my feet. We didn't wait to watch the devastation. We ran.

Our breaths were ragged by the time we reached Syrra and Gerarda at the cliff edge. Riven's legs shook and he leaned against the rock to steady himself.

Syrra frowned as she threw a rope around his shoulders.

"I can climb down on my own." Riven wheezed between each word.

Syrra tightened the loop across his chest. "You can barely stand, Riventh."

Gerarda and I helped lower Riven to the shore below. While the rope spun through my hands, I saw that the canoes and paddle-boats Gerarda had made us bring were floating along the hull of the ship. Shades were already climbing to the deck and pulling others aboard.

Disbelief and worry pierced my heart. If we managed to get them out alive, I would never be able to thank Gerarda enough for her relentless stubbornness. She had saved them all.

With Riven secure, I did a final scan of the island. The beacon still burned along the Order, backlighting the stone castle in orange flames. Torches all over the city had been lit to witness the devastation along the beach and I knew somewhere in the distance Damien was quaking in anger.

I smirked and grabbed my guideline. My feet landed softly on the sand and we moved in silence to load Riven into the sole canoe that was left behind.

Gerarda picked up one of the paddles but I shook my head. I focused on the rippling sea beneath us. I used everything Feron had taught me to find the flow of magic within the sea itself. It spun and swerved with the freedom of a child playing in a field.

I set our boat upon it and the current let me control its movements as it carried us toward the ship more quickly than any amount of paddles could manage.

Syrra cracked a rare smile as she pointed to the sea. Swirls of turquoise and gold fluttered through the waves like schools of fish. "I have not seen such magic in a long time."

I laughed as a school of swirls leaped from the sea like dolphins.

"*Miinidiivra*," Syrra muttered under her breath.

Gerarda stared wide-eyed as a turquoise orb broke through the surface and arched through the air like a seal. "A miracle indeed."

I glanced at her. I had never heard Gerarda speak Elvish but she was obviously learning quickly in Myrelinth.

I slowed as we approached the ship. Syrra and Gerarda grabbed the ladder of Elvish rope and held us steady as Riven and I made the first climb. I pulled myself over the edge of the ship and then pulled Riven too. His breathing was heavily labored despite the help.

"Do you need more?" I asked as he winced, holding up my hand.

Riven shook his head. "You need to get us away as quick as you can." He held his ribs as he spoke. "I will manage."

I shook my head. "Their beaches and port are flooded. Damien can't follow us now."

"Unfortunately, he can," Nikolai shouted with his arm extended toward the one large ship that had survived the wave. Large oil lamps hung from the sail posts, making the countless canons and catapults stocked along the bottom deck visible.

Gerarda turned to me. "Can your gusts outrun them?"

"I don't know." I looked to Nikolai. "Do we have any weapons to fight them?"

Nikolai shook his head. "This isn't a battleship."

"Stop with your worrying!" a strong voice boomed from above. I turned and saw Myrrah wrapping her wrist in a strand of the custom rigging Nikolai had installed. She cut through one piece and a heavy bag of earth fell to the bottom deck, hoisting Myrrah high enough into the air that she could soar on one arm between us. She curved around the sail post, slowing enough for her to drop into the chair that Gerarda had placed at the base of the ship wheel.

Syrra and Nikolai stepped back in shock but Gerarda and I were not surprised. Myrrah had more flair than anyone at sea. She looked to both of us. "What do you do when you're out-armed?" She'd become our teacher once again.

I laughed while Gerarda straightened her back and answered at once. "Outmaneuver them."

A proud smile spread across Myrrah's face and she nodded. "Do what you can, Keera, but trust I have control of this ship." She unlocked her chair and pushed herself in the direction of the large wooden wheel. "Raise the anchor!" she shouted over her shoulder.

Nikolai tilted his head. "Is she talking to us?"

Gerarda elbowed him in the gut. Vrail stepped protectively in front of Nikolai as he folded over, but Gerarda didn't care. "Shades at the ready!" She called over the deck. Every Shade that could, stood at once. My eyes stung as I realized just how many we had saved. The entire second deck was full.

"Raise the anchor and gather any arrows you have. We need to fill my quiver and the warrior's across the deck." She pointed to Syrra, who nodded and took her place at the starboard side of the ship. Her bow was already in her hand.

Damien's ship was getting closer. Another minute and I knew we would be in range of the canons. I ran to the middle of the deck. "We don't have time to waste pulling it up!" I sliced through the thick Elvish rope with my bloodstone dagger and felt the anchor drop back into the sea, no longer attached to the ship at all.

The Shades collapsed against the anchor wheel as our ship picked up pace. I glanced at Damien's; it was turning so its side was facing us. They were readying the canons to shoot.

I waved my hands and shot a huge gust of wind at our sails. Myrrah's chair rolled backward as the ship lurched forward. "I know we're in a rush, but a warning would've been nice!" she shouted as she locked her chair into place.

"Here comes another one!" I shouted back at her as I sent another gust of wind at the sails. I held the magic as long as I could, feeling Myrrah correct the ship under my feet as the wood groaned against the sea.

My legs trembled under the use of my magic. I searched for Riven, but he was laying at the edge of the deck, unconscious. We only had my powers to rely on and they were almost depleted. There was no way I could sustain the gusts long enough to widen the distance between us and Damien's warship.

We needed to disable them. That was the only option left.

"Myrrah, lower the sail!"

Syrra's head snapped back at me, but I ignored her shocked look.

But Myrrah couldn't hide her doubt. She straightened the ship and shouted across the deck loud enough for everyone to hear. "Keera, I know you haven't spent much time at sea, but that would only bring us *closer* to the men with the canons."

"Precisely!" I jumped on top of the anchor wheel and climbed the mast as quick as the children who endlessly climbed the vines in Myrelinth.

Gerarda stuffed a bundle of arrows into her quiver. "Keera, what exactly are you doing?"

I smirked down at her. "Outmaneuvering!"

Gerarda blinked once and then a feral grin split across her face. "Get us as close as you can as quickly as you can!" she yelled at Myrrah.

Myrrah used her entire body to steer the ship toward the shore. "I knew the two of you would be the death of me!" She pointed at the sail and a Shade ran to unleash it. Not a Shade—Elaran Curringham.

Our unexpected move distracted the soldiers long enough that they didn't fire the canons. From my perch at the top of the post, I could see them frozen along the decks as they stared down at our green sails barreling toward them.

I looked down at Gerarda and Syrra. "Nock your arrows!"

"And aim for the sails!" Gerarda shouted as she and Syrra launched four arrows each at the black sails of Damien's ship. I closed my eyes and felt the spark of fire ignite within my veins. I had just enough magic left to light their arrows. One at a time, the eight of them ignited, turning to bright flames against the night sky that streaked across the black fabric of Damien's ship.

Stoked by the last of my magic, the flames tore at the sails like sharks at feast. They devoured them, eating through the linen until large, smoking holes were all that was left.

My grip on the rigging loosened, but I still had one more thing I needed to do. "Myrrah, are you ready?"

She pulled on a thick rope and the sail dropped to the floor of the ship. "Now!"

With every last bit of energy I had I called a final gust through my body and threw it against the large green sail. It was barely more than a breeze, but it pushed us forward just as a canon boomed. Splintered wood flew from the stern of the ship. Nikolai ran to assess the damage.

"It's high along the hull!" He turned with a smile so wide I thought his cheeks would tear. "We can repair it before it poses a problem."

Safe. He was saying we were safe.

The Shades.

My family.

That was the last thing I thought before I collapsed into nothingness and plummeted to the deck.

CHAPTER TWENTY-ONE

THE SCENT OF WINE filled my nostrils before I opened my eyes. My throat burned instantly, diminishing only slightly when I realized I was in a room I'd never been in before. The floor was a perfectly polished white stone with thin threads of gold, violet, and silver fanning out in all directions. A pool of burgundy liquid coated the floor and opened door. It looked like someone had thrown their goblet and stormed down the stairs.

I glanced up the wall in front of me. It was painted with a beautiful depiction of an Elder birch. Along the topmost leaves were three frames painted amongst the red. I recognized the first immediately. Aemon's proud face stared down at me with his large crown settled along his thick brow. Beside him was a scorch mark slightly smaller than his own portrait.

My stomach hardened.

Killian had told me his father had burned his mother's face off the wall. My gaze dropped to the portraits below. A young Killian sat sullen and almost fearful in his portrait. His large jade eyes looked up at the painter under curls so blond they were almost white. Next to him was Damien, his grin just as crooked as the gold circlet around his head.

My heart hammered against my chest as I pushed myself from the floor. I was in the king's chambers. The same chambers Killian had described to me. The same ones his brother slept in now.

I turned around, grabbing my dagger from my belt even though I knew this was a dream. A grand bed lay on a golden dais in the middle of the circular room. But apart from the small patch of wall near the door, the rest of the walls were made of glass.

Not just any glass—Elven glass.

It magnified everything in its view a hundredfold. I walked toward the right side of the room and a frigid wave slowly crawled down my spine. The Order was visible from the window, though it was shrouded by the smoke from the burning port.

Damien could watch anything that happened on those grounds from his window. I swallowed my fear and reminded myself that Riven's shadows had cloaked our movements. And even magnified, Vrail and I would have appeared as nothing more than little ants along the grounds.

Damien wouldn't have known what we were doing even if he had been watching us.

My heart stilled. This was Damien's room, which meant it was Damien's mind. I spun around to see Damien's cold, predatory stare across the room. I instantly tugged at my sleeve that had bunched around my elbow but Damien's good eye didn't notice Brenna's name down my arm.

I glanced at Feron's ring on my finger and relief bloomed in my chest. I had underestimated Damien's skills of observation before, but I would not make that mistake again. I stood tall knowing he would not be able to see any of the names written on my skin or the magic flaring in my silver eyes.

Damien's eye patch shifted as his good eye narrowed. "Are you here to relish in your *small* victory?"

Damien stalked toward me. He lifted his hand and for a moment I thought he was going to grab my throat, but instead he placed it on the back of the golden chair beside the window. His neck flexed as he observed the sight below.

"I wouldn't call that a small victory."

Damien lifted his chin. His tunic was loose and unbuttoned in the same disheveled way he'd kept it when he was prince.

Damien hadn't planned this dream.

My muscles tensed as I spotted the thin line around Damien's neck. It was faint like a scar, barely noticeable in the oil lamps that lit the room, but I recognized it for what it was. Gwyn had a similar line around her ankle. The physical proof of a magical bond.

Is that how Damien was always able to find me in my dreams? Had he created some kind of connection that drew him in every time I went to sleep?

Damien drummed his fingers along the back of his chair. His words were cold, unfeeling, but I could see the rage burning in the amber ring of his eye. "You did me the service of killing whichever guard let it slip that the Shades were still alive."

I turned toward the window so Damien wouldn't see the victory in my face. If he believed we had come for the Shades, then he didn't know about the seals. Our plan was still safe.

"That was an impressive display of water magic." Damien stepped in front of the chair with his hands behind his back but did not sit. "Very impressive considering the Fae gifts faded some time ago."

My certainty crumbled, but I lifted my chin and didn't bother to hide the sideways tug on my lips. "My reports of the loss of their magic were exaggerated."

The only reaction Damien gave was a brief flex of his jaw. He sat in the chair, his back perfectly straight as his hands turned to fists on the armrests. "You may have taken my supply of Halfling blood, but it will only take my guards hours to pull Halflings from the streets."

My chest heaved at the thought but I didn't show it.

"I rescued a legion of your best trained soldiers." I crossed my arms. "They are not so easily replaced."

Damien's lip curled. "Most are girls who have never left that island let alone drawn blood."

I gritted my teeth at how easily he was able to dismiss what he did to them. What he'd done to *children*.

"You have seen what we are capable of." I turned back toward the flooded beach. The flames reflected in the water that now reached the garden walls of the palace. It was a terrifying sight, the shore at once underwater and engulfed in flame.

Damien scoffed. "Water magic will not save you when we meet inland. All you have shown me is that I need to reinforce my assets by the sea. And despite your *measly* display"—Damien flicked his hand like the burning ships and drowned soldiers meant nothing to him—"I have more than enough men to defend *my* kingdom."

I sat on the small table directly across from Damien since he'd only outfitted his room with a single chair. I leaned back and rested my ankle on my knee. Casual and open, unworried about an attack.

Damien's eye narrowed.

"We have much more than water magic at our disposal." I drummed my fingers against the dark wood.

Damien's lip twitched upward. "And how long will that water wielder need to recover from a single wave? A day? A week?"

The blood drained from my face.

Damien stood, peering down at me with the cold hardness of a statue. "You forget I am well studied in the art of Fae. Every use of magic has its cost."

His boot nudged mine and a cold shiver went down my spine but I refused to move.

"You can attack my armies by sea, by air, with flame or earth. It does not matter." Damien let out a dark chuckle. "Twenty thousand more men are reaching my shores as we speak. Do you think I care how many I lose in your pitiful attacks?" He smiled down at me like a cat, a curious and patient killer. "I can withstand them. Drown a battalion and I have another that will charge your fleet while your magic wielder is made useless. Burn the soldiers where they stand and another troupe will be at the field of battle before the first sun rises."

I swallowed at the utter lack of fear in Damien's eye.

"I can wait while your Fae fall one by one. And then I will kill everyone they hold dear while they watch. You have won the round, Keera, but I intend to win the war." There was a vile edge to his voice, a part of him that relished this back-and-forth.

"You haven't called your banners." I stood, pleased that without his dais Damien had to look up at me. "All you have is empty threats."

Damien grinned and reached for the bloodstone dagger at my waist. My mouth went dry as he studied the blade that had killed Brenna. He drew it across my throat, light enough to tickle but I felt the amber blood drip down my skin.

Damien's pupil expanded as he watched it fall. His stony face was wild when he looked at me. "Do not test me, Keera. You have no idea what I am willing to do."

He turned the blade onto himself and pushed it into his own chest. In the same spot that I had done with Brenna. I let out a gasp and the room went black.

CHAPTER TWENTY-TWO

I woke on a soft bed of faelight with a dozen curious faces peering down at me. My entire body ached from exhausting my magic, but all my bones were intact. A miracle from a fall so high. I blinked up at the eagle's nest swaying above my head. It blocked out the light of the suns already past their peak.

"How?" I wheezed.

Gerarda smirked as she elbowed Vrail in her side. "She's a quick thinker. Had the faelight covered before you hit the deck. Though you've been out for hours."

I felt like it. Vrail bit her lip, her dark eyes dancing all over my face as she made sure I was okay. I adjusted myself on the bed and my arm grazed something hard. Riven lay next to me, his face twitching in pain even though he was unconscious.

My head spun from launching myself off the faebed. "What's the matter with him?"

I turned to Syrra and Nikolai. They glanced at each other glumly before Syrra finally answered. "We think it is exhaustion from the magic use. But . . ."

Nikolai crossed his arms and pulled on his hair. "He's never been so uncomfortable in his sleep before."

I brushed my fingers over Riven's sharp cheek. I tried to call forth my magic that usually rippled just under the surface of my skin, but his didn't answer the call. The bond between us was just a whisper of its usual hum. I frowned, looking up at Nikolai. "It's happened before but never like this. Do you have any elixir for him?"

Nikolai swallowed thickly. "We've already given him everything he brought aboard."

My body went cold. If Riven's pain was this bad while medicated and sleeping, I couldn't fathom what he must have been feeling on that island. I'd pushed him too far. I reached for his hand, pleading with my healing gift to give him whatever he needed, but Syrra wrenched my hand away.

"He needs to be seen by the healers." Syrra knelt so we were speaking at the same level. "We will be at sea for weeks if you expend all your magic trying to numb his pain." She looked up at the sail; the wind had not been in our favor. And I had been unconscious long enough that Damien's spare ships could have closed the distance between us. We only had the speed advantage while my gusts filled the sail.

"There's nothing more we can do for him?" My words scratched against my throat, coming out breathy and shaking.

Syrra lowered her head. "I am not a healer. Even if I was, this is something I would only trust to Feron."

"Do you think he will last the trip?"

Syrra's frown was all the answer I needed.

I took a slow gaze at the deck. The Shades were patched and mended as best as we could manage, but there were too many of them to disembark anywhere in the kingdom. We needed to sail for the Faeland where Damien's navy and soldiers were not around every bend.

Myrrah was sitting in front of the ship wheel, steering us into the wind. I stood and waved my arm. "How far are we from Koratha?"

"We've just passed the south eastern tip." Myrrah pulled on some rigging and the sail swooped to the port side of the ship. "From here onward, we sail southwest until we pass Exiles Rest."

Hope fluttered in my chest. My head snapped back to Nikolai. "Do we have any canoes aboard?"

He tilted his head in the direction of a tiny vessel at the bow of the ship. We hadn't towed it to the Order with the others because it only had enough seats for two. Now it was the only vessel left aboard.

It would have to do.

I called over my shoulder at Myrrah. "How close can we get to shore at Faevra?"

Myrrah locked the ship wheel and pushed her chair to the edge of the upper neck. Deep lines hovered over her brows as she peered down at me. "I must admit, Keera, I thought your rescue mission was a bit more detailed than bringing us to a ruin. Nothing grows among those stones and the king's soldiers are stationed along every road."

I crossed my arms. We didn't have time to argue if Damien's ships were in pursuit. "Can we sail close enough to paddle a canoe to shore or not?"

Syrra grabbed my shoulder. "One canoe cannot ferry all of us to the portal. We would be sitting defenseless with no way to escape if a ship were to appear."

"We won't set anchor, only slow long enough for you and Nikolai to get Riven to shore." I turned to Nikolai but he was already uncovering the canoe.

Syrra straightened. "You expect me to leave you and all these Halflings when your magic is not fully restored?"

I nodded. "Yes."

Syrra shook her head. "Damien could have a ship just behind us. Slowing down to save one life while risking so many is not the wise decision."

I placed my hands on Syrra's shoulders. "If this were a ship full of refugees, I would agree with you. But look around, Syrra." I waved my arms in both directions. Every Shade that could was busying about the boat, armed and ready for a fight. "You are the finest warrior I have ever met. And that is why I trust you to get him back safely. But I am in good company."

Gerarda appeared at my side with Elaran right behind her. They lifted their arms and placed an open palm across their eyes and then their chest. It was the salute of an Elvish soldier. Syrra blinked back tears as she returned the gesture and nodded once.

"I will get him home by daybreak."

I watched through Syrra's spyglass as she and Nikolai paddled Riven to shore. He was bent along the shallow bottom of the canoe so only his head was visible between Nikolai's back and Syrra's knees.

Myrrah locked the wooden steering wheel into place and moved her chair beside me. "He means a great deal to you."

My breath shook as I nodded. "He does."

I didn't need to say anything more. Myrrah could read it on my face. "I'm glad you have opened yourself up again. You are stronger than me."

I turned to Myrrah and grabbed her hand. I had so many things I wanted to say to her, so many ways I wanted to apologize, but none of them crawled up my throat.

"Damien brought her to the Order after everything." The words were so cruel, Myrrah had to whisper them to the sea and not at me.

The blood drained from my face. "He did *what*?"

Myrrah's chin trembled in disgust. "He said that it was important that the Shades knew what had happened to their teacher. That they knew *no one* was coming for them and that we would serve him just as loyally as we served his father." Myrrah's lip curled up like she had a putrid taste in her mouth.

"What happened to her . . ." I couldn't bring myself to say the word *body*. "Did you bury her?"

Myrrah shook her head. "We weren't allowed on the grounds. Damien was very strict about it. We lost a dozen Shades those first few nights." She looked up at me and patted my arm. "Elaran has some knowledge of Elvish burials. She was able to preserve the body until you came for us."

"You have her here?" I choked.

Myrrah took a deep breath and nodded. "Perhaps we can set a pyre wherever you are taking us?"

My heart snagged at the broken way Myrrah's brows quivered as she looked up at me. All her easy laughter was gone, left in the kingdom as yet another tribute Damien had demanded. I kneeled and held both her hands across her lap. "Of course. I will speak to the Elverin as soon as we return."

Myrrah cupped my face in her hands. "Hildy was right about you, Keera."

I froze against her palm. Hildegard had too many opinions about me to narrow down a single one.

Myrrah's icy eyes glinted in the light of the suns. "She always knew you would be the one to bring the Shades out of the kingdom."

I swallowed the tightness at my throat and shook my head. "She was wrong." I looked down at the lower deck where Gerarda was bandaging one of the younger initiate's legs. "I fought Gerarda every step of the way here. It was *her* who demanded this. *She* saved you all."

Myrrah blinked. "The world really must be changing if you're giving Gerarda the credit."

"We don't need to tell her how much it's changed." I winked. Gerarda looked up at us as if she knew we were talking about her.

"If you're done gossiping," Gerarda shouted, standing beside a different initiate wincing in pain, "there are a few down here who probably shouldn't wait for a healer, Keera."

Myrrah raised her brow and I fluttered my fingers. "I have a few new tricks up my sleeve."

"Apart from the wind and the fire?" Myrrah quipped.

I flicked my wrist and a small gust of wind blew Myrrah hard enough that her chair rolled backward. When she was done blinking she smiled so widely I thought her cheeks would burst. "How long can you hold that for?"

I smirked at Myrrah's quick mind and nodded for her to grip the steering wheel. "Brace yourselves!" I called across the lower deck before casting a braided orb of wind into the sails. Even though it had been less than a day since I depleted my powers, I felt strong. I didn't know if it was renewed hope at bringing the Shades home or the release of magic from the second seal, but I knew we would get home quicker than when we left.

Myrrah stared up at the sphere of wind in awe. She glanced along the horizon and realized we were sailing faster than she ever had before. She pulled on one of the custom riggings Nikolai had installed and opened the sail as tall as it could go.

A childlike grin spread across Myrrah's face and it numbed some of the guilt in my chest. "I like this ship," she whispered to herself.

"Gerarda, stop glancing at the door." I gritted my teeth for the third time. "Myrrah has everything under control."

Gerarda straightened her back. "You have an initiate on lookout."

I closed my eyes and took a long, steadying breath. Gerarda had been nothing but anxious since we left the capital. To her the mission wasn't over until the Shades were asleep in their new beds thousands of leagues from Damien or his men.

"I have *three* initiates on lookout." I crossed my arms behind the small desk in the captain's quarters. "Three pair of eyes are better than your one."

Gerarda's lip fell flat, obviously insulted.

"Gerrie, sit down," Elaran said, patting the tiny bit of spare cushion on her chair.

My neck tensed, still not sure how I felt about the former Lady Curringham, but I was grateful to see Gerarda take a seat.

"What do we have to discuss that cannot wait." Gerarda's tone was exasperated as she took another glance at the door.

"Keera doesn't trust me yet." Elaran ran her fingers through the back of Gerarda's hair. "This is where I plead my case and she decides whether to throw me overboard."

I frowned. "I was never considering throwing you overboard."

Elaran broke into a smug sideways grin. "Then you do not know what I am capable of."

"Is that a threat?" I raised a brow.

Two flashes of silver spun through the air. I turned to see Gerarda's knives embedded into the wall, piercing my cloak between them.

"Enough chat." Gerarda folded her arms. "El isn't a threat, she just likes to be in charge."

Elaran flipped a pile of curls to the side of her head. "True."

"And Keera"—Gerarda turned to me—"is not going to throw anyone overboard. Forget the theatrics and ask whatever questions that will get me out of here."

"Fine." I leaned on the edge of the desk and locked eyes with Elaran. "You are wearing the clothes of a Shade, but they're fitted for someone much shorter." I glanced at Gerarda whose cheeks flushed. "And until you made yourself known in Cereliath, I had never seen your face. You certainly didn't train at the Order with the rest of us. So if not a Shade, who are you?"

Elaran pulled something from her pocket and placed it in my palm. I turned to Gerarda. "This is just like the arrow you gave Syrra when we got to Myrelinth."

Gerarda shrugged. "I tried to explain it to you. You didn't listen."

"I'm listening now."

Elaran scooped up the arrow and tossed it into the air. "I was never formally trained as a Shade, but I was trained by Hildegard. She was the last leader of the Guild."

"The Guild?" I crossed my arms. "She never mentioned this to me."

"She wouldn't dare." Elaran shrugged. "You were watched from the moment they pulled you from that Rift. A member of the Guild needs to be a ghost. They need to not exist."

I stared at the piece of gold in her hand. "To what end?"

Elaran waved her hand. "To whatever end was needed. Thieves sent to raid someone's bedchamber. Chefs ordered to poison a lord or two. A wife sent to spy on her husband." Elaran's voice turned hard and Gerarda squeezed her hand.

"When Aemon first reached these shores," Gerarda continued for her, "he came with a small group of men. He told them that they were traveling to a land only his family knew existed. A land where the people lived forever, where they never aged and never died because of the fruit they ate. He convinced them to make the journey in search of everlasting youth."

I scoffed. "But Aemon was a Halfling. He knew a Mortal could not eat himself to immortality."

Neither of them seemed shocked by this information.

"It was a ruse," Gerarda agreed. "But one that took some time for those men to uncover. They spent years, decades believing Aemon's lies, and in that time they built temples and preached their mission to all the other Mortals Aemon brought to these shores." There was something bitter in Gerarda's words, her dark eyes were glazed like she was living through a memory rather than sitting in this room.

"Those men built lives in Elverath. They befriended the Elverin and took wives of their own. All while eating the food and believing that they would live forever. Just as Aemon had told them. But eventually they noticed that while their hair grayed and their backs weakened, Aemon held onto his youth. Knowing they would only hear more lies, they plotted to find the truth. And when they did, they turned to the only one they thought had a chance at stopping him."

I shook my head. Gerarda couldn't mean—

"My mother?"

Elaran's eyes widened. Her hand in Gerarda's hair stilled.

Gerarda nodded. "These men had become a part of the Elverin. They had children and some had grandchildren by the time Aemon started vying for control. After the first of the Blood Purges, they told El'ravaasir what Aemon had done. All but one died on the battlefield."

I eased back on the desk. "And he formed the Guild?"

"Yes. El'ravaasir had told him that there would come a time when Aemon's age would begin to show. That someone with the power to kill him would emerge and his followers would have to do everything they could to help her."

Elaran crossed her leg over her knee and raised her brow at me. I raised my brow back. "So you were married off to Curringham to protect me?"

Gerarda's jaw clamped shut.

"In a sense," Elaran said, twisting some of Gerarda's hair between her fingers. "Hildegard was suspicious of Damien for years, particularly his need to insult my late husband in front of his father yet spoil him with riches at his parties. She couldn't send a Shade to spy on him without Damien finding out about it."

I blinked. "So she sent you first—"

"And made sure Damien knew of your mission to the House of Harvest." Elaran leaned back in her chair. "And when you left—"

"He never thought to suspect Curringham's new bride," I finished for her.

Gerarda bounced her leg. "Hildegard and I fabricated the reports about the Shadow and Curringham working together."

"And your apparent trade connections to the other realms?" I raised a brow. "You are obviously not the daughter of a trade lord you sold yourself to be."

"Threaten the right people and you can become anyone, especially with enough money." Elaran shrugged. "I was quite good at it though, wasn't I?" She wrinkled her nose as she smiled. "I always loved the undercover missions best."

"I could've done without it," Gerarda mumbled under her breath.

Elaran tugged on Gerarda's hair and looked at me. "Ger's still a little sour about it all. But I was born into the Guild. I knew what I might be asked to do when Hildegard started training me."

I jutted my chin at Gerarda. "So you were recruited when you reached the Order?"

Gerarda shook her head. "No. I didn't know anything about the Guild until the day you were named Blade."

My jaw hung loose. "Why would Hildegard risk such a secret?"

"Because the king had ordered me to kill you." Gerarda shrugged. "Aemon had stopped believing that you were a sign of magic returning to the land. I think he hoped that when he found a silver-eyed little girl that it meant he wasn't going to die after all. But by the time he named you Blade, he had lost hope. He was willing to keep you as long as you stayed sharp and—"

"Loyal." I finished. Aemon had ordered Gerarda to strike me down if I ever stepped into the Faeland.

Gerarda nodded. "Hildegard put together what Aemon had demanded of me and she decided to tell me the whole truth."

"Against her better judgment," Elaran injected with a teasing smile. "But fortunately Ger proved herself trustworthy."

"She certainly has," I agreed.

Gerarda shifted in her perch, uncomfortable, but she couldn't hide the glimmer of pride in her eyes.

I crossed my arms. "Are there any more Guild members who are going to make their way to the Faeland?"

Elaran shook her head. "Hildegard always kept it small. Everyone who knows is either on this ship—"

"Or dead," Gerarda finished bluntly.

Elaran's head fell against her shoulder and she nodded. Gerarda's entire body tensed. My chest tightened. I knew what it was to live in a world after the person I loved most was taken from it. I could see the fear swirling in Gerarda's chest. She was filled with joy and relief, but terrified of ever feeling that grief again.

For her sake, I hoped she never would.

I stood from the desk. "There's no place for the Guild where we're going. A fragmented rebellion is one destined to lose."

Elaran shook her head. "The Guild fulfilled its purpose. Aemon is dead."

"Yet not by my hand." My fingers flexed against the white hilt of the dagger that had been meant for him. "I'm sorry to disappoint you, but Hildegard was wrong. I am not a kingslayer. I am certainly not some savior meant to free the Halflings on my own. I never wanted that role and I reject it."

Elaran bit her cheek but didn't say anything more.

"But"—I held out my hand—"I will do everything in my power to bring magic back to these lands and end the Crown's tyranny once and for all. And I would be honored if you joined me." I turned to Gerarda. "*Us.*"

Elaran's smile was demure, nothing more than she wanted to show. "I wouldn't have it any other way."

CHAPTER TWENTY-THREE

"DO YOU EVER SLEEP?" a soft voice asked from under my feet.

I yawned and looked down to see Fyrel clinging to the small pegs sticking out of the mast. I reached out my hand and pulled her up into the eagle's nest with me. "I will sleep when I get you all home safe."

I kept my gaze locked on the east. I hadn't lied, but the truth was more complicated than I wanted to burden Fyrel with. I had searched the ship high and low for Nikolai's store of wine but hadn't found it apart from the two skins he had left on my bed. I knew the rest must be glamoured but without a way to ask Nikolai where they were, it was pointless to look.

Without anything to keep the dreams away, I wasn't going to risk falling asleep so close to Volcar. Half of Damien's armada was stationed at the snowy city and while we were moving faster than even the falcon flies, I was not going to assume news of our attack hadn't reached the armada in the west.

Damien had proven that he had moved beyond Mortal inventions. He had schemed with Curringham from halfway across the kingdom and received reports that came from the Faeland itself. I didn't know what tools he had at his disposal, but I knew we needed to be on alert. The ships at Volcar would be armed and waiting.

Myrrah believed the same and gave the coast a wide berth. Wide enough that we sailed against the current, but my gusts pushing against the sail made that possible.

"I haven't seen the other initiate you trained with." I nodded down at the group below. "Saraq, if I remember her name."

Fyrel stilled beside me. "A small group of Shades tried to fight on that first night—once they realized what Damien had planned. Rohan told us what happened in the throne room and said that an Arrow should always be the first line of attack." She wiped her eyes. "I told Saraq that it wasn't a good idea, but she made her choice."

I didn't need to hear the rest to know that none of them had survived.

"I never thanked you for healing my arm," Fyrel said, changing the subject. She took the spyglass from my belt and peered into it from the wrong end.

I shook my head and flipped it the right way for her. "No need to thank me."

She closed one eye and looked into the distance where the smoke from the fiery mountain in Volcar was visible along the horizon. "You were sweating when you did it. Does it hurt?"

"To heal people?"

Fyrel nodded, still looking through the spyglass.

I sighed, considering the question. I didn't want to tell Fyrel the real reason for my sweats had nothing to do with magic, but a lack of wine. "No. Though it makes me tired and I need to rest if I do it too much."

"Can you use it to heal yourself?" Fyrel leaned far enough against the banister to make me nervous.

I pulled her back by the scruff of her tunic and looked down at all the Shades sleeping on the deck huddled together in groups. In that moment the warmth of my magic flared in my chest and soaked through my bones. I couldn't deny that there was something healing in seeing the Shades safe in their makeshift beds.

I'd finally done something right.

"Yes," I whispered, answering Fyrel's question, but the young initiate didn't hear me. She had lowered the spyglass and her eyes were wide. Her arm extended out, pointing to where black sails were peaking over the horizon.

I grabbed a knife from my belt and threw it at the post just above the steering wheel. Gerarda's head snapped up. I called as quietly as possible, "Sails on the starboard side."

She nodded and unlocked the wheel, steering us farther west. My gusts were still swirling against the sails but I didn't trust our speed. The masts on Damien's ships were taller so their scouts would still be able to spot us.

"Watch the sails," I ordered Fyrel. She straightened her back and nodded once.

Whispers echoed from the lower decks as the Shades woke from Gerarda's stark maneuver. The older Shades threw off their cloaks and blankets, grabbing for whatever weapon was nearest.

I hoped we wouldn't need them.

The suns were just beginning to set along the eastern horizon. Soon it would be too dark for the ship to see us, regardless of how high above the sea their scouts flew. I just needed to give us the advantage until then.

I thought of Riven and knew that he would already have the ship cloaked in a haze of shadow. But I didn't have the gift of darkness.

My skin tingled as an idea rushed forward. Riven's fog hadn't been fog at all, just whisps of shadow mimicking a fog from a distance. But I could make a real one.

I closed my eyes and focused on the thrashing flow of that new magic under my skin. I felt the water stir underneath the ship and let it rise. I focused on my breath just as Feron had taught me and instead of pulling the water together to make one strong blast, I stretched it as far as it could go. The water lifted and pulled across the horizon, tendrils disintegrated into tiny droplets that hung in the air.

Fyrel gasped beside me and I opened my eyes.

The fog had surrounded the ship and expanded forward until the black sails were no longer visible by eye or spyglass. Droplets of all sizes hung in the air, floating like the tiny faelights in Myrelinth. A chorus of shocked whispers circled underneath my feet and Fyrel popped one of the larger bubbles with her finger.

It splattered like rain onto her boot.

She looked up at me and cackled with glee. She popped another and then another. She even tried catching one in her mouth.

I leaned against the post, feeling the drain on my magic as I fought to keep the shield of water around us and as far across the sea as I could manage. I inhaled the salty air as deeply as I could but then it was my turn to gasp.

The second sun had dropped below the horizon, sending a barrage of golden light directly at our ship. Each droplet reflected the rays into the next tiny orb until the entire ship was surrounded by miniature rainbows.

Fyrel hopped over the bannisters and sunk down to the deck below on a rope. I followed and landed on the deck. The Shades were moving in slow circles with wide eyes. A young girl, no more than eight, reached out her hands and held a large dewdrop in her palms. A ray of rainbow light shot through the top of it and she fell to her knees in a fit of giggles.

"I love magic!" she screamed as she ran from Shade to Shade, showing them the tiny miracle she held in her hands.

Elaran stepped beside me, her green eyes reflecting the scene in front of us. She pulled out a small blade I recognized as the one she'd taken from the guard at the Order. She lifted her chin and ran it across her palm. Amber blood coated the blade, staining her clothes as she laid it across her knee in front of me.

I blinked in surprise. I looked up and saw that all the other Shades had taken their swords out too, coating them in their own blood despite months of having given too much of it. The older initiates found whatever weapon they could and did the same.

"We pledge our swords to you," Elaran called loud enough for the entire deck to hear.

The Shades stamped their hilts into the deck five times.

I turned to Gerarda and Myrrah at the stern of the ship. Myrrah smiled proudly and bowed her head. Gerarda gave a tight nod over the steering wheel, but her lips were in a smile.

I shook my head. None of this was right.

"I refuse your pledge," I told Elaran, loud enough for everyone to hear.

Fyrel stood up with the fiery indignation only a teenager could muster. "But we *want* to fight!"

A cascade of agreements rippled through the deck.

"And you can." I took out my bloodstone dagger and cut a line along my palm, coating the blade with my own blood. "But the days of the Shades are over. Your days fighting for someone are finished. From this day onward, you fight for yourselves. We fight for *our* people. I am not your Blade and I am not your Mistress. I will not hold you to any pledge. The choice is yours. To choose today, tomorrow, and the next. You may choose to fight. You may choose to not. But whatever you decide, there will always be a home for you amongst our kin."

"But I liked our old home," the little girl with the rainbow whispered.

I knelt to the ground and cupped her hands in mine. "What did you like about it?"

Her bottom lip jutted out and her black curls fell to the side as she tilted her head. "My friends were there and there was always food." She rubbed her belly. The canon strike had spoiled a good portion of the rations for the journey home. "And I had a bed." Everyone laughed as she pointed to the pile of hoods some of the older Shades had given her.

I chuckled. "What's your name?"

"Orrin," she said proudly.

I smiled at the way she put her hands on both hips. "Well, Orrin. In Myrelinth there is food better than any that exists in the kingdom. Better than the king eats."

Her brown eyes went wide.

"And there are *hundreds* of children there for you and your friends to play with. You can swing from trees as tall as mountains all day long if you like."

She blinked in awe. "Can I climb them?"

I laughed. "You can sleep in them. You can have your own room. Or share one with your friends and sleep amongst the stars."

Her jaw dropped. "Truly?"

I nodded. "I promise."

My eyes burned as I said the words, knowing it was the least I could offer a young girl from whom the world had already taken too much.

Elaran stood with her blood-coated blade. "Then we pledge our swords to each other and promise that none of us will ever be forced to serve again."

She lifted her blade into the air and the others followed suit. Droplets of water left tiny rivers of amber against the steel as I finally dropped the shield of fog and raised my own hand.

"For all Halflings and our home!" Gerarda called out from the upper landing.

"All Halflings and our home!" I shouted in unison with the others.

Damien would rue the day he ever touched one of my sisters.

CHAPTER
TWENTY-FOUR

We reached the port a few hours after daybreak. Myrrah and Gerarda expertly directed the ship to the end of the long dock. Syrra and Nikolai were waiting with a ramp ready to help the Shades disembark. There expressions were hard, but not grieved, my shoulders relaxed knowing that at the very least Riven was alive. Gerarda stood behind Myrrah and propped the front of her chair over the small ledge and crept down the slope.

Nikolai stood beside a custom-made chair of his own invention. Its wheels were wide and covered in thick, pliable leaf that would add better traction along the beach and trail. Myrrah hoisted herself onto the cushion seat and pushed forward in three easy strides. She pursed her lip at Nikolai. "You outfitted my ship?"

"*Your* ship?" Syrra raised a brow.

Myrrah didn't hide the way she was staring at Syrra's scars. I knew she wanted to hear the stories behind how the Elf had gotten every one. "Keera says your kind are missing a few captains. I'm just happy to stake my claim where I'm best suited." She grabbed Syrra's hand and kissed it.

Nikolai shot Myrrah an approving look.

Syrra barked a laugh. "Then we are happy to have you."

Myrrah leaned over her armrest to whisper, "The toughest ones always cave the quickest to flattery. It's how I got my wife." She frowned for a moment, and my heart tore for her. It had been years before my own moments forgetting Brenna was gone had finally stopped.

I walked beside Myrrah and waved at the Shades to follow. A host of Elverin were waiting along the beach with large tables set into the sand covered in food of every kind. I turned back to the group and saw their nostrils flare at the rich, warm scents hanging in the breeze. But their eyes were locked on the multi-colored beach, no one daring enough to step onto the sand.

I yanked off my boots and took the first step. A unified gasp released behind me as the Shades watched my footprints change color from pink to a bright green. Syrra's gaze flicked from my prints to my face with a soft smile. The gray had almost entirely gone and even some of the black.

Gerarda knelt and untied Elaran's boots before slipping off her own. My shoulders fell in relief when I saw that her footprints were a vibrant mulberry without a hint of gray. Elaran laughed freely as her toes touched the sand and left five orange dots along the beach. The tone reminded me of the leaves that wrapped around the purple flesh of a dew root.

"Time to feast!" I shouted, and the Shades raced across the sand, pulling off their own boots and gasping at the colors they left behind.

They flooded the tables and a chorus of introductions and bows took place as the first of the Elverin welcomed the Shades home.

Syrra stood beside me as the others got their food. "Thank you," I told her. Her brow furrowed in confusion. "Only you would have the foresight to prepare such a feast," I explained.

"I can cook more than rabbit you know."

I raised a brow. "I never see you in the kitchens."

She chuckled. "Lash'raelth and I trade off every few decades. We are not allowed to share them." She pointed to the beach and all the footprints left behind. "It seems the false king has not branded them as badly as you feared."

A sob cracked through my chest. I turned into Syrra's shoulder to muffle the sound so none of the others would notice. Almost none of the footprints were heavily grayed or blackened. None were as vibrant as they could be, but it was far better than I could have ever hoped.

Syrra wrapped her arms around my shoulders. "You did well, child. The *Faelinth* will cherish them. They will prosper here."

I wiped my eyes and nodded. "How is Riven?" My stomach hardened, preparing itself for whatever had kept Riven away.

Syrra smiled and nodded. "He's not well enough to travel. But Feron seems to have helped him get his powers back in control. He'll be waiting for you in Myrelinth when we arrive. Maerhal and Rheih are watching over him until then."

"And Killian?" I had noticed the prince was not part of the welcoming party.

Syrra followed my gaze to the table where Nikolai and Vrail were helping serve the youngest of the initiates. Her jaw pulsed once before turning back to me. "Someone needed to help Feron prepare for your arrival." She lifted her arms at the hundreds of Halflings we had saved, their laughter and wide-eyed wonder covering the entire beach.

She wiped a stray tear along my cheek. The roughness of her callouses didn't match the gentleness of her touch. Her dark eyes studied my face. "You have not slept."

I grunted a laugh. "Not since I fell from that mast."

Syrra narrowed her eyes. "There was trouble?"

"Nothing I couldn't handle." I swallowed the dryness in my throat. All I wanted was to sleep, but Damien would be waiting for me there. And considering the threat he had levied the last time, I didn't want to provoke him any further.

Syrra's mouth dropped as understanding settled on her face. "Nikolai never showed you the wine." He had brought enough for the journey but had hidden it under a glamor that only he knew about. In the rush to get Riven back to Feron, I hadn't thought to ask.

I gulped, not knowing how much Syrra had guessed. This was not the place for that conversation. "I had the elixirs. They've kept the tremors and sweats at bay though I will need to resupply once we're back."

Syrra gave a tight nod. "I will gather them myself." She went to one of the tables and pulled a small bottle of wine from one of the baskets. She brought it over and handed it to me. "There are hammocks through the woods there. It will be a few hours before everyone is fed and rested for the trip home."

I stared down at the bottle. It felt wrong to take it from her of all people, but Syrra wrapped my hands around it. "You cannot overcome it without sleep." She rubbed my arms gently. "But if you are ready to try, just say the word and we can get things sorted when we return."

I nodded and left her to take a few hours of undisturbed sleep in the hammocks. The wine had barely filled my belly before the need for rest overtook me.

Gerarda came and woke me hours later. She shook my shoulder until my eyes slowly opened. "We're ready," she whispered.

I grabbed her arm as she turned to leave. "I'm glad you didn't lose what you thought you had." I nodded in the direction of Elaran's booming laugh.

Gerarda's lip twitched to the side. "If only all my losses could be false ones." She bowed her head and didn't say another word. I pulled on my boots and fixed my braid before heading down the trail myself.

Nikolai was helping Myrrah onto a manual lift that he'd designed for her chair. She slowly rose until the lift was level with the carriage and she could take her place at the reins.

"I have designs for a saddle if it interests you." Nikolai gave Myrrah his most charming smile.

She shook her head. "I'm sure it's lovely, but an old sailor can only learn so many new tricks at a time. Let's get to wherever we're headed first."

Nikolai grinned and I could tell he was taken with the gruff Halfling. He raised a brow. "Would you like some company for the journey?"

Myrrah patted the bench next to her and Nikolai hopped on. I nodded to them as I walked by and Fyrel grabbed my arm. "I'm riding in the front with you." She stood tall but her voice shook.

I chuckled. "Are you?"

Fyrel gave a resounding nod. "Gerarda told me that you haven't an apprentice. I would like to claim the role . . . if those exist here." She glanced at the towering trees as if a dark creature was going to jump out of the wood.

"This forest is rather safe. It's the trees that talk back that you need to be worried about."

Fyrel tensed. "They *talk*?" she mouthed silently.

"An apprentice of mine can't be fearful of trees," I teased.

Fyrel straightened her back once more. "I'm not fearful. Not at all. I can handle some whispering trees."

Gerarda dropped down from a large branch and landed gracefully on one of the carts. "And what about the ones that eat passersby?"

Fyrel gulped. "If Keera will face them, then so shall I."

I tilted my head up at Gerarda and laughed.

"It wasn't meant to be funny." Fyrel's shoulders drooped.

I grabbed a bow and quiver from the cart and passed it to her. "You just remind us of someone. You'll get to know her soon enough." I glanced down the line at Vrail who was in the middle of a long-winded story about the wood with her own quiver slung across her back. "I can trust you to keep watch along the front of the caravan?"

Fyrel's smile was wide and toothy. "Yes, Mistress."

"Keera," I said quickly. "There are no titles here."

It was dusk by the time we reached the outskirts of Myrelinth. Syrra led us down the trail that followed the lake. When we turned at the portal the entire caravan gasped up at the Burning Mountains. The suns had just lowered beyond their peaks, so the leaves of the Elder birch along the ridge looked like molten gold.

I dismounted my horse and walked backward so I could take in the faces of wonder as the Shades looked at the city before them. Fyrel dismounted her ride beside me and she stepped over the small hill with eyes wider than I had ever seen.

The entire city was decorated in beautiful artwork that spanned down each grove. Long banners embroidered by talents that didn't exist in the kingdom. They depicted stories of renowned hunters and magic wielders, even warriors who had studied at the Order when it was called *Niikir'na*.

Some young girls pointed at the circle flame along the tree trunks, cobalt and scarlet burning without wood or air in their own magical orb as they always had. Others pointed up at the treetops where young children were waving and laughing at the group below.

Feron stood in front of the Myram tree and lifted his hands. The faelights seemed to awaken from their slumber, floating out of the branches and leaves below and lighting the darkening sky.

I walked over to Feron and he pressed a gentle kiss to my cheek. "Good work, Keera," he whispered. He turned to the group as they crowded around the giant tree and stared at its swirling arms. "Hello, cousins, I am so glad you have finally made it to our city. You may call me Feron and this"—he waved his arm in the direction of the groves—"is Myrelinth."

The whispers rippled through the crowd of black, some excited and some cautious. Feron cleared his throat. "You are welcome to stay together in whatever groups you choose. We have more than enough accommodations." Feron's gaze landed on Myrrah, who was looking up at the burls with obvious doubt. "We have rooms in the trees and in the lower city, enough that everyone should be comfortable."

Fyrel pointed at the long drape of linen painted to depict a warrior hanging over a trunk. "What are these?"

Feron smiled. "Each of these groves belong to a line of *ikwenira*. Their descendants are painted to keep their stories alive and hung on occasions as special as this. And once you are settled, we have a way to decipher what, if any, bloodlines you belong to. If you wish to know."

Fyrel stuttered as she spoke. "You mean we could have *family* here?" My chest ached at the hope that blossomed in her face. It was the one worn by all the orphans that stood behind her, children and grown.

Feron nodded. "There is no rush, young one. And if we cannot find your bloodline, know that to us you are already family. Fae, Elf, or Halfling." Feron waited as the Shades took a closer look among the city dwellers and realized most of them were Halflings just like they were.

I stepped forward and smiled so wide it stung my eyes. "Here, we are all Elverin. One kin. One family. One home."

CHAPTER TWENTY-FIVE

RIVEN WAITED FOR ME in his burl until the Shades had chosen their rooms and explored the city as best they could by faelight. The moon was already beginning to set by the time I climbed up the Myram to our grove. Riven's shadows spiraled out of his burl, reaching for me as I crossed the bridge. He leaned in the doorway wearing nothing but a pair of trousers.

I collapsed into his chest and took a deep breath of his birchwood scent. "You're okay," I whispered in relief.

Riven wrapped his arms around my shoulders and nodded against my head. "Thanks to you. Feron doesn't think I would have survived another night at sea."

I lurched back. "What happened?"

"Exhaustion." Riven shrugged as if he wasn't talking about his own death. "Feron thinks that the increase in pain is related to the increase in magic. The Fae powers are growing; my powers are not exempt from that."

My blood ran cold. "And your pain isn't either."

Riven shook his head.

"And it will only get worse with every seal?" I grabbed his hand. "We have three more, if this happened after just the second . . ."

"*Diizra*, all will be well." Riven pressed a kiss to my forehead. "The magic has to return." His voice was so calm, almost peaceful. Like he had already accepted his fate.

I shook my head and stepped out of his grasp. "You expect me to just move onward. What if the next seal kills you?"

Riven stepped to the side and pushed my back against his burl. My heart raced and I was thankful the others preferred to spend their nights elsewhere. "I cannot change the future, *diizra*. But whatever happens, it will not be your fault."

I opened my mouth to protest but Riven held a finger against it.

"And I will do *everything* in my power to stay." Riven's gaze turned hard, knowing there was only one word that would quell my protests. "I promise."

I relaxed into the bark behind my back and Riven pressed a gentle kiss to my neck. Tears pricked my eyes as I remembered the way Riven had lain on that ship, spasming in pain. I had been useless, unable to protect him. Just like I had been unable to protect Brenna.

"I can't lose you too." My lips barely moved, as if saying them too forcefully would set a curse upon us.

Riven grabbed my hand and kissed my palm and then my wrist and then he kissed the sleeve of my tunic directly over the scars where her name was carved. "I will fight until my last breath to make sure you never go through that again."

His gaze was heavy, it thickened the air until I was aware of my own breaths. Suddenly, we were not having this conversation on a solid branch, but a vine strung precariously over the plummet below. Both of us stepping to each other's dance, both of us knowing that there was more to the story of Brenna's death than Riven knew, both of us waiting to see if this was the moment I would finally tell him.

I opened my mouth, but the truth abandoned me.

"Let's go inside." Riven intertwined his fingers in mine and tugged us toward his burl. "I have something for you and there's something we need to discuss."

"A present?"

Riven smiled down at me without a shadow of pain in his face. "Of sorts."

"You're starting to sound like Nikolai if you're calling *that* a present." I smirked and tugged at the waistline of his pants. "But I'll happily unwrap it."

Riven barked a laugh and ducked under my arms before I could grip his waist. He pulled something out of a pouch sitting on the table and tossed it to me.

It was a small vial of clear liquid but it moved like thick sap from a tree. I held the glass up to the faelight by my shoulder and saw that it had tiny flecks of violet floating in the liquid.

"Rheih finally settled on a recipe she thinks will work." He pulled the cap free from the vial and a long glass stem came out with it. "Three drops should be enough for a full night's rest."

I curved my hand around the vial and choked on my breath. "Thank you, Riv. I don't know what else to say."

Riven's brows furrowed as his gaze fell on my wet eyes, but he didn't comment on it. Instead, he took a deep breath and pointed to the bed. "You should sit down."

Riven pulled the small chair from the corner and sat directly across from me, close enough that our knees were touching, but formal enough that I knew he wanted to talk.

My heart swelled looking at him, his shadows literally twisting into knots as he tried to find the words to say. He had let me live with my secrets for so long that I'd forgotten how it must have weighed on him, watching me struggle without knowing how to help. He kept so much of himself open to me, even while the darkness wrapped around his throat. It was selfish to not tell him what he needed to know.

He opened his mouth to start but I spoke first.

"Damien can access my dreams." Riven froze mid-breath. I waited for him to blink or move, but he gave no sign of living at all. I tapped his shoulder. "Riven?"

His chest heaved at the feeble way I said his name. His eyes were violet storms, swirling just like the shadows along the ceiling. "What do you mean?" He said every word slowly, like he was fighting the urge to throw something across the room, or take the nearest portal to Koratha.

I straightened my back. "That day in the throne room. When Killian and I were captured?"

"I remember." Riven's jaw clamped shut.

"Damien injected something into my arm before he ordered his new Arsenal to take me to the dungeons." I took a deep breath. "I didn't know until a few days later because I barely slept in all the chaos. But when I finally did, Damien was there. Waiting for me."

"In your dream?" Riven's hands turned to fists along his knees.

I nodded. "He could talk to me as we are now, but he could also show me things. He could change the dream to be whatever he wanted, just like Feron did when he projected those memories into our mind." The truth rammed against the dam that I had been keeping it behind. I could feel it cracking inside me with every breath until my breaths became sobs.

Riven dropped to the floor and grabbed both of my hands. Thick tears fell onto his skin but he didn't care.

"He showed me what he had done to the Shades. The way he tortured them. The way he had hung them to collect their blood until they died. I know now that they were only fantasies, that most of it wasn't true, but . . ." I leaned my head against his shoulder needing to catch my breath.

"But with the reports of the island being deserted you had every reason to believe him."

I wiped my nose on my sleeve and nodded. "Some nights he replayed Hildegard's death over and over again until I screamed for him to kill me." My chin trembled as I let all the truth spill out of me. "He made me kill Brenna over and over again. Just like the first time, but worse."

"*Diizra*. I had no idea." Riven lifted his hand to my cheek. "Why didn't you tell me?"

I looked down at my lap, twisting my fingers underneath Riven's hands. "I didn't know what else Damien could see. I didn't know if he could access my mind outside of the dreams or if he could access my thoughts while I was in his nightmares. I was worried that if I tried to tell anyone, it would somehow endanger us more."

Something like a growl came out of Riven's chest.

"At first I thought the connection was like Feron's mindwalking, that he could only show me memories and he was the one in control. But I don't think it happened the way he intended. When I collapsed after we escaped the Order, I had another dream. But it was different than the others. I don't think he expected it to happen." I took a much-needed breath. "And obviously he wasn't showing me true memories at all, just whatever he could to hurt me. But I had no idea until we found the Shades alive."

Riven's fists shook on my knees, but his shadows caressed my arms. "He probably had experimented on dozens of Halflings before he injected his twisted magic into you." Riven spat out his words like they were ash in his mouth. "He didn't know about your gifts. I doubt he ever considered how the injection might differ in the blood of a magic wielder."

My stomach hardened to think how many people had gone through the same terrors night after night not knowing it was Damien who was feeding them, just to appease his vile pleasures.

I wiped my eyes. "I barely lasted a fortnight before it became too much. I was so tired and I knew I couldn't keep seeing those memories, those scenes again and again each night . . ."

"That's why you started drinking." Riven's voice was rough and jagged, but his touch was gentle against my cheek. "To stop yourself from dreaming?" Riven's eyes fell on Feron's ring and understanding settled on his face.

I nodded. "I wish I could say that this elixir will be enough for me to stop." My hand shook and a thick tear fell onto my lap. "But I don't know if I can. The cravings are just as bad as they were before. Worse. It's all I think about, even with the elixirs you gave me." I wiped my nose. "Sometimes I wonder if Damien designed it that way on purpose. If he knew what I would do if he made me desperate enough."

Riven pressed his forehead against mine. His hand found its way to the back of my neck and I eased into the caress of his thumb behind my ear. I felt hollowed out with the truth no longer buried inside of me, but I was lighter too.

"Syrra and I can help if you want." Riven pulled back just far enough to look directly in my eyes. "If you want to stop, there are methods that can help. They aren't easy, but I suspect they would be easier than whatever you did before."

I shivered, remembering that ride from Cereliath to Koratha. There had been more than one night that I had contemplated ending the pain once and for all.

"How long?" I looked out the window where I could still hear the whispers of laughter from the Shades in their beds. "I can't abandon them now."

Riven gripped both sides of my face. "You could never abandon them. You brought them out of that place and gave them a second chance at whatever life they want, *diizra*. You can take three days."

"Three days?"

Riven nodded.

I looked down at the vial in my hands. We had already broken two seals and brought every surviving Shade to the Faeland. However Damien was tallying this war, somehow we were coming out on top. And for the first time, I believed we could stay there. As long as I was as strong as I needed to be.

I turned to Riven. "Can we start tomorrow?"

Riven pressed a gentle kiss to my lips. "We can start whenever you want to." He sat next to me on the bed and wrapped his arm around me.

"I want to speak to Nikolai, but then we can begin."

"Then that's what we'll do." Riven grabbed my chin and turned my face to his. "Keera Waateyith'thir, I am more proud to love you with every passing day."

My heart ached at his words. I pulled myself onto his lap and wrapped my legs around him. "I am proud to love you, too." I pressed a kiss to his lips. "I felt you there on my lowest days and I will love you through whatever lows come for you."

Riven's hands hardened along my waist. We both knew what his tainted powers could mean and how quickly that might come. Riven tucked a piece of hair behind the point of my ear and kissed my nose.

"Do you want to sleep here tonight?" He glanced down at the vial. "Or would you prefer to try it on your own."

I answered by throwing us both onto the mattress. Riven chuckled but his brow was furrowed.

My throat tightened. "Is there something wrong?"

He bit his lip. "*Diizra*, I love you no matter what . . ."

I raised a brow, my grip on his collar loosening.

"But you *smell*." He grinned down at me.

I shoved him in the shoulder. "I have been at sea for ten days!"

Riven sat us both up. "Which is why I didn't mention it until now."

I stood and scowled down at him. He grinned until I pulled my tunic off my body and flung it at his face. His expression turned feral as I unbuttoned my trousers. I stepped toward the shower and slowly lowered them past every curve of my body.

Riven reached for me but I smacked his hand. "Since I smell so bad, I'm showering *alone*."

Riven nodded, his eyes lingering on every bouncing part of me as I disappeared into the shower. I took my time, relishing not only being clean for the first time in a fortnight, but for *feeling* clean. There were no longer any secrets between me and Riven, nothing weighing me down.

When I stepped back out into the room, Riven was under the blankets with a nightgown stretched across the bed. I raised a brow. I hadn't heard him leave.

"I had Nikolai stock my closet with some when he filled yours," he explained with a shrug. His eyes dropped to the hem of my towel. "Though I'm regretting it now."

I grinned at him and took my time layering the jade nightgown over my body. Riven flipped the blanket up on my side of the bed and patted the mattress. I slipped between the warm sheets and relaxed against the soft bed.

"Three drops." Riven opened the vial and I opened my mouth. He let three thick drops fall onto my tongue, each one tasted sweet like fruit, but distinct.

"How long until it's meant to take effect?"

Riven gave me a wicked grin. "Just long enough for me to help you fall asleep." He lowered himself down on the mattress, so close to my body that I could feel the warmth of his breath through my gown and see the thick muscles tense along his shoulder blades.

He grabbed my knees and spread them open. He took a deep breath of my scent and licked his lips. "I have craved the taste of you every day since Wenden."

I jerked against the mattress as Riven's teeth scraped the inside of my thigh. A wave of heat overtook my body in a single touch.

A tendril of shadow traced circles at my hip before slowly trailing up my torso to my breast. The warmth of Riven's magic along the neckline of my nightgown sent a flutter of heat down my spine. Riven pressed a kiss to my other thigh. "I want to taste you until you moan my name."

I swallowed. I was already closer than Riven knew.

He wrapped his arms around my thighs, his fingers leaving dimples in my skin. "Do you want me to lick you until you beg for release?" He pressed a gentle kiss to the new scar on my thigh, knowing I had needed Hildegard's death to mark me without a word. His teeth scraped the inside of my thigh.

I squirmed against the mattress.

Riven reached up and tugged the top of my nightgown until I had nowhere to look but him. "That's not an answer, *diizra*."

"Yes," I breathed.

Riven was feasting on me before the word had fully left my lips. The hand wrapped around my left thigh pulled my leg wider as his tongue cut a line through the core of me. His other hand pulled down the front of my nightgown and cupped my bare breast, while his mouth explored all the ways it could bring me pleasure.

I whimpered when Riven finally brushed up against that small bundle that throbbed with my need for him. He circled it with his tongue and pulled at the bud of my breast until my body curved to his whim. He kissed me there with just as much hunger as he had for my lips, deepening his feast with every soft moan he tore from my body.

He pulled away and I wrapped my leg around his shoulder, coaxing him back. But Riven only grinned up at me as he let go of my thigh and pushed two fingers inside of me. He moved them in gentle, easy strokes until I gasped. My muscles flexed and Riven could see that he'd already brought me to the edge.

He increased the pressure of his fingers. "Strong. Beautiful," he whispered, lowering his mouth to me once more, as slowly as the suns.

This time when Riven's tongue swirled around the most sensitive part of me, he didn't stop. My legs thrashed against the mattress but Riven didn't waver. I groaned as he pressed harder with each stroke, matching the rhythm with his tongue, but Riven held me back from that cliff's edge, waiting for something.

My hips bucked along his mouth and he chuckled against my skin. His teeth brushed against that spot and a wave of goosebumps scattered across my stomach. The pressure built until it bordered on pain, until I couldn't take anything more.

"Riven," I moaned, begging for him to end this.

Riven's eyes flashed bright with violet and his shadows held me in place against the mattress. He flicked his tongue again and again, while his hand pumped inside of me. Something warm gathered in my chest and I could feel Riven's shadows reaching out for it, wrapping around my torso. Riven reached up with his free hand

and scratched the skin between my breasts, releasing my power and my pleasure in one final touch.

I let out a moan and a gust of wind blew through the burl, throwing Riven's belongings to floor. The vase along the table shattered into tiny pieces as the whirlwind whipped around the room. I didn't even pretend to care.

Riven didn't glance at the room to see the damage I'd done. He only lifted his head and licked his fingers clean. A feral part of me wanted to pounce on top of him, but my body was entirely spent. I could barely keep my eyes open as Riven crawled on top of me and pressed a kiss to my forehead. I turned my head against his chest and fell asleep to the rumble of his laughter.

CHAPTER TWENTY-SIX

I woke in a pool of my own sweat. Riven's arm tightened around my waist as the sunlight roused him from his sleep. He felt the bed and his eyes snapped open.

"Keera." His voice was thick with sleep. "Did you have a nightmare?"

I shook my head. "No, the elixir worked." I rubbed my temples with shaky hands. Riven helped me ease out of bed but it was too fast. I wretched onto the floor and covered the rug in vomit.

My cheeks heated but I was in too much pain to care. Riven ran to the cupboard and grabbed a glass. He held it under a lone branch that stuck out from the window and a stream of cold water poured out, filling the cup. He lifted it to my lips and helped me drink it.

I could only manage a sip. He placed the cup on the table beside me. "Should I fetch some wine?"

My body wanted nothing more than for him to do just that, but I had meant what I said the night before. I needed to do this. Not for the Shades, the war, or even Riven. But for me. I grabbed his arm. "No. Syrra said that she had elixirs for me. Those will work for now."

Riven's jaw pulsed. "They're meant to prevent the withdrawal from getting this bad." He picked up his tunic from the floor and wiped my brow with it. "They may not help now."

I shrugged. "I meant it when I said I was done. I've let Damien control my life for too long. I'm not giving him another hour."

Riven's hand balled around the fabric. I could see in the way his lips twitched that he wanted to argue. "I'll pack our bag while you shower."

I nodded and mustered the will to stand. Every heartbeat nailed a spike deeper into my head, making the room swirl, but somehow I got to the shower with only a bruised knee. The warm water eased the ache in my skull by a fraction, but I was more than grateful for it.

I limped down the Myram tree. I didn't have the stomach to drop from my burl and my shins burned in protest. I had only reached the bottom when something launched at me from behind the spiraled branch.

I grabbed for my blade but quick hands had already reached there first. "That's no way to greet a friend," Dynara whispered in my ear as she gave me a coy smile. She waved the bloodstone dagger in her hand with a smug grin.

I blinked. "What are you doing here?" I looked around the groves for any Halfling faces I didn't recognize.

"The courtesans are still in Cereliath." Dynara handed my weapon back to me. "Though not for long."

"What reason did you have to leave them?" I straightened my back. "Do you need help bringing them here?"

Dynara gave me a dramatic pout. "I thought you said I was your best spy?"

"You are."

She flicked the point of my nose. "Then don't assume I need your help. If I do, I will ask for it." She wrapped her long arm around my shoulder and I caught the rich floral scent of her chestnut hair. "Nikolai sent word that you rescued the Shades from under Damien's nose. I figured that was worth a visit." Her dark eyes trailed along my body and then my face. "I thought you'd be in better spirits on the cusp victory."

"I'm ill."

Dynara raised a disbelieving brow. "Is that what you're calling it?"

"Either way I'm dealing with it." I clasped her hand as we walked. "I'm glad you're here, but won't your presence be missed?"

Dynara twirled a strand of her hair. "The lords that Damien allowed to keep their heads may be under the impression that I have been *commissioned* to Silstra for a short visit." She smiled devilishly. "I won't be missed for a week or so."

"I'm glad I know you'll be safe for a week." I squeezed her hand. "Remember how you dressed me that night in Aralinth?"

She shoved my hip with hers. "I'm not sure there's enough time for me to forget how wonderful you looked in that bodice."

I grinned. That night had been one of my favorites since coming to stay in the Faeland. Dynara had become one of my favorites too. "Would you want do to something like that again? But *bigger*?"

Dynara's eyes flashed with excitement. "How much bigger?"

"As grand as you and Nikolai could possibly imagine."

She stepped down from the last step. "That's a dangerous combination."

I followed her across the large hall and my lungs filled with the inviting smells of Lash's baking. "That's what I'm hoping for."

We stepped into the kitchens and Nikolai and Gwyn were sitting at the table exactly where I had asked him to be. Gwyn's blue eyes landed on me and she stood.

I stepped in front of her. "I will not make you stay, but I would like to introduce you to someone I think you'll like very much."

Gwyn moved her hands in a quick slash through the air. I turned to Nikolai, who frowned. "She says she doesn't care to meet any of your friends."

Dynara stepped around me, making a point to let her leg slip through the slit in her skirt. Gwyn's eyes couldn't resist taking in the beauty of the layers that flowed like a waterfall down Dynara's leg.

Dynara smiled, knowing exactly how to crack the thick wall Gwyn had built around herself. She slipped the gold flower from her small braid and tucked it into Gwyn's fiery curls. "This is the sister you've been telling me about."

I stilled. I had never used that word to refer to Gwyn in her presence. Only in the notes Dynara and I passed back and forth to each other when I was at her bedside with the healers. I tried not to look at Gwyn.

Dynara pulled one of the copper curls from behind Gwyn's ear. "A beauty and a warrior, I see."

Gwyn stepped back with wide eyes but didn't sign anything.

"This is Dynara," I interjected before Dynara could say anything else. "She's the one who procured the beads I gave you to call me back to Koratha. She's the reason Gerarda was able to . . . get you out."

Gwyn's brows furrowed and she stared at me like a painter lost in her unfinished portrait, looking for something that wasn't yet realized. My heart quickened. I would have given anything for her to speak one word to let me know what she was thinking.

Gwyn turned back to her chair and pulled it completely free from the table. She gave a small nod to Dynara and pointed at the seat.

Dynara sat gracefully and flicked her skirts over her knee. Gwyn looked at the door behind me and I watched the debate rage in her eyes. Then she grabbed the chair next to Dynara and sat down.

My shoulders relaxed. I turned to Nikolai, who was pretending not to be interested in what had just occurred. "Glad to see my message reached you, Dynara," he said with a stiff nod.

She smiled back at him. "I appreciate you thinking of me. It seems I arrived just in time. Keera was telling me about some kind of fashion disaster."

Nikolai tilted his head at me with curiosity. He grabbed his ankle over his knee. "This is the first I'm hearing of it."

I rolled my eyes. "I told you last night."

"No, you asked how many stuffed closets I had among my grove, my room, and my apartment." Nikolai flicked a stray piece of thread from his pants. "And the answers depends on whatever this so-called *disaster* is."

I took a deep breath. "I know Feron is planning on hosting a welcoming ceremony for the Shades and I would like the three of you to help him."

Gwyn's head perked up as Nikolai and Dynara exchanged glances. Dynara spoke the question they were both thinking. "There are many you could ask, why us?"

"There are few I would trust with something as important as this." I pulled on the ends of my sleeves. "And Riven and Syrra have their own task to occupy them for the next few days."

Nikolai leaned back in his chair and gave me a soft, proud smile. Syrra had told him where we would be going and why. "We can have the ceremony when you return. I'm sure the Shades would want you here."

My chest tightened, unsure if that was true. "I don't know if it's feasible, but I think the Shades would appreciate having something else to wear apart from their black garb. They've worn black for too long."

Nikolai's smile fell to a serious line. "Yes. They have."

Dynara grabbed my hand. "I think that is a lovely idea, Keera. But are you sure you don't want to be the one to lead it?"

I shook my head. I looked at Nikolai and saw the Elf who had everything taken from him but had never stopped laughing. Even going as far as to adopt his own Halfling son, knowing that he would far outlive him, knowing that he would carry a piercing stitch in his heart after only a few short years. In Dynara, I saw a Halfling who had fought for her freedom with everything she had, to the brink of death, and made herself a home amongst the Elverin while still doing everything she could to liberate the Halflings she had been forced to leave behind.

Neither of them had succumbed to their vices. Neither of them crumbled with the weight of their grief and loss. That was who I wanted the Shades to look to now that they had the chance to put their pasts behind them.

Not me, who was still haunted by her ghosts.

"I know what it is to be broken, but you know what it is to be mended." I grabbed both of their hands. "*That* is what the Shades need most and I can't think of two people more fit to provide it."

Nikolai stood and slapped his hands against my upper arms. "You speak as if you aren't mending right before our eyes, Keera dear."

I glanced at Gwyn, hoping she would find the same strength Nikolai and Dynara had given me. I took a deep breath and gave them the only truth I had. "I'm trying."

Dynara's wide lips broke into a rosy grin and she nodded approvingly. "You won't even recognize the Shades when you return."

They stood and Nikolai walked alongside Dynara, keeping a respectable distance as they mapped out their plans. They turned, glancing back at Gwyn. "Are you coming?" Dynara asked by both tongue and hand.

Gwyn stood and nodded, but she didn't cross the room. Instead she twisted her fingers and stared at the floor. After three tantalizingly long breaths, she darted around the table and wrapped her arms around me in a tight embrace.

I was still catching my breath when she let go and scurried out of the room. I stood there, smiling long after they had disappeared into the tunnel. A spark of hope flared through my chest as I realized Gwyn was trying too.

CHAPTER TWENTY-SEVEN

Riven was waiting for me in the grand hall. He held up a small vial of a yellow elixir as his shadows curled around my feet. Riven uncorked the vial and handed it to me. I took a quick swig and instantly felt my headache settle to a manageable pulse.

Riven raised a hand to my forehead. "The sweats seem to have stopped."

"I ate some birch berries from the kitchen." I corked the vial and tucked it into my belt. "Rheih taught me they helped with nausea too."

Riven's fingers laced through mine as we walked to one of the staircases. It was strange, holding his hand so openly, without fear of who would see. My transition to living in the Faeland had not been an easy one for either of us and then I had made things worse. This time it felt like we were just existing like anyone else in the city. My heart swelled with the unfamiliarity of it all. I had never been able to be so open in the short time I had with Brenna.

I tried not to think about how my time with Riven could end up being short too.

Riven noticed my slow pace as he stepped onto the curved stairs. "Are you having second thoughts? If you want to stay with the Shades—"

I shook my head. "They're in good hands."

Riven peered at the sunlight shining from above. "We should hurry then. Syrra has already left to prepare and we have two daylight portals to travel through if we want to make it to Vellinth by dusk."

"Vellinth?" I tilted my head. I had never heard of the place before.

Riven's violet gaze was full of mischief. "The secret city. And my first home."

We traveled in an easy silence for the rest of the morning through the Dark Wood along the northern ridge of the Burning Mountains. The golden leaves of the Elder birch cast auric rays on our backs as we rode through the trail. Large teal birds the size of dogs flew overhead, following us as we journeyed onward.

"Do they want food?" I called to Riven, pointing at the feathered beasts.

He chuckled and shook his head. "Those are *osthira*. Syrra calls them guardians of sorts. They do not sing, but if they open their beaks to speak it is loud enough to be heard for a hundred leagues or more."

I blinked up at the bright orange beak of the bird closest to me. He craned his head to the side and his rose-colored eyes blinked back at me. He followed us all the way to the portal, which was a small pond in the middle of the wood.

Riven tossed the *winvra* berries into the pool and the water rippled with golden rays of magic. The pool swirled as Riven dismounted his horse and led him through by the reins. He stepped into the water and sunk below the surface like he was walking down a set of stairs.

I hopped off my saddle and followed behind him. My horse did not flinch as we stepped into the water but remained completely dry. She tugged at the reins, quickening our pace as we stepped out of a small spring-fed pond.

The Burning Mountains were to the west of us now, their snow-capped peaks looked more like clouds along the horizon than rocky giants. To the east was the large lake that fed the Three Sisters of Silstra. I squinted through my lashes and could see the outline of an island through a thick, gray fog.

My chest tightened. One of the seals lay on that island. Riven stepped beside me, looking out at the Pool of Elvera too, and I knew we both were wondering if that would be the seal that pushed his magic over the edge.

He brushed his hand down my arm and pointed to the south. As far as my eyes could see, the field we stood in was covered in small flowers of every color. There was no breeze but Riven pulled a scarf around his face and passed me another. A single gust of wind could blow the flowers' pollen onto our skin and cause a festering rash that lasted for weeks.

We wouldn't meet any travelers walking through the field. Riven clipped a small bead to my horse's bit and then an identical one to his. "It will keep them safe until we reach the portal."

The first sun skimmed the eastern horizon by the time we reached a small grove of trees in the middle of the meadow. It was like an oasis in a desert, lush and thick with Elder birch. Two of them twisted together to form a long oval across one side. Within their trunks was a thin veil of mist. Riven placed two *winvra* berries in the crux of a branch and the mist turned gold.

He paused with one foot in the veil and turned back to me. "Just in case you didn't learn from last time. No noise and no lights."

I gritted my teeth but didn't say anything as I followed Riven through the portal. We were in the Singing Wood. There was just enough light filtering through the thick canopy of vines and swirling trees to see the path that cut through the forest. My mare's ear flicked, listening for the creatures that called this place their home.

I rolled my shoulder defensively remembering how it felt to be sliced through by the claw of an Unnamed One. Riven marched on without a worry. Somehow his steps felt lighter here in the dark than anywhere else. Perhaps his magic called out to the shadows and they welcomed him too. In the darkness, the twisted trunks of the Singing Wood seemed to shift and sway.

A light breeze blew through them and the haunting song of a Fae echoed down the wood. I reached out, the voice had taken hold of my body and all I could think of was finding whoever was singing that melody. A shadow curled around my arm and stopped me.

I opened my mouth to protest, and Riven covered it with his hand. His touch broke the spell on my body and my mind cleared just enough to realize how close Riven's mouth was to mine. He drew his thumb over my bottom lip, slow and tantalizing, before he trusted me enough to drop his hold altogether.

I leaned into the absence of his touch as he started down the path again. My body turned cold enough that my teeth chattered and my brow began to sweat. Riven glanced at me over his shoulder and pulled out another small vial of pale green liquid. He dropped two doses on my tongue and then said something in slow stilted movements with his hand.

I shook my head. I hadn't learned any of the signed language the Elverin used. Riven's jaw pulsed and he nodded down the path once more. I shrugged and followed him.

A few minutes later the path opened up to a large valley in the middle of the wood. The thick canopy hung across the wide expanse, shielding the city from the bright rays of the suns. The clearing was lined by large trees that were just as tall and thick as the ones in Myrelinth, though these came in every color of sunset. Small silver balls of faelight floated through the thick canopy of treetops, casting the entire city in eternal dusk.

Like Myrelinth, the trees were home to many dwellings, but they were not large burls emerging from the trunks themselves. Instead, the twisted branches braided together along the middle and tops of the trees to form homes of every size.

They were beautiful but empty.

As we walked through the city, we passed pool after pool of water along the ground. They shimmered under the balls of moonlight, each one a slightly different shade of blue. They reflected our faces as our horses walked along the curving path to the heart of the city.

A large orb of water hung above us, suspended by a thin net of vines that seemed too weak to hold this lake in the sky. It shimmered with silver light, swirling inside of itself like one of my braided gusts.

It was larger than both the suns combined and reminded me of the grand chandelier Lord Curringham had installed in the House of Harvest. I stared up at it and realized that it was placed directly in the center of the circular city so that it could be seen from any spot. Just like the Myram was the heart of Myrelinth and Sil'abar was the heart of Aralinth, the orb was the heart of Vellinth.

I turned to Riven and pointed to my mouth, unsure if I could speak. He nodded and I glanced around the city once before asking my question. "Does it have a name?"

His smile was proud as he nodded. "*Miikibi'thir miichi'vra.*"

"*Water hands?*" My nose wrinkled as I tried it for myself.

Riven leaned his head to one side. "In a rough sense, though Vrail would give you a better translation."

"And a four-hour lecture on the history of this place." I peered up at the orb again.

Riven huffed a laugh. "This is likely the *one* subject I know more of than Vrail. Vellinth was my home for a long time."

I turned on my heel. "I thought Feron raised you in Aralinth?"

Riven's brow knotted together and he shook his head. "My existence was kept a secret from everyone." The muscles in his neck flexed and he kicked a stray pebble into one of the pools. "The story goes that it would have interfered with what my mother was trying to accomplish in the kingdom. She didn't want to give Aemon any reason to reject her proposal. She was the only Fae left that could give him an heir and she knew she couldn't do anything to compromise that chance." Riven's lip curled into a thin line of disgust.

I grabbed his hand. "She left you here?"

"I wouldn't say that." Riven cleared his throat. "Feron took me in and stayed here with me and Darythir." Riven pointed to a tall tree that housed three dwellings along its trunk.

My chest cracked at the thought of Riven being hidden for his entire boyhood. I knew the scars that could leave on a person. "That must've been lonely."

Riven gave me a stiff nod. "As my magic grew, it became obvious to Feron that it was dangerous. He didn't let me into the other cities until he *knew* I could control it."

I squeezed his hand. "How long did it take you?"

"Thirty years." Riven sighed up at the orb.

My jaw fell open.

He jabbed my side with his elbow. "It wasn't all bad. Nikolai and Syrra came to visit me here as much as they could. Syrra's training saved my life. I don't think I would have learned how to cast a net over my powers without her help."

I leaned against his shoulder. "Nikolai told me Syrra only trains people she cares greatly for."

"In your case perhaps." Riven pressed a kiss to my hair. "But Syrra and I did not care for each other in the beginning. She only trained me out of fear that I would hurt someone she cared about."

Syrra appeared beside Riven. "And in time, you became one of them."

We both stepped back in surprise, neither of us having heard a sound.

"How do you do that?" I gasped.

Syrra grinned and pointed to the thick branch that trailed from her right shoulder down to her elbow. "I earned this marking by protecting the young child of a Light Fae who was in my care at *Niikir'na*. She imbued the carving with a spell." Syrra crossed her arms and shrugged. "It muffles the sound of my feet."

I turned to Riven. "Is that true?"

He only shrugged.

"I would think you would rather believe my tale. Otherwise you would have to admit that my natural talents as a spy are better than yours." Syrra's smile was the picture of innocence, but I recognized the competitive flame in her eyes.

I crossed my arms to match hers. "Do you have any more secret talents I should know about?"

"Yes," Syrra said with a nod. She didn't add anything more.

Riven laced his hand through mine before I could pull the truth from Syrra by force. "Is everything ready?"

Syrra nodded and pointed to a small tree at the edge of the city. "We can conduct the ritual in there." She turned to me. "If you make it through all five rounds, we should be done by the third daybreak."

I swallowed. "*If?*"

Syrra's face was as serious as I had ever seen it. "This will not be easy, child. The elixirs will burn through your cravings in a series of five rounds. Each will be longer and more painful than the one before it."

I swallowed. "And that will cure me?"

Syrra chuckled softly under her breath. "No. There is no cure for a vice like ours, but it will clear your physical body of every trace of wine and let you focus on healing your mind and spirit."

"You did this?" I asked. "When Feron helped you with the *winvra*?"

Syrra nodded.

I took a deep breath. "How bad is it?" I trusted her to give me an honest answer.

She bit her cheek. "It is the hardest thing I have ever done."

My stomach plummeted to the ground. I'd been hoping for a better answer than that.

Riven's shadows curled around my legs and he squeezed my hand. "This is your decision, *diizra*. Syrra and I will not judge you if you decide to return to Myrelinth."

I looked up at the softness in Riven's violet gaze and knew that he wouldn't think any less of me. But that wasn't true for myself. I knew my odds of surviving the war were slim. Damien liked to toy with me, but eventually the toying would end and he would want my head. I'd be damned if I died with wine in my veins because Damien had set a curse upon me.

If I lived, I wanted to live in peace. And if I died, I wanted to die sober and protecting my kin.

I had gotten through it before knowing that's what the Shades needed from me and with the support of Hildegard. I squeezed Riven's hand and nodded at Syrra. I had more support than I ever had before, and while I was terrified at what the next three days held, that truth gave me comfort.

"Let's begin."

CHAPTER TWENTY-EIGHT

My blood was made of liquid flame. Every pulse stoked the fire until I could see my flesh bubbling but somehow not burning. I screamed into the darkness, wishing for the pain to stop. I didn't care if the only way to end it was death, I would gladly take that final reprieve to end my suffering.

My throat ached as I shrieked but then the darkness swirled and took shape around me. Syrra had warned me that this final round would be the hardest. I wouldn't only face physical pain under the last elixir, but every kind of pain my mind could muster. The part of myself that didn't want to give up the wine would fight me with everything it had and if it succeeded in tempting me, I would have to start the entire process again.

I didn't have the strength for that. Or the time. The Shades were waiting for me.

I gritted my teeth and prepared myself for whatever was about to come. My vision blurred but I could see the shadowy figures that had haunted me for decades. The children I was forced to bring to the Order and then couldn't keep alive. The families that I had been ordered to destroy and did to keep my title. Every one of my names dripped from my skin and transformed into a shadowy silhouette to witness what I deserved.

A goblet dropped in front of me. The lush scent of wine filled my nostrils and with it came a momentary lapse of pain. My body thrashed along the ground, inching closer to it without control. I kept my hands back, waiting for the vision to fade.

It's not real.

It's not real.

It's not real.

I chanted it over and over again to myself, but it was hard to believe when the pain was undeniable. My mind, my body, every part of myself wanted to give in to the craving, but that wine was just part of the illusion. If I couldn't say no to that, I would never say no when true hardships fell on me again.

I clenched my jaw, shutting my eyes so I didn't have to see the burgundy liquid swirling in the large cup.

"But this is real," a voice I'd almost forgotten whispered beside me.

Tears welled in my eyes before I even opened them.

Brenna stood in front of me. Her blond waves framed her face and shoulders as she kneeled. She wasn't wearing the black garb of an initiate or the bloodstained clothes Damien had been making me see for weeks. She wore a long Elvish robe, in a petal blue that brought out the honey color of her eyes. It was what I would have wanted for her, if we ever had reached the Faeland together.

She cupped my cheek and wiped the tears away. I whimpered at her touch. It was too real. Not cold like a memory or burning like my flesh, but the soft lukewarm temperature her skin had always had. I closed my eyes and I could smell the brine and salt wafting from her hair.

When I opened them again she was smiling. The scars down her eyes tugged along her dimples in the same way they had whenever she laughed. My stomach clenched, remembering how many afternoons I had passed with that being my only goal. To do something, say something, that would pull that fiery song from her chest.

Brenna picked up the goblet and held it between her palms. I thought she was going to carry it away but instead she held the brim to my lips.

"Drink."

I pulled back from her but she only leaned forward with the cup.

"Drink."

I shook my head and my heart raced against my chest. "No. I can't. I *won't.*"

Brenna's face darkened. She stood with the goblet in her hand, staring down at me like I was a worm struggling through the dirt. "I thought you'd do anything for me."

"I would—" I stammered.

Her voice broke. "I thought you cared about me."

"I do!"

Her lip trembled. "I thought you loved me."

My heart broke as I thrashed against the ground. Seeing the hurt in Brenna's face was worse than any of the pain pulsing through my body. "I did," I whispered. "I did."

Brenna's shaking breaths stilled and her face fell into a cold mask of disdain. "And there it is. *Loved.*" She stepped back from me so I couldn't reach out and touch her. "That's all I am to you now? I get to be a scar on your arm while you move on with *him.*" Her thin top lip curled over her teeth as she said the word.

Somehow I had gathered the strength to pull myself to my knees. "You're dead!"

"Because you *killed* me." Brenna pounced and grabbed me by the throat.

My body went limp with guilt. The cut of her robe showed a deep wound along her chest where my blade had ended her life.

I hung my head in defeat as the shadowy figures surrounding us started to move and whisper. Soon their whispers grew into chants.

Drink, drink, drink.

I shook my head. Tears splattered the dark ground. Brenna's finger looped under my chin as she forced me to meet her gaze. "Keera the disappointment," she whispered as a shadowy figure of Hildegard stood beside her.

I choked on a sob. "I'm sorry."

Brenna shook her head and held the goblet of wine to my lips. "Keera the promise breaker."

I bit them to keep from drinking it even though I agreed with the disgust and rage on Brenna's face.

She lifted the cup, wetting my lips but I didn't open them.

And then she said the words that had haunted me most of all.

"Keera the killer." The shadowy figures of Collin's family appeared beside her. Then the Shades I'd killed in Silstra. Hundreds of them flashed before me as Brenna cruelly smiled down at the crumpled pile I'd become, rejoicing in their new chant.

Killer.

Killer.

Killer.

I covered my ears, trying to drown them out. I rocked back and forth on my knees but nothing could block out that sound. My teeth chattered together in pain, pushing me beyond any limit I had ever tested. Then like the string on a bow pulled too taut, too many times, I snapped.

"Enough!" I pulled myself onto unsteady feet. "I will not drink."

Brenna's hand slipped from the goblet, it crashed at her feet and stained the skirt of her dress, but she smiled. She stepped toward me and I flinched at her touch, but the moment her hand pressed against my cheek the pain in my body vanished.

The shadowy figures were no longer made of darkness, but fully realized memories of the ones I couldn't save. All of them were smiling at me with looks of relief.

I huffed a laugh, realizing that everything that had happened my mind had done to itself. It had tried so hard to keep a grip on my craving, to keep a grip on *me*, that it had created a lie to keep me in its hold.

But now I was free.

Brenna wiped the stream of tears along my face with her sleeve. She pressed the softest kiss between my brows and leaned her head against mine. "Don't feel guilt for something I did, Keera." She grabbed my arm and traced the letters of her own name along my skin, sending shivers through my body. "Let go and be happy."

She leaned in and pressed her lips to mine. They were softer than a pillow after a month's ride. I leaned into the kiss, savoring that sweetness that I had never tasted anywhere else. Brenna was branded on my tongue just like she was in my memory.

I opened my eyes and she was gone.

I woke to the smell of fire smoke and cedar. Syrra darted from the far side of the room as I opened my eyes and rubbed my temple. She placed a cool cloth on my brow and I realized how damp my clothes had become.

"Did you succeed?" From the edge in her voice, I knew that Syrra had an inkling of what I had faced.

I rubbed at my dry throat and Syrra handed me a cup of water. It tasted cool and fresh on my tongue and didn't spark a craving in my chest. I turned to her. "You had to face something like that?"

Syrra slumped beside me on the cot, breaking from her perfect posture for the first time. "I did not complete the ritual until my third attempt." She swallowed, eyes misted as she relived some memory of it. "It takes much strength to succeed."

I shook my head and grabbed her hand. "I could never have faced that again. You need to give yourself more credit."

Syrra's lip twitched to the side before her head snapped to me. "You *did* refuse then."

"How did you know I would be tempted?" I tucked my legs into my chest.

"The mind and body are a powerful pair." Syrra patted my knee. "They can accomplish the most vile things if threatened."

I shivered. I never wanted to think of the way Brenna had stood over me again.

Syrra filled my cup with water once more. "I am proud that you trusted me to get you through this safely and that you had the strength to do so."

I wrapped my arms around Syrra and we held our embrace longer than ever before. "I will need your support to make it through this war."

Syrra chuckled. "And I yours. Your resolve will strengthen, but even after six hundred years, I still have days that tempt me."

I grabbed her hand. "Then we shall be strong together."

"*Apavra'kir.*" Syrra nodded.

Always.

I glanced around the room. "Where's Riven?"

Syrra stood from the bed and walked over to a small pool of water nested in one of the branches. "I told him to leave. His power was growing too dangerous while watching you struggle."

I swallowed guiltily. "How long did that round take?"

"Eight hours."

I blinked. The other rounds had just been pain that seemed to never end, yet every time I woke, Syrra said the session had only last an hour or two. My body was exhausted but there was a clarity in my mind that I couldn't remember feeling before. I leaned back knowing the poison of my vices had been fully leeched, at least from my body.

Syrra swirled the water with her finger three times sunwise. The liquid rippled before glowing with a soft emerald light. Something shifted out the window and I saw that the large orb of water hanging from the city center was glowing with the same soft light.

Syrra peered over the pool in our room but her face also appeared in the orb above. She made three quick gestures with her hands, projecting them across the entire city for Riven to see, no matter which part he had ended up in.

I stared, wide-eyed, as Syrra swirled the water in the opposite direction and the glow faded away. Riven's shadow curled around my feet a few moments later, soon followed by the Fae himself.

He whipped open the door and his entire torso sagged with relief when he saw me standing. "You're well," he whispered as he wrapped his arms around me.

I nodded against his chest. "Are *you*?" I glanced at the way his shadows shook and the sweat along his brow.

Riven's jaw stiffened but he nodded.

"Very clever magic." I tilted my head in the direction of the orb.

Riven smiled proudly at the watery sphere. "Vellinth was the stronghold of the *niibivra'thir niimi'vra*."

"Singing fingers?" I echoed, unsure of my translation.

Syrra nodded. "There were a few bloodlines of Elverin who were born without the ability to hear as we do. Most of them were unable to speak by tongue so they created a language by hand." Syrra moved her hands in the same gestures as before, but more slowly. I could see that there was an intricate way she held both hands for each sign and the way she positioned them in front of her seemed to change the meaning.

Riven understood her hands as easily as he could read words on a page or hear me speak.

"They used the orb to communicate," I whispered in awe. The Elverin kept on surprising me in all the ways that they had used their magic to help their people. And that was only the magic that still survived. My skin tingled in anticipation at what might be done if we successfully unlocked those seals.

But then my gaze settled on the empty households. Hundreds and hundreds of them sat vacant in the ghost of a city. "Everyone who lived here was deaf."

Syrra shook her head. "Not all, but most. Some of their children were born able to hear but longed for nothing but the comforts of home."

I paused, not sure I wanted the answer to this question. "What happened to them?"

A shadow swirled along Riven's brow. "The *miikibi* is not only connected to the pools of Vellinth, but all the water in Elverath. And the pool beneath it"—Riven pointed to the large teal pond rippling along the ground—"is connected to every portal. It is one of a kind, but it also meant that when the Blood Purges began the Elverin of Vellinth were the first to receive the call. And they always answered."

Syrra crossed her open palm over her eyes and then her chest. "They suffered the most losses of anyone. Entire bloodlines gone in a matter of days. The only survivor was their Elder who was too old to fight."

My stomach twisted into knots. "Darythir."

Syrra nodded glumly. "She is not the most pleasing of our kind, but she has lost more than any other."

"But why leave it empty?"

Syrra shrugged. "At first I suppose it was too painful for anyone to return. Then by the time anyone considered it, they already had built their nests somewhere else in the *Faelinth*."

I sighed and looked down at the large pool with new reverence for the memories that still echoed here. "Do you think it's possible to reclaim everything they took from us?"

Syrra stilled. "No. Some stories and names are lost to us forever." I hung my head against my shoulder and Syrra grabbed my hand. "But a new forest can always grow where an old one burned. And the ground remembers the roots even if the trees do not."

I furrowed my brow at her riddle-like answer. "I think you've been spending too much time with Maerhal."

Syrra threw back her head in a hearty laugh.

Riven wrapped his arm around my shoulder. "Would you like to rest here tonight and journey back on the morrow?"

I shook my head. "We've been gone long enough. I want to see the Shades."

CHAPTER TWENTY-NINE

We made it back to the Faeland by daybreak. My bones still chattered from the hours we had to spend waiting in the snowy hills of Volcar for the suns to rise and the portal to redirect to the Dark Wood. From there it was a short ride to Myrelinth that we spent in silence.

Riven rode behind me, his shadows stroking my back endlessly to keep me steady on my horse while the fatigue crept over my body. When we reached the stables, he was there to help me dismount, pressing a kiss to my forehead.

"Do you want to try to sleep?" He pulled out a vial of the clear liquid that would keep the dreams at bay.

I shook my head. "Not until I see the Shades. I don't want them to think I abandoned them."

Riven tugged the end of my braid and nodded. He bent down and pressed a hand to one of the roots along the stable doors and his brow flickered. "They're in the hall," he whispered with an uncertain air to his voice.

"The Shades?"

He nodded. "And a few others. But it feels . . . chaotic."

That was all I needed to know. I bolted down the nearest twisting steps of the Myram and pulled out my dagger, ready for whatever was waiting for us below. I skittered to a stop when I saw that the main hall had been transformed into a giant dressing room. Tall looking glasses were scattered about with small podiums in front of each one. In between them were roots that had been pulled up from the earth and used as long poles to hang clothes of every size and color.

A group of young initiates raced passed me and started pulling at long dresses made of rich silks. They giggled as they stuck their heads through the hangers and twirled in circles without even putting the dresses on.

Nikolai waved at me with a pin sticking from his mouth. His short curls were pulled back into a clip to keep them from falling in front of his face as he marked the hem of Fyrel's new robe. It was a vibrant green shade with yellow stitching along the hem and sleeves. She beamed at me in the mirror, her hands grazing over the soft length of her new clothes. Nikolai had pinned the hem to just above her ankles so her new boots were visible. "I've never worn a color before."

My heart burst as I saw the same joy on the faces of the other Shades.

Nikolai stood, tucking the pin in his mouth into the pad tied along his wrist. "This shade of green is not worn well by many." He tapped Fyrel's nose and winked. "That is something you and I have in common."

She turned to me. "What color should I try next?"

I blinked and turned to Riven. He was dressed in his usual black garb and my own clothes were dark enough to be mistaken for it. "I would trust Nikolai's judgment with that."

Nikolai gave me a sideways smirk and squeezed my hand before disappearing behind the mirror to fetch something from the racks of clothes.

"Are you adjusting well?" I asked Fyrel, trying to keep my tone light. "Is there anything you or the others need?"

Fyrel continued to stare at herself in the mirror. Her hair fell around her shoulders as she swayed. "Everyone has been very kind. Yesterday, Lash and Gerarda taught us how to use the vines and climb the Myram by faelight." She turned to me. "We were *flying*."

I laughed and fixed the back pleat of her robe. "Did you choose a room in the lower city or the groves?"

Fyrel rolled her eyes. "Who would refuse a chance to sleep amongst the stars?" She glimpsed Riven in the mirror and stilled. "Gerarda told me that you're the Shadow."

Riven's jaw fell slack to the side. "I'm sure that's not all she said."

Fyrel shook her head. "She also said that you did it to rescue Halflings and bring them here. Just like you did with us."

Riven's face fell into a soft smile and he nodded. "And I won't stop until they are all free."

Fyrel straightened at those words. "I will help." She peered up at him and the swirling cloud of shadows behind him. "And you should know I don't find you that gloomy at all."

Riven's smile fell to a flat line as I burst out laughing.

His shadows twisted around the end of my braid and gave it a playful tug just as Nikolai appeared with a bright clementine dress. Fyrel's eyes went wide as she beheld the silks. "Now this is a dress fit for a young warrior." He hung it behind a red curtain and nodded for Fyrel to change. "Be mindful of those pins."

She scurried inside without protest. Nikolai wrapped his arms around me and lifted me off the ground in a big spin. I would have laughed but his squeeze was too strong. "Are you well?" he whispered as he put me down.

"Well enough." I gestured to the entire hall. "Where did all these clothes come from?"

Nikolai rocked back on his feet. "Donations. Feron had a lot of older robes stored in Aralinth from Elverin who have passed. He thought this was the perfect occasion to bring them out of hiding." Nikolai grazed a wistful hand along a hanging silk.

I laughed. "You're enjoying this."

"Too much," Riven quipped.

Nikolai ignored him. "Hard not to when everyone is having a great time. All the Shades have filled their closets and then some." His face dropped for a single moment.

I raised a brow. "Except . . ."

Nikolai pointed across the hall with his chin. On the farthest platform stood Gerarda, who had a miserable look on her face as Elaran held up what seemed to be another rejected shirt. I turned to the pile of pinned clothes that were strewn across a stool next to Nikolai.

"Who is hemming these?"

Nikolai took a deep breath. "Feron. He has a group of Elverin in his chambers."

I turned to Riven. "Can you bring these to him? I'm going to try to . . ." I trailed off and just pointed in Gerarda's general direction.

Riven looked relieved to have a reason to leave the hall and all its color. He gave us both a quick nod and carried the garments across both arms.

I slowly approached Gerarda. Dynara came by with a handful of dresses and long robes but Gerarda instantly refused. "No dresses. And I prefer trousers to robes."

Elaran shot Dynara an apologetic look. Dynara sighed but smiled when she noticed me. "I didn't think the Dagger would be more stubborn than the Blade, but I've been proven wrong."

I chuckled under my breath. "We've been butting heads for almost sixty years."

"I heard that," Gerarda called from her podium.

I smirked. "You can still wear black if that's the problem."

Gerarda's shoulders sagged. "It's not the palette, though Nikolai seems to favor colors that burn my eyes."

Elaran shook her head and sat down on the stool. "Perhaps you can help where I cannot."

I glanced at the two piles of clothes next to the mirror. One was mountainous and made of every kind of garment while the other was a tiny pile of trousers and the occasional tunic. "I'm guessing these are rejections." I pointed to the larger of the two.

Gerarda nodded. A faint line had appeared between her brows and her eyes were flicking from point to point over the mirror in a rhythmic pattern. My chest swelled for Gerarda as I recognized the same caution in her gaze as mine every time I tried on new clothes. Just like I had to check again and again for someone not to see my scars, she was checking for something too.

But that problem could only be solved if she told me. I knelt to the small pile of clothes she had accepted and began folding them neatly. Gerarda watched as I folded the pants but didn't say anything. They were all long and contained a multitude of pockets where Gerarda could store her blades. The leather guards she had found had slits along the arms for her throwing knives and were a warm red as opposed to the black ones she currently wore. The shirts were all loose, some with long sleeves and others short.

I noticed none of them had a low neckline. "Have you tried the shirt with the stiff collar?" I pointed to one hanging from the mirror beside us. It was made of wool and had a rounded collar that closed directly over the neck.

Gerarda's cheeks flushed. "They're too tight."

I blinked. Gerarda had always been small and lithe. Nikolai had gathered clothing in every size, certainly enough to fit Gerarda properly. She looked down at her boots and I realized the problem was the fit. Her weeks in the Faeland had changed her frame. Living a life without rations had brought a fullness to her cheeks that made her look more youthful than she ever had before, but that fullness had also found its way to her chest.

"I'll be right back." I rummaged through the racks, looking for something that wasn't tulle or silk when Dynara found me.

She tapped my shoulder. "What are you looking for? I've been through these racks a dozen times by now."

I sighed. "Do you have anything that looks like Riven's leathers? A vest that ties at the sides instead of down the middle."

"I did see one . . ." She walked over to another rack full of leather training clothes and started pulling them over the thick root. "Here!"

She handed me a dark leather vest with sharp shoulder caps that were made of five layered pieces cut to the shape of leaves. A design of interwoven vines was pressed into the leather in a similar pattern to the one Riven wore. It was cut in the same fashion as the armor the *innithira*—Elfmen—wore.

"I think that might work." I kissed Dynara on the cheek and grabbed a matching tunic.

I brought the pieces to Gerarda and sighed with relief when she agreed to try them on. Elaran watched her walk behind the curtain with wide eyes and she mouthed *thank you* to me as Gerarda changed.

Gerarda stepped out of the dressing room with a satisfied look on her face. She stood up on the podium just as Syrra appeared silently at my side.

"I like this much better." Gerarda was too shy to meet my gaze. "Thank you."

I smiled.

But Syrra stepped behind the Halfling and lifted her hands to Gerarda's short hair. "May I?" she asked in Elvish.

Gerarda nodded.

Syrra combed her fingers through the thick black tresses and pulled the top half of Gerarda's short mane into a braid. It was the same style Riven and Feron often wore. And now I realized that Syrra always wore too.

"Do you like that better?" Syrra stared down at Gerarda through the mirror.

Gerarda lifted her hand to her hair. "I'm not sure if it's appropriate—"

Syrra placed gentle hands on her shoulders. "That is not the question that was asked. Do you like it, child?"

Gerarda nodded.

"Then you shall wear it and wear it proudly." Syrra pulled the front piece of the vest along the bottom so it fell in line with Gerarda's shoulders. "We can fashion you a few more of these. Tell Nikolai what designs you would like and he will see that it gets done."

Gerarda turned around to face Syrra directly. "There's no need. I don't want to be a burden."

Syrra shook her head with one hand on Gerarda's shoulder. "This is your *home*. You must be comfortable here. The world has not been kind to Elverin like you and me."

Gerarda blinked. "Like us?"

Syrra's face softened. "Aemon built a world with only two paths and decided who should walk along each one. Those that strayed were forced to hide or died along the way." Syrra sighed deeply. "But here, Elverin may walk along both paths as they like, or forge new ones altogether. That is not something to be ashamed of. Choose whatever path speaks to you and walk along it with whoever you wish."

Gerarda's brows trembled. "Thank you, Syrra." She hung her head in a deep bow and stepped off the platform.

Syrra returned the gesture and went off in search of Nikolai.

Elaran slipped her arm around Gerarda's neck. "You look delicious," she whispered in her ear. Gerarda nudged her hip with her elbow, but the smile tugging along her lips was pleased.

I grabbed the pile of discarded clothes and left, pretending I hadn't heard them.

Nikolai's room was chaos. Fine silks and luxurious robes were scattered on every piece of furniture and sticking out of the four large closets on the farthest wall. Any space that wasn't covered in clothing was littered with random tools or discarded ideas etched onto sheets of parchment.

"Keera dear." Nikolai popped out from one of the enormous piles of clothes. He waved his hand over everything. "You should know it's *never* like this."

I picked up a burnt orange robe from the floor and held the lace collar to the light. "Of course not, you'd never let something this nice be this wrinkled."

Nikolai let out a low breath. "You understand me perfectly."

I laughed and tossed him the robe. He carefully put it on a pile of equally wrinkled clothes and nodded down the tunnel. "Vrail's study is free and much less cluttered."

I raised a brow but didn't say anything. Nikolai led me down the hall to a small room by the library that was littered in books and scrolls.

"I said *less* cluttered," Nikolai quipped, reading my thoughts.

I shrugged. "At least this has chairs you can sit in." I picked up three scrolls from the seat and set them on the ground. Nikolai stopped me, placing one of his larger handkerchiefs underneath them before he let me set them on the ground.

"You look dreadful." Nikolai slumped back into the chaise across from me.

I huffed a laugh. "You can be so charming."

"You should be sleeping. It's already midday." Nikolai looked up as if he could see the suns through the layers of earth between us and the open air.

"I'll be plenty rested before the ceremony." I grabbed something from my bag and Nikolai's eyes went wide.

He reached for his notebook. "I thought I'd lost that under the piles of clothes."

"That's my fault." I nodded at the leather-bound book. "I needed something to keep me occupied when the Shades and I were sailing back and I found that you left it aboard."

Nikolai flipped through the pages, checking on his designs like a parent checking on a child. "I was focused on more important things." He opened the later pages and noticed where I had sketched my own design. "What are these?"

"I thought you could make them. For Maerhal." I swallowed, suddenly embarrassed that my idea wouldn't work. "She always has trouble with the faelights when I go to visit and she won't go outside until after sunset. I thought these would make it easier on her eyes."

Nikolai bit his lip and studied the different versions of the design I'd scribbled on the pages. "It's like a mask, but made of glass."

I nodded. "I know that the Elverin can imbue their glass with different dyes and properties." I pulled a vial from my bag. It was filled with tiny yellow blooms still attached at their stems. "Rheih taught me that shade petals darken under sunlight. I thought you could make something that could keep Maerhal's sight dark enough that she doesn't get any more headaches."

Nikolai took the vial like it was the most precious item he owned. His eyes were lined with tears, but they didn't fall.

"I was just visiting your mother and Rheih. Maerhal said she wasn't going to come to the ceremony until after the suns had set." I tucked my hands under my thighs, unsure where to put them. "But she's already spent so much of her life underground. I don't want her to miss out on one more thing."

Nikolai's chin trembled and a tear ran down his face. "I can make a model this afternoon." He stood and wrapped me into a tight embrace. "Thank you, Keera." He squeezed even tighter. "Thank you for still fighting to bring my mother out of the darkness."

My throat tightened and my own cheeks were wet. "And thank you for doing everything to make sure I didn't lose myself there."

Nikolai pulled out a handkerchief for each of us. "I will get this started, but you need to go to sleep, Keera dear." He walked me as far as his room and then went inside to begin tinkering with the initial prototype.

I walked down the tunnel with a small faelight hovering over my shoulder to light the way. I thought I was alone until I saw a quick flash of light down the far end of the tunnel. I slowed, grabbing the hilt of my blade as I walked that way.

The large stone door was opened as I peered into the room. Killian was standing at the hearth, leaning onto the mantel with his chest rising heavily. I knew he had been scurrying along every inch of the city to prepare for the feast and the Shades' arrival, but I hadn't seen him since I'd returned. It was as if he was purposely making himself scarce.

"Killian?"

He jumped up. "Keera," he rasped when he realized it was me. "Maerhal had said you'd gone to bed."

"Not yet." I smirked and leaned against the doorway. "Is everything fine?"

Killian straightened. "Yes. Why wouldn't it be."

I eyed the broken lantern in the fireplace.

"That was an accident." Killian's finger picked at the skin around his thumbnail. "Please, sit." He pointed to the chair next to the cabinet that he didn't know I had ransacked only a few short weeks before.

"Tell me why the Shades haven't seen you once since they arrived?" I raised a brow playfully. "They're calling me a liar for saying I know the good prince."

Killian's jaw flexed. He awkwardly paced along the edge of his bed before leaning against the mattress. "I didn't think my presence would be a welcome one."

My heart fell. I had known the real Killian for so long that I'd forgotten it wasn't who he was allowed to be outside the Faeland. To me, he was just as much a part of the Faeland as any other Elverin, but to the Shades, he was still Damien's brother. Aemon's son.

To them he still wore the mask of the enemy.

I leaned forward. "I'm sorry, I should have realized earlier." I reached my hand for his, but Killian didn't take it. "I will introduce you to them tonight. You will be at the ceremony, will you not?"

Killian gave me an unconvincing nod. His jade eyes lingered on my outstretched hand as it fell to my lap. He looked at it like he didn't know if my touch would hurt him. My cheeks flooded with embarrassment, realizing I was the reason he didn't trust himself alone with me.

"Killian, I am so sorry for what happened in the kitchens." My shoulders fell, but I made sure to meet his gaze.

He blinked, eyes widening as the words settled between us. "Keera, you do not need—"

"Yes, I do." I shook my head. "I was acting selfishly. I wanted to hurt you and I wanted to hurt Riven through you. It was unfair and I am deeply sorry for putting you in such a position."

Killian gritted his teeth. "You have nothing to apologize for."

I opened my mouth to argue but Killian stood.

"Keera, if there is anyone who has regrets for what happened it is me. In that moment, I was focused more on my wants than your well-being." He walked toward the door and didn't turn around. "I am sorry in more ways than you know."

CHAPTER THIRTY

I MANAGED A FEW HOURS of sleep before the groves filled with laughter and music. Riven chuckled as I blinked against his chest. I had been alone when I got to my burl. "I'm so irresistible you can't help but watch me sleep?"

He pressed a kiss to my palm. "I wanted to be here in case the nightmares came." He didn't phrase it like a question, but I knew it was.

I wrapped my leg higher along his chest. "I didn't dream at all."

He pulled me on top of him and cradled my face in his hands. "Are you sure about that?" He pressed his lips against my neck and pulled at the string of my nightgown with his shadows. "I'm certain I heard you moan my name in your sleep."

I smirked. "I think you're confusing my dream for your fantasy."

"Is that a challenge?" Riven trailed a sharp finger down my spine until my skin prickled with anticipation.

"How long do we have?" I peered out the window to see the suns but Riven blanketed my entire burl in shadow.

"They won't start without you." His hand caressed my thigh, moving closer to the dangerously short hem with each stroke.

I pressed my hips into his and grinned at the groan that issued from his chest. I swayed my hips once more and lifted Riven's hands above his head so he had no choice but to relive that night in his burl. Then I nipped his ear until I knew he would give me anything I wanted.

"We can't leave them waiting." I smirked and hopped off him.

Riven's eyes turned feral. "It will be quicker if we shower together."

I threw him a disbelieving look. "We both know that isn't true. You wouldn't stop until we had run through all the water in the grove."

Riven's voice was suddenly low. "The city."

I pulled off my nightgown and tossed it onto Riven's face before he could follow me. I heard him clamber out of bed and I made a point of locking the door.

Riven didn't try to open it, but his voice was thick with wanting as he spoke through the bark. "I'm glad you're rested because you will be up *late*." His shadow slipped under the door and poked my side before he left.

I wore one of the long silk gowns Riven had ordered for me. Its sleeves were light and airy, but covered my scars in layers of translucent fabric that extended past my wrists. Dynara helped settle my hair into gentle waves that rolled down my back. She threaded tiny faebeads of sunlight into the strands that matched the thin faebead necklace trailing down the slit between my breasts.

She flitted her hands under my skirt, letting each layer settle on top of the other. The entire dress was constructed of silk leaves that mimicked the look of an Elder birch. Most of them were a deep red, but the ones that connected along my waist were a bright gold.

It was like wearing art.

Dynara's thick tresses were braided in thin loops behind her head with strings of pearls hanging from each of them. Her gown was made from structured silks to form a crashing wave that fanned over one shoulder and transformed into a sea-foam spray along the skirt. The high slit at her hip showed that she wore no shoes but ribbons of glowing blue that churned against her skin all the way up to her thigh.

I blinked, realizing that they were water. "Magic?"

Dynara smirked. "I had to trade Nikolai my best broach for them." I watched as the water lapped against her skin, always in a beautiful pattern that reminded me of the long lines of Elvish embroidery. "I wanted my last night here to be one to remember."

I gripped her hand. I had already spent the better part of an hour trying to convince Dynara not to go, but she wouldn't budge. She had laid the groundwork to free the courtesans once and for all and she wasn't going to abandon it now. No matter how dangerous.

"Do not fret over me. Nikolai designed exactly what I need and the plan won't fail." Dynara squeezed back. "Enjoy tonight, Keera."

She pulled me out of the burl by my hand and walked us down one of the swirling branches of the Myram. Riven and Nikolai waited for us at the bottom. Nik smiled happily up at both of us, but Riven's violet eyes were wide as they drifted over every inch of my body. His jaw went slack but then his eyes narrowed as he pulled me into his arms.

"I see you aren't done with the teasing," he whispered hotly.

I gave him a coy look. "I have no idea what you mean."

Riven's eyes flashed as his hand found my neck, his thumb caressing my jaw. "You look absolutely stunning, *diizra*."

"You're welcome," Dynara chimed before slipping her arm through Nikolai's.

He lurched in surprise but then a kind smile settled across his lips. He pointed at the rows and rows of tables that lined the grove. "Shall we?" His arm extended into the direction of his mother who was chatting excitedly with Syrra and Rheih with her new spectacles over her nose.

Uldrath waved excitedly across the meadow with his father behind him. I caught Pirmiith's gaze and lifted my hand. The Elf's warm smile faltered as the Halfling woman beside him sneered in my direction. She scooped up the young boy and I saw the resemblance between them. I glanced at Riven. "Is that Uldrath's mother?"

His jaw hardened as he nodded. "Noemdra."

My brows furrowed. "Is she angry with you?"

Riven wrapped his arm around my shoulder and turned us away from Noemdra's feisty glare. "She is Tarvelle's niece and she has . . . questioned the legitimacy of what we discovered in the capital."

"She doesn't believe Tarvelle was the mole?" I stole another glance at the Halfling, seeing Tarvelle in her green eyes and long brown hair.

Riven shook his head. "She says it is impossible."

"Nothing is impossible when someone is desperate enough." My chest tightened. In some small way I understood what Tarvelle had been trying to accomplish. He had no reason to trust me or the alliance I had forged with Riven and Killian. He would have done anything to destabilize the Crown, even helping Lord Curringham, if it gave him a chance of saving his people and his land. But it was easy for a stranger to believe the worst of someone.

Riven guided me through the rest of the crowd and found a table full of friends. Syrra was speaking with Elaran at the end of it, introducing her to some of the Elverin, while Vrail and Collin sat at the other end. Vrail was chattering away, oblivious to Collin's dazed expression. His eyes fell on me and the spell broke. He didn't grimace but bowed his head, knee bouncing before he excused himself and left without another word.

Vrail lifted her hand to follow him but he was already gone.

She turned and saw Nikolai helping Dynara into her seat. Vrail's brow furrowed before quickly looking away. "You look lovely, Keera. I'm glad you're well."

I wrapped my arms around her and sat on the bench. "We visited Vellinth."

Vrail's eyes sparkled. "Isn't the magic system there amazing? Its history far exceeds the Age of Wielding. There are scrolls at the library that date back to . . ." Vrail launched herself into a ten-minute history lesson on the libraries of Vellinth.

I glanced at Riven, who snickered, but neither of us interrupted the Halfling. I had grown fond of her tangents, and they passed the time as Feron took his place at the front of the Myram tree. Pirmiith stood beside him, ready to interpret whatever he had to say.

"Welcome," Feron called, and the music slowed to a halt. "It has been an honor to help our cousins make a home here these past few days. You all look lovely."

The Shades erupted into cheers. "We love you, Nikolai!" someone screamed from across the clearing.

Nikolai stood and took a bow before pulling Dynara up to take her own. The entire city cheered and laughed as the Shades twirled in their new robes and dresses.

Feron raised his hand and the crowd quieted once more. He pointed to the large pedestal in front of him. "This stone is imbued with the memory of every bloodline to ever have walked along these lands." His hands drifted over the red lines that trailed along the white stone like marbling. "It has the power to show which bloodline any Elverin is from."

Feron poured a small cup of water onto the concave top of the pedestal. He nodded to Lash, who took a small knife from his belt and pricked his finger. The Fae held his hand over the water until a single drop of red blood sent a ripple through the small pool. The water began to churn and bubble. Then it rose into the air, churning into a deep red shade as it took the form of one of the blue birds I had seen on the way to Vellinth.

Feron pointed to the tree that was decorated in the long banner with the same totem. The Elverin underneath it cheered and whistled as the watery totem fell to the ground and disappeared.

Feron placed the waterskin on top of the pedestal and addressed the crowd once more. "I know you have spent months having your blood taken from you and gave much more in your years of service to false kings. If you do not wish to give any more, know that does not make you any less welcome."

The tables of Shades murmured as they whispered to one another. "But for those who do," Feron continued, "you can find your mother's bloodline tonight."

The Shades were struck into silence. Each of them, young and old, gazed at the pedestal with wide eyes. The ones whose families had left them to their fates stared in fear, while the ones who had never known their families stared in blatant curiosity. But none of them dared to move closer to it.

Fyrel stood from her table. "And what if you have a Mortal for a mother?"

My chest twinged as the crowd went silent. Such children were not talked about in the kingdom; it was rare for a Halfling to be born to a Mortal woman, and they were often met with violent ends. Fyrel herself had been left at the end of the glass bridge as an offering to the Order. How she had come to know who her mother was, I didn't know.

Feron didn't hesitate to answer Fyrel's question. There was nothing but kindness in his voice when he said, "Your father belongs to a bloodline too, young one. You would discover his mother's totem."

Fyrel sighed with relief and walked up to the pedestal. Feron laughed and filled it with a splash of water. Fyrel scratched her hand too deeply and a stream of blood fell into the pool. Lash pulled one of Nikolai's handkerchiefs from his robe and passed it to her. Fyrel took it without looking at him, her eyes glued to the bubbling water suspended above her head.

It took the shape of an owl mid-flight with its wings extended and its horns projecting out. The table under the matching banner broke into a chorus of owl calls. Riven nudged my arm and glanced down at Syrra, who shuddered at the end of the table.

"Unnecessary," she mumbled under her breath.

I watched as Shade after Shade completed the ritual. Tables of eagles, deer, fish, trees, and flowers erupted each time as their bloodlines grew. I recognized the little girl, Orrin, from the ship as she cautiously walked up to Feron and Lash.

Lash knelt and tickled her belly before pulling out a thin, sharp pin. "It will only hurt for a second," he said as he held her hand.

"I'm not scared."

Lash laughed and pricked her finger before lifting her up to the pedestal. The water shifted into a fire lion and the crowd gasped. I had only ever seen such a creature once. Feron smiled widely and pointed to a table at the far end of the grove. Their cheers hadn't been heard over the shock of the crowd because only three Elverin sat at the table.

The little girl burst into a run and was tossed into the air by the Elf and two Halflings. Her giggles echoed through the trees.

I turned to Vrail. "What line do you belong to?"

"The wounded willow." Her face fell. "Though I am the last of them now. My grandmother taught me everything she could about the libraries before she passed. In the years before Aemon, our clan ran all of them."

"And now there are no scroll keepers at all?"

"There are still some from the other tree lines, but no keepers for Volcar."

I leaned on Vrail's shoulder and turned my sights on Riven. "And what are you? A chipmunk?"

"I could see it." Nikolai smirked, tossing a toasted nut into his mouth.

Dynara narrowed her eyes. "He's more of a field mouse, I think."

Riven shook his head in amusement. "That isn't even a totem." He turned back to me. "I'm part of the wolf line. There are more of us than Vrail's but most died in the Purges."

"Warrior lines." Nikolai tossed another nut into his mouth.

I glanced around the grove. "But Killian must be a wolf too."

Riven gave a stiff nod.

Dynara grabbed one of Nikolai's nuts. "I haven't seen the princeling at all this week."

Vrail's head snapped up. "He was helping us set up earlier."

"I think he feels like his presence isn't welcome with the Shades." I glanced around the grove looking for Killian's black garb and blond head but didn't find him. "I told him I would help make the introductions but he didn't seem willing to take my offer." I didn't add what else had occurred in our conversation.

Vrail's brow creased as Nikolai stood, holding his hands to her and Dynara. He nodded to the crowd of dancing Elverin by the Myram. "Shall we?"

Dynara smiled and grabbed his hand. Vrail stared at the open palm before shaking her head. "I'm going to go check on Killian," she mumbled. She watched after Nikolai and Dynara with a forlorn look and then disappeared into the crowd in the opposite direction.

They passed a group of initiates and Shades crowded around Lash and Feron. Flames and smoke danced through the air in the shape of terrifying monsters as Feron told the story of the first Fae—Faelin and her daughters with their golden eyes who had banished the shadow creatures for good. Lash raised a sphere of bright flames into the air and separated the orbs into two, creating the second sun just as Faelin had, as the crowd around him gasped.

I smiled seeing Gwyn amongst the crowd. She was standing next to Fyrel, signing away to a young Halfling from the *Faelinth* who was happily interpreting a conversation among the three of them. There was a hint of a smile on Gwyn's lips as Fyrel rattled on about life in the Order.

Elaran slid down the bench beside me. "It seems you have an enemy?" She peered at the Halfling across the grove.

It was Noemdra, Pirmiith's wife. Whether it was me or Riven she was watching, she hadn't left us alone all evening.

"She is the niece of Curringham's mole." I grabbed Riven's arm to keep him from walking over to her.

Elaran laughed. "My late husband had no moles. He barely had reports."

I tilted my head. "Curringham was working with an Elf name Tarvelle. They ferried the rebellion's secrets to Damien."

Elaran's full brows creased. "Those meetings were not reports, they were barely even discussions. Damien spoke and Curringham listened."

I bit my lip and turned to Riven. "Have any other secrets been leaked?" I hadn't missed many meetings.

He shook his head and it settled the worry in my stomach. "There must have been more to their correspondence then you knew."

Elaran's eyes narrowed, but Gerarda clasped her hand and she softened. "Believe what you wish. But I was sent to Cereliath to know Curringham's every move and I did not fail at my post."

I blinked as she stood to dance with Gerarda. A thought flittered across my mind. The same reservation that had struck me the day I saw Tarvelle's body hanging from the throne room. Why would the mole have been so brazen in his dislike for me? It was like he had wanted to get caught.

Riven stood and grabbed my hand. My arm was stiff as he pulled me onto the dance floor. His hands wrapped around my waist but his mind was somewhere else. His eyes looked through me as he twirled us around the grass.

I ran a finger down his cheek before slowly stepping around him in two tight circles with the other dancers. "I hope you're thinking of those promises you made to me about *later*," I whispered into his ear.

Riven's focus snapped back to me. His lips twitched as he extended his arm and I spun across the grass before falling back into his arms. "I was thinking about our last dance." He lifted me into the air and my body slid against his as he slowly lowered me to the ground. Riven grinned and let my body fall toward the ground before pressing his lips to my neck.

My breath hitched. We had been in Cereliath, barely allies and certainly not friends. We had come so far since then even though it had been only a few short months. *I* had come so far. I took a breath and it felt easier than the one before. There was still so much I had to do, so much hardship to march through, but there was a spark of hope that I might be able to do it. With Riven and the others by my side, I might not fail again.

CHAPTER THIRTY-ONE

Nikolai hadn't said a word since Vrail entered the library. She barely noticed us, running in with one stack of books only to fill her arms with another. She was spending every spare minute looking for a solution to Riven's magic. Poring over every book and scroll she had to see if she could predict what would happen to him as we broke the seals and if there was anything we could do to prevent it. My stomach tightened into knots, knowing the answer to that question was far out of my depth. Perhaps too far for even Vrail and Feron to find.

She nodded at us with tired eyes before racing out of the room. Nikolai collapsed back into his chair, staring at the door Vrail had left from.

I snickered and stole one of the nuts he had plated on his lap.

"Do you have something to say?" He tossed a nut into the air and leaned back to catch it in his mouth.

I raised a brow. "I think the person with something to say is you."

The nut hit Nikolai square between the eyes and fell to the floor. "I don't know what you're inferring." He quickly straightened his back and crossed his leg in an obvious attempt to seem casual.

I pointed my chin in the direction of the door. "You flirt with everyone who crosses your path, but you refuse to tell Vrail your true feelings."

I expected Nikolai to deny it, or to be flustered, but he only smiled in the same slow manner of the older Elverin. "Sometimes I forget that you've only known the impatience of Mortals when it comes to such things."

I stole another nut. "The Elverin don't seem to have any trouble making their intentions known." I eyed Nikolai's half-tied and crumpled tunic that I knew he had pulled off Lash's floor that morning. "You, especially."

A mischievous look flashed in Nikolai's eyes as he chuckled. "Mortals fret their entire youths over finding a partner to share their short lives with."

The nut cracked loudly against my teeth. "Only those who have the power to make that choice."

Nikolai's gaze flicked to the east as if he could see every person in the kingdom who had been forced into a union they did not want. "Yes. Another difference between our kinds."

I spanned my arms across the back of my chair. "But there are many Elverin who find partners to spend their lives with just like Mortals do."

Nikolai nodded. "Yes, many do. Eventually. But until the first Halfling was born, all the Elverin lived for millennia. And many of the first Halflings are with us still." Nikolai stretched his arms wide to demonstrate the length of that time. I leaned back, unable to imagine so many lifetimes, so much pain. "For those that feel such hungers," Nikolai continued, "we are encouraged to spend the entirety of our first millennia on our own. We take lovers and enjoy the company of many, but it is a time to explore our tastes and our passions." Nikolai leaned back in his chair and winked.

I pulled my boot onto my knee. "In the eyes of the Elverin, you and I are considered youth?" I made sure to coat every word in sarcasm.

Nikolai choked on his drink and broke into a fit of laughter. I crossed my arms when he slapped his thigh mid-wheeze. "Keera dear, I may flirt and joke with you because it amuses both of us, but there would be many hot words flung in my direction—and more fists than just Riven's—if I were to *do* anything with someone as young as you."

I leaned forward on the table. "You are just over seven hundred years. We're both are in our first thousand years."

Nikolai had the decency to cover his mouth as another chuckle burst through his lips. "I will try to explain the difference to you in terms you may be more familiar with. To the Elverin, my seven centuries would make me something of a gangly young man, old enough to marry in the strictest sense, but it would attract many shocked gasps if I did."

My face and voice were deadpanned. "So I would be a child."

"An infant."

I shoved his shoulder. "The Elverin view me as a child yet allow me to be part of a rebellion?"

Nikolai sighed and tilted his head. "It was the Halflings who first encouraged the rebellion to begin with. The rest of the Elverin could not stop them . . . and war changes many things. But not *all* things; it would not be allowed for someone as old as I to be involved with someone as young as you."

I crossed my arms, feeling indignant. "Lash is thousands of years older than you are."

"I know," Nikolai said with a wicked grin. "But we are not partners. He does not map the decisions of his life by my compass and neither I with him. We enjoy each other's company and that is all. And until I reach my thousandth year, that is all the Elverin would allow between me and anyone his age."

I slumped back in my chair to gather my thoughts.

"This surprises you?" Nikolai's brows disappeared under his tight curls.

I shrugged. "As a Shade I never thought about marriage. It was something only the Mortals did. But I've seen marriages between men with heads of gray and girls just past their first bleed. Such unions are not treated with contempt."

Nikolai couldn't hide the disgust on his face. "How could Aemon have allowed such a thing?"

I scoffed. "He presided over a few of them himself." My mind wandered to the faces of young girls who had been married to rich lords to secure their families' wealth and status.

I twisted my braid in my fingers, remembering the caring way Riven had weaved it that morning. "If this is the Elvish view of life, many must be horrified by Riven and I."

Nikolai shrugged, throwing another nut into his mouth. "You and Riven are both very young. I don't think many would see your union as serious."

My stomach turned to rock at those words.

Nikolai quickly swallowed. "But knowing you both, I think it is a gift from Elverath herself to have found each other so early in life. Especially when none of your tomorrows are assured."

"Even if we win this war, I may not live for millennia," I whispered.

Nikolai's arm froze midair. "Keera do not joke about such things. I thought you were feeling better."

My brows knitted together, not understanding the horror in his voice. But then the truth fluttered inside my chest. "I forgot," I whispered, and Nikolai's worry softened.

I flexed my hand on my lap, feeling the magic coursing under my skin. My amber blood marked me as a Halfling, but my magic meant I was something else too. I was a Light Fae. I had never stopped long enough to consider what that meant for my mortality. If we won this war, I wouldn't have decades of peace. I would have millennia.

Forever.

I pushed the thought away. All it did was stoke the storm already rumbling in my belly.

"Your tomorrows are not assured either." I turned to Nikolai. "I see the way you look at Vrail. And the way you often *don't* look at her. Why not tell her?"

Nikolai let out a deep breath and rested his neck on the back of his chair. His fingers found the stretched strand of hair over his brow and he tugged on it.

His brown eyes swirled with worry, trying to find the right words to answer my question. My shoulders fell, realizing his worry wasn't for him but for Vrail.

"Because she's your compass?" I answered for him.

A mix of joy and fear crept over Nikolai's face. He reminded me of one of the baby birds perched outside my burl preparing himself to jump off and trust his wings. A cautious smile tugged at his lips.

"I hope so." His eyes glazed over and I knew he was remembering the way Vrail had carried the pile of books out of the room. He shook himself free of the memory and stood. "But she deserves the time to draw her own map." He held out his own hand for me to grab. "And I will wait for however long that takes."

"Straighten your stance, Fyrel!" Gerarda shouted from the sideline of the training grounds. A crowd of Elverin, mostly Shades, stood around the perimeter of the field five bodies deep. Everyone wanted to see the spectacle Feron and Syrra had devised to help me train my magic. It would be vital to tear through Damien's soldiers at the next seal.

Fyrel swung again with her long, curved blade. I jumped over it easily but when I landed, the ground started to shake. I only had a moment to roll along the grass before Feron shot a pillar of earth forty feet into the sky.

That only brought me closer to Vrail who had a large mallet in each hand. She swung and I dodged. She swung the other and I bent my body backward, watching the hammer graze the air just over my nose. A spout of hot flame exploded beside my ear. My skin bubbled as I waved my hand and doused the fire with my magic.

I glared at Lash's smug face beside Feron's. "Just because I can heal doesn't mean it doesn't hurt!"

He crossed his gigantic arms. "If you were more instinctual with your magic the flames wouldn't have lived long enough to burn you."

Vrail slammed the mallet down between my legs and I twisted my calf around her shoulder, throwing her to the ground. "Instinctual," I muttered under my breath. "You've had three thousand years of practice and I've had three weeks."

I tried to put some distance between Vrail and I, ducking Fyrel's swing that narrowly missed my head. I sent a gust of wind into her chest and she fell to the ground.

I caught my breath and readied my sword but Feron lifted a single hand and eight pillars of earth penned me in on all sides. In the gaps between them, Lash ignited fires that raged over my head, making my brow sweat. I closed my eyes and focused on the scorching power that flickered under my skin. I smoothed it out in my mind, like taking a pot from a boil to a manageable simmer. The flames turned to red embers on the ground and I stepped through the pillars.

But Riven was there to meet me with his shadows. He blanketed the entire field in his darkness as the crowd gasped.

I couldn't see anything. I reached out, trying to grasp a tendril of shadow, but nothing slipped through my fingers.

Something knocked into me and I fell to my knees. I focused on the beat of Riven's heart and heard him circling around me in slow, silent steps. I matched the rhythm of his breaths to mine and used that as my anchor. I imagined each of his steps, mapping out our distance as his heartbeat thumped beside me.

I felt the softest breath of movement to my left and pounced.

The whirlwind that had been building inside my chest roared. Sweat pooled along my brow as I fought to keep control, pulling the air from Riven's lungs. Slow and careful, not pulling so hard to hurt him, but enough that his power faded.

The shadows around me turned to gray fog. Riven's black figure was kneeling on the ground across the field.

I pounced, pinning him to the grass.

"Got you," I whispered, unable to hold back my smug grin.

But Riven only grinned back as a sharp jab pressed between my shoulder blades.

"And I got you." Vrail pulled back on her short sword and smiled triumphantly at Syrra and Gerarda. They both nodded with approval, which only sent Vrail into a frenzied dance across the grass.

I sighed and rolled off Riven in defeat. Fyrel brought me a waterskin and helped me off the ground. "I should have had you," she said. "Twice."

I patted Fyrel's shoulder. "You will in time. I reckon you're good enough to best Gerarda."

Gerarda rolled her eyes. "We will work on some more advanced footwork tomorrow. Then you'll run circles around Keera."

Fyrel beamed and ran back to her friends in the parting crowd.

I poured the water over my face and then into my mouth. Feron raised a root out of the ground for me to sit on. "You have made much progress this week, Keera." His lilac eyes narrowed. "How are you feeling."

I shrugged. "I feel fine. No strain on my magic at all."

Lash perched on the armrest of Feron's self-made chair. "I think it's time we moved past defensive skills then." He looked down at Feron, who leaned forward on his cane.

"Those skills will save many lives," Feron replied slowly.

Lash shook his head. "The false king's armies are too large for foot soldiers to fight. But a magic wielder as gifted as her"—he nodded at me—"could change the tide of this war."

"And what about wielders as strong as you?" I glanced between them. The Fae had yet to declare their support for the rebellion.

Feron lifted his chin. "I will not leave the Elverin defenseless. The Fae will remain here."

"Until when?"

Feron's mouth was a straight line. "Until our prospects strengthen."

After training all day, I longed for some peace. I loved having the Shades in the city, I loved seeing them play and laugh with the other Elverin as if they were lifelong friends, but monitoring every one of their needs was more tiring than any training session Syrra could design.

I walked along the lake, occasionally stopping to skip a flat rock across the glass-like surface. Something moved in the corner of my eye. I turned and realized I had walked to the north side of the lake. The usually empty clearing was to the east, but there was someone in it. At first I thought it was Nikolai, leaving flowers at his mother's statue out of habit, but as I neared closer I saw her chair.

Myrrah sat under the statue of Maerhal and the shade of the tree that was the living memorial of Nikolai's son. She sat facing the city with her head craned upward at the burls and connected bridges along the upper branches.

"Nikolai could find a way to get you and your chair down if you wanted to go up by faelight," I called out from the far side of the meadow. "If not, Feron certainly could."

I sat down in the grass next to her and watched as another group of initiates emerged from the hollow trunk of the Myram tree in a fit of shrieks and giggles.

Myrrah smiled softly. "I was never fond of heights even when I could've made the climb. Besides, seeing it from the ground is thrilling enough."

I turned back to the city and tried to view it with the same sense of awe that filled Myrrah's face. My first impression of Myrelinth had been clouded with the threat of mutiny and banishment, but even I couldn't deny it was beautiful. The second sun had just dipped behind the Burning Mountains, darkening the gold leaves of the Elder birch along the peaks and streaking the sky with copper. The faelights that rested in the branches during the day had lifted from their nests and floated like stars waiting to greet their sisters that hung from the sky.

"Hildy would have loved this city," Myrrah whispered, more to herself than to me.

My throat tightened and I pretended to still be studying the swaying treetops.

"Every day, I see something that I wish I could show her." Myrrah's chin trembled as she turned the gold ring on her middle finger. It had been a gift from Hildegard for completing her first mission after her accident. Every time she shifted it out of place, the pale indent that was left above her knuckle was visible. I doubted Myrrah had ever taken the ring off.

I tried to imagine Hildegard spending her days training with Syrra and laughing with Nikolai, but the painting in my mind was hazy, like a canvas left unfinished. Perhaps it hurt too much to imagine knowing she would never have the chance, or maybe I knew that for people who had worn a hood as long as we had, that we would never truly belong in a place so beautiful and untouched by misery.

Hildegard would have felt just as I did, like a figure painted into a portrait long after it was rendered, forever separated from the other figures by layers of dust and time.

"She would have loved the trees and lights, but the vines—" My lip perked to the side.

Myrrah laughed so hard she snorted. "She would have found it utterly ridiculous having to fall to your death each time. She'd never stop mentioning it—"

My belly filled with laughter too. "Every jump would leave her bun undone."

Myrrah wiped her eyes, half in laughter and half in grief. "There isn't enough tea in all the Faeland to fix the temper that would follow."

We sat until our laughs faded and the sky blanketed us in darkness. The silence pulsed between us, beating against my chest until the words I wasn't sure I should say sprang forth. "I'm sorry that my taunt cost you your wife."

Myrrah went completely still. I would have counted my heartbeats, but I was sure my own heart had stopped waiting for her to speak. Instead, she pulled the brakes free from both her wheels. Her callused hands pushed against one wheel and my heart split, thinking she was leaving me alone in my guilt.

But Myrrah's face was soft as she positioned herself directly in front of me. Under the faelights, the gray strands of her hair almost glowed against what was left of the black, all of it wild and unkempt in a way that her wife would have never allowed.

Myrrah took a deep, raspy breath. Her gray-blue eyes were no longer misted but were rippling pools of uncertain waters. "Keera, I know."

My shoulders relaxed into my knees, but Myrrah shook her head.

"I don't mean your apology"—she lifted her chin to the sky and started whispering to herself or to someone above her—"I know I promised never to speak a word of it, but we both know she won't hear what she needs to without knowing the truth."

My skin prickled like a cool breeze had blown across it. I knew exactly who Myrrah was whispering her quick prayer to.

"When did she tell you?" My throat had dried completely so each word cracked as I spoke.

Myrrah's head snapped back down at me. Her brows were wrinkled with worry and pity. It was wrong that she should be so concerned with my grief when hers was so fresh. "The night it happened," she whispered gently.

I wiped at my eye before a tear could fall. "I'd always wondered, but you never said anything. Never even hinted."

Myrrah made a noise that sounded like a grunt. "There were many close calls. Hildy and I had several fights about it over the years, but she knew you best and she thought a confrontation would only make it worse."

My chest splintered, splitting like a base of a tree, jagged and fractured as the weight of everything Hildegard had done for me came crashing down. Myrrah pushed herself closer, until the wheels of her chair scraped against my knees. She pulled my head onto her lap and stroked my hair.

Brenna was the only one who had ever comforted me like that. Somehow, finally talking about her death to Myrrah made it feel like it was her hand on my head. When I closed my eyes I could feel the warmth of her skin and the way her blond locks tickled my back as she curved her calves around my waist.

"Hildy knew she would never take off her cloak. That decision was made before she met you or me." Myrrah sighed, but there was no bitterness in it. "We knew that each day we got to spend together was a blessing and we both considered ourselves very much blessed." Myrrah's strokes slowed and we both listened as the wind blew through the tall trees like a soft lullaby. "Neither of us were angry at you for how you handled yourself in that throne room. Damien meant for his question to be cruel and shocking, but *you* bested *him*."

I scoffed against her knee. A rough finger tugged at my chin as Myrrah lifted my head to meet her gaze. "Do you agree that I knew Hildy best out of anyone?"

I nodded.

"Then believe me when I tell you that she did not die meek or angry, she died *proud*. Proud of *you*, Keera." Myrrah's hand shook as it held my cheek. "If everything had gone to plan, I would have died with her. But I'm glad I'm here to tell you this."

I tilted my head to the side and blinked back the last of my tears. "That was never her plan."

Myrrah's laugh caught in her throat as I pulled a piece of parchment from my trouser belt. Its folds were so worn the scrap had almost split in multiple places, but the words she had written were still legible. It had not left my person since Gerarda had handed it to me.

Myrrah's hands trembled as she delicately unfolded the letter and read it again and again.

I trust Gerarda with your life and the lives of the Shades. Listen to her for once in your life. I know I couldn't save your love, but please do what you can to save mine.—H

"I can't say I'm surprised . . ." Myrrah's voice caught as she lifted the letter. "Can I keep this?"

I closed her fingers around the parchment. "It's yours."

I stood and wiped the dirt from my trousers as Myrrah read the letter one last time. I gestured to the back of her chair, offering my help and she nodded. We walked down the path back to the city as I slowly pushed her chair through the well-worn earth. "Did you ever picture yourself a life without a cloak or that Shield pin around your neck?"

Myrrah chuckled. "All the time. Every mission I took, I'd imagine what would happen if I sailed my ship away from the kingdom's shores for good, left it all behind. How much worse could the other realms be for a Halfling?"

"You never tried?"

"Never." Myrrah looked back up at the starry skies. "I suspect it's the reason I couldn't get Hildy to sail with me. She knew that I would never leave her, just like I knew she'd never leave that island."

My fingers gripped the handles of her chair so fiercely the front of it tipped up. I loosened my hold and kept us going along the beach. "I know the feeling. Even though I left my title behind, I can still feel the weight of that blade pushed against my throat. I don't know if it will ever go away."

Myrrah lifted one of her hands over her shoulder to tap my hand. "You and Hildy were always so alike. Thick-headed and strong-willed with a tendency to pick up every tragedy as your own. Don't let your need to save everyone strangle you."

I squeezed her shoulder. "I won't."

"Or drown you."

That would be much harder.

CHAPTER THIRTY-TWO

NIKOLAI HAD CLOAKED the entire city in shades of crimson for the funeral. Long thick trails of red silks hung from the upper branches and burls, others were wrapped around vines that swayed just over the ground. He had even fitted some of the faelight with the same filter he had made for Maerhal's spectacles, this time the material was stained so the orbs lit the procession with soft scarlet rays.

The entire city surrounded the Myram tree, some looking down on the large pyre from above while others crowded at the base of nearby trunks. They were dressed in gowns of every color of flame, as was the tradition in the Faeland, but it only made the circle of black around the pyre more severe.

"Are you ready?" I whispered over Myrrah's shoulder from behind her chair.

She swallowed once, just as the first sounds of low flutes and hard drums echoed through the meadow. Her hair had been cut short that morning, her peppered tresses braided into Hildegard's grayed locks. Myrrah's hand lifted to her ear, as if forgetting that there was no longer any hair to tuck behind it and nodded. "Take me to her."

I gripped the leather handles of her chair and slowly walked us down the path marked on either side by Shades. They had been given clothes in every color, but today they wore the same black that was wrapped around Hildegard's body. The same color they had worn beside her for every day of their lives.

We marched forward slowly. Myrrah did not speak or whimper but kept her eyes on the pile of wood in front of us. She locked her chair as we reached the edge of the pyre and turned to Elaran who was waiting for us with a sharp knife in her hands.

Today the traditions of the Elverin would be blended with the traditions of the Shades.

Myrrah took the blade by its wooden handle. Her jaw pulsed and her eyes searched the crowd for someone, softening for just a moment, before Gerarda opened her mouth and began to sing.

"Ish'kavra diiz'bithir ish'kavra." From flame to ash to flame again. The words themselves were not sad, but in Gerarda's low tone they were devastating. Despite her small stature, Gerarda sang with the presence of a seasoned warrior and entertainer all in one. Her voice was thick and rich like honey, but then would crack and sting like the venomous kiss of a bee.

Myrrah held up the knife as Gerarda's song shifted to a gentle melody. She pulled the black cloak she rarely wore out from behind her back and sliced a large piece off from the bottom. Then she sliced open her hand and soaked the black fabric with her own amber blood. She looked up at me and I pushed her as close to the pyre as possible for her to lay the piece of her cloak across it. She laid it to the left of Hildegard's head, the same place Myrrah had rested her own every night she had shared with her wife.

The Shades moved as a group, pulling out their blades in one quick motion before slicing their own hoods from the backs of their necks. They laid their blood-stained garments across the pyre, one by one, not only to show their respect for the Halfling who had trained them, saved them, and died for them, but as a promise to never note their black hoods again.

Today marked the death of Hildegard and the death of the Shades.

I stepped back from Myrrah's chair and unsheathed my bloodstone dagger. I sliced through the fastener at my neck and let the entire piece fall from my shoulders. I ran my blade over both palms before picking up the crumpled pile of black and staining it with my own blood. I carried the hood that Hildegard had crowned me with and the cloak she had wrapped around my shoulders only a few years later to her feet. I laid the entire cloak at the base of the pyre and looked over the wood to where Myrrah whispered her last words to her love.

When she was done, she nodded once.

"*Ish'kavra diiz'bithir ish'kavra.*" Gerarda's song broke into a crashing crescendo as I raised my hands and felt the warmth of the flames flicker inside me and then deep inside the belly of the pyre. The first cracks of wood were haunting harmonies to Gerarda's farewell ballad, the song ending just as the pyre fully ignited in shades of crimson and gold.

We watched the fire burn until the flames had all but gone. Even after most of the Elverin had left to attend to their tasks and the children had run to swim in the lake, the Shades stood guard as the greatest of us was turned to ash.

Riven kept his distance from me but his shadows swirled at my feet, curling around my ankles as I watched the embers fade from bright red to white. The Shades knelt on the ground in a final act of respect and dispersed hours after we'd taken our post.

Syrra and Gerarda stood on either edge of the ashes with white rakes made of birchwood and finished with gold tines. They pulled the ashes into a small pile in the middle of the burnt circle the fire had left behind.

Syrra knelt in front of Myrrah and presented her with a white-wood box. Myrrah opened it with trembling hands to reveal a velvet cushion that held a small pouch. It shimmered like glass imbued with flakes of gold, but its edges were flexible as Myrrah grasped it and opened its mouth by the golden string.

Syrra stepped behind her and moved Myrrah's chair next to the pile of ash. The ground around the pile shook, breaking free from the earth and rising into the air just high enough for Myrrah to use the small gold spoon Gerarda handed her to fill the pouch.

I searched the clearing for Feron and saw him perched on an extended root next to the Myram tree, half concealed in its shadow. I smiled at him, grateful that he could use his powers to help Myrrah finish the ritual herself.

Riven appeared at my side and I reached for his hand, lacing our fingers together as I leaned on his shoulder. "That pouch will be used to plant Hildegard's tree?"

Riven squeezed my hand gently and nodded. "Twelve moons from now, we will hold another ceremony to mark the new life that will grow from her death."

"If there are any of us left to see the moons to come."

Riven's grip tightened, even his shadows curled more tightly around my legs. "That only gives us another reason to win."

We watched in silence as Myrrah finished filling the last of the ashes into the bag. Syrra pulled her blade from one of the orbs of fire around the Myram tree and used it to sear the opening shut. Then she pulled the gold chain on the bottom free and placed it around Myrrah's neck so she could protect it for the next year.

"What is that pouch called?" I asked Riven as the others helped Myrrah to her room.

Riven chuckled underneath his breath and looked down at where my head still laid against his shoulder. "It is one of the most sacred items of our people because it contains a person's entire life, one's entire being."

I lifted my head. "So special it doesn't have a name?"

His face cracked into one of those rare smiles, unburdened by pain or duty. The one he only ever wore for me. "It is called a *diizra*."

My heart fluttered in my chest as the meaning of the word washed over me. It was the name Riven had been calling me for months, so casually I had thought it was a common name used between lovers here. But I could see in the intense way Riven's eyes shifted that there was nothing causal or common in the way he meant it.

His hand found its way to my throat, tangling into the hair at the base of my neck. He bit his own lip as if restraining himself from doing anything unseemly at the edge of a funeral pyre. Instead his thumb brushed against my mouth, a promise of more to come.

"If I perish in this war—"

"Riven, don't say such—" He silenced me with another brush of his thumb.

"*If* I perish and you survive, then you should know that it is your hair I want braided into mine. You shall light my pyre and collect my ashes and carry my life around your neck until it is time to say farewell to me. It is only right, *diizra*, that you be the one to hold my life in your hands because it has always been yours. In life just as it will be in death."

Riven pressed his lips to my forehead. His touch heated my skin and I leaned against his chest. "Will you be the one to braid my hair and collect my ashes if I am the one to perish?"

"No." Riven's answer was hard and cold, as if the thought of my death chilled his body to ice. I leaned back and saw the determination flash across his face before he looked down at me. "There is no path forward where I survive the war and you do not, *diizra*." Riven's hands knotted behind my back, anchoring me to him in a way I hadn't allowed myself to crave. "I shall protect you with everything I have, with my dying breath if I must, and if fate is determined to make me a liar on that promise, then I will die collecting the last breaths of whoever dare take you from me."

I ran my finger down the sharp bump of Riven's nose, tapping the end of it. "I do not want this war to end with your ashes hanging around my neck, Riventh Numenthira. There will be times when I will need to trust you will do your mission and not worry about protecting me."

Riven didn't make any more promises but only pressed another kiss to my head. There was something defiant in its sweetness I didn't trust, but I knew there was nothing more I could say to change Riven's mind. In that way we were the same, fiercely loyal and defiant when it came to the ones we loved.

I just hoped it wouldn't cost us our lives.

CHAPTER THIRTY-THREE

"WE'RE SAILING ANYWAY, I don't understand why Volcar isn't your preferred choice!" A voice echoed through the tunnels as Riven and I reached the door to our usual meeting room. I glanced at his hardened jaw and saw his shadows darken as he whipped open the door for us both.

"The fact that I have to explain why to *you* of all people . . ." Gerarda threw her hands in the air in exasperation. Elaran only glared down at her, unmoving in her position.

Nikolai sat in his chair watching the fight like a play while Syrra leaned against the mantel cleaning her blades. Killian's head popped out of the book he was reading the moment I took my seat.

"They've been at this for ten minutes already," Nikolai whispered, leaning over his armrest to offer me that morning's selection of snacks. Today, it was cured meat and cheese.

"Do I look to be in the mood for whispers and jests?" Gerarda turned on her toes, slicing the air like one of her knives to snarl at Nikolai.

Nikolai raised a brow. "Are you ever?"

Elaran chuckled under her breath.

"You state your opinions very loudly for someone only invited to this meeting out of courtesy to Gerarda." I crossed my arms. "I could hear you both from the great hall."

Gerarda straightened and tucked her arms behind her back. Elaran pressed a hand onto the round table and shrugged. "I assumed I was invited for my opinions."

"You were." I leaned back in my chair. "But your opinion is wrong. We are sailing to the Fractured Isles."

Gerarda's throat bobbed in victory but she didn't break her stance.

Elaran crossed her arms. "Half of Damien's armies are stationed at Volcar. Why wait when we could fatally wound his cause by the morrow?"

"And you think we can take that many with a legion of seven?" I rested my arm over the back of my chair.

A fine line appeared between Elaran's brows. "Look at what we were able to do at the Order."

"What Keera was able to do." Riven's shadows swirled around my chair.

Elaran's lips fell to a straight line. "We have other magic wielders at our disposal." She glanced at me. "I mean no offense."

I shrugged. "And I take none. But the other Fae will not join our cause until their magic is strong enough to secure a certain victory. We give ourselves the best chance by restoring as much magic as we can and attacking Volcar with a fuller force. I will not risk the survival of everyone on my magic alone."

Riven flinched beside me. I didn't say it to wound him, and Riven knew his magic could not be relied upon. Especially not as his control continued to slip.

I unfolded the map of Elverath across the table. I pointed to the Fractured Isles. "Our reports indicate that Damien has fewer ships docked along the islands. The ports are smaller and there are only three dozen in total."

"Not a small number," Killian interjected, his knee bouncing as he leaned over the table to see the map.

"I was hoping Nik would have some idea on how to deal with that problem." I raised my brows at where he was still slumped over in his chair.

"I have many ideas, Keera dear," he mumbled through his food.

"If you all are able to destroy the ports and the ships while I break the seal then Damien will have no choice but to split up his armada." I pointed at the large ports at Volcar. "It will be distraction enough for us to break the two other seals and will give us the advantage of forcing Damien's ships to sail for the east while we attack the west."

Elaran's bottom lip protruded slightly as she nodded. "You make a reasonable point."

"Yes, I do." I crossed my arms and tried to make my smile less smug. "And I don't want to provoke Damien so close to the *Faelinth* until we have as much magic as possible to defend it."

Gerarda nodded her head. "The exact point I was trying to make."

Elaran cocked her jaw and rested her arm on Gerarda's shoulder.

The faelight that had been circling her head swirled out from the movement and danced over the map. Syrra's eyes widened and she pointed at the parchment.

"Could that be correct?" She looked up at Killian.

Killian's eyes fluttered as he studied the map for something I couldn't see. "You said they faded over time. Perhaps they can come back."

The table creaked as Riven leaned on it. His eyes scanned the parchment for a moment before widening. "How many more could reopen?"

His shadows swirled around the new symbol at the Order. It was no longer black, a sign that the portal had stopped functioning. It was inked in gold and silver light, indicating two portals had reopened over the lake.

Syrra shrugged. "We lost dozens when the magic began to fade. These"—she pointed to the two connected portals—"were some of the first to close."

"Even more reason to break the seals." I stood up from the map and looked at Nikolai. "How long do you need to make your preparations?"

His dark eyes looked at the ceiling while he did some quick calculations in his head. "Three days."

"Three days it is. Get Vrail to help you." I nodded my head at her empty seat. "If she hasn't found an answer by now she isn't going to find one." Riven put a gentle hand on my back.

Nikolai's brows fell as he glanced between Riven and Killian, but he didn't argue. "I'm sure she won't mind." He tossed his last piece of cured meat onto the table and sauntered out of the room.

I lifted my chin to the others. "Syrra and Gerarda will map out a plan of attack."

Elaran loudly cleared her throat.

"And you are more than welcome to assist them."

Her answering smile was poised but smug. "Of course." She lifted her hand and Gerarda took it before they walked out of the room together.

Syrra's jaw flexed once before she followed them. "We still train at dawn," she shouted as she stepped out of the door.

I slumped back down in my seat and cocked a brow at Killian. "Will you be joining us this time?"

"No," Riven answered before his brother could speak.

"Maybe we should discuss alternatives—" Killian crossed his arms, not even flinching when Riven's shadows flared.

I tilted my head at him, but Riven's gaze didn't leave Killian's. "Keera, can you give us a moment?"

I nodded and walked out of the door though the curious part of me was screaming to stay. As soon as I stepped through the doorway, Killian's voice exploded into a barrage of fury. "Riven, how much longer can you expect me to put up with this?"

I could hear the steel in Riven's reply. "I didn't realize you thought there was an expiration."

Killian sighed. "You're being ridiculous."

"I have my reasons." Riven's words were dark and daring.

My cheeks flushed. I could only think of one thing that would make Riven refuse to allow Killian to accompany us on the mission. Guilt pricked my throat and I swallowed. I had been so happy to accept Riven's forgiveness that I had never stopped to think that he might not have been so forgiving with his brother.

I wanted to barge back into the room and console Riven. Make sure he knew there was nothing he needed to worry about, but this mission was a matter of life and death. For everyone, but especially for Riven. If leaving Killian in Myrelinth would help Riven focus then I wouldn't push him.

My goal was for both of them to live. They could sort out the rest after.

Three days later we were back on the ship. It was safer to travel by water than by portal for such a long journey and it allowed everyone to rest before we landed on the northern shores of the Fractured Isles.

Gerarda stood at the helm of the ship as the first stars began to line the sky. The others disappeared below deck to rest while I kept watch along the horizon for any sign of black sails we needed to hide from.

The sea was silent and still. The moon shone over the water, rippling across it like stippled glass. I sat along the floor of the eagle's nest and let my feet dangle from the landing. My braided gusts filled the wide sails though the thin ship barely made a sound as it raced across the open sea.

The only sound was coming from Gerarda's relentless tapping.

Tap, tap, tap, tap. Pause.

Tap, tap, tap, tap. Pause.

"Is something on your mind?" I called down to her.

Gerarda ignored me.

My lip tugged upward. "Trouble with your lady?"

Her finger did one more round of tapping and then stopped. "No." Her jaw pulsed as she glanced at the upper cabin where Elaran was resting. "It's not a story worth telling."

I huffed a laugh. "I'd rather listen to a boring story than have you continue with the tapping. I'd like both of us to see the suns rise."

Annoyance pulled Gerarda's lips into a frown as she glanced up at me. Her eyes focused on the bright star behind my head and she adjusted our course by half an inch. "I am nervous for what we'll find when we get there."

"I've never known you to be scared of some soldiers."

Gerarda embedded a knife in the railing above my head. "I'm not."

I waved my hand down at her.

She took a deep breath. "The Fractured Isles are my home. I'm anxious to know what Damien has done to them."

My brows lifted on their own. "Your *home*?" I'd never heard a Shade use the word before to refer to anything other than the Order.

Gerarda gritted her teeth and nodded. "I lived there as a young girl until Aemon's soldiers came. Then I was brought to the Order."

I tilted my head. "But you are only a few years older than me. The islands were taken in the conquest."

Gerarda huffed a laugh. "They were put under Aemon's control, but it was very different than the scourges that happened in the mainland. The islands are wild lands and Aemon's men did not know how to tame them. It was easier to have the locals farm the land to fill his pockets so he allowed us some freedom . . . until he didn't."

I shook my head. "But he burned their main city to the ground. There is a painting of the siege along with the other raids."

"*Iq'akir.*" Gerarda's fingered twisted around the wooden wheel she was holding. "He did burn it to the ground, but centuries after the Blood Purges." She swallowed thickly. "My parents died in those fires."

My heart pounded against my chest. I had known Gerarda for over fifty years and she had never once hinted at the life she had lived before the Order. I had always assumed that she had come too young to remember any other life than the one in black.

"You were orphaned and sent to the Order." I bowed my head. "I'm sorry."

Gerarda inhaled a shaky breath through her nose. "I wasn't alone. Not at first."

I held my breath, waiting for her to continue.

"I had a sister. Her name was Gabrellen." Gerarda swallowed, her throat bobbing. "We were raised as farmers and had no reason to think our lives would be any different than our parents'. Four generations of Halflings had tended those fields after Aemon's conquest."

I lowered myself onto the quarterdeck and perched on the railing in front of the wheel. "What happened to her?"

Gerarda wiped her eyes and stared down at her boot. "She pulled me out of the fire and knew what would happen when the soldiers came. I was too young to understand what happened to Halflings in the kingdom, what our *options* would be as females."

My stomach plummeted, knowing that her sister had acted the way countless other siblings had in the face of my blade before.

Gerarda lifted her hand to the ends of her hair along her jaw. "She cut through my hair with a paring knife. Lobbed thick chunks of it onto the ground and caked my face in mud." Gerarda looked up at me with strained eyes. "I think she knew that the only hope for me was at the Order. I think she sensed that I was . . . different and would not take well to the dresses and duties of a courtesan."

A chill ran down my spine. "She made you ugly for the guards and hoped they would leave you at the Order's doorstep?"

Gerarda nodded through her trembling chin. "And that's what they did. But she hadn't had enough time to do the same for herself, so I was dragged into one carriage and she another."

I placed my hand over Gerarda's along the wheel. "That last memory must be a heavy one to carry."

"It wasn't the last time I saw her." A tear rolled down Gerarda's cheek. "I spotted her in the streets of Koratha during my first patrol as an initiate. Carston almost killed me with the lashing she gave me for leaving my post, but I had to follow her."

I blinked. "You spoke with her?"

Gerarda nodded. "I told her as much as I could in those few minutes and she listened just like she always had. But then I grabbed her hands and realized they had taken one from her."

I winced. It was a common punishment for courtesans who tried to run away from their houses. There were dozens working the streets of Koratha who no longer had hands at all.

I grabbed Gerarda's arm. "I'm so sorry, Ger." Somehow the shortened name felt right on my tongue.

Her lips twitched but her dark eyes were glazed with a veil of memory. "There was nothing I could do for her as an initiate. I couldn't sneak her onto the island, and that had been the first night I had ever left it. But I promised her that I would return. As soon as I earned my hood, I would find a way to free her. Use whatever leverage I had to get her a placement with a kind lord on a small parcel of land. Days of laundering clothes was not freedom, but it would have been something."

There was a sharp edge to Gerarda's voice that cut through my hope.

"And I did." Gerarda adjusted the wheel along the sea without looking at me. "The day after I passed my Trials, I told her of my plan. She was so happy she wept. And then I finally earned my cloak and found her a placement. I returned and found her dead."

My breath hitched. "That's why you always fought to—"

"Be the best." Gerarda nodded in disgust at her own foolishness. "I made it through the Order quicker than any other initiate, trained harder than any other Shade to earn a title, but in the end it didn't matter. The cough took her before I had the chance to save her." She grabbed the ends of her short hair and my chest cracked open. She had kept it the same length for over sixty years.

The night air turned cold and abrasive against my skin. I reached my hand out to comfort Gerarda but she stepped away from me. "That's why I was hard on you before we went to Elandorr." She glanced up at me with hard eyes, but there was a fondness there that had never been before. "I won't apologize for what I said; you needed to hear it. But now you know that I wasn't trying to be cruel. I had lost people too."

I swallowed thickly as Gerarda made another tiny adjustment to our course. She was right. She had come to the Faeland with the same losses as me—her mentor, the Shades, her family, she even believed her love had been taken from her. She knew that I could survive the weight of that grief because she was carrying the same load.

My lip twitched; somehow knowing that made me understand her in a way I never had.

"You are much stronger than I am." I planted myself beside her, not touching but close enough that Gerarda was letting me into the wide berth she kept around herself.

Gerarda lifted her chin. "I'm aware."

I flicked her on the head before I could stop myself.

Her jaw hung at the side as she glared at me. "Do you want me to cut you?"

I shrugged. "I heal fast."

I half expected Gerarda to pull out one of her thin blades, but instead she laughed. Light and airy at first but then it bellowed deep from her belly and out into the sea. Her grief-stained cheeks were washed away with lighter tears as her laughter mellowed.

I turned back to the mast, readying to climb up the pole to the eagle's nest, but there was still a question tugging at my mind. I turned back to Gerarda. "How did you find the strength to keep going, to keep *leading*, in the face of so much proof that there was only more pain to come?"

"Spite."

I chuckled, thinking she was kidding but Gerarda's face was entirely serious.

"There's a reason Aemon designed the Order the way it was, the way he designed the entire kingdom. The ones with the most power to use against him always suffered the most. So we can't succumb to our losses, Keera, because there will be no one left to fight. Aemon counted on that, and so does his son."

CHAPTER THIRTY-FOUR

WE REACHED THE FRACTURED ISLES at dusk just as Gerarda had planned. Our ship was shallow enough to sail into the inner bay between the southern islands, out of sight from the armada that was docked along the southernmost shore.

The same shore that Vrail and Nikolai were certain was the location of the third seal.

We were hiding in the long shadows of the forest that Riven had darkened though there were no soldiers in sight. I glanced at Vrail. "You're certain that the seal isn't on the northern island?" That would make our mission much easier.

She bit her lip. "I don't like to deal in certainties."

Nikolai nudged her with his elbow. "It's there, Keera. Water takes the path of least resistance and there are no barriers to magic."

I nodded like I hadn't heard this several times in the past week. The other seals had been located at the closest point from where the initial spell was cast. And the royal ports were the closest to the Ruins of Faevra.

The second sun sunk below the horizon and I gave the nod. "Then we proceed."

I filled the sails with a small braid of gust. Elaran adjusted its size as we slowly cruised through the bay into the small mouth along the top of the southern island. I raised my hands and called the flow of my water magic forward. It churned in my belly until it was pressing against my lungs. I held my breath, closing my eyes, before slowly letting the magic flow through me and into the bay.

A thin mist rose from the water's surface, creating a natural fog. I extended it in front of our ship and reached for the sea. All the soldiers would see was an evening fog rolling in with the tide. I turned to Riven. He called forth his shadows, covering the fog in a thin gray smoke.

In the darkness, no one on the island would be able to see the shape of our sails through the haze. Syrra stood at the bow of the ship with two faelights, leaving enough light for Gerarda to maneuver us out of the strait.

She raised her hand and closed it into a sharp fist. I held the mist in the air and untangled the braid of wind, letting the sail fall limp. Gerarda and the others moved without speaking. They lowered two slim canoes into the sea with a bag of Nikolai's inventions between the seats.

I just hoped they worked as well as he promised.

My chest tightened as Vrail and Nikolai dropped into the front of both canoes. They were each traveling with seasoned warriors, but I knew I wouldn't breathe easily until they were both back on the ship and safe.

Syrra nodded at me and Riven. She pulled a vial from her trouser pocket and shook the pale liquid inside until it turned a deep blue color. "Wait until it is translucent. No matter what you hear." She looked directly at me.

My neck flexed but I nodded. She hung the vial from one of the pegs in the mast before disappearing over the ledge with Gerarda and Elaran. There was a faint splash of water and then they were gone in the cloak of darkness Riven and I had created.

"They will be okay, *diizra*," Riven whispered from behind me.

I gulped and leaned against his chest. "You can't be certain."

"Vrail says certainties can't be trusted." I could hear the smirk in his voice. Riven stroked my shoulders as I stared at the vial, waiting for it to lighten to cerulean then fade to a pale lapis.

Something exploded in the distance.

I straightened my back, calling my water magic forward and lifting the ship onto its current. Riven grabbed my shoulder. "Wait, *diizra*."

He pointed to the vial and I held my breath.

More explosions sounded followed by a loud battle horn.

The liquid was barely tinted now. I lifted my hands but Riven shook his head.

The smell of smoke filled the air as another explosion sounded. This one was close enough that the flash of bright orange flames was visible through the haze, lighting the fog like lightning through clouds.

Finally the last of the blue dye cleared and Riven moved to the front of the ship. He lowered his shadows, navigating through the mist as I called a current underneath the thin hull. We lifted a few inches as we cruised onward with our sail filling backward.

The soldiers' shouts filled the beach as they loaded rocks from a ready-made pile into the buckets at the front of the catapult. Their slings were already loaded with sharp projectiles and large stones just as they had been in Koratha.

I watched, unable to do anything as our ship nestled along the shore. One tug and the catapult would fire directly at us.

I slowed our pursuit as the captain lifted his arm and the men stood with the rope between each fist. He slashed it through the air and his soldiers yanked on the trigger lines. But the catapult didn't budge.

An arrow had sliced through each of the ropes. I smirked proudly and watched as the load crashed to the ground behind the catapult. The soldiers shouted in terror and ran, but not fast enough to save them from being crushed under their own ammunition.

In the chaos, the soldiers along the second catapult pulled their cords too early and sent their rocks tumbling into the empty sea in front of us. I gripped the hold on my magic, causing the ship to lurch. I closed my eyes hoping the others had made it unscathed too.

A flare of bright blue fire exploded at the end of the burning docks. I let the veil of mist fall back into the sea as four glass vials flew through the air toward the beach. Riven blanketed the shore in darkness as orange smoke trailed out of each vial. He grabbed my hand and we dove into the water. He squeezed my arm and swam under the hull of the ship, waiting until it was safe for him to surface.

I snatched one last breath as I called a whirlwind along the beach. The vials of orange smoke grew into a cloud that covered every grain of sand. The soldiers coughed, falling to their knees as they grabbed at their throats, slowing suffocating.

Only when the beach was silent did I push the orange air up into the sky, too high to hurt us. Then I grabbed the vial Nikolai had given me and poured the contents into the sea. The magic of the water gravitated toward the elixir in glowing spirals of blue and silver. Riven broke through the surface beside me as four heads appeared close to shore.

I used my currents to carry us to the beach and bring the ship as close as possible while we stomped along in our wet clothes. Vrail and Nikolai looked up to the sky while Elaran searched the ground for the third seal. Gerarda grabbed her arm. It was a useless endeavour until I broke the glamour.

Vrail pointed to the small curve along the west side of the beach. Behind a wall of large stones that had been placed to break the waves coming from the channel was a narrow stretch of land. The southern tip of the southernmost island.

I nodded just as a chorus of screams sounded from the beach. A group of forty soldiers stormed onto the sand with swords in their hands. I lifted my arms to grab both blades strapped to my back but Gerarda shook her head. She pulled a short sword free in one hand and four throwing knives in the other. "We'll take care of this, Keera. You go to the seal."

The guilt of leaving my friends paralyzed me. We hadn't been expecting another troupe of soldiers. A horn sounded in the darkness and my stomach dropped. Damien had more ships stationed along these islands than our reports had led us to believe.

Riven grabbed my hand and pulled me into a run. Large black sails covered the stars as they approached from the western side. Riven cloaked the sea in a wall of shadow so their archers could not aim at the beach without hitting their own men and forcing their captain to sail without eyes.

We leaped over the first partition of rock and then climbed onto the second wall. My breaths wheezed as I pointed to the ground at the shiny seal marked in the sand. Tiny pools of water were placed along the circular pattern like sea glass. I leaped from the wall and rolled as I landed. My bloodstone dagger was already in my hand and I plunged it into the first pool at the edge of the seal.

Its magic wrapped around my arm and blade, anchoring me to the spot as I cut the perimeter of the spell. I pointed to the rocks with my other hand. "You're in range. Ready your bow."

Riven's jaw flexed. "Keera, I'm meant to help you." He nodded in the direction of the ship we could not see.

"There's nothing you can do for me but keep everyone alive!" I huffed a breath, refusing to look away from Riven until he agreed.

He pulled his bow from behind his cloak and waded into the water to peer around the wave wall. I drew a deep breath as I heard his arrow fly and finished tracing the outline of the seal. It pulled at my magic more than the others had, perhaps because there was more to drain. Before the circle was done, my eyes and mouth were dry and I could barely keep my sight focused on the intersecting lines and webbing of the inner pattern.

An arrow landed three feet from me along the beach. A soldier charged at me with an arrow against his cheek. Riven's shadows curled around his throat and the snap of his neck echoed off the stones. "Keep going!" he urged, firing another arrow at the scene along the beach.

My heart pounded against my chest, slow and heavy like even it was fighting to keep moving. I dragged my blade through the sand but it felt like stone, the river of silver liquid behind my blade became dammed by my slow pace.

I stepped between the pattern and a blotch of amber blood landed on the sand. I wiped my nose and cursed. This seal was taking more than either of the others and I was only halfway done. I gritted my teeth and pulled until the fiber of my muscles snapped. I knew the surge of magic would reinvigorate my powers and give me the energy to protect my friends. I just needed to break the seal.

I groaned as I cut the last intersecting line and the rivers of silver turned to gold. The hold on my arm released and I lifted the sandy blade to my palm, coating it in amber. I slammed the point of the bloodstone blade into the middle of the seal and a burst of silver light exploded over the beach.

I smiled at the bushes of magical berries that appeared along the shore and tasted iron. I wiped the blood from my nose already feeling my healing gift stitching my body back together. I didn't care as the blood merely smeared across my sweat laced face.

I only had eyes for Riven. The moment seemed to stretch on forever as Riven's back arched and he let out a blood-curdling howl like a wounded beast. I screamed his name so loudly it tore through my chest and echoed into the night.

He collapsed and his shadows faded revealing the three ships that had anchored themselves along the shore and had their canons pointed at the beach.

I charged at them and leaped over Riven's unconscious body. I lifted my arms and there was sudden flash of bright light. I soared above the wall of rocks, in disbelief at this new surge of power that let my body fly before I realized I wasn't in my body at all. Where my arms had lifted at my sides were now wings.

Mighty, golden wings of a soaring eagle.

I laughed but it only came out as a high-pitched whistle. I soared above the beach and saw all the chaos at once.

Syrra and Gerarda had lured the soldiers in between four large rocks so they were forced to charge in twos. Elaran sunk her arrows into them as the others picked off the rest. They would hold long enough for me to take care of the ships.

I dove. I tucked my wings against my new body on instinct and let myself fall toward their sails. I tried to feel the new magic underneath my skin and realized it was the only magic I had in this form. I let the flow of it surround my entire being and then I stretched my arms out one more time.

Lightning cracked from cloudless skies as I landed on the deck, in my own form again, with both my blades in my hands. The bolts of lightning set their masts ablaze. I fought the soldiers with steel and tendrils of fire that plucked their burnt bodies into the sea to be eaten by whatever fish didn't mind the taste of purchased swordsmen.

A large crack echoed through the night as the middle ship's mast fell onto the one beside it, splitting both ships in two. The soldiers fled their stations, jumping into the water for a chance at survival. But that was not a chance I was willing to give.

I plunged my blade into the back of a fleeing soldier and used his body as a shield as I raised my left arm. Thick walls of water lifted from the sea until all the men were caught in the still surface between them. Their squeals of terror were muffled as I let the water fold on top of them, crushing the ones who hadn't drowned.

Somehow my powers had yet to feel the slightest bit emptied. I dropped the dead soldier on the deck and holstered my blade. I jumped from the ship and let the fires flame bright behind me, so high they almost touched the stars. I didn't check to see if there were any survivors. I knew there were none.

I let a small wave of water wrap around my waist and carry me to shore. The few soldiers that were left turned to charge at me but I pulled the dozen arrows from my quiver and threw them into the air. My gusts launched them quicker than any bow and each man fell with an arrow in his neck.

I ran to Riven, rolling him onto his shoulder to check his breathing. It was slow, barely discernible, as was his faint heartbeat. He twitched from pain that left his face in a scowl; I knew there was nothing we could do for him here.

I lifted his knees together and stepped on the toes of his boots. I took one deep breath and pulled him forward, using the momentum to lift him onto my shoulders. I grabbed an abandoned spear and shook off its dead owner's hand as I walked. The surge of magic was finally settling and I knew we needed to get aboard.

For both my and Riven's sakes.

Gerarda walked backward, loosing arrows at the few straggling soldiers emerging from the fort to the north of the beach. "Is he dead?"

I shook my head as Vrail and Nikolai pulled one of the canoes onto shore and helped me lower Riven into it. A tear fell from Nikolai's face and landed on Riven's black leathers.

Syrra glanced down at Riven as she loosed another arrow. She and Gerarda flanked me on either side, flinging arrows into the remaining soldiers, but it served no use. We needed to go and we couldn't be followed.

I let the whirlwind in my chest grow until it sparked. Two bolts of lightning flooded the sky and set the long barracks ablaze. The soldiers dropped their weapons and raced to protect their stores.

I lowered my arms, exhausted, as a silhouette appeared against the smoke. Syrra raised her weapon but Gerarda frantically held out her arms. "That's not a soldier," she said with a wistful edge to her voice.

I leaned against my spear as Gerarda took cautious steps toward an elderly woman. She walked with a stick that was taller than her curved back. It was painted in layers—green, purple, red, orange, and yellow—the colors of the five Fractured Isles.

Gerarda lifted her left hand in front of her chest and swirled her right hand around it as she lowered into a bow. When she spoke, the rhythm sounded like Elvish but the words were different.

"Gerarda is of the islands," Syrra whispered, lowering her bow. I nodded, too tired to answer.

Gerarda's voice got louder, bordering on shouting, but the woman only shook her head. The headpiece she wore trailed down the two parts of her hair and was braided into her gray tresses. She raised her hand and said one word in the King's Tongue.

"Go."

My heart broke for Gerarda, but Elaran got to her first. She wrapped her arms around Gerarda's shoulder as she kicked and screamed, begging the elder to come with us in every tongue she knew. But the Halfling only lifted her chin and walked back into the flames. I didn't need to speak her dialect to understand.

She would not abandon her homeland just as we could not abandon ours.

CHAPTER THIRTY-FIVE

"THERE'S NO TIME," Gerarda shouted, leaping from the edge of the ship to adjust the sails. "Leave the canoes."

Vrail and Elaran abandoned the canoes and helped pull Riven onto the deck. His face was still twitching in pain while unconscious. My vision blurred as I grabbed his hand but all I could feel was cold, stinging magic through our bond.

Nikolai ran to my side with a pile of vials in his arms. "I grabbed them from your room," he whispered frantically, opening one of the stoppers of the elixir to dull Riven's powers.

I lifted Riven's chin and gently pulled his bottom lip down as Nikolai let the liquid trickle down his throat. The crease in Riven's brow settled though his face still twitched.

Vrail knelt beside us and something cracked under her knee. She leaned over onto Nikolai's lap to reveal a shattered vial. The clear contents were specked with violet.

"Don't worry about it." I sighed in relief. "That's not one of his anyway."

It was the only elixir I had brought for the trip, but I didn't care about that now. If we couldn't get Riven's pain under control I was never going to be able to fall asleep anyway.

I grabbed the pale blue elixir and popped the lid free. Nikolai held open Riven's mouth as I poured the painkiller down his throat. Finally, the tremors stopped but Riven did not open his eyes.

"We need to get him to Feron." Syrra frowned down at us with her arms crossed. "He is the only one who will be able to help."

Nikolai pulled a notebook from his bag. "I will send Feron a message now." He scribbled something on the paper and looked up at Syrra and I. "Where should he meet us?"

"The portal north of the hook."

Nikolai quickly finished the message and set the page aflame.

"Keera, the sails!" Gerarda yelled from the wheel of the ship.

I wiped my eyes and let the whirlwind gather in my chest. My magic was straining after everything I had done on the beach, but I had enough to weave a large gust. The ship lurched forward and Elaran and Gerarda expertly steered us around the wreckage.

I lay back onto the deck with a heavy chest. Vrail passed me a skin of water and I finished it in a single swallow. When I wiped my mouth, a streak of amber coated my sleeve. I'd forgotten I had blood all over my face.

"This happened when you were breaking the seal, didn't it?" Vrail asked, wetting one of Nikolai's handkerchiefs for me.

I took it and wiped my forehead. "It's nothing I can't handle."

Vrail frowned.

"How can you possibly be worried about me right now?" I pointed at Riven.

Vrail's eyes narrowed. "Each seal seems to take a greater toll. We still have two left, Keera."

I shrugged. "Whatever happens, my powers grow the moment the seal opens. The pain doesn't scare me."

Vrail leaned back, unconvinced, but unwilling to argue.

"Your powers did more than just grow." Nikolai was staring like he had never seen me before. "Forgive me, Keera dear, but did I not see you sprout wings?"

I huffed a laugh. My thoughts had been with Riven from the moment he fell. In all the chaos I hadn't had time to process my new magic or the new form that came with it.

"I think I was an eagle," I whispered in disbelief. I turned to Syrra. "I thought transformation was a Dark Fae power."

Her dark eyes assessed me curiously before she answered. "It is one of the gifts that was shared between the Light Fae and the Dark Fae, though it was extremely rare among magic wielders."

I swallowed. "Was my mother a shape shifter?"

Syrra shook her head. "El'ravaasir was a powerful wielder, but she only had one form. As I said, it is a rare gift."

I finished cleaning my face. "Can any of the other Fae shift into a creature?"

Nikolai's jaw pulsed but it was Vrail who finally answered. "No, the last of those to take a creature's form died some time ago." She glanced down where Riven lay at her feet.

My chest heaved as my gaze followed hers. Riven looked as if he was resting, but I could see the hints of pain still carved into his face. I knelt and the others left me to keep watch over him on my own.

Without my elixir I couldn't sleep, but I didn't want to. I sat beside Riven until the suns began to rise, stroking his hair and gripping his hand through every twitch.

Elaran came and wrapped a warm cloak around my shoulders and took the first watch in the eagle's nest. I hadn't moved by the following dusk when we reached the hook along the northern shore of Elverath.

Pirmiith and Lash were waiting for us with Fyrel and some of the other Shades. They helped carry us into the carriage while the others rowed their small boat back to the ship to sail it home.

"Lay down, Mistress." Fyrel patted the makeshift cot she had made beside Riven's.

I raised a brow.

"Keera, sorry." She patted the cot once more and I relented. Fyrel gave me a serious nod before she closed the doors and took her post at the front of the cabin. I knew her watchful eyes would keep us safe as we made the journey to Aralinth.

It was only a few short hours away, but I couldn't keep my eyes open any longer. The rocking of the carriage made my eyelids heavy enough to close. I still held Riven's hand as the darkness claimed me too.

CHAPTER THIRTY-SIX

My flesh was burning. I opened my eyes and saw planks of burnt wood under my hands. I flexed the hand with Feron's ring on it, grateful I had brought it with me for the journey.

I lifted my head and saw Damien sitting on a throne in the middle of the burning ship. Flames licked the deck, but no smoke filled my lungs. As soon as my mind accepted that this was a dream, the pain disappeared. I pushed myself off the deck and walked through the flames to reach him.

"I will kill ten Halflings for every soldier you drowned on that beach." His jade eye shifted over his snarl. The statue Damien had made himself into was beginning to crack.

"And what will you do when I kill all your men?"

Damien stood and pulled the end of his sleeves so his black jacket lay perfectly flat. "You do not have the numbers and I can always buy more swords."

Damien waved his hand and the burning ships changed to the streets of Koratha. Soldiers dressed in royal armor were scurrying in every direction, grabbing people from their homes and cutting their arms to draw blood.

Children screamed as their parents were ripped from them. Those with red-stained arms were thrown to the sides to weep while the amber blooded were loaded into carts with bound limbs and gagged mouths.

Some were too young to walk on their own.

My eyes welled but I refused to turn away.

"Then we shall kill those swords too." I lifted my chin to make sure my voice didn't tremble.

Damien snarled. "Have I not made myself clear?" He waved his arm and the Shades appeared. Not dead and hanging over buckets the way they had in those first nightmares, but beaten and bruised, pricked with needles again and again to spill their blood. Their eyes were red from crying, staring at me like I was the one who was doing this to them. "What will you tell the Halflings I arrest for *your* crimes? That you were too concerned with bringing back magic for your new more powerful friends to wield than you are with saving their lives?"

A cold wave washed down my spine.

"Did you think I didn't know?" Damien's snarl turned into a vile grin. "It took me longer than it should have to realize you didn't come to the Order on a rescue mission. I had to torture dozens of guards before I learned the truth."

The screaming figures of men being prodded with hot swords filled the space behind the Shades.

"Why else would you come with a single ship to ferry so many?" Damien waved his hand again and the watery seal along the ground of the Order came into view. "So I investigated myself. The spell was almost faded by the time I arrived, but I recognized it for what it was. You coming to the Fractured Isles and leaving all those Halflings behind only served to prove my suspicions."

"Yet you stand here taunting me?" I raised a brow.

Damien's smile widened. "I'm impressed, Keera, that you have finally put aside your quest of being a savior and started going after an ounce of the power I have. You've almost become a worthy adversary. Almost. But there can only be one me."

I spat at the ground. "I am *nothing* like you."

Damien sat back down on his throne, relishing the tortured screams that echoed around us. "No? You seek to gain power for Fae friends. Do you hope they will forget what you have done if you restore their magic? Do you think they will forget all the ones you've killed?"

Damien lifted his chin and the images around us shifted again. Now we were surrounded by countless Halflings, some with faces I recognized, others nameless Elverin from Damien's imagination. All of them had a thick line of amber running down their necks as they fell to the ground.

My hands turned to fists and I fought the urge to strangle Damien. But he was wrong. I had already faced these ghosts and won. These faces and images Damien wanted to pass off as memories did not scare me now.

I was free.

It was my turn to laugh. Damien's lip curled as I stepped toward him. The bloody Halflings disappeared and instead were replaced by the burning images of Damien's ships and drowning soldiers. I waved my hand to make it clear to him that it was my mind that was controlling our shared dream now and cast an image of the palace of Koratha falling into the sea and Damien's body hanging from the white stone walls of the city.

The eye patch was gone, so the entire world could see his true self in death.

A smug satisfaction flowed through me as Damien paled.

I grabbed my dagger and held it up to his chin, forcing him to look up at me. "You think you scare me with your threats and lies?" My breath was so close to his face that it fogged the red steel of my blade. "I have bested you not once, but twice. Why should I heed your warnings that I am incapable of a third?"

I looked around the dream and smiled. "You have spent too long messing with my mind." I pushed the tip of my dagger into his throat, not enough to end the dream, but enough to haunt Damien when he woke. "Now it is my turn."

Damien leaned back in his throne trying to get away from my blade. I waved my hand and his golden chair disappeared, sending him crumpling to the floor. Damien lashed at my legs with his arm, flinging spit at me as he looked up at his hanging corpse.

"I dispatched my Arsenal to Volcar the moment I realized what you were trying to accomplish." He coiled his limbs around himself. "Once they destroy it, I will destroy you."

Damien let out an unhinged laugh and fell back onto the ground.

"Then I will get there first," I promised, and slashed my blade across his throat.

CHAPTER THIRTY-SEVEN

I COUGHED MYSELF AWAKE. A strong hand slapped my back, helping the rest clear my airway.

"You inhaled too much smoke," Rheih said in between the slaps. "Your healing gift couldn't fully clear your lungs."

I coughed again and black liquid splattered onto the ground.

"Tea from Elder birch bark." Rheih poured it down my throat until my sheets were splattered with black specks. "Clears ash from the lungs. Inhale too much and it can fatally strain your heart." She tutted her tongue to the top of her mouth. "But I don't think you will die in your sleep tonight. Thanks to me."

I wiped my mouth with my sleeve and swallowed another swig of the tea. A vial of clear elixir with swirls of violet shadow fell onto my lap. Rheih folded her arms, pleased with herself. "The fast talker told me you needed more of it."

I didn't even have time to feel relieved. I stashed the vial in my pocket and pulled myself up from the cot. We weren't in the infirmary in Myrelinth. The room was small and bright, made entirely of wood so thick that I could see the tiny veins of water pumping through the grain.

"Where is Vrail?" I spotted my weapons belt beside the cot and put it on. "I need to speak to everyone. Now."

Rheih clucked her tongue and shook her head of gray curls. "No one appreciates a healer." Her yellow eyes narrowed at me. "Not even healers themselves."

"You're the best healer I know." I bent down and pressed a kiss to her cheek. I only had a moment to enjoy the apparent shock on Rheih's face before she settled back into her grumpy state.

She pointed to the door. "They're waiting for you in the council room."

I ran out before she could say anything more.

Sil'abar was much brighter than it had been the night of that first dinner Feron had invited me to when I'd crossed into Aralinth. The wood split along the tunnels within the massive trunk to let sunlight into the paths. There were no doors in the palace, but wider and taller splits in the grain that led to different rooms. I pressed my fingers to one and it snapped shut, leaving nothing but a thin seam of wood where the opening had been.

I raised a brow at the magic and pressed my hands to the seam again. It opened once more to display a small sitting room filled with books. I had not noticed the rooms the last time I searched through the palace. They had all been shut to keep an outsider from breaching their walls.

But I wasn't an outsider any longer.

I ran down the hall, listening for voices I couldn't find. I crossed over to a second hall and found a large room at the end of it decorated with weapons I had never seen before. Shields made of ice that did not melt. Arrows made of flowing water that held their shape, reflecting the warm light from the large faelight in the middle of the ceiling.

But that was not what drew me into the room. In the middle of the wall was a long sword. Or what once had been a sword. Now it was a collection of tiny fragments, too many to count, arranged in the shape of a long blade. Each piece of metal glowed and matched the lines of gold pressed into the white marble handle.

It was the most beautiful weapon I had ever seen.

"Faelin's sword," Syrra said, appearing beside me without a sound. "The only blood-bound weapon still known to us. Though obviously fractured beyond use."

"Faelin . . ." I recognized the name from one of Darythir's stories. "The first of the Fae."

Syrra nodded. "*Niinokwenar.*"

Fae mother.

I lifted my hand to traced my fingers over the glass protecting the sword. "Was it made gold to match her eyes?"

Syrra shook her head. "Faelin was the last to wield it, but it belonged to the Elves long before her time. It is said it turned gold the day that she cast the spell that made the shadow sun and shattered the day she left this life. It stays here as a reminder of what Faelin did for us, how she and her kin vanquished the *waateyshir* for good."

I shivered, remembering the shadow creatures Lash had painted with his flames and smoke. They had been the adversaries of the Elverin for eons. I drummed my fingers along the glass and felt something pulsing from the sword through it. "It has magic." My eyes went wide with wonder.

Syrra smiled. "A mighty weapon for only the mightiest of warriors. Perhaps one day we will learn how to forge such blades again."

She placed a hand on my shoulder and gestured to the hall. "Everyone is waiting."

I nodded and followed her into what appeared to be the center of Sil'abar herself. I could hear the hum of voices from behind the sealed doors, more than the group I'd sailed here with.

Syrra lifted her hand to the trunk and the wood split open.

There were dozens of Elverin inside. Each one fell silent and lowered their head as we walked into the circular room.

Feron sat at the center with Darythir and Lash beside him. Syrra took a seat in one of the empty chairs and I realized what was happening.

A council had been called.

Feron raised his hand and every pair of eyes fell to him. "Keera, welcome." I glanced around the room and saw other purple eyes mixed in with faces I recognized—Nikolai and Pirmiith, Gerarda and Elaran, and Fyrel and Myrrah too. I looked behind them and saw they weren't the only ones from the Order in the room.

"I called a council after receiving reports of Halflings being—"

"Grabbed from the streets by the carriage load?" I finished for him. My stomach churned into tight knots. I knew Damien would make good on his threat, but I didn't realize it would happen so quickly.

Feron's brow furrowed. "Yes." He leaned forward to look at Syrra.

"I didn't tell her." She stared at me curiously.

I took a deep breath. I hadn't planned to announce this to a packed room, but we were running out of time every moment we wasted.

"Before Gerarda was able to get me out of the capital Damien injected me with an elixir of his own making." I pointed to my arm where his needle had gone in. "It created a connection between our minds, allowing us to communicate while we dream."

There was a long silence where dozens of blinking eyes stared at me with their brows half raised. Then the room exploded into a fury of questions.

"Enough!" I shouted as loud as I could. "We do not have time. Damien knows about the seals and somehow he knows their locations. His fleet waits for us in Volcar and his new Arsenal is on their way to destroy the seals."

"Damien told you this?" Gerarda flipped one of her thin blades through her fingers.

I nodded. "He discovered the faded seal at the Order and discerned our plans when we came for the Fractured Isles."

Gerarda's eyes narrowed. "Or he put it together in the dream. Damien sits on a throne won through lies, why should we not assume he is lying now?"

Elaran ran her hand through her mane of curls and wrapped her arm around Gerarda as she stared me down.

"We can't be sure." I turned to Feron and Syrra. "But do we want to risk the chance to restore magic on the hope that Damien has spun yet another lie? If we are wrong, his men will reach Volcar first and they will destroy the seal before we get a chance to break it."

"Is that possible?" Syrra asked, interpreting her own question for Darythir as well as everything I had said.

I scanned the room for the one person I thought could answer the question, but Vrail only shrugged.

"A spell of that nature is like any other living creature." Feron rested both hands on his cane. "It has methods of defending itself, but it can fall prey to the right weapon used at the wrong time."

"A blade?" Killian stilled in his place along the circle.

Rheih huffed her own laugh. My brows crossed, wondering how she had reached the room before I did. "Poison would be the wiser choice." Her yellow eyes met mine. "And it seems the false king has a habit of concocting his own recipes."

I swallowed thickly knowing Rheih was right. I turned to Feron. "Can the spell be poisoned? Would that be enough to destroy it?"

Feron's full lips almost disappeared into a straight line across his face. "It would depend on the poison, but if Aemon's son was clever enough to learn of the seals on his own, we must assume he knows enough to destroy them."

Darythir waved to get Feron's attention. When he nodded, she asked her question by hand.

"I would assume the magic would be sealed away forever," Feron answered in both languages.

My shoulders fell. "Then we must make haste to Volcar." I faced the pairs of Shades across the room. "That is our best chance at protecting everyone. Once the seals are broken, then we'll work on getting those Halflings back. Every last one of them."

Myrrah gave a stiff nod and the Shades behind her followed.

Feron stood from his seat. "The Fae shall join you. If Damien plans to defend Volcar with his full force then we shall meet him with ours."

Myrrah unlocked her chair and moved it into the circle so she could be seen by everyone else standing along the edge of the room. "And the Shades will fight alongside you both."

Tears welled in my eyes as Pirmiith stood and placed his hand over his face and then his mouth. "And the Elves shall join you."

My breath caught. I reached out, instinctively feeling for Riven's hand, but it wasn't there. Riven wasn't in the room at all to witness the Elverin finally uniting in this fight, just as he had always wanted.

My chest heaved but I nodded, accepting each of their swords.

I turned to Nikolai. "How long will it take to prepare the ships?"

He bit his lip before answering. "By suns down tomorrow."

My stomach plummeted.

Gerarda grabbed my arm. "Even if Damien dispatched his Arsenal the night we left the Order, they still have not reached Volcar yet."

I tried to do the calculations in my head, but I couldn't. I had spent too many nights fighting my own battles to count the days, nor did I know how quickly the trip could be made by sea. I turned to Myrrah. "How soon can we expect them?"

Myrrah folded her arms across her chest. "It will be tight, but they should still be at sea for five more days. Two if the winds were nothing but favorable."

The muscles in my back eased by the smallest fraction. It was a window. A tiny window, but better than nothing.

"Nikolai, make the necessary arrangements." I turned to Syrra. "Work with the Fae and Myrrah and make sure everyone is equipped with whatever weapons and armor they need." They both nodded and the crowd began to disperse.

Rheih started out of the room but I grabbed her hand. Feron had somehow sensed that I wanted to speak with him. He waited, perfectly still in his chair as the room emptied.

His gaze flickered to Killian's and then to his own ring on my finger. "I trust this *connection* is why you asked for my ring?"

My cheeks flushed and I nodded.

"Can I also trust that whatever this connection is, you are certain it is not putting the Elverin at risk?" Feron's voice carried a serious tone that lacked its usual warmth.

I nodded again.

"It didn't work the way Damien anticipated." I swallowed, not wanting to get into the details of what had been happening in those dreams. "I can control them as much as he can. And Rheih's elixirs have stopped them completely."

Feron's chin lifted. "Not completely. You knew about the Halfling attacks before we did."

I cleared my throat. "My vial of elixir was damaged on our way out of the Isles. I tried to stay conscious, but—"

Killian grabbed my hand and squeezed. "You did nothing wrong, Keera. You got everyone back to the portal safely."

My throat seared for the first time in days. "Not everyone." My vision blurred, but I refused to let my fears overwhelm me. I wanted Feron to confirm them first. "Where is Riven?"

Feron's gaze fell to the floor. Rheih clucked her tongue in a dejected tone that made my skin shiver.

Killian stepped between us. "Feron thought it best for Riven's magic to be fully suppressed," Killian answered, squeezing my hand. "That way the pain can't affect him nearly as much."

I swallowed a sob and nodded. "Will that protect him? What will happen when the next seal breaks?"

Feron flexed his jaw and shrugged. "There is no way to know. There are no remedies to Riventh's fractured magic. As the magic grows, his pain may only get worse. He could succumb to it completely."

My entire body froze. I was unable to breathe, unable to think. My feet were not touching the ground, instead I was drowning in a pool of my worst fears.

"Or," Feron said, grabbing my shoulder. "When the magic is restored, a balance may be reached across Elverath. Perhaps his magic will be balanced too."

Killian's jaw hardened and I could see the doubt settling into his face. He didn't dare meet my eye.

"I may be able to help." Rheih gave a loud huff and folded her arms. "Riventh helped create that elixir of yours." She nodded at my pocket. "He let me bottle some of his magic to add to the recipe. Perhaps yours will extend him the same relief your bond does."

"Take it." My voice was a desperate rasp. "Whatever you need. Take it all."

Rheih's lip trembled as she patted my arms. "I will fetch you in the morning. The most important thing you can do for him is rest."

Rheih left the room with a nod.

I turned to Feron. "Can I see him?"

Feron's brows knitted together as he glanced at Killian. "I don't think that is best," Feron whispered.

I stepped out of his grasp. "Why?" I turned to Killian, my joints bent and my muscles tight like I was preparing for an attack.

Feron's pale purple eyes were swirling storms of pity.

Killian cleared his throat. "Riven's magic has always reacted to your presence, Keera. You can't see him without causing a spike in his pain."

All the blood drained out of me. "Me being close to him will hurt him?" The words scraped against my throat like shattered glass refusing to come out.

Killian's arm dropped and his mouth hung open though no words came.

My lip trembled. "I cannot say goodbye?"

Killian's eyes were misted but he straightened his back and shook his head.

My chest cracked in half. Rivers of tears ran down my cheeks and my head spun until I couldn't see the ground underneath my feet. I knew if I closed my eyes my knees would give way and my body would collapse on the ground, but I didn't so much as blink.

Crumbling into my despair would do nothing for Riven. Even though my throat burned and my mind mapped the exact path I needed to take to the kitchens for a casket of wine, I didn't move. Riven had been my strength for too long for me to waver now. He had stood by me through the darkness and kept his burl lit even when he had no reason to hope.

I couldn't let myself succumb. I had to hold onto the light for both of us even when the tiniest spark seemed too hard to grasp.

I wiped my eyes and faced both of them with a strength I didn't know I had. "Make sure someone is always with him from the moment we leave." I turned around and headed out the door. "If Riven dies, he shouldn't die alone."

CHAPTER THIRTY-EIGHT

I DIDN'T NEED THE MAP in my pocket to take me where I needed to go. I ran out of Sil'abar without care for all the eyes I attracted and didn't stop until I reached the garden. I pulled the vial from my bag that I kept for portal travel and placed a berry in the small pool between the two Elder birch that twisted together.

I didn't take the trail into Myrelinth, but instead marched north to the small pond that had just reopened its portal. I didn't know where to place my *winvra* so I threw it into the water without care. The pool swirled with auric ribbons, and I stepped into it but remained perfectly dry.

When I surfaced, I stepped out of the lake at the Order. The same place I had learned to swim as a child. The familiar scent of brine and salt pierced through my chest and made my red eyes sting even more than they already did.

The guard tower was empty and there were no lanterns lit along the grounds of the keep. I wrapped my cloak around my body to shield me from the evening gusts and marched toward the north side of the island.

The part I never went to.

The spot where she was buried.

My Brenna.

No one would know that her grave was a grave at all. But even with the overgrowth of grass, I could feel her presence in the earth. Her bones called out like they belonged to me. In every way that mattered they did. Brenna had no family to remember her, no mourners to kneel at her grave and water the wildflowers with their tears.

I collapsed to my knees beside the small roll in the hill along the cliffside and screamed. My gusts whirled around me, lashing out in every direction just like my pain, carrying my shrieks out to sea.

I pounded my fist into the ground and sobbed. "I can't do this," I yelled to the sky. To my ancestors. To my mother. To whoever was listening. "Not again."

I had already been forced to plunge my blade through one lover's heart and now I had to do it once more. Even though Riven would be miles away from me, even though his chest would not bleed as Brenna's had, whether it was the next seal or the last, when my bloodstone dagger sank into the ground his life would end just the same.

And I would be the one to take it.

The walls that I had packed my grief behind crumbled and buried me. I bent over my knees until my forehead scraped the earth as I begged the sea herself to end this. When she didn't answer by pulling me into her depths, I yanked the red dagger free from my belt and threw it on Brenna's grave.

"I don't want this anymore," I screamed. The image of my mother's face in the garden fluttered across my mind but my pain shredded it to pieces. She never had to live with the guilt of the Light Fae's sacrifice. She never had to carry the weight of it for decades because she was gone in a matter of days.

But I had to carry it all. The weight of my decisions, the weight of hers, and the weight of the ones I would be forced to make. My heart was shattered and I knew there was no way to put the pieces back together. There was no way to heal from this once it was done.

I would finish my job. I would break the seals, but then I would plunge that dagger through the pile of pieces that was my heart. That blade had taken so much from me; it was only fitting that it should be the end of me too.

The dagger that took the Blade and both her lovers.

A warm breeze flittered across my cheek like a soft caress. I choked on a laugh, picturing Brenna wiping away my tears. "A promise is a promise," I whispered, an echo of the vow we had made to each other.

Someone approached behind me. The scent of parchment and fire smoke wafted through the air and I knew I was safe. My body hardened, waiting for Killian's touch, but it wasn't his hand that fell on my back.

Gerarda knelt on the ground beside me and passed me one of Nikolai's handkerchiefs. I grabbed it but didn't wipe the dirt or tears from my face. "How did you find me?"

"It wasn't hard to figure out." Gerarda nodded at the grave.

My breath hitched mid-sob. "You knew?"

Gerarda's sharp brow pricked upward. "That you loved her? Or that you buried her here?"

"Both."

"Everyone with eyes knew the first, Keera." Gerarda's gaze went soft. "That you loved her and that she loved you."

A new stream of tears rolled down my cheeks. That love had gotten Brenna killed. "And the second?"

Gerarda swallowed guiltily. "I watched you bury her that day."

I winced. Gerarda had never said a word.

She flipped a tiny blade through her fingers and stared at it as she spoke. "I didn't tell you because I thought it would make that day harder for you given my and Brenna's . . . shared history."

I huffed a laugh. I had almost forgotten about that night in the corridor.

Gerarda threw her blade over the cliff edge and turned her body to face me. Her small hands grabbed mine and she finally met my gaze. "I know we weren't on the best of terms, but I have always been sorry that you lost her in the Trials. Brenna deserved so much more than this island."

I blinked, letting Gerarda's words sink in. Figures moved in the distance. Syrra and Nikolai stood with Vrail, far enough away to give me space but close enough to hear. Beside them was Killian, folded over and out of breath.

Without any other reason than knowing I was in pain, my family had come for me. That gesture filled some of the empty parts of me with warmth, but the hollows still echoed with loneliness and grief.

It was time they knew the whole of it. If they were to stand with me, I wanted them to know everything they stood beside.

I tugged at the end of my sleeve along my left wrist. Somehow, I gathered the strength to begin. "Hildegard never told you how Brenna died?"

Gerarda tilted her head. "She failed her Trial of . . ."

"Loyalty." I nodded. "Was yours an easy one to fail?" The Shades weren't meant to discuss their Trials with initiates and many of the Shades kept the practice well after they earned their hoods. The Trials weren't something any of us wanted to remember.

Gerarda's brows knitted together. "I was fed poison and the person with the antidote would give it to me if I disparaged the Crown. I obviously did not."

I huffed a laugh. If only we had been given that option. I pulled up my sleeve and ignored Gerarda's gasp as she read Brenna's name. "Brenna didn't die in her Trial of Loyalty—she died in *mine*." I swallowed the thickness at my throat. "Damien and Brenna had history from before she came to the Order. You knew her well enough to know that she didn't care he was a prince."

Gerarda gave a half-hearted chuckle, clinging to every word. Her dark eyes seemed to flick from mine to my mouth, unsure of where to look or what she was hearing. Killian stared at me with deep pity; he already knew how this story ended.

"He spent years tormenting her even after she came," I continued, my tongue sharp with venom as I remembered the way she would come back bruised and broken. "She wanted to end him, end all of it. She joked about how two Shades could take down the entire regime, but soon that joke grew into something more . . . It grew into a promise. A promise that we would do *everything* in our power to end Aemon's reign, but we grew too confident, too quickly."

Gerarda's breath stilled. "Damien suspected you?"

I nodded. "He told his father that it was too high a risk to have such talents be so fond of each other. He said we needed to be loyal to the Crown and there was only one way to prove it." My voiced cracked and I ran my finger over Brenna's name.

"Oh, Keera." Gerarda sighed, grabbing my hand.

I looked down at my lap knowing if I saw any of their faces I would crumble into another fit of sobs. "When I was called to my Trial the room was empty. Aemon and Hildegard were there and so was Damien. He took great pleasure in explaining how he thought the Trial of Loyalty was the most important of all. *Where heroes were made* is what he said. And then he pulled down the curtain and she was there."

Gerarda squeezed my hand. My tear fell on the back of her palm but neither of us moved. The story was like a rock rolling down a hill and it had picked up too much momentum to stop now.

"He told me the task was simple. I could kill Brenna and claim my hood or refuse and his father would take my head. But it was clear only one of us was walking out of that hall alive."

Gerarda's shoulders fell. "And you made the choice to live?"

"No." The word was harsh coming out of my lips. "Brenna had already made the choice. She pleaded for me to kill her and I drove this dagger through her chest." I pointed to the bloodstone blade where it still laid across the grave. My lips trembled as I faced Gerarda with a harsh truth only a Shade could find comfort in. "I gave her a quick death."

Gerarda's eyes swam with sympathy. "You made a choice. One many would make."

I shook my head. "I never had a choice. Brenna had already taken it from me. Damien never knew, but I was close enough to see the staining on her lips. Somehow, she had expected him to do what he did . . . She poisoned herself just before the Trial and her last words were the ones she knew would convince me to do it."

Gerarda lowered her head to meet my gaze. Her brows were crinkled as she waited to hear what words could cause one to shove a dagger through their own lover's heart.

"You promised." The same words that had haunted me since that day.

Tears streamed down Gerarda's face. I turned to the others and theirs were misted too.

"That's why you won't make promises," Killian whispered, his eyes were red and hollow.

I nodded. "I was already trying to pay one debt. I don't have room for another."

Killian's gaze trailed down my arm to where he knew the names of innocents were carved into my skin. I undid the lacing at my neck and my dark brown cloak fell to the ground. I pulled my tunic free from my trousers and turned to expose my back.

Nikolai wretched onto the ground, tears already soaking his cheeks from my tale, but Syrra's gasp was the deepest. She cursed under her breath as I felt the weight of her stare on my scars. "Who did that to you?"

"Damien," I answered, without turning around to face them. "Each Shade is inked with the symbol of their most impressive Trial. Damien decided that he wanted to call on old traditions to celebrate my *special* achievement. He carved it himself."

Gerarda's breathing stopped and her face paled as she took in the scars. Vrail choked on the bile in her throat and Nikolai kneeled to hand her a waterskin.

"After he had finished, I took Brenna's body to bury her. I had the mage pen Damien had used on me in my pocket and decided that I wanted a scar that *I* had chosen. A scar that showed he hadn't broken me. A scar that meant the promise was still alive."

"So you carved Brenna's name," Gerarda whispered in awe.

"Her name was only the first." I turned slowly. I had no shame that they could see my bare chest. Their eyes were trailing along other parts of me anyway. "Every time Aemon ordered me to take a life. Every time I was forced to slay an innocent. I carved their name into me." I turned to Syrra, embarrassment heating my cheeks. "I was inspired by the traditions of your predecessors. Each name was a tiny little rebellion and way to reclaim what had been taken from me. I made the ritual my own."

Syrra placed an open palm over her eyes and then her heart. "It is an honor to see your scars of battle."

I scoffed. "They are a record of my failings, not my survival."

Syrra shook her head and closed the distance between us in four paces. "They are the markings of a warrior who made herself into a shield for her people."

My rebuttal caught in my throat.

Gerarda's cold hand grazed across my upper arm. "Some of these names were not yours to take." Her dark eyes snapped to mine. Gerarda had been the one to scribe the execution orders for the king. "That Halfling told me what you did for his family and those Shades. How many times did you bear the brunt of Aemon's order?"

I swallowed. "I knew how badly taking a life could scar. After Brenna, I tried to save as many as I could. Sometimes that meant funneling Halflings into safe houses and sometimes it meant taking execution orders so the Shades need not carry them out."

A tear ran down Gerarda's cheek. "You never said anything."

"And you never said anything about your losses either." I smiled as warmly as I could manage. "We were raised to think of each other as opponents, not to share in each other's weaknesses."

Vrail's voice was a dark rasp over the wind. "An army of competitors can be wielded; an army of comrades can overtake."

Gerarda and I glanced at each other and nodded.

I pulled the tunic back on and stood. "I will do my duty to the Elverin and make sure the seals are opened. But"—I turned to face them all, knowing they knew the truth of it now—"I will not survive killing the person who matters most to me again. When the seals are broken, I will consider my promise kept."

Nikolai glanced at Killian almost like he expected him to say something. But the prince was silent, as if speaking would ink his brother's death into the histories and carve it into my skin. At least one of us held onto a glimmer of hope.

Nikolai kneeled beside me and grabbed my hand. "Riven would not want you to put him above everyone else." Nikolai's jaw clenched. "But there is more hope than you know."

"I don't have the strength for hope." My entire body sagged toward the ground. "It seems fate has dealt me the same hand again. I know how to play it."

And then the game will be done.

CHAPTER THIRTY-NINE

NO ONE SPOKE as we traveled to the ports. It felt like the entire city had joined us for the journey, the trail ahead was full of children and families in constant embrace. The war had finally come to knock on the doors of the *Faelinth* and too many of its residents had already lived through the perils to come.

It was painted on their faces. Grief and fear that stirred inside each of them until it turned into resolve. There was no other choice, but it didn't make it an easy one. The united tension made it hard to breathe as the convoy reached the beach.

The children were already barefoot, running across the sand and leaving footprints of every possible color. Bright and shiny under the light of the setting suns. I took a deep breath at the sight and knew the others saw it too. This is what we were fighting for. The time to protect ourselves from the miseries of the Crown had gone, but perhaps if we fought hard enough we could spare the next generation of Elverin from the same fate.

I swallowed the burning sensation in my throat and recognized it for what it was. Fear of failing again. It terrified me, the thought of what Damien could do to this place, but I would do everything in my power to prevent it.

Killian rode beside me. He had become something of a shadow ever since we returned to the *Faelinth*. Rarely speaking, but always there. I wondered if he felt like he owed it to Riven to protect me. My stomach lurched at the thought. Riven had spent so much of his time trying to spare me any harm, but when it mattered most I couldn't do the same for him.

Killian opened his mouth to speak but I spoke first. "Is it about this mission?"

Killian's jaw snapped shut and he shook his head.

"Then it is a distraction." I dismounted my horse and unlatched my saddlebags. "And we cannot afford any distractions."

I didn't need to look back to know my footprints had turned almost gray. I had no space for any other emotion beyond grief. But I would reshape it, mold it into something sharp and dangerous, use it to stoke my power and destroy whoever waited for us in Volcar.

I reached the dock along the port and saw a group of Shades dressed in brown cloaks the same color as my own. Fyrel stood with them and next to them was Gwyn.

My heart raced as I saw they were both dressed to fight.

"Is this meant to be a joke?" I turned to Myrrah and Gerarda behind them. "They are barely sixteen!"

Fyrel lifted her chin and straightened her back like an initiate waiting for her command. Gwyn's blue eyes narrowed and she dropped to the ground, slashing at my leg with hers. By the time my eyes opened, she had a knife pressed to my throat.

I took a deep breath before gently pushing her off me but Gwyn took the opportunity to pin my arms.

Gerarda smirked proudly.

"You've been training her?" I snarled.

Gerarda crossed her arms. "She was angry. I merely gave her a place to channel it."

Gwyn waved her hand at me and then signed several things very quickly. I didn't need an interpreter to know what she meant when she dragged her hand across her left eye.

My shoulders fell. "Gwyn, Damien will not be there."

Her cheeks turned pink and she stomped her foot. I tried to remain calm, but there was no way I was going to let her on that ship.

I placed my hands on her shoulders, grateful she didn't immediately shove them off. "I am not discounting all the training you have done. Gerarda would only spend time with you if you showed promise."

Gwyn smiled and it almost took my breath away. But it still was not enough for me to let her risk her life.

"If you want to meet Damien on the battlefield then I will not block your chance, but you will need to go through the same tests every Shade takes *after* we return from Volcar."

Gwyn shook her head, her hands gesturing wildly in front of her. I cupped them in my own and bent so we were speaking eye to eye. "Gwyn, I love you." I swallowed a thick breath. "And I *will* come back and help you train. And when you are ready you can join us, but until then you must remain here. I will not be able to focus if I am worried about you."

Gerarda stepped forward and placed a hand on Gwyn's shoulder. "That is a fair deal, Ring."

"Ring?"

Gerarda shrugged. "Seemed a fitting name for the one who plucked out Damien's eye."

Gwyn's lip twitched upward in a proud grin. Rheih appeared at our side and nodded at her. "Come, youngling. There are plenty of tasks to be done." She gave me a knowing look over her shoulder as they both walked back down to the beach. "I will teach you how to make healing ointments and how to stitch the skin together quicker than Keera's hands can manage."

I watched them until Gwyn's red curls disappeared into the edge of the forest with the other Elverin who were staying behind. Then I turned on Gerarda like an angry dog. "Why would you tell her she could come to Volcar? Two months of training and you think she's ready for a mission?"

Gerarda rolled her eyes. "Of course not. I never told her she could come. She showed up here in this one's armor." She shoved Fyrel, who had the decency to blush.

"Why not send her back the minute you saw her?" I seethed.

"Why should I play the villain when I knew you would do it so well?" Gerarda patted my shoulder with the hand that wasn't flipping her throwing knife. "Keera, she is already angry at you. Why should she be angry at us both? The training is helping her. She has *friends* and the other morning when I got to the training ground she was singing."

I stilled. "Singing?"

Gerarda nodded. "I only want the best for her too."

I sighed. "And what about this one?" I jutted my chin in the direction of Fyrel who was trying to hide amongst the other Shades.

Gerarda tilted her head. "I told that one she could fight."

My jaw snapped shut, but Myrrah whistled drawing our attention to her. "Fyrel is ready. Gerarda and I did not make that decision lightly."

I crossed my arms. "When you pledged your swords, I thought you meant the *Shades*. Fyrel never earned her hood. She is too young to fight."

Fyrel shoved the others out of the way. "I was not too young to fight the soldiers when they came for the other initiates in the middle of the night. I was not too young to stitch their arms back together and hum them to sleep as they cried. And I was not too young to fight when we left that island to come here. This is my home as much as it is yours, and I wish to fight for it." She cleared her throat. "And if you tell me no, I will just sneak onto the ship."

I scoffed.

Myrrah pushed her chair forward. "Keera, you are no longer Blade. You fought to free us, so we did not have to answer to anyone, but you freed our swords as well. You cannot be surprised that some of us will choose to use them."

I pinched the bridge of my nose. "You will stay on the ship with Elaran and Myrrah. You will do anything your superiors tell you *without question* and that includes any command to save yourself and leave the others behind."

Fyrel's brows knitted together.

"Am I understood?"

"Yes." Fyrel nodded enthusiastically. "Thank you, Keera."

I turned to the rest of them. "You understand the risks. This will not be like any other mission. We are not fighting with the resources of the Crown, but against them. All of them."

Myrrah shrugged. "I always thought I would die at sea."

I ignored her comment and stared down the Shades behind her. Each flexed their jaw and stared right back at me. There was no hesitation, no reluctance in their eyes. They knew what lay ahead because they were soldiers, soldiers who wanted to fight.

Myrrah pulled a white box from the bag hanging off her chair. She opened it and handed it to me. "Since there are no leaders among us, I made sure everyone got one." I looked up and saw that each of them was wearing an identical pin around their necks. It was cast in white metal, carved into the shape of the Order. Its three towers stretched across the fastener with tiny gemstones atop each one to represent the glass emblems.

Myrrah grabbed the fastener and threaded the lace of my cloak through its center. "We wore weapons around our necks for so long I think it's time that we wore a symbol of home to remind us what we're fighting for."

My throat tightened as Gerarda lifted her chin. A bright white pin was around her neck too. She gave me a knowing look. "We all deserve to fight for a worthy cause, at least once."

The scars along my skin tingled and I nodded.

We stepped onto our ships and my breath hitched as I looked out at all the faces along the three decks. Halfling, Fae, and Elf fighting together as one. We were no longer a band of rebels trying to destabilize the Crown, we were a united front.

The rebellion was over and the war had officially begun.

CHAPTER FORTY

WE ARRIVED JUST BEFORE DAWN with black sails along the horizon. Thirty ships circled the east side of the island and I knew we would find more along the western shore. Gerarda and Syrra flanked me on either side.

"It's as we expected." Gerarda assessed the canons and archers along the ships with a spyglass. "Our best bet is to go through the channel and hope that we can get our ships out before the rest of the fleet can close in on us."

I took the spyglass for myself. "How long would it take for the others to circle around?" Each ship had two hundred soldiers along the deck and even more waiting along the shore.

"Thankfully, the winds are against them." Gerarda clipped the spyglass to her belt. "An hour at most."

I nodded. "Then we have to disable their ships first. Break the line. Then I will go in while the rest of you deal with the threat along the shore." I nodded at Syrra who still had a spyglass to her eye. "Do you see those bolts?" There were large mechanical bows lined up on the beach with arrows as long as the tallest Mortal and thicker than his arm.

Syrra clenched her jaw and nodded. "Damien has fitted them with glass bulbs. We should assume they are filled with one of his new inventions."

I gritted my teeth. "Violet flame." The liquid in the glass was a dark purple color.

Syrra placed her hand on my shoulder. "We are not raiding their city, Keera. We only need to hold our own for an hour and ensure their ships cannot follow us home."

Gerarda huffed a laugh. "Only?"

"Think of it as a chance to outshine Keera." Syrra's brow rose.

Gerarda grinned. "That does make me feel better."

Syrra nodded at the first sun rising over the western horizon. "We will not find better cover than that."

I nodded and grabbed the vial of water Nikolai had given me. It was infused with the same auric swirls as a portal threshold, swimming inside the jar. Gerarda stepped on a tiny faebead and let the light flash once before extinguishing it again. The signal for the other ships to ready their own bottles.

I poured the liquid into a wooden pedestal next to the ship wheel. There were three hollowed circles for me to split the water among. I swirled my finger in each pool three times until the faces of Elaran and Myrrah appeared in one and Feron and Lash appeared in the other.

"The sunlight will give us an advantage once I cast the fog." I peered down at their nodding faces. "Feron and Lash, this will be your chance to disable as many of their ships as you can. We attack their sails and we send their weapons into the sea."

I turned to Myrrah and Elaran. "I won't drop the fog until Nikolai's weapons are in range. When the horizon clears be ready to shoot."

They nodded as Nikolai's head popped into their pool. "We've loaded the bolts to the starboard side of the ship and every arrow shaft is coated in oil. You and Lash only need to ignite them. Save your magic."

We both nodded and Nikolai poured another substance into his pool. The water bubbled with golden light before floating into the air like a faelight. It rippled and then split into two orbs, and then they split too. And again and again until the pools were tiny droplets hanging in the air.

Two floated by my ear and I could her the whispers of Myrrah and the others, while a third hovered by my lips. The magic would last for just under an hour, giving us time to communicate across the three ships with ease.

At least in that way we were at an advantage.

"Open your sails," I ordered. The sound of three giants sails dropping low echoed behind me as I raised my arms and pulled the sea into the air, concealing the horizon in a morning fog. The sunlight would make it hard to see our sails through the thick of it until we were well in range of their ships.

My brow trembled as I kept the fog around all three vessels and beyond while I called that whirling power forward in my chest. I cast three eternal gusts and sent them into each ship's sails. We moved through the water like a blade, silent and deadly.

"Wielders at the ready," I whispered as I let the fog disperse by a tiny fraction. Not enough to reveal our position but enough that we could see the black sails coming closer along the horizon. I turned to the right and saw Feron at the stern of the ship. He was seated in a wooden chair with his cane tied to his hip.

When the black sails were close enough to see the shiny emblem stitched into them, Feron stood and turned to me.

His eyes were a bright violet, glowing in the distance.

I nodded and he raised his hands.

There was no turning back.

A deep rumble like far-off thunder rippled from the sea. The calm surface began to thrash—the only warning Damien's ships had before three giant pillars of rock erupted from the sea.

Feron was cunning in his use of his power. Each tower of sea-floor was erected right under one of the largest ships, shattering its hull like glass and sending its battalion into the raging water. He waved his arm and the towers fell, plummeting onto the sails and decks of the ships beside them.

Feron had managed to destroy seven of the thirty ships in one attack, but the drain on his power was already showing. He sat back down and wiped the sweat from his brow.

A battle horn cried from the smoking mountain. The soldiers might not be able to see us yet, but they knew we were here.

"We're in range." Nikolai's voice boomed in my ear.

Killian raised his hand and issued the command. "Archers and bolts at the ready." He dropped his arm and I dropped the veil of fog around us.

Canons exploded in the distance. Myrrah lurched her ship to the left, dodging their blows and aligning our own weapons at once.

"Fire!" Killian ordered as Feron used his power to shield our ships from their canon strikes. Our large arrows flew over the wall of earth between us. I dispersed my gusts, letting each ship coast, and climbed to the eagle's nest.

Some arrows fell to the sea, short of their targets. But some landed on the decks of their ships. I smirked as the soldiers cheered, unaware of how much danger they were in. Lash cracked his knuckles in the nest beside me and waved his arm.

The arrows lit in slow succession, like candles reigniting after a breeze. The oil sparked to life along each arrow, burning white hot, enough to catch the wet wood and rigging aflame. Men shouted for buckets of water to douse the flames, but with a push from my own fire powers they spread to their masts and twenty-three became twenty.

Feron lowered his shield just as the stern of the ships came close to crashing against it. A barrage of arrows flew into the sky, flying at us like a flock of pointed black birds. I waited until they started plummeting toward us and used one strong gust to throw them off course.

Myrrah opened her sails and overtook my middle ship. Feron followed her lead as Damien's soldiers prepared another canon attack. I raised a fog around the closest black sails, obscuring their aim. The Shades loaded Nikolai's mechanical bows once more and then nocked three arrows each.

Killian gave the order to fire and we sent our own flock of fatal birds upon them. Lash lit the arrows one by one and two more ships were set aflame. Their soldiers jumped into the thrashing water before we could stoke the flames like we had on the first ships.

Feron stood from his chair and closed his eyes. When he opened them thick strands of seaweed uncoiled from the water and wrapped around the necks of soldiers. Strangling them like tentacles and pulling others into the depths below.

We had taken half of the ships on this side of the city. Now all we needed to do was make a gap wide enough for me to cross the threshold.

Myrrah turned her ship sharply again, and Nikolai shot one of his bigger arrows. It pierced the hull of the closest ship and set an anchor with the same spikes he had used that night in Silstra. A rope tied their two ships together and I filled Myrrah's sail with the power she needed.

Her boat took the lead of our tiny fleet as she pulled one of Damien's ships into the hull of another. Its stern pierced through the wood with a loud creak. Elaran waited until the broken ship had turned enough to set its course toward a third and sliced through the rope altogether.

Feron's ship was close enough to the others that enemy arrows could fall upon their decks. Pirmiith stood at the mast with a long bow almost as tall as he was. He aimed five arrows at a time, taking a soldier with each bolt.

Lash incinerated the enemy's arrows before they could reach their sails or pierce the Elverin's chests.

My shoulders relaxed as I took in the destruction. We had successfully destroyed the ships along the middle and created a space wide enough for my canoe to breeze through undisturbed.

I leaped down from the eagle's nest and used a rope to slow my fall. Just as my feet hit the deck something sparked in the distance and a loud hiss sounded across the sea. My blood chilled, thinking there was some kind of ancient serpent under our ship, but instead the sea was lit in purple flame.

A line of violet fire ignited along the water and I noticed the sheen in front of each of Damien's ships. That was why they weren't crossing the threshold of the channel. They had other means of enforcing it.

"Gerarda, turn!" I shouted, but it was too late. The flames ignited underneath us like a lit fuse and the ship was blown in two.

Water filled my lungs as I was thrown into the sea. I surfaced to see the green sails of a ship lit with purple flame. The heads of the

Shades surfaced on the western side of the wall of flame while our two other ships sat on the east.

"I can't control the flames." Lash's voice sounded in my ear. I was grateful the orbs of water hadn't dissolved the moment I touched the sea. "They're too strong and too wild."

"Then we will swim under." I let that thrashing power build in my belly and the water around me bubbled until I was lifted from the sea. The Shades looked up at me as I gestured my plan to them. When they nodded I dove from my high point along the surface and we swam below.

The flames descended into the water's surface deep enough that some of the Shades had to cut themselves free of their cloaks to sink low enough.

I gasped for air as I breached the surface on the other side, my hair drying in the heat of Damien's tainted flames. Feron was pulling Shades onto his ship using the weeds while I pushed them onto the deck of Myrrah's with my waves.

Killian grabbed my shoulder, pausing for a moment to make sure I wasn't injured. His jade eyes were full of worry until I squeezed his wrist.

"You need to leave now." His words were stuttered from the swell of the waves.

I thrust us toward the rope ladder along Myrrah's ship. Gerarda and Syrra were already climbing onto the deck while Vrail and Nikolai pulled Shades over the ledge. "Is everyone accounted for?" I asked Elaran and those on the other ship.

Gerarda had already begun her count. "We have eighty-three here."

"Sixty-one here." Lash's report was cut off by his sudden need to turn a barrage of arrows to ash.

I did the math in my head. “That leaves us one short.” I scanned the deck for the brown hair and lanky limbs I was looking for. “Fyrel!” I screamed in a desperate plea.

Gerarda turned frantically looking for her in the sea but Nikolai lifted his head and shouted. “There!”

Fyrel was standing at the top of the mast with a bow in her hand. She shot in such succession that I could barely count her arrows as she emptied the three quivers along her back. Each shot struck her target in his chest.

I sighed with relief.

Myrrah steered the ship toward the shores of Volcar. Damien’s own fleet would have trouble turning to face us. I ordered the Shades to ready a canoe. When I turned, I saw that line of oil, barely visible floating in the waves of the sea. We would be on it in seconds.

“Flames in the water!” I shouted at the top of my lungs. “Turn!”

Myrrah didn’t ask questions. She cranked on the wheel. “The anchor!”

Gerarda leaped over the upper deck of the bow and landed on the lever along the anchor wheel. The heavy piece of carved stone dropped into the sea with a resounding splash. The Shades fell to the deck as the ship lurched, narrowly missing being consumed by a wall of Damien’s inextinguishable flames.

We were boxed in on two sides. This was Damien’s plan. His soldiers might not be a match for our magic, but they would swarm us once our powers were exhausted.

“Mind the surface of the water,” I shouted over the deck and into the orb hovering by my lips. “The flames with look like oil on the sea. You’ll only notice the reflection in the right light.”

“There!” Nikolai pointed to another line beside us. If the soldiers lit the flames, the ship would be fully boxed in.

My back tensed as I spotted more lines of dormant flame in the sea. "Feron, keep your ship close. They're trying to separate us."

He ordered his ship to sail for us and I held my breath. There was nothing I could do if Damien's flames consumed his ship like it had ours.

"Archers aim for the captains!" Myrrah locked her wheelchair and pointed at the three black sails drawing closer. She met my gaze and her face crumpled with confusion. "What are you still doing here?"

I pointed to the wall of flame. "I can't go anywhere!"

Myrrah's frown only deepened. "I did not kick you into that lake as a child for nothing!" She pushed her chair to the edge of the quarterdeck. "And there's nothing stopping me from doing the same now." She pointed at the rippling water. "Go!"

"I can't abandon you now!" My head shook. "We didn't plan for this."

Myrrah nocked an arrow and fired. "A plan only ever goes so far. We've out-trained them."

Gerarda dropped her quiver and ran over to me. She pointed to the small canoe that Syrra had already launched into the sea with a team of Shades. They levied their arrows at one of the catapults along the deck of a ship and it released into the sea. "They have this, Keera."

"Someone needs to go with you." Killian stepped forward, pulling off his wet boots.

Gerarda crossed her arms. "That will be me, *princeling*."

Killian's jade eyes turned hard and for a moment I thought he was going to strike her. His jaw pulsed as he picked at the skin along his thumb. "Keera can decide."

I glanced between the two of them before pointing to Gerarda. Her lips twitched upward in a snarky grin. "She's the more seasoned warrior," I said to ease Killian's disappointment.

"And if you exhaust yourself?" Killian eyed Gerarda from boot to brow. "Can she even lift you?"

Gerarda dipped into a spin and kicked Killian along the knees. Before he had completely hit the deck, she hoisted him into the air and marched out four steady paces.

"You made your point," Killian grumbled, still laying across Gerarda's shoulder. She dropped him onto a pile of rigging.

There was no way around by canoe now. The towering walls of flame blocked our passage, but Gerarda had already resolved herself for a swim. She secured her bow and quiver on her back and tied her cloak around her waist so it wouldn't drag.

She grabbed my hand and pulled me to the edge of the deck. "Feet first!" She shouted before dropping into the sea. I glanced over my shoulder at Killian, his jade eyes glinted in the violet flames but he nodded, trusting the choice I'd made.

"We'll defend the ship," he promised as I plunged into the icy sea.

Lash's voice sounded over the small bubble that now clung to my ear like a droplet of water. "Be safe, Keera."

"Burn them to the ground," I answered.

He chuckled and set another ship's sails alight.

Gerarda and I swam as close as we could to the wall of magic flame. She dove under the surface to surveil how deep the flames sunk beneath the water.

"Thirty feet deep," she gasped, surfacing after a minute. "We can't waste energy attempting that more than once. We'll have to swim under on the way back too."

I dunked my head into the water and saw the flickering line where the violet flames started along the channel. "Do you trust me?" I spat salty water from my lips.

Gerarda didn't hesitate. "With my life."

I grabbed her hand. "Dive as low as you can and whatever you do—don't let go." We both took a final breath before thrashing our legs in wide circles behind us to dive below the depth of the flames. Then I squeezed Gerarda's hand and called the current of my magic forward. Pressure swirled around our legs, propelling us onward without the need to kick. Gerarda relaxed into the current and I propelled us under the flames and into the channel.

I squeezed her hand asking her if she needed to surface.

Two squeezes back.

No.

I kept us flying through the water until my lungs were pierced by a thousand tiny blades of ice and I thought they would explode from the weight of my own blood. I released the current and let go of Gerarda's hand, needing both my arms to reach the surface before I ran out of air.

I gasped as I broke through the sea at the edge of a small peninsula. The smoking snowy mountain loomed high overhead and the western ports of the channel were far behind us.

"Why didn't you suggest that earlier?" Gerarda gasped.

My shrug was hidden by the wave. "I didn't know I could do it until I tried."

I swam until my boots rested along the ashy bottom of the channel. I waded through the water as Gerarda swam beside me and we both collapsed on the beach.

"I think the seal is just on the other side of here." I pointed up at the snowy rocky shore that created a barrier between us and the eastern edge of the island.

Gerarda crawled over to the rocks and peered over the edge. "Keera, there are at least thirty ships out there and who knows how many soldiers waiting on the island."

"There aren't many places to hide." I pointed at the ashy beach and snow-covered rolls along the base of the mountain. An ambush was unlikely.

Gerarda unlatched the leather straps along her chest and wrenched her bow free. "Ready?"

I nodded and climbed over the frozen rock behind her. Gerarda moved almost as quietly as Syrra through the snow. Her head scanning in every direction like a swing swaying back and forth in the wind.

I pointed in the distance. Gerarda couldn't see it yet, but along a flat piece of the snow was a seal made of deep blue ice. I gripped the bone hilt of my dagger and pulled it from its sheath. We crouched, stalking toward the seal with our eyes locked on the horizon. No horns had sounded yet and I prayed that meant we had reached the seal first and hadn't been spotted.

I kneeled at the edge of it and Gerarda gasped as it came into view for her, the glamour shattering like glass. I mapped my path over the webbed designed and the circular edge as I gathered the courage to begin.

I closed my eyes and hoped that Riven would survive what I was about to do. A warm tingle flooded through my skin that felt just like the bond between us, as if Riven was telling me to do it.

A slash across the ground made me spin on my knee. My chest heaved as I lifted my dagger into the air.

Gerarda shook her head as she stabbed another short blade into the ice around me. "In case we need them," she said over her shoulder. The handles were sticking out at waist height, ready to grab if we found ourselves under attack.

I tilted my head, appreciating Gerarda's strategy. No matter where I was in breaking the seal I would be within easy reach of a weapon.

"Get on with it," Gerarda urged, pointing to the seal with her chin.

I took a final breath and slammed my red dagger into the ice. A cold pressure pulled at my arm until it felt as if my limb had been swallowed by the mountain. I cut through the circular edge of the seal first, feeling the drain on my powers as my blade moved through the ice. The fire under my skin burned down my arm as a whirlwind pounded against my chest. It was as if my magic was fighting me, begging me not to continue but I persisted.

I cut through the second of the eight intersecting lines when something hit me on the back of my head. My vision blurred but I could see Gerarda fending off two soldiers dressed in black. The tallest of them was almost as large as Lash and had a long cloak that billowed in the night air.

A silver shield glinted in the light of the torch he held in his thick arm.

Damien's Arsenal was here.

I turned my head, my hand still locked against my blade, to see another cloaked figure standing above me with a thick chunk of ice in his hand.

"Did Damien bother to learn your name before he named you Dagger?" I eyed the silver fastener at his neck. I lifted my gaze and recoiled in horror as I realized his left eye was completely black. Not inked by a loose fist, but inked by magic. The green hue of his other eye was gone, as were the whites around it, there was nothing but black and a small pupil the color of amber.

It sent a chill down my spine. The new Dagger had a scar that cut across his lip. It turned white as he scowled. He dragged a hand through his ginger curls and took a swig from a small flask. He spat his swallow onto the ground, leaving my captured hand dark and sticky.

His lips curled into a predatory smile. "They will sing songs of how Henris killed the Banished Blade."

I feigned what I hoped was a desperate, terrified look as I called every last bit of power that wasn't being drained by the seal. Henris pulled his sword from its sheath. "Have any last words for me to give my king?"

I fluttered my lashes innocently. "I have some for you."

Henris's brow twitched upward and his sword stilled above his head.

"Sing for me." I let the turbulent power in my chest cascade down my arm like a gentle breeze. It whipped in a tight loop so small Henris could barely see it until it hovered just above his throat.

He opened his mouth to shout but that was all I needed. I quickened the pace of the tiny whirlwind and pulled the life from his lungs. He choked on the air flowing out of his body as he collapsed to his knees. His hands grasped at his throat for a rope that wasn't there, not understanding what was happening to him.

I didn't stop until red blood splattered across the snow and Henris lay dead at the edge of the seal.

My body crumpled. I turned to see Gerarda charge the Shield. She leaped, wrapping her legs around his shoulders before whipping herself above his head. A glint of silver was all I saw and then Gerarda's knife was protruding from his eye. She pushed off his shoulders, rolling through the air, as he landed in the bloody snow next to his comrades.

Gerarda was barely out of breath as my chest heaved. "They were waiting until you started," she said with her lip curled over her fangs.

I shook my head at my own folly. "They only had an idea of where it was. There was no way for them to know until I broke the glamour."

Gerarda kicked his boot. "Their eyes."

"One of Damien's experiments, I'm sure." I slumped against the ground, not sure how much longer I would be able to speak.

Gerarda's eyes widened and she started emptying the Shield's pockets. She pulled out a small dagger with a black blade and a bloodred hilt.

"Bloodstone," she whispered.

"Keep it." I winced as I moved my blade three more inches along the seal. "That must be how Damien thought he could break it."

Gerarda stuffed the blade into her belt. "Keera, you're bleeding."

I wiped my nose with my free hand but didn't waste my energy to respond. I needed all of it to finish the seal. Gerarda paced around the perimeter, watching the horizon for any more soldiers climbing up the embankment or the shore.

"Only one line left," Gerarda whispered, urging me onward.

My jaw clenched and my wrist shook along the earth. My vision blurred and foamy bile spilled out of my mouth. I would have let go of the blade if the seal had let me, instead my limbs shook violently as Gerarda shouted my name.

I was only partially aware of her stepping onto the seal, careful not to disturb the silver liquid, and wrapping her hand over mine. I felt the seal claim her power as she pushed my arm forward. My eyes closed and my head exploded in pain but Gerarda kept going.

A battle horn sounded in the distance. "What's happening?" I rasped.

Gerarda groaned but I could feel her head shift as she pushed us another inch along the ground. "The ships are moving around the island to help the others. If we don't hurry we won't be able to outrun them."

My eyes fluttered open and amber blood dripped from Gerarda's nose. The seal was draining her life source much more quickly than it did mine. I opened my mouth to tell her to stop, but no words came. They would have been useless anyway because the pull of the seal was not something either of us was strong enough to fight.

Gerarda crawled forward, somehow not disturbing the edge and yanked the blade into the last cut. She coughed and blood bubbled out of her mouth. Her hand dropped from mine and the seal turned gold.

I somehow found the energy to pull the blade free and coated it in the thick layer of blood that covered my neck. Gerarda wheezed on the ground beside me as I plunged that bloodstone dagger into the ground and a flash of light sailed over the sea and turned the shore to ice.

CHAPTER FORTY-ONE

"GERARDA, KEEP YOUR EYES OPEN!" I shrieked in desperation. The shocked gasps of the others sounded in my ear and then went silent. The magic had faded. We were alone.

Gerarda's head lolled to the side and her chest did not rise. I pressed my ear to her flat chest piece, almost unable to listen for her heartbeat over the thunderous pounding of my own. It was faint and failing fast.

My magic surged inside me, completely restored by the seal breaking and with a new icy chill that tickled my spine. But I fought the urge to use my healing gift and examined Gerarda just as Rheih had taught me.

I rolled her onto her side and cleared the thick glob of blood and vomit from her mouth. Once I knew she wouldn't choke I let that warm magic flow down my arm and into Gerarda. I could feel her body stitching itself back together, along the flesh I could see and the flesh I couldn't. When my gift slowed, I pushed Gerarda onto her back and punched her in the chest.

She exploded into a fit of coughs. They settled as my magic made quick work of the rest. "Are you okay?" I asked, my voice still panicked.

Gerarda shoved me off and stood. "I should be asking you." Her eyes fell on the silver fastener along Henris's neck. Her lip curled in disgust. "A pitiful replacement."

I turned to the others to see their titles.

"Shield and Bow," Gerarda answered, rubbing the back of her head.

I pursed my lips. "Odd that he wouldn't send all five."

Gerarda shrugged. "Perhaps they captain this fleet." She pointed at where the black sails were disappearing around the smoky mountain. "We should go, if you're well enough."

"If *I'm* well enough?" I scoffed. "You almost died."

"You had a seizure." I recognized the mix of rage and fear in her face.

I turned away, unable to deny it.

Gerarda smacked me across the head. "You did not suffer all these years to be so happy to die."

"I shall not to die today." I sheathed my dagger. "Take it and be happy. We need to go."

Gerarda grumbled but started toward the shore where we had surfaced. I clucked my tongue. "We won't be going that way."

Gerarda raised a brow and I pointed to the last black sail along the southern horizon. She grinned and nodded.

"Ruin the sails and leave the men." I tightened my weapons belt and cloak.

Gerarda flipped a dagger in her hand and tilted her head to the side. "I'd prefer to leave them dead."

I rolled my eyes. "Stand there." I pointed to a spot on the ground and began backing away.

Gerarda's eyes narrowed. "Keera, we're running out of tim—"

Her last words were cut off as I charged at her with full speed and extended my arms out beside me. I closed my eyes as a flash of light flared and my body crashed into the frozen beach. Gerarda lifted a brow but knew enough to stay quiet.

I wiped the snow off my knees and tried to concentrate on that new part of my magic. Shifting forms had been harder for me to master than any other power. I gritted my teeth and charged toward Gerarda once more. A quick flash of light exploded and my body transformed to one with wings. I soared high, letting myself adjust to the power of my new form and then I dove for Gerarda.

She lifted her arms in a brace and my sharp talons wrapped around her forearms. There was a loud rush of air with every beat of my wings until we were high enough to soar. Gerarda marked the ship trailing behind the rest of the fleet and we dropped.

I let out a high-pitched call and felt Gerarda ready herself in my grasp. I let go and she tumbled toward the sail of that first ship, slowing her fall by piercing the sail with two long blades and leaving two jagged gashes behind.

I flapped my wings and soared to the next ship. A flash of light and I transformed too soon, falling high above the deck. I pulled out two long blades and drove them into the linen of the sail, using the friction to slow me down enough to roll along the planks. I stood and the soldiers gasped in horror as I set their black sail alight. I leaped from the ship and transformed once more before my boot struck the water. I pumped my feathered limbs and climbed high above the scene to see it all.

Gerarda had laid a dozen soldiers to rest. I called once more as a signal and transformed high above in the sky. As I fell, I let that newfound magic stroke my spine until it was made of ice and then I released my power. The back half of the fleet was frozen into place as the water underneath their ships turned to ice. I waved my hand and created a ledge for Gerarda to climb along each one before another flash and I was a bird once more.

I soared high above the front sails and disappeared into the clouds. I flew past the ships and saw that the others were fighting three sails of their own. Though both our ships remained intact.

I turned my attention back on the first ship of the eastern fleet and dove. The air whipped against me, but this body was made for speed. Even as the sides of my vision blurred beyond the point of comprehension, my target seemed to move in slow motion. I transformed just above the mast, cutting the sail with my blade just as Gerarda had.

I singed the edges of my slice with the flames underneath my skin. The remaining hole was much too big to stitch. The ship would never be able to follow us back to *Faelinth* in such a state. I scratched along the mast and set the pole aflame for good measure.

The captain swung his sword at me but I dodged it with ease. I rammed my sword upward, slicing through the man's forearm and pinning him to the mast. I didn't turn as his screams filled the air. I merely leaped from the quarterdeck and let my wings take me to the next ship.

Within a matter of minutes, the ships were disabled beyond quick repair. I pierced the hull of the frozen ships by extending those slabs of ice into the wood. When the sea melted back into itself, the ships would become wrecks along the bottom.

Gerarda ran for the edge of ice as I flew to her. She lifted her arms and my wings carried us away. Relief flooded my body just as Gerarda yelped beneath me. I looked down and saw an arrow embedded in her leg.

"Keep flying," she urged. "It won't kill me." Her lip curled in pain and I only beat my wings faster.

I let out another high-pitched call and watched as Lash turned the barrage of arrows aimed at my chest to smoke. I slowed enough to drop Gerarda onto the deck and soared above the rest. I landed on the eagle's nest and my heart fell. Both ships were encased by violet flame.

Three of Damien's ships sat untouched by our magic or weapons, ready to attack. I transformed back into my own form. "We could commandeer a ship."

"No," Lash shouted from his own deck. "You disable those three. I can clear the flames for us to sail ahead."

My chest tightened. It didn't take an eagle's eye to see that Lash was already on the verge of exhaustion. Feron sat crumpled in his chair beside him. "You said the flames were too wild to tame?"

Lash shook his head. "It only takes more power to tame them and you broke the seal. I can get us across." He folded his arms over his chest, slowly like a mountain growing higher along the horizon.

Killian pulled the rigging along the sail to prepare for the new course. "If we time it right, it shouldn't take more than a few seconds."

I swallowed. And if we didn't, every single person on our ships would be risking their life.

Killian's jade eyes locked on mine. There was something warm in them, a complete trust in this plan, a complete trust in me.

At least that made one of us.

Vrail pointed at the edge of the ship. "We can tether our ships together. Shorten the distance Lash has to quell."

"Do it." I nodded down at them. I turned to Lash. "You're certain you can do this safely?"

Lash nodded, his violet eyes hard with resolve. "Those flames will not touch our ships."

I took a deep breath, feeling the edges of my magic. I still had more power than the others, but not for long. We needed to be precise and we needed to be quick.

"You've trained me well." I smiled down at Lash and received a boyish smile in return. He nodded and tied the rope that Nikolai threw at him along the edge of the ship.

I jumped from the mast and let my wings carry me to the enemy once more. I soared toward them, relishing the feel of this body, so powerful yet completely cut off from my magic. In this form, I had no healing gift, I had no flames or gusts, I only had my wings.

But they were enough.

I disappeared into the clouds and dove. This time I didn't rake my blades down the long black sail, but let my body plummet into the sea. The cold, icy water wrapped me in its clutches and I transformed.

My cheeks bulged as I held my breath under one of the hulls and swirled my arm, collecting sharp shards of ice to form a giant arrow's head around my hand. I slammed it into the wood and felt it splinter.

I pulled myself free and swam a few feet before doing it again and again and again. The ship was already sinking by the time my head popped out of the sea. The soldiers along the other decks pointed at me and fired, but I waved my hand and a wall of water shielded me from their arrows and swords. I let the wall grow higher and higher until it towered over the mast of their ship and then I let it fall.

The water sliced through the wood like an ax. The ship splintered in two and the soldiers shrieked as they slipped along the deck and into the sea. I pulled myself onto the third ship and froze the surface of the sea completely, leaving the men to drown.

The remaining soldiers were readying their swords as I climbed, but with a single push of my power a gust of wind lurched into their still-intact sail. The soldiers fell to their knees from the sharp movement, some falling on their own blades. I pulled the gust out of the sail and it split into dozens of tiny streams that wrapped around each soldier's neck.

I took a deep breath as I pulled those men's last breaths from their chests. They crumpled as one. I ran my hand along the ship and left a line of flames that rose behind me until the mast and sail were lit. Then I jumped off the stern and let my wings carry me to my kin.

They had passed the wall of violet flames unscathed, but from the air I could see that most of them were huddled along Feron's ship. Nikolai's wail echoed over the burning fire and the screaming soldiers. It pierced my chest before I saw its cause.

Lash was laying on the deck. His violet eyes open but pale.

I dropped to the ship in my Fae form and ran to him. "No!" I shouted. "No!"

I called that warm flow of power forward, but there was nothing warm left for it to latch onto. It stopped, stagnant, unable to do anything for the brave Fae.

Tears welled in my eyes as I turned to Feron. "Do something!" I begged.

Feron merely shook his head, a tear rolling down his cheek. "There is nothing to be done, child."

"But he said . . . he said he could do it." I choked. "He said we would all be safe."

Syrra's gentle hand found my back. I turned and saw that her dark eyes were red and filled with tears. "He said the flames would not touch the ships and they did not. He knew the choice he made."

Nikolai wailed harder, and Vrail wrapped her arms around him in some attempt at comfort. Elaran found Gerarda's hand and didn't let go.

I leaned back, the grief and exhaustion hitting me all at once. I closed my eyes and they didn't open.

CHAPTER FORTY-TWO

DAMIEN'S HANDS WERE AROUND MY NECK. I thrashed underneath him, but his knees pinned my arms and he sat too high on my chest for my legs to reach him. His fingers tightened until my vision blurred.

He snarled down at me. His eye patch slanted along his cheek to reveal the depth of the scar underneath. "I will end everything you hold dear."

My fingers scratched at his hands. "An empty threat made from a soon-to-be empty throne," I wheezed with a smile on my face. Damien couldn't kill me in our dream. His hands would only end this torture chamber he had created in our minds.

His lip curled as if the same thought whirled across his mind. He let go of my throat and slammed my head into the floor. I blinked from the shock of pain and then it disappeared. We were in a black room. There were no windows or doors, only us. Somehow we could see each other as clearly as if the suns shone overhead but there were no torches hanging in the room.

"You burned my ships!" Spit flew from Damien's mouth as he spoke. He circled me like a lone wolf, wounded and desperate. "You killed my Dagger!"

I sat up from the floor and spat. "He didn't put up much of a fight."

"How could he when you sucked the air from his lungs." Damien tried to straighten his back, but it was curved and bent like one of the trees in the Dead Wood. "*Fae*." He said the last word as a curse.

I stood slowly, prepared for a sudden attack. "How could you possibly know that?" I turned around the room, looking for clues about where Damien's mind may have taken us. "You're in Volcar?"

It didn't make sense. Why would Damien risk his own life in a battle he thought he would win?

Damien's cruel grin sliced across his sharp face. "I am everywhere." He removed his eye patch and I gasped. His other jade eye was still gone, but Damien had replaced it with something else.

His new eye was black with no whites along the edges. In the center the pupil was a dark amber color that continuously shifted shape. It was the same as the eyes the Arsenal had. Identical copies.

"You saw it happen?" My blood chilled as I stared at Damien's discarded eye patch.

"I see everything." Damien took slow, sidelong steps about the room. I followed his head and we circled each other like two soldiers waiting for the other to strike.

I tilted my head to the side. "Did you inject their eyes with something like you did to me?"

"Yes." Damien picked up his eye patch. He didn't put it back but instead placed it in the slim pocket along his tight jacket. "I made an improvement on the elixir." He waved his hand around the room to gesture at our shared dream. "I thought I had gotten something wrong when that first dream started happening. The others were never aware of my presence, but not you . . ."

I braced myself. "Others?"

Damien fixed his collar and brushed his jacket as if he had not savagely attacked me on the floor. "Keera, you didn't think that was my first attempt?" He tucked his hands behind his back. "I've been studying the Fae gifts for a long time."

"Years?" I swallowed the bile that rose in my throat at the idea of how many Halflings Damien had been experimenting on.

"Decades." Damien's cruel grin made my stomach churn. He stepped toward me, his chin lifting. "There's still one more seal left, Keera. Remember if you break it, there will be consequences."

I narrowed my eyes and refused to react. There was no way Damien could know about Riven. He might suspect that my powers grew stronger with every seal I broke, but he couldn't know the cost that Riven would bear because of it.

He raised a cold finger to my neck and traced the faint line across my skin. A ghost of the cut I had made across his own throat the last time we found ourselves in this nightmare. "The more magic you bring back, the more I have at my disposal too. Be careful what you wish for."

Damien's black eye flashed amber and then he was gone.

CHAPTER FORTY-THREE

Nikolai was still quietly weeping when I woke. Syrra passed me a skin of water without a word and I drank it all, wiping my mouth with the back of my hand. My mind was spinning from the fatigue and the dream. Something Damien had said left my scars tingling and my back tense.

He had been crazed with anger when he first saw me. I rubbed my throat as if his hands had left a mark. I had glimpsed the part of Damien he worked hard to keep leashed, the part of him that craved violence with every breath. It was terrifying.

Yet he had bottled that rage just as quickly as it appeared. He wasn't acting as a king who had just lost a third battle against a rebellion he had tried so hard to smite. His confidence was entirely unearned.

That didn't match the Damien I had come to know. The Damien who spent years plotting against his own father to steal the throne.

Damien was patient and calculating, and whenever something went awry he always had a plan. A card to play that no one was expecting.

And he had one now.

My breath hitched at the realization. I hadn't been the only one whose dreams Damien had been haunting.

I jumped up from the deck. "Where is Collin?"

Gerarda's eyes widened as she joined the group. "He stayed in Aralinth with Rheih and Maerhal."

"He was in no state to come and fight, Keera," Vrail said gently, nestled beside Nikolai. "He's been ill for months."

"No, he hasn't been." I gritted my teeth. How could it have taken me so long to see the truth? Collin had been avoiding sleep for just as long as I had been. Why hadn't I considered that he was equally afraid to reveal his reasons?

I turned to Killian, who was still sitting on the rigging I had been lying on. "Did Collin ever travel with you to the palace?"

Killian's brow furrowed.

"It only had to be once," I added, impatient.

Killian glanced at Syrra and then back to me. "Not the palace. But he would join us whenever I needed to be in the capital. Several times."

I turned to Syrra. "Were you always together at a safe house?"

"No, we each had our own duties to attend to." She folded her arms. The scars along her shoulders stretched and shimmered in the midday sun.

"He would frequent one of the pubs in the third circle," Nikolai cut in, his eyes were bright red as he looked up at me. "He could pass as a Mortal easily enough and it was a good crowd for overhearing things useful to the rebellion."

"The Silver Crown?" I guessed. It was a favorite place of respite for the royal guards. We had Shades stationed in their midst each night keeping their ears open for useful information to report. I had been thrown out of it on several occasions.

Nikolai nodded.

My stomach dropped. So Damien would have more than enough opportunity. Any of those guards could have been under his command and if Collin had drank enough, he might not even remember a small prick to the neck.

Syrra grabbed my hand. "Keera, what did you see in your dream?"

"Riven was right." I huffed. "Whatever Damien did to me, he did to other Halflings first. And I think he did it to Collin."

Five pairs of eyes stared at me in disbelief.

"Damien said the others weren't aware of his presence. What if he could shift through their minds unnoticed? Pose as people they knew and have them confess information in their dreams?" My heartbeat quickened and I started to pace along the deck of the ship. "Collin wouldn't have known, not until—"

"Keera, what are you saying?" Killian grabbed both my arms and stopped me. His jade eyes were filled with worry but all I could see was the deep amber rings around their pupils. It was the same color as Damien's new eye.

"Collin was the mole. All along." I turned to the others. "He was the one feeding information to Damien, but he never knew it. The storehouses, the Halflings, the rebellion's missions. Collin was privy to almost all of it."

Vrail shook her head. "Tarvelle was the one passing information along to Curringham."

I snapped my head to Elaran. "You were certain those meetings never took place. That you would have known about them. And Tarvelle's own family has never believed it. We only did because we didn't know the truth was possible."

"But how do you know it's Collin?" Killian crossed his arms. "By that logic, Damien had access to anyone who frequented the capital." He turned toward the group. "That's almost everyone aboard this ship."

I shook my head. "But how many of us have done whatever it takes to keep from sleeping?"

Nikolai's jaw dropped. "None of the healers have been able to heal him."

"Because guilt is not something you can heal with a concoction." My voice rasped at the realization of how much guilt Collin had been carrying. "Collin and Tarvelle were close. Close enough for him to know he couldn't have possibly been the mole. I doubt it took him long to suspect what really happened once Tarvelle's body had been left hanging in that city."

Syrra tilted her head to Killian. "He has recused himself from almost every meeting since. He refuses to go on missions. He could have been trying to—"

"Protect us," I finished for her. The word felt heavy on my tongue, like a truth I couldn't swallow. I had let my own fears and my own vices obscure what was right in front of me. I was so willing to believe Damien's lies because one Elf had been brazen enough to show his distaste for me.

Tarvelle had been nothing but a ploy. An easy target for Damien to lay the blame on while still keeping his eye on the Faeland.

I bit my lip and turned to Pirmiith. He was standing by the mast, leaning on it like his legs could not fully support his weight. "Noemdra was right." I bowed my head. "Tarvelle was loyal to his last breath."

His lifted his square chin. "Then his death must be avenged."

"And it will be, but first we need to make sure Collin is safe." Killian nodded to Nikolai. "Write to Rheih and make sure Collin stays at Sil'abar."

Nikolai pulled out his notebook and began scribbling.

"Damien also saw what I did at the seal," I admitted. "He knows I am a magic wielder."

Gerarda stopped flipping her blade. "What do you mean he *saw*. We're the only two who left that island alive."

I pointed to my eye. Gerarda lurched back and she looked like she wanted to vomit. "Three of Damien's Arsenal were there," I explained to the others. "They each had one blackened eye. I didn't know what to think of it until I met Damien in that dream just now. He's replaced the eye Gwyn ruined with his own invention. He can see whatever his Arsenal sees."

Gerarda's upper lip curled back. "Or however many soldiers he does it to."

Nikolai stood from the deck and tugged on his hair. "We have a problem." He handed Killian the notebook. I leaned over his shoulder and saw that Rheih had written back in her tiny, jagged scrawl.

Collin offered to take Maerhal to pick lilthira.

Nikolai scribbled along the pages again, asking where they had gone. I could hear Rheih's annoyance in her reply.

I am a healer not a minder of Elves and Halflings.

Damn that Mage.

I turned to Nikolai. "Where do those flowers grow?"

He tugged on his hair so tightly it was perfectly straight. "Along the outskirts of Silstra."

"Damien has five thousand soldiers in Silstra alone," Elaran said, tying her thick curls back.

Gerarda sheathed her dagger. "And Damien could have injected any of their eyes."

Syrra wrapped her cloak around her arms and pulled her quiver over it. "I need to get to a portal."

"Wait!" Vrail shouted over everyone's bickering. She pulled out a map of the portals and laid it on the deck. "*Lilthira* grow on either side of the Three Sisters. It would be smarter to send two teams. One through the portal north of Wolford and the other to the portal on the outskirts of the Dead Wood. If we hurry both paths can start here." She pointed to a sunlit portal along the western edge of the Singing Wood.

Killian pointed to the Dead Wood. "Keera and I will go here. I doubt Collin and Maerhal would have traveled so close to the city, but if they ran into trouble, my crown and Keera's powers may buy us enough time to get them out."

Syrra's jaw flexed. I knew she wanted to rip herself in half so she could assist both teams, but she knew quick action is what counted most. "I will go to Wolford."

"And we will assist." Gerarda and Elaran stepped forward in unison.

I nodded. "Everyone else needs to sail for the ports and ready any weapons we have left. I don't doubt Damien has already sent troops to Elvera too."

"I'm coming." Nikolai's voice was barely a rasp after all the tears he had shed.

I grabbed his hands. "I say this with love, but you're in no state to help. Bring Lash back to Myrelinth and we will bring your mother home. *I promise.*"

Nikolai's lashes fluttered at the words. He knew what they meant for me to say. He let go of his hair and nodded. "I'll tell Feron to steer his ship home while we head inland." He pressed a firm kiss to my forehead. "And make sure you come home too, Keera dear."

"Please tell me you didn't have to kill anyone?" Killian whispered as I passed him the reins to his new horse.

I mounted my own. "The stable boy will wake up with a headache and assume it was the ale he was guzzling." I patted the satchel under my cloak. "And I left him more than a fair payment."

Killian's shoulders relaxed and he climbed onto his own horse. We left the edge of the Dead Wood just as the suns were beginning to set. Still, I pulled my hood far over my face to shield it from any passersby we met on the road.

Killian removed a gold circlet from the bag he had packed on the ship and put it over his grown-out curls, then pulled his hood over the top.

I eyed the thin line of gold still visible across his forehead. "What use is that to us now?"

Killian lifted his chin, though his finger picked at his thumb along the leather rein. "There are still many that would hesitate to disobey a prince. That hesitation could save your life or mine."

I gritted my teeth, but couldn't argue his point. Especially since my powers had not fully recuperated.

The lights of the city were visible along the darkening horizon. The tall cliffs of Silstra and its ruined dam were lit like a beacon at all hours of the day.

"Aren't you tired of putting on that mask?" I turned to face Killian only to find his eyes already on me.

He went so still he almost fell off his horse. "Mask?" he echoed, after realigning himself in the saddle.

I pointed at his hood with my chin. "Your crown."

Killian's stare hardened. He didn't speak for a long while, but I could hear the thoughts swirling in his mind like water through a creek. "I never thought of my crown as a mask." He rubbed the reins between his fingers as he spoke. "My crown is more like the red-hot sting of a brand. No matter where I am, regardless of whatever masks I wear, the mark of my birthright can never be expunged." Killian's voice was hoarse with guilt. The guilt of a Halfling who had been given so much, but felt as if he helped too little.

I knew that feeling well.

"But a legacy can be destroyed," I whispered, recalling our conversation in the safe house of Koratha only a few short months before.

Killian swallowed. "Yes, but the cost is steep." He stared at me without blinking, without breathing, locking me in some kind of trance. His jade eyes almost glowed underneath the last streaks of warmth in the sky.

My chest loosened as we watched each other. In some ways, Killian understood my past more than anyone. He had barely noticed my scars when he first saw them that night in the Singing Wood because he had his own scars too. No one left the kingdom unscathed, but especially the palace.

There was something comforting in knowing we had both gotten ourselves out of there, scars and brands be damned.

I gave Killian what I hoped was the genuine smile he deserved. "I believe you will live to start a new legacy."

Killian's throat bobbed at the words. His brows furrowed in disbelief and perhaps a little pain. When he spoke, his words were a harsh whisper. "I hope the same for you." His lips kept moving as if he had something else to say, but he stopped himself.

That unsettling silence fell between us. The one that wrapped around us every time Killian's eyes lingered too long on my lips.

I turned away, cutting through the silence with an exasperated sigh. "If they were here, we should have seen them by now. The portal's about to close." I nodded at the eastern horizon. Only the very top of the second sun was visible. We had been searching through the fields of *lilthira* since we arrived, but Maerhal and Collin were nowhere to be found.

"Elaran and Gerarda must have them." I nodded at his bag. "Write to them to confirm and then we can head north for the moonlit portal to return home."

Killian reached for his bag. He pulled out the notebook just as an arrow struck the ground between our horses. Killian looked up at me but I was focused on the glass bulb that had shattered the moment the arrow hit the ground. Dark fumes rose from the broken glass and filled my nostrils with the scent of *winvra* and dew rose.

Killian pulled his cloak over his face, but it was no use. He reached out for me. "D—" he gasped before falling backward off his horse. I didn't see him hit the ground. I coughed and then everything went white.

CHAPTER FORTY-FOUR

I WOKE IN A CHAIR with my hands bound behind my back. A thick knot pulled along the skin of my wrists, the bindings so tight my fingertips were entirely numb. My vision was blurry but I could see that the floor was made of planked wood decorated in paint.

A fist collided with my jaw. I looked up and saw a beast of a man standing over me with one gray eye and one of pure black. A silver blade fastener hung at his neck, holding the long black cloak onto his broad shoulders.

"My father was so confident the day he named you Blade." Damien sat in the middle of the room on a golden throne. He nodded up at the towering frame that took his position behind him. "Kairn is a great improvement. Brutal *and* loyal."

The new Blade puffed his chest and smiled wickedly down at me. My own blood covered his fist but I felt no pain.

"But then again"—Damien straightened his back in his gilded chair—"my brother has always been a disappointment. I shouldn't be surprised that is who he chose to align himself with."

Damien kicked his foot and someone groaned. Killian was tied at his brother's feet. His eyes were closed and his face was red with blood. My heart pounded in my chest as I squirmed against the bindings, but then I realized it was pointless.

"You're not really here." I snarled up at Damien.

He raised the brow over his tainted eye. "Neither are you."

"You injected Collin with your elixir." I stood from the chair, the bindings disappearing as my mind commanded of them. Damien wasn't the only one who could control this dream. "You've been poisoning his mind?"

He shrugged. "If it's wanted, is it poisoning or helping?"

I scoffed. "Collin did not want you in his mind."

"No." Damien leaned back against his throne with a ghost of a smile on his lips. "But he did want Killian." He spat his brother's name like it tasted foul. "How easy it was to stage his dreams and pretend to be his lover. He told Killian everything, and never suspected any of it because he was so desperate for the dreams to last." Damien looked down at the image of his crumpled brother and snarled. "Pathetic, but useful."

"How much did he tell you?" I seethed.

Damien laughed. "Keera, why would I go to all this trouble of killing him if I were to tell you that?"

I flinched.

"Did you think I would spare him?" Damien waved his hand dismissively. "He was a tool. He had his use and now he is better to me dead. It was only a matter of time before you put together Collin was avoiding sleep just as you had. Thankfully, he was so desperate to do something *good* that he didn't even notice I had planted the idea of bringing Maerhal to Silstra in his head. The dreams had been so short, he didn't know he'd been sleeping at all."

Damien's eyes trailed over me hungrily, taking in my fear.

"That's what this was?" I narrowed my eyes in disbelief. "You lured him out of the Faeland to kill him?"

Damien grinned with glee. "You have no idea how happy I was to see you along that trail." Damien's black eye flashed with amber. "One trap and I managed to capture five prized hens."

"Five?" I echoed. Even if Damien had managed to captured Collin and Maerhal, Killian and I only made four.

Damien leaned forward in his throne and licked his lips in anticipation. "It seems that the Shadow couldn't stay away. He decided to chase that damned Halfling himself." Damien giggled like an excited child. "Years of him slipping through the Crown's fingers and all I had to do was bait a single Halfling."

I crossed my arms. "It isn't possible. The Shadow did not know about any of this."

Damien's lip twitched upward as he looked down at Killian again. "Yes, I was told that the Shadow wasn't present in Volcar. A curious decision. Unless his powers had been drained in some other way. Unless he was healing somewhere in the Faeland when your message came and he decided to answer the call."

I swallowed thickly. I had no way of confirming any of it. I had been miserable with the thought that Riven had died the moment I broke that seal, but what if Feron's theory had been correct? What if the closer magic came to balance, the easier Riven's burden was to carry. Maybe he woke the moment Volcar was broken, not cured, but well enough. If he had thought Nikolai's mother was in danger, he would have done anything to get her back safely.

But none of that meant it was true. And I was not going to believe another lie from Damien's lips.

I spoke through clenched teeth. "I don't believe you."

Damien waved his hand dismissively. "But you will."

Killian coughed onto the floor. I took a step toward him, even though I knew it really wasn't him. Just the image Damien wanted me to see. He pushed Killian onto his back with his boot.

"Don't touch him," I barked. I imagined a different scene and the room disappeared, taking Killian and Kairn with it.

Damien smirked at the change of scenery. It was the first place I had thought of. Somewhere I felt safe and in control that wasn't in the Faeland. Damien took a seat behind the desk of Hildegard's office. "You're so protective of my brother." Damien's eyes narrowed suspiciously. "I wonder how *his* brother feels about it? Do you drift from one's bed to the other?"

I froze.

Damien huffed a laugh. "Of course I know my bastard brother has a bastard brother of his own. That lovesick Halfling never stopped talking about it. I think he hates the Shadow almost as much as he hates you."

"But you let Killian in and out of the palace?" I shook my head. "When you knew he was working against you with the Shadow? Why?"

"It served a purpose." Damien crossed his leg, tightly folding the left over the other. "The more people working against my father the better. And once I took the Crown, it served a greater purpose."

Damien drummed his fingers along the armrest with a smug grin on his face. "Would you rather go into battle with an opponent you've spent years studying or a stranger?"

I cocked my jaw.

"The Fae were strangers to me, but when they let my brother into their ranks that gave me a way to glimpse their logic. I became a master at guessing their next moves. And then you joined them. And you are nothing if not predictable."

I closed my eyes. "Play so your opponents lose, not to win," I whispered Damien's own words back at him.

"I told you life was nothing more than a vicious game." He uncrossed his legs and leaned forward in his throne once more. "A game that you must now play."

Fear ran down my spine with a jolt, but I stood my ground. "I no longer play your games."

"You will play this one." Damien stood and straightened the interwoven clasps of his black jacket. "I had meant for this to be a choice between Collin and that chattering Elf he brought with him, but it seems fate had a much more interesting game for you to play."

Fear flooded my chest, pressing on my lungs until I couldn't breathe. "I will cut out your other eye before I let you hurt Maerhal."

Damien ignored my threat and pulled on his sleeve. "The choice of who dies is yours." His cruel lips trembled in anticipation. "When you wake you will find yourself in the city center. On the east bank of the river you will find the Elf you stole from my dungeons. Unharmed as long as you get to her in time." He waved his hand and a tall townhouse appeared. I recognized it from the market street of Silstra.

I straightened my back. "I will."

"Keera, you can't save them both." Damien chuckled to himself. He waved his other hand and a second house appeared. This one more rugged than the last and only one story. "On the west bank is your Fae. Riven, I think is his name?"

My heart dropped to the floor. I couldn't move. I couldn't breathe. All I could do was stare at the decrepit house. "What are you going to do to them?"

Damien ran his tongue along his flat teeth. "I think you mean, what will *you* do to them." Smoke began to billow from each roof. "When you wake, the flames will have already been lit and you can make your choice. The Elf who spent so long alone in the dark or the Fae that drips in shadow."

My mouth went dry. I turned away from the violet flames that had consumed both houses. "I won't choose. I refuse." I had played this game before and there were no winners.

Damien stalked toward me. He didn't stop until our chests were almost touching. "Remember what happened the last time you refused to play?"

Hildegard's bloody face flashed across my mind. Tears welled in my eyes.

"Play or don't." Damien's finger curled under my chin. "I win regardless. But I know you will always settle for one death over two."

"This could all be a ruse. You may not even have them." I spat.

Damien's nail scratched the skin under my jaw. "Perhaps. But I believe you will be convinced when you wake."

There was an earnest anticipation in his voice that made my skin crawl. Whatever game Damien was playing, I knew it wasn't a lie, at least not entirely. The pleasure was in watching me squirm, in trying to guess which choice I'd make.

"Kill me." I rasped. "Let them both live and I will not fight your Blade when he comes for me."

Damien's cold fingers wrapped around my throat but he didn't squeeze. "You don't get to die today." Damien's lips were so close to my cheek I thought his tongue would brush against my skin. "You have destroyed my ships and killed my men with no regard for my power. Such treachery does not earn you an easy death. I will break you before I take your head." Damien's words were cold and calm, it made the threat that much more dangerous. "You are not allowed to die until you have watched everyone you love perish. You are not allowed to die until that Shadow you love so dearly burns in a fire so bright his shadows can't save him. I will use his screams as fuel for your nightmares for months, if not years. Then I will cut the skin off your eyelids so you can watch every Shade you stole pay for your treason as I slice your front just as I did your back."

Damien's hand cupped my cheeks and squeezed, pushing the tears from my eyes.

"Only then will I kill you." He ran his hand over my cheek to wipe the tears away, like a friend issuing a promise instead of a threat. "When you beg for death, I shall be merciful enough to give it to you."

Damien threw me to my knees and stood over me as I caught my breath. "The choice is yours, Keera. The Elf to the east or the Shadow to the west." He gave me a gentle smile and stepped back into the violet flames behind him. "Play well."

CHAPTER FORTY-FIVE

I WOKE IN AN ALLEY in the middle of Silstra. The smell of shit and stale water filled my nostrils and stung my eyes.

On my lap were two items. The shaded spectacles Nikolai had made for his mother and a thick black cloak I recognized immediately as one of Riven's. It was stitched with the same Elvish pattern of small leaves and swirling stems as his leathers. I leaned down and the scent of birchwood was faint, but it was there.

My blood pounded as the truth stared me in the face. Maerhal and Riven had been captured, and now I needed to choose.

I stood and tripped over something soft. The palms of my hands tore as I caught myself on the stone wall of the narrow alleyway. I looked down and saw Killian unconscious at my feet. His hands and legs were bound, but his chest was rising in even, steady breaths.

His hands were undone with a quick slice of my dagger. He could untie the rest when he woke, I didn't have the time. I ran to the street and looked at the skies. The night was clear but I could see two thin wafts of smoke beginning to billow. One to the east and one to the west.

Tears streamed down my face as I stood, paralyzed. No matter who I chose, I would never recover. No matter who I picked, someone's death would be my fault.

My stomach churned. My heart already knew I wanted to run for Riven, that I couldn't live with myself if he died and I had the chance to save him. But would I survive if Riven perished when I unlocked the last seal? Would Nikolai be able to survive it if I traded his mother's life for a few short days with Riven?

Guilt tore at my throat as my eyes shifted from the east to the west. I could hear Damien's cruel laugh in my ear, taunting me that no choice would leave them both dead.

My hands were so tight the scratches on my palms bled but I didn't feel the pain. I knew what I wanted to do. I knew from the moment Damien had stated the choice who I would pick.

I just didn't know if I could live with it.

Damien's words echoed through my mind. *I play for my opponents to lose.*

I looked to the west where Damien said Riven would be and ran the other way. I tried to shift my form, mustering the strength to soar above the crowd and into the smoke, but no flash of light came. I was already too exhausted and my body too stressed. I ran as fast as I could, tears streaming down my neck as I sprinted through the growing crowds to the townhouse. Not because I was leaving Riven behind, but because I believe Damien had switched their locations. I could only pray I was right.

I had left Maerhal to burn without more than a moment's pause. Without care that she had only been given three months of life after centuries sleeping in a dungeon. Without care that she had offered to mother me like her own, with nothing but love in her heart. All I could think about was Riven and that I could never choose another. I knew what it made me, but Riven had come to love me anyway.

Keera the killer.

I had reached the townhome within minutes. The roof was already engulfed in thick violet flames. I let that hot sensation bubble through my blood, but I couldn't control the blaze. I pushed myself to the front of the crowd that had formed around the burning building and let the whirlwind build in my chest.

A powerful gust blew along the flames, but it only let the fire claim the next house. Damien's flames were too powerful to tame and too hot to pull water from the air. I had to go inside.

I ignored the shouts behind me as I kicked the front door into the house. Black smoke billowed from the new opening, denser than any normal fire, a new tweak to Damien's invention. I covered my mouth with my cloak. I bent low and felt along the ground with my sword.

A loud crash sounded from outside and was emphasized by terrified screams. A flash of purple flame had me dropping to the floor. The second story was already gone. I swallowed, knowing that meant Riven could already be gone.

I crawled along the floor until I saw the dark shape of a boot. My chest heaved with relief when I saw the size of the black leather and grabbed the foot. Riven was tied to a chair, that fell backward and scraped along the floor as I started to drag us out of the house. I cleared the smoke away from both our faces with my gusts, unable to look back before the rafters above us began to creak.

I grabbed his legs and the legs of the chair all at once and ran. I leaped from the building just as it exploded behind us, devouring the house in flame and ash.

Black soot fell from my mouth as I coughed. The crowd had run for the riverbank when the explosion sounded, but now they all stared at me and the unconscious body tied to the chair beside me.

The warm power of my healing gift stirred. Then I sat up and the world fell away.

My heart stopped beating and my lungs no longer held air. It was as if the entire world had been burnt to ash and was carried away on a breeze. I had no needs, I had no wants, I had nothing. Because the body in the chair was dead and it wasn't Riven.

Collin's wide eyes stared up at me, but saw nothing. His shirt had been slashed in two and the words *Halfling Scum* were carved into his flesh in large amber-filled letters. His left hand was stained with his own blood and on his right arm he had left a message of his own, just one word long:

Sorry.

I beat my fist to the ground and the sky above me cracked with lightning as I screamed. The thick smoke across the river was visible even through my tear-filled eyes. Fear pricked my chest as I realized Damien could still have Riven in that house. The cloak had been his, I was as certain of that as I was that those had been Maerhal's spectacles.

My powers were almost expended but somehow this time I found the strength to transform. The crowd screamed beneath me.

"The Fae are here!"

"We're under attack!"

Their voices boomed through the city, but I didn't care. I didn't care that the king's guard were filling the streets with loaded quivers and bows in their hands. If I didn't make it to that burning building in time, I'd let their arrows pierce me.

My winged form took me to the source of the smoke. I rose high above it and tucked my wings as tight against my body as I could.

A high-pitched shriek escaped my beak and I dove straight through the smoke.

My own legs hit the ground and I rolled to smother the flames on my cloak. The house was filled with smoke but I pushed it into the roof with a gust of wind. It only gave me a moment to take in the room but that was enough to see Maerhal tied in the middle of the room.

I sliced through her bindings and by some miracle she was still breathing.

"Is Riven here?" My words were loud and desperate.

Maerhal's shoulders slumped onto mine and I repeated my question again in Elvish. She coughed red blood onto my cheeks and shook her head before going limp in my arms.

My lip trembled. I wanted to keep searching but I could feel the burns along Maerhal's body. Without my healing gift, she only had minutes left. The beam of the roof cracked and I pushed Maerhal to the ground. I sat up and my cloak was stuck underneath the beam.

One quick slash of my Elvish blade cut through the pinned fabric and I wrapped Maerhal in my arms. The house overlooked a bank along the river. If I could run fast enough, we could jump into rushing water from the back window and escape the city.

I clenched my jaw and sprinted toward the back wall. A single gust splintered the glass and burnt wood and we plunged into the Silstra River. I gasped for air as my head breached the surface and looked for Maerhal.

A singed yellow flower was in her hair, bobbing along the surface down the river. Seconds from the thundering crash of the waterfall that had overtaken the dam we had blown. I wasn't fast enough to reach her and pull us from the coursing waters.

I kept my eye on Maerhal and swam toward the cliff edge. Her arm lifted into the air as she tumbled off the ridge and I was engulfed in a flash of light.

I beat my wings with as much power as I could. My new muscles protested until I dove down into the thrashing water searching for that yellow flower. She was feet from the jagged rocky end. I tightened my wings until I could feel the heat radiating from her burnt skin.

I extended my wings and clasped Maerhal's middle with my long talons. A gasp of relief escaped me, echoing through the night as an eagle's screech.

I flew us toward the Dead Wood where I knew the moonlit portal would make for a quick path home. I dropped Maerhal to the ground as gently as I could along the outskirts of the wood, about a thirty-minute ride from the city. If the soldiers did come for us, we could slip through the portal well before they reached us. I hoped Killian had awoken and found his own escape.

The hair Syrra had worked so hard to braid for her sister was charred and smelled of smoke. One half of her face was burnt so badly her skin bubbled and hissed. I ripped open her shirt and was relieved to see that Damien's Blade had not carved into her skin the way he had done with Collin's.

I grabbed her hand and let that warm healing gift flow through me and into her. My chest broke with a sob as the magic took. I had been too late to save Lash, but at least I could save Maerhal. My head ached as Maerhal took what she needed from me, but I didn't let go. Her burns popped and then stitched together. Soon her eyes fluttered open and her lips moved but nothing came out.

She coughed as the magic reached her throat and looked up at me once more. "*Miiran*," she whispered, "I was so scared."

My heart split down the middle as I realized she thought I was her son. "I'm here, Mava," I whispered back to her in Elvish. If pretending to be Nikolai gave her comfort then I would say whatever she needed.

Her lips twitched into a smile as her eyes closed once more. "*Kiiza dii'thir, Miiran.*"

I love you, my heart.

I stroked her cheek and let the last of my magic heal her. Only when her chest rose and fell in steady breaths and every inch of her skin had closed did I finally let go of her hand.

A horse grunted in the distance. I turned and saw Killian hunched over his saddle, riding toward us. I ran for him. I left Maerhal behind the boundary of the glamour, resting and safe behind the concealment. The tears that had dried were wetting my cheeks once more as I let him wrap me in his arms.

"Damien killed Collin," I wept. "He took Riven and Maerhal and left them to burn."

Killian stilled. His hands gripped my arms so hard I knew they would leave indents in my skin. "Where is Maerhal?" His words were full of fear.

I shook my head and Killian's head fell. "I got to her in time." I took a deep breath. "I healed her. She's asleep just beyond the glamour, safe." I pointed to the edge of the wood. We were too far back to shatter the glamour so all we could see was burnt trees. "But Riven." My chest heaved.

Killian's hands cupped my face so all I could see was the earnest care in his jade eyes. "Riven is safe."

"You don't know that!" I thrashed against his hold but Killian didn't relent.

He only repeated the same words until I heard them. "Riven is safe." My eyes fell to his bag. The hard edge of his notebook was visible through the leather. My shoulders fell and I slumped against Killian, made of nothing but relief.

"Riven is safe." I chanted until my heartbeat settled.

"Did you see Damien in Silstra or—"

"A dream." Killian's entire body was tense as I spoke. "He's been waiting for Collin to leave the *Faelinth*. His Blade is in Silstra. He's the one who ambushed us. Though I suspect he will head to Elvera next, to try to beat us to the final seal. Damien didn't want us asking Collin questions. He knew I had discovered the truth and decided Collin was better off dead." My voice broke as I remembered what Collin had written into his arm. "They tortured him first, Kil. They carved *Halfling Scum* into his chest before they killed him. And Collin knew why. He had painted the word *sorry* on his arm before he died."

Killian's face paled and for a moment I thought he was going to be sick.

I squeezed his hand, but Killian did not squeeze it back. "I'm sorry I left you alone in that alley."

His jade eyes flared and he shook his head. "Don't ever be sorry for that. You did what needed to be done. You got Maerhal out alive."

"How did you know we would be here?" I asked, seeing that the horse Killian had rode here was not the one we had stolen that afternoon.

He shrugged. "I didn't. I woke up to find that cloak and Maerhal's spectacles." He patted the front of his saddle and I saw them both sitting there. Riven's cloak draped over the horse's neck and Maerhal's spectacles looped over the horn. "The fires had already started and the streets were teeming with soldiers. I took the first horse I found and fled. I was going to go back to Myrelinth to get people to help search for you, but you were here." Killian's brow crumpled and his rocky tension cracked. Tears welled in his eyes but he turned away before they could fall.

I took the reins of his horse and stroked a hand down Killian's back. "You needn't worry now. We made it out. We're safe."

Killian cleared his throat. "I'm so sorry, Keera."

I shook my head as we started back toward the edge of the wood. "You do not need to apologize for the games your brother plays. You did nothing wrong."

Killian was silent for a long time, standing still next to his horse. He finally opened his mouth to argue but his words were drowned out by my scream as I crossed the boundary and the glamour shattered once more. I dropped the reins in my hands and ran to where I had left Maerhal laying on the grass.

"No!" I screamed as I fell to my knees beside her. Maerhal's skin was still perfect and unmarked, just as I had left it but her mouth was coated in black soot. I yanked her to the side and pulled the sludge from her mouth with my bare hands, but I couldn't feel a heartbeat. I pressed my ear to Maerhal's chest and sobbed.

I grabbed her hand and called my magic forward. Barely a hint of warmth flowed through my arm, I was so exhausted, but the way it dammed where my skin met Maerhal's pierced my heart like a blade of ice.

She was gone. I had never cleared her lungs of the smoke and Maerhal's heart had been too stressed. I should have rushed her through the portal and not stopped until we reached Rheih in Aralinth.

"It's my fault," I whispered in a broken breath, slumping back onto the grass.

Killian kneeled at my side. "Keera, you couldn't have known." He placed the gentlest of hands on my shoulder.

"Elder birch tea." I shook my head. "Rheih used it on me. I should've thought of it. I should've known. I never should have left her side."

A thick tear dropped onto Maerhal's cheek leaving a blackened river down her neck.

"Keera, no one would expect you to act as a healer after only a few short weeks training." Killian's voice was hoarse fighting his own sobs.

I shoved his hand off me and cradled Maerhal in my lap. "It doesn't matter. I didn't choose her. She was in that damned house for so long because I went to Riven first. *I chose him.*"

Killian froze, still as a rock. Only his eyes shifted to me, filled with the questions he wanted to ask but was too scared to voice.

I answered them anyway. Each word coated in the hatred I had for myself.

"Damien told me Riven and Maerhal had been left in those fires to burn. He made me choose which one to save and I went after Riven. I didn't care that the only proof I had was that damn cloak, I made my choice. I left Maerhal for dead. And this was my punishment. To save her life only for her to die because of me."

I slumped back on the grass, entirely undone. There was no part of me that wasn't shattered. There was no part of me that hoped Nikolai and Syrra would come to understand, because of course they wouldn't. They had opened their arms to the Blade and their own kin's throat had been sliced because of it.

I may have shed my title, but Damien had made sure I was still a tool for the Crown. Killian didn't say a word. He only sat there, perfectly still and perfectly silent, as the last bit of warmth left Maerhal's body.

CHAPTER FORTY-SIX

I REFUSED TO CARRY MAERHAL HOME on the back of a saddle. I carried her in my arms while Killian rode on the horse. Unmoving and silent. I didn't feel the strain in my legs or the sores that grew on my feet.

I was hollow. The only thing that kept me anchored to the ground was the Elf in my arms who deserved to come home one last time. We stepped through the final portal only a short ride from the treed city, but it felt like a world away.

There the Elverin laughed and children played. There they believed that Maerhal had come back from death and had millennia left to live in freedom. That world had not yet been shattered and drained of all its color.

I was the rock that would fracture an entire world.

Killian did not speak. He did not eat. He only stared, wide-eyed, at whatever was in front of him, never truly seeing at all. He sat like a dusty, empty book with no care for the world around him. From the moment he'd laid eyes on Maerhal, Killian had turned into nothing but a shell.

His grief seemed severe for one who had known the Elf so briefly, but I had no will to try to coax more from him.

The horse walked beside me without the need of directions from its rider. The first sun had just begun to rise as the end of the Dark Wood came into view. The strands of red still hung from the trees of Myrelinth from Hildegard's funeral and my stomach tightened into a knot when I realized there were now two more funerals to plan.

Lash and Maerhal.

My lip trembled as I tried to think of what to say to Nikolai. I knew that pain was cruel and sharp and I had nothing to blunt the blows.

I spotted Gerarda first. She was cloaked in a dark blue vest with her short hair pulled back in the same style as Syrra's, who stood beside her. Vrail waited next to Nikolai, her leg bouncing wildly with impatience. I knew they had been waiting from the moment we stepped through that portal.

Feron had told them we were here. But he had no way of knowing the devastation we brought with us.

I searched for Riven, but no shadows swelled around my legs, no darkness welcomed me at all. Even though I longed for the comfort of his touch, I was glad Feron didn't wake him. It would be cruel to make him face the pain of his magic only to be met with something even sharper.

Nikolai wasted no time running to me and pulling me into his arms. "When you didn't make it through the portal, we thought the worst. I waited in Aralinth when the others came through but Feron said you were here." His hand caressed his mother's face and I realized he thought she was resting.

I had wiped away the soot so her skin was clean and her expression peaceful. But there was no way to hide the cold from Nikolai's gentle hand.

His eyes widened as he turned to me. My lip trembled but I still had yet to find the words to tell him. He pulled back on his mother's bottom lip and saw the faint black line along the inside of it. The relief that had built up in Nikolai leaked from him and drained the warmth from his face. His arms lifted, as gentle as a breeze, as he took his mother into his grasp.

My body trembled as my arms hung in the air unsure of what to do. I had ended so many lives with my blade, but watching Nikolai was a life ending in a different manner.

"Mava?" He pressed his forehead to her own and two thick tears streamed down his cheeks and onto hers. It was as if Maerhal was crying with her son for all the years they would never have together.

But all I could see was an Elf caught between time. A time *before* this moment and the time *after*. I pulled the spectacles he had made her from my pocket and placed them on Maerhal's chest.

"I'm so sorry, Nik," I whispered hoarsely, trying to hold in my sobs. "I'm so sorry I didn't save her."

Syrra dropped to her knees. Two rivers flowed down her cheeks and neck, covering her scars in the dew of her loss. Her gaze was locked on Maerhal's burnt hair. Her entire body trembled. A wild, terrifying sound escaped her lips that sent the morning birds in a flight of panic. Syrra beat the ground with enough force that, had she been gifted the ability to wield magic, she would have split the world in two.

Nikolai's bottom jaw trembled. He reached for something in his pocket but he couldn't grab it while holding his mother.

I grabbed the handkerchief for him. He glanced at me with dead eyes before wiping the tears from his mother's face. "And Collin?"

"Dead."

Vrail fell to her knees and sobbed silently. Gerarda stroked her hair but her gaze stayed on me, ready to help in any way I needed.

"I'm sorry I didn't get there in time." I didn't know if I was trying to apologize to Nikolai or to Maerhal herself.

Syrra folded into herself on her knees, too exhausted from grief for any more tears. "Who did this?" Her hand curled dangerously around her curved blade.

Guilt lashed at my throat. That was a complicated question.

"Who did this?" Syrra repeated in a voice that was more dangerous than any weapon she held.

I gave her the easy answer first. "Damien."

Her hand wrapped around the hilt of her blade so tightly the veins on the back of her hand erupted from her skin. She had a name but no one to strike. Syrra scowled and looked down the path behind me to where a portal waited that would take her to the one who killed her sister.

But then she tilted her head to the side and turned back to me. "Why would the false king want anything to do with my sister?" Her voice broke on that last word. "She was not a warrior."

I glanced back at Killian. He was still staring at nothing, completely undisturbed by the torment playing out in front of him. I ran a hand through the top of my braid and fought the urge to scream. To take one of my blades from my hip and plunge it into my chest just to feel a reprieve from the guilt.

"Keera." Gerarda took a slow step toward me, sensing the darkness burrowing inside me. "What did he do?"

I shook my head, wanting to run from the truth. I wanted to hide in the Dark Wood and never return. Telling my friends that their mother and sister was dead was scarring enough. How badly would I ruin them if they knew *I* was the one who had sealed Maerhal's fate?

Gerarda lifted her hands to my face and gripped my cheeks, pulling my gaze to hers. "*He* did this, Keera," she whispered. "This is not your fault."

I shook my head, fighting to release myself from her grasp, but Gerarda held onto me with everything she had.

"He made me choose." It was all I could say before I collapsed into Gerarda's arms. She slowly lowered me to the ground and let my rasping sobs settle to slow breaths. We sat there until the suns had risen over the wood behind us—me against Gerarda, Nikolai laying in Vrail's lap, and Syrra standing all on her own while Killian watched nothing at all.

Gerarda glanced up at him cautiously before tucking a strand of my hair behind my ear. She asked in the most gentle voice I'd ever heard from her, "Are you ready to tell us now?"

I pulled myself onto my knees and stared at the ground while I spoke, too much a coward to look at Syrra or Nik while I told them the truth. "The rest of Damien's Arsenal was in Silstra. Damien led Collin there to kill him. He didn't want us finding out how much he had gleaned from haunting Collin's dreams." I shot a look at Killian, but he had still not moved once since we'd arrived. I didn't know if he could hear me at all.

I took a deep breath and told them how we were ambushed and captured by the new Blade. My blood pumped through my veins with rigor as if I was reliving those moments again.

"When I woke, Damien was there. He was almost giddy." Nikolai sat up though he still leaned against Vrail. Syrra lowered herself to the ground and sat as still as Killian.

"What did he want with you?" Gerarda asked with venom on her tongue.

"To play a game." I turned to her, knowing she would understand the wicked way in which Damien played. She swallowed in revulsion before I continued. "He said I had to decide."

Syrra's hands turned to fists. "Decide what?"

My sorrow stung my eyes as I looked at her, knowing she would never forgive me. "To choose between saving Maerhal or saving Riven."

I didn't need to say who I had chosen. The tears staining my cheeks and the guilt lacing my words were more than enough for them to know.

Syrra's breathing stopped. Nikolai's head snapped to me. "What did you say?"

Guilt pierced my chest but I didn't shy away from the question. Not now that the truth was laid bare. "He told me that he had set two houses aflame on either side of the city. One had your mother inside and the other had Riven." I swallowed once, my hand balling into a fist beside me. "I didn't want to believe him at first, but when I woke from the dream, Maerhal's spectacles and Riven's cloak were on my lap. I didn't have time to think. I only had time to choose, east or west. I went east."

Nikolai blinked, the words refusing to penetrate. "And Damien had Killian too?"

I shook my head. "Killian was in the same alley as me. I left him there unconscious." I reached for him, but Nikolai pulled away.

He stood, his limbs trembling with anger. "You made that choice while he was laying at your feet?" His nostrils flared as he pointed up at Killian.

I straightened. "He was unconscious, Nik. The choice was mine alone."

Nikolai turned to me with a feral look on his face. It sent a shiver of fear up my spine. "But he was there?" Nikolai asked, flashing his fangs like a cornered beast.

I pushed myself from the ground. My eyes narrowing in confusion. "Yes—"

The word had barely left my tongue when Nikolai launched himself at the horse. He whipped Killian to the ground so hard the mount ran toward the lake. Killian grunted but didn't make a sound as Nikolai sat on top of him with his fists pulled back.

"You lying sack of shit." Nikolai shrieked between blows. Killian didn't even care to guard his head. "I told you your lies would cost us." Nikolai's fist connected with Killian's jaw and a mouthful of blood sprayed across the grass.

I grabbed Nikolai by his shoulders and lifted him off Killian. "Enough, Nik!" I yelled as he kicked Killian in the gut. "This is not his fault."

Nikolai scoffed and kicked Killian one last time. "You *still* haven't told her!" Nikolai spit on the ground where Killian was lying in a crumpled ball, bruised and cut, but not making a sound.

I froze. "Tell me what?"

Nikolai turned to me and I watched as his rage cooled to pity. Not for himself but for *me*. Thick tears fell down his cheeks as he looked at the spectacles in my hands. "I should have told you myself, Keera."

Something in the way he said my name, no *dear* added onto the end of it, made me more frightened than anything else he'd done. Gerarda gripped one of her knives beside me as Nikolai turned around and kicked Killian's boot. "Do it," he spat, with no warmth or care in his voice. "You owe me that much."

Killian slowly pulled himself onto his hands and knees. I reached out to help him but Nikolai held out his arm to stop me. Every one of us watched in silence as Killian stood to his full height, his blond hair red with blood and his right eye swollen shut. He didn't look at Nikolai, not because he was too scared to face his friend, but because his functioning jade eye was locked on me.

My entire body shook as if it could sense I was in danger. "What is going on?"

But Killian only dropped his head in shame and whispered, "I'm so sorry, *diizra*."

Then he balled his hands and disappeared into an explosion of light. I lifted my arm to shield my face from the sudden blast.

Gerarda gasped beside me and I dropped my arm. Thin tendrils of shadows swam around my feet, but didn't dare touch me. Understanding coursed through me like lightning along a treetop. Every nerve in my body was left raw as I stared at the truth.

Killian no longer stood in front of me. His black jacket had torn at the shoulders from being stretched so quickly. It had been fitted for the prince but now the Shadow stood in his place.

Riven.

CHAPTER FORTY-SEVEN

EVEN THE BIRDS were silent as Riven stood in the middle of the clearing, his shadows lashing uncontrollably behind him as he tried to keep them where they couldn't hurt anyone. His face twitched with pain and his shoulders caved into his chest as he fell to his knees.

"I didn't expect *that*," Gerarda mumbled. Her brows lifted and she pointed to the others who stood behind us. "But apparently they did."

I turned and saw what Gerarda meant. There wasn't a hint of shock on Syrra's or Vrail's faces. Each of them were staring at their boots, suddenly more interested in the dirt at their feet than the prince who had magically shifted into his half-brother.

"You *all* knew?" I stepped back, needing distance from any of them so they weren't close enough to strike. I turned to Riven. "How is this even possible? I've seen you both in the same room dozens of times."

Riven's hand shook as he reached for me. "Keera—"

I took another step back, shaking my head uncontrollably. "Does everyone know?" My pride burned through me with that question as I stared at Riven.

"No!" Riven replied too forcefully. He dropped his hand to his side and bowed his head. "I promised you I wouldn't keep secrets from just you. I have kept that promise."

I scoffed. "Explain. *Now.*"

Riven turned to Vrail with desperate eyes. I followed his gaze and saw her cheeks were red and her jaw was chattering, unable to find the words. She didn't need them. Instead, she pulled out a thin chain from her pocket with a small pendant along the end. It was made of the same green stone as the ring on my hand.

Feron's ring.

The glamoured ring.

"A glamour?" I huffed in disbelief. "But you and Killian study in the library together. I've *seen* you."

The glamoured necklace shook from Vrail's arm. "Sometimes Riven is the one wearing Killian's face. And sometimes it is me."

I glanced at Syrra and then at Nikolai. "And you've known the entire time?"

Nikolai's jaw shook as he nodded. Syrra nodded too, but her gaze was on her sister as she caressed her hair.

"But why?" I turned back to Riven. I needed to hear it from him.

"Protection." His jaw pulsed. "I was twelve when I first turned. I had no idea what was happening to me and my new body was so consumed in pain I thought I was dying. It was months before it happened again and by then I had made it to Volcar. I told my father it was to study under the tutors there, but really I wanted to find answers to what was happening to me. I snuck out one night and made the journey along the edge of the Singing Wood by the sea. I was halfway through the Fool's Trap when Syrra found me. Feron had sensed my presence and sent her to me.

"He knew I needed to train my powers. I couldn't be transforming into a purple-eyed Fae at a moment's notice. And the pain that came with my Fae form bothered him. He wanted to take the time to train me himself. A decoy was the only the way I could spend the time I needed to in the *Faelinth*. A prince cannot disappear for years at a time without being noticed. That was all Vrail's glamour was meant to be."

"And Vrail wanted to spend her days in the library of Volcar." I turned to her and she nodded. I had known Killian was her advocate in getting Feron to allow it, but I never realized it was because she was pretending to be the prince. "But what changed?"

"My *father* changed." Riven said the word like it was poison. "By the time I had leashed my power, he was letting his people starve. And as he grew weaker, he became more paranoid of the Halflings. All he needed was the smallest excuse and he would hang them from the wall."

My neck flexed. "I'm well aware."

"I knew I had to do something to stop him. I had to try." Riven coughed and his shadows sliced the trees behind him. "Then a decoy became convenient. It made it easier for me to stoke a rebellion as someone other than the prince and safer for the Elverin, too."

I paced in front of Riven, trying to understand. "The Elverin were not suspicious when a new Fae the same age as the prince showed up in the *Faelinth*?"

Riven's brow twitched. "Feron used his gifts to plant a seed in the minds of the Elverin. He didn't want to, but he believed it was the only way to keep his people safe."

I scoffed. "Safe from you?"

"My father." Riven winced but kept going. "Keeping my two identities separate helped waylay suspicion, especially once I'd decided to actively work against the Crown. Could you imagine what he would've done if he found out he had sired a Fae for a son? If he had discovered that very same son had aligned himself with his mother's kin and was working to overthrow the kingdom?" Riven huffed a dark laugh. "Aemon would have gathered every guard, Shade, and sellsword he could and had taken the Faeland for his own before the Elverin had any hopes of escaping."

My mouth dried. Aemon would have killed everyone in the Faeland just to spite his son.

Riven doubled over and Vrail ran to his side. "This conversation can be had just as easily as Killian."

Riven's jaw bulged as he shook his head.

"You feel no pain as the prince?" I couldn't bear to call Riven by any other name.

The crease in his brows deepened as he looked up at me. "Not until the seals started breaking. As Killian, it's manageable."

I lifted my chin. "But still there?"

Riven nodded solemnly. At least the threat against his life had not been a lie too. "Whatever tainted methods my father used to grow his own power tainted my gifts too. I was born to Man and Fae. I should have been born a Halfling, with amber blood to mark it as true, but I wasn't. Instead I was given a Mortal form and a Fae form. But both carry a price."

I tilted my head to the side. "But the other Dark Fae who died, he was not fathered by Aemon."

"He did not exist." Riven looked at the others as they gasped. I turned and saw confusion painted on each of their faces. "Another one of Feron's seeds. If I had been the only Fae with tainted gifts, then the Elverin would have grown suspicious. Feron made it so everyone believed my mother had birthed a Fae son before she left, a few years older than the prince. That boy had been kept away because his powers were tainted just like the other Fae born since the Purges."

"And you said he died," I added. "Because that would've required another decoy." I didn't care about the bitterness in my tone.

Riven nodded. "That story only worked if as many people as possible believed it. Only Feron and I knew the entire truth."

I crossed my arms. "Only Feron and you decided to lie to everyone."

Riven's jaw pulsed and his head hung between his shoulders. "I thought I was protecting them."

I shook my head. "You were protecting yourself. You decided to stake the well-being of the Elverin on your secret and didn't care how it festered." I turned to Syrra. "*A secret is like a poison.*"

She frowned but didn't argue. She had made the choice to keep Riven's secret too.

I kicked a rock along the ground. "But you didn't protect them. You were right there, Riven. At my feet." I pulled at my hair, unable to contain all the emotions swirling inside me. They thrashed and scraped at my hollowness. "I would've known. I would've been able to get to her in time."

My shoulders slumped and I fell back down to the ground under the weight of what that meant. "He knew," I whispered.

Gerarda's breath hitched but my eyes were locked on Riven.

"Damien knew," I repeated when his brow furrowed.

"No." Riven's shadows thrashed behind him. "Damien couldn't have known. Apart from Feron, everyone who has ever known is right here."

My nose wrinkled. I knew I was right. "Collin?"

"No." Riven shook his head. "Collin never knew."

"But Damien does." I straightened my knees. "He has known. Why else would he leave you there in that alley. He could have killed us both, but he didn't."

Riven blinked, his head still shaking. "My brother and I have had little contact since I left the capital as a teenager. If that was true he would've had to have known for—"

"Years," I finished. "Decades. He's known the entire time. I'm sure of it."

My mind spun with Damien's smug face. He had sent me to kill the Shadow, he let Killian leave the capital after he murdered the king, and then he had us both in his clutches but he still let us go. It didn't serve a purpose for him unless he knew. Unless he had known the entire time, that he held a truth that could shake us to the very core and unravel the rebellion in one fell swoop.

I play for my opponents to lose.

"He wanted this." I stood with barely any air in my lungs. "He wanted all of this. That's why he chose Maerhal."

Syrra picked up her sister in her arms. Her eyes were red but hard. "He used the truth as a weapon and he used it well." Her hands tightened their hold on her sister. "Maerhal deserves better than the ground to rest." She turned away and Nikolai and Vrail followed.

"Why now?" Riven rasped. "Why do it now?"

"Because we are winning," Gerarda answered. She stood and took her place beside me. "United we were strong enough to face him, so he needed to make us crumble."

We had given Damien the time he needed. The new Blade was already on his way to the last seal. Our Fae were expended and our hope lost. Exhaustion pulled at every joint in my body; I was stiff and in need of a long sleep. There was no way I had the stamina to break that seal.

Damien had the head start he needed.

My fists clenched at my sides. Riven collapsed onto the ground and yelped. There was another flash of light. Killian lay at my feet, exhausted but no longer in pain that overwhelmed him. The jade eye that wasn't swollen shut looked up at mine. "There are no words in any tongue I know that could ever begin to describe my regret."

I crossed my arms and glanced at Gerarda, whose dark eyes were a hard glare looking down at the prince. "You needn't worry," she said to him. "The dead can't hear them."

A thick tear dropped from Killian's—Riven's—cheek and onto the ground. Part of me longed to say something that would ease the pain of that regret, but I knew there was none. Gerarda looped her arm through mine and we left the unmasked Fae prince on the trail.

CHAPTER FORTY-EIGHT

FERON STOOD AT THE EDGE of the treed city as Gerarda and I walked out of the Dark Wood. His lilac eyes were lined with tears and I knew he had seen the truth in Syrra's arms. I had no pity for him. The hollowness the guilt had burrowed through me had filled with anger that I didn't know would ever cool.

Feron reached for my hand but I did not take it. I stood tall, making a point to have my head rest higher than him and waited for his weak words to come.

His lips pursed to the side. "Thank you for bringing Maerhal home."

My lip curled in disgust. "Did you think I would leave her there? Her sister and son deserve to bury her properly. She deserves to be *home*, even if it is in death."

Feron's head drooped. "You are angry with me."

I scoffed and stepped back. "Anger does not do my feelings justice." I gritted my teeth as I looked at him. "Ten thousand years is not enough time to learn that you cannot control the way a secret festers?"

"It was not my secret to tell." Feron's words were shaky, as if even he didn't believe them.

"Fuck that." The words were sharp enough to make Feron wince but he did not turn away from me. "You had a duty to our people to make sure that Damien didn't have leverage over us. You witnessed what he's capable of when he knows his opponent's weakness. You knew he was worse than Aemon ever was. I warned you."

For the first time, I glimpsed fear in Feron's face. He was no longer blessed with his youthful glow and quiet joy, instead I saw him for what he truly was: an ancient Fae terrified that he would live through the last days of his people. "You are right. The blame lies with me."

I took a deep breath, my gaze locked on the way Feron's knuckles bulged over the top of his cane. I straightened my back and met his violet gaze. I wanted to throw more sharpened words his way, make him feel each one until my grief gave way to something more useful. But that is what Damien wanted. That would be playing into his hand once again.

My throat burned and I thirsted for wine. It was too easy to place the blame on Feron. Damien had not won because he had known a single secret, he had won because all of us had kept the truth from one another.

"Yes, it lies with you," I said, my voice hoarse and quiet. "And it lies with me for not telling you all about the dreams sooner. And it lies with Collin for the same. And Nikolai, and Syrra, and Vrail, and Riven, and whoever else could have spared Maerhal's life if they had only taken the time to tell the truth."

I sighed. The truth was little comfort now.

Feron turned toward the Myram tree where a group of Elverin had joined Syrra in preparing Maerhal's body for burial. The ritual would happen over the course of several days. Feron cleared his throat. "We shall mourn her properly."

I scoffed. "We have no time. We leave for Elvera at first light."

Feron frowned. "Keera, there is a funeral to plan and none of us are in any state to fight."

"And I am?" I crossed my arms, the heat returning to my words. "The seals did not wait while I was drowning in guilt. They could not wait while Riven was supposedly dying in your care. And they do not wait now." I started walking to the spiraled branch of the Myram where Gerarda was whispering to Elaran. "We can mourn the dead after tomorrow. If we haven't joined them."

Feron did not speak for a long moment. My heart thrashed against my chest but I did not balk. He finally nodded. "I will prepare the others."

"Good."

I only slept for a few hours, but I could feel my magic pulsing under my skin when I woke. My sleep had been dreamless, thanks to Rheih's elixir. The suns still shone outside as faint cries carried up from the grove below. News of Lash's and Maerhal's deaths had reached the city.

My heart ached. I didn't have the energy to move let alone grieve them. All I had to do was survive until tomorrow and perhaps my grief would take me too. The thought felt easier and took the weight off my chest.

I inhaled slowly, stretching my lungs so they took more than the shallow breaths they wanted to. My nostrils filled with the scent of parchment and fire smoke wafting in through the small window of my burl.

"I know you're there." I didn't say his name because I didn't know what to call him.

Killian dropped in through the window. He only wore a white tunic with the arms stained from ink and his black trousers. He hadn't had time to stitch the seams of his jacket that had busted when he transformed into Riven. He had visited a healer because his swollen eye had settled and his cuts were stitched.

"I wrote you a letter." He ran his palm through his hair; it was covered in ink too. "A lot of them."

"I don't want to read them." My words were cold just like the icy tension in the room.

"None of them were good enough anyway." He perched on the armrest of the chair.

I sat up. His eyes didn't widen at my bare chest. I hadn't bothered to put on a nightgown or cover my arms. All my secrets had been told. I remembered the way Killian had not even flinched that day in the portal when my sleeve had torn. The scars couldn't be a shock if you already knew they were there.

I brought my knees to my chest and rested my chin on them. "That day we rode into Myrelinth the first time. That was you."

Killian nodded.

I huffed a breath. "That was you the entire time? The speech in the Singing Wood. All those meetings after when you told me Riven was gone."

Killian swallowed and nodded again.

"Why?" My nose wrinkled to stop the tears. I had already cried enough. "Why not tell me?"

Killian sighed and his jaw pulsed. There was something familiar about it and the way his eyes darkened that looked like shadows. Now that I knew the truth, I could see the traces of Riven in Killian's form. It only made me angrier that I had fallen for his deceit.

"How much of the truth do you want?" His jade eyes were soft but determined as he faced me.

"All of it."

Killian took a deep breath and started. "I didn't tell you when we first struck our deal in Aralinth because I didn't trust you. I didn't even like you, though that had more to do with my faults than with yours." He sat back down on the chair properly and leaned on his knees. I inched to the end of the bed, not wanting to miss a word of it.

"Everything changed after Silstra—it had been changing for weeks, but I couldn't deny it then. You had risked *everything* for that mission and holding you in my arms, thinking you were dead was the worst day of my life. I felt like I had only just found you and that you had been taken from me. It felt like a taunt from fate, a punishment that I deserved. But then you lived." His jade eyes were misted when he looked up at me.

I balled the sheets in my hands. "And then you chose not to tell me."

"Maybe if I loved you less I would have." Killian ran his hands through his hair and the crease between his brows deepened. "What I told you in the Singing Wood was true, Keera. I thought you were safer if you went into Aemon's throne room not knowing the truth. Yes, I thought it was the best for the Elverin and the rebellion, but really I thought it was the best for you and that was all that mattered." Killian let out a long breath. "I had no idea what my father was going to do. He had grown so paranoid in those last years and I was terrified he was going to hurt you or worse. I didn't want you to carry the burden of all my secrets when you gave your report. You already had enough to hide."

I swallowed, remembering that same fear. That day had been like a dance, swinging and blocking threats with my tongue. I had been hiding so many secrets, and Aemon and Damien had been hiding many too. I shouldn't have been surprised that Killian was staging his own dance in the company of liars.

"But we had a whole night in that cave, and you didn't breathe a word of it."

Killian bowed his head. "Nikolai and Syrra advised me to tell you, but I thought I was right. I knew that your transition into the *Faelinth* would be difficult because I had done it myself. I knew how watched you'd be in those first few days and I thought it would be easier to keep the secret from the rest of the Elverin if you didn't know. By the time they had grown used to you, we knew we had—"

"A mole," I finished for him. "Did you suspect me?"

"It crossed my mind," Killian answered truthfully. "But no, the attacks were targeted against you. Still, I knew the mole had an interest in watching you. It didn't seem prudent to tell you the truth. Then we went to the capital and everything changed."

I gasped. "That was you. In the throne room, that day. You were the one who was there when Hildegard died."

Killian paled and he nodded.

My chest heaved. "But you heard what Damien said about me. About Brenna. I looked at you and thought you were disgusted."

"I was." Killian sat up straight. "But not with you. With Damien. I had never imagined there was more to the story than what you told me about your scars. I was fighting the urge to transform right there and kill them both."

"Why didn't you?"

Killian scoffed. "What do you think the Mortals would have done if the king and the prince died the same day a Dark Fae was spotted in the throne room? There would have been an uprising we had no hope of controlling. Mortals would have killed Halflings in the streets while the lords decided who was best suited to the Crown." Killian grabbed my hand. "I never wanted Hildegard to die."

A quiet sob escaped my lips. I hadn't wanted it either.

"I would have told you the moment you returned to Myrelinth, but you never left Gwyn's side. And then you started to pull away. I thought I had done something, that you had decided that whatever had been happening between us was done. I was scared telling you the truth would make you despise me as much as I despise myself."

"Why would I ever despise you? I only wish that you had told me without being forced."

Killian cleared his throat. "Do you know why I hated you when you first came to the *Faelinth*?"

"I had disrupted your plans and I was arrogant." I shrugged.

Killian laughed. "No, those would come to be some of the things I loved most about you." His jade eyes hardened and his finger picked along the cuticle of his thumb. "I saw you in your cloak and fastener, brandishing your title, and I saw myself. The version of myself that stumbled into the *Faelinth* all those years ago. I had not come for some righteous reason. I came because I needed answers, because it was my only hope of surviving. All those years I had spent in the kingdom, knowing my mother was a Fae, I never questioned it. I never worried about the Halflings that lived in the palace or the ones that starved in the streets. I never cared to know what cruel things my father had done and continued to do to them. I just wanted my books and a full belly. I was a naïve, ignorant prince whose life was made possible from the pain and suffering of his own kin." Killian's lip curled back in disgust.

"So when you came, throwing your boots onto the table and demanding to help our cause, I thought your motives were the same. I thought you enjoyed your wine and royal spend account and didn't care what it took for you to keep it."

I bit my cheek. "I was an act I had to play."

"I know that now." He slumped back. "And you played it well. But you couldn't hide yourself completely those days along the road. I saw glimpses of Keera underneath the Blade's cloak. Then you pulled out that medallion in Caerth and I knew. The Rose Road is older than my rebellion. You had been fighting for the Halflings for two *decades* before the thought had even occurred to me. When I saw you for who you were, pained and trialed, but *fighting*, I couldn't hate that. That was what I had been trying to be for so long."

"But you did start fighting."

"Eventually." Killian sighed. "But it shames me to know how long it took. When I was Riven, the Elverin accepted me without qualms. Because I was Fae and because they didn't know the truth. So when I decided to fight against my father, I knew I had to use everything at my disposal and that meant introducing Killian to the Elverin too."

"They were cautious at first." It wasn't a question, I knew it well enough.

"Yes, but not for long. But that feeling of proving myself never disappeared, it only grew. The shame I had for living a half-truth, the guilt from knowing that while I might have a legacy to the Elverin, I had a legacy in their horrors too. I was convinced I wasn't good enough for them and when you crashed through that window and into my life, I started to convince myself that I wasn't good enough for you either. I made excuse after excuse, Keera. Until everyone I love most paid the price."

"Yes, we did." It wouldn't ease his pain to decorate the truth in softness. A blade with roses on its sheath still cut just as deep.

"Does it ever get easier?" Killian's gaze was desperate. "To live with the choices you made?"

I pressed my cheek to my knee, unsure of the answer. "Yes and no." I sighed against the sheet. "Your regrets will mark you. Change you in ways you never imagined because now you know the truth of what you are. The lines you're willing to cross, the people you're willing to sacrifice when the scales weigh out against them. And those decisions can haunt you if you let them and then you'll never be free."

Killian's chest broke and he nodded to his lap.

"But"—I reached out and lifted his chin—"you have some control over how they change you. You can learn this lesson once and never make the same mistake again. You can bring those you harmed some honor by *fighting*. Keep fighting to make the world better for having made that choice."

"That still won't bring Maehral back."

"No, it won't. But she lived most of her life praying to see the sun. If you have the power to bring a little more light into world she loved so much, you owe it to her to do so."

A hoarse rasp escaped Killian's throat. "I can try."

"That is a brave thing to do." My jaw hardened. I knew too well all the ways a secret could spoil. Enough to know I was done carrying them any longer. "I have lived in the darkness for too long. Burdened by my guilt and shame in ways not so different from you. But I meant what I said in Vellinth. I am done hiding behind my past and I am done keeping secrets. I will not keep yours, not after knowing what the cost may be."

Killian swallowed. "I would never ask you to."

"I have one more question." I wrapped the sheet around my forearm, unable to look at him. "What should I call you?"

No name left his lips. He sat there, still as a statue as his jade eyes swam at the meaning of that question.

I stood from the bed and walked into the shower. Living a lie made it hard to parse out the person from the act. I left him to take all the time he needed.

CHAPTER FORTY-NINE

I WALKED OUT OF THE SHOWER and Killian was gone. The scent of parchment and smoke still hung in the air as I dressed myself in a simple long-sleeved tunic and pants. I found solace in the training grounds. I wrapped my wrists, wanting to punch something but instead I lay on the grass, staring up at the burnt streaks the setting suns had drawn across the sky. I heard soft footprints overhead and a black whirl somersaulted overtop of me.

Gwyn landed at my feet.

"Another trick Gerarda taught you?"

She shook her head and scratched the letter *F* through the air.

I smiled as best I could. "I'm glad you've made a friend. Even if she did try to sneak you onto that ship." I raised a brow and was glad Gwyn had the grace to blush.

She plopped onto the grass beside me and pointed at the Myram with her chin. Her knees were tucked underneath and she swirled a long blade of grass between her fingers.

I leaned back onto the grass. There were so many emotions swirling inside me, I didn't know what to feel first. But I knew if I didn't do something soon I was going to explode. "You heard about Maerhal?"

Gwyn frowned and nodded.

Tears pricked my eyes. The guilt over what had happened in Silstra had hollowed me out so completely that I didn't think there was anything of me left. I was just a shell, filled with useless rage about Riven's lies and secrets. I wanted to scream until my voice tore to shreds and I could spend the rest of my days in silence.

I would just lay on the sand like the discarded shell I was and wait for the tide to wash me away.

Gwyn's wide eyes tracked me as I rocked back and forth in the grass. I tried to find the words to explain it all to her, but she was just sixteen. Why should she be burdened by the woes of the world? By the terrible things I'd done. It was my job to keep her safe, not burden her with my regrets.

She pushed a stray strand of hair behind her ear. Her red curls were not loose and bouncing as they always had been, but pulled straight into a tight bun at the back of her neck. Her fingertips were calloused from hours of sword work and there was a breadth across her shoulders that hadn't been there before.

My stomach tightened. Gwyn was not a child in need of protection, she was no longer a child at all. Perhaps what she needed, what we both needed was for me to speak to her as I would my other friends. Let her know everything and come to her own conclusions.

Everyone else was too close to this for me to trust their answers. And Gwyn had been the one to come and find me.

I opened my mouth and words cascaded from my tongue like the thundering falls at Silstra. I told her everything. The alliance that I had struck months before, the bond between Riven and I that had only grown. The secret he had been keeping from me the entire time. Her eyes widened and blinked with every new piece of the story, but she never turned away. Not even when I told her what Damien had done. To Brenna and Maerhal both.

Her blue eyes only softened and she grabbed my hand. "Don't hold onto guilt for playing games that Damien made you play."

I lurched backward at the sound of Gwyn's voice. It was raspy, from lack of use, but also from age. Her cadence had changed too, no longer a girl's high pitch, but something darker. Something more mixed.

She kept speaking as if she hadn't spent the last three months in silence. "I was so angry when we made it out of that palace. I was angry at myself for not fighting hard enough, for only taking an eye when I should have taken Damien's life." She plucked a handful of grass from the ground. "But I was angry at everything else too. It was all I could be. Every time I saw one of the children swinging from the vines instead of cleaning a chamber pot, the anger grew. Every time someone asked what I wanted to do, reminded me that here I had a choice, I just wanted to flip the table over and run. It all happened too quickly, too suddenly, like the years I had spent tethered to that place were insignificant. Like everything he had done to me didn't matter. How could I let it? I survived. I was free, when so many are not."

I swallowed and brushed her fingers in the tangle of plucked grass between us. "Those years mattered, Gwyn."

She sniffled and her nose twitched. "I know that now, but it didn't feel that way. It just felt wrong. And then Rheih told me that the slash he made had left me barren." She ran a flat palm along her lower belly. "And that made me angrier. I had always known I didn't want to bear a child. Not in the kingdom, not under that curse. But then when my dream finally came true, better than I ever could have imagined, Damien had taken that choice too." She scowled at the ground.

My heart splintered for her. "I'm so sorry, Gwyn. I wish I would have known before I healed you."

She shook her head. "You saved me. And I am very grateful." She gave me a stern look that said she would not allow me to take any of that blame.

I nodded. "Did the rage ever end?"

"It lessened." Gwyn leaned back on her hands. "Gerarda's training helped. It gave me a place to channel it. To imagine that maybe I would get the chance to carve that blade of mine across Damien's throat yet."

Blood drained from my face. I never wanted Gwyn anywhere within Damien's grasp again.

"But it didn't end until I realized that rage was just another part of Damien's game."

My head snapped to the side. "What do you mean?"

"If I stay angry. If I stay *silent*. Then he wins." Gwyn chuckled darkly. "He is thousands of leagues away, but I still plan out my every move at his whim. That's what he wanted before he thought he'd killed me. And it would give him too much joy to know he controls me still." She turned to me and looked back at the Myram. "That's what he's doing now, Keera. He set up his game and you all are still playing it as long as you let this break you. Damien wins if you can't find a way to move past this."

I scoffed. "You think I should forgive Riven out of spite?"

Gwyn shrugged. "There are worse reasons."

"You sound like Gerarda."

Gwyn grinned. "There are worse people to be." Her smile fell and she nudged my boot with her own. "What exactly do you need to find the strength to forgive Riven for?"

My face fell. "Maerhal is dead."

"Yes." Gwyn nodded coldly. "As are many."

"I cannot be angry over one death if I am not angry for them all?" I rolled my tongue over my teeth.

Gwyn shook her head. "You can be as angry as you like. But to me, I see little difference between what Riven did and what you have done."

"I wore my mask as Blade because I had to." My jaw clenched. "Because it was *right*."

"Didn't Riven do what he thought was right?" Gwyn's red brow arched. "You may not agree with his choices, but do you think he was acting only for himself?"

"No." I picked grass from the lacing of my boot. Despite the words I had thrown at him, I knew Riven had weighed every choice he made. It was his choice of scale that stoked my rage. "Riven would never act only for himself."

Gwyn gave me a knowing look. "There are many who would not have acted as Blade in the way you did. There are many who disagree with how you used your title, but your choices have always been in the interest of the Halflings. I think it is the same for Riven and I think it only benefits Damien to overlook that."

My breath hitched as I realized Gwyn was right. All this squabbling and fighting was exactly what Damien wanted. And if I let it fracture us, then Damien won. There was a truth to that I could not ignore.

I wrapped my arms around her shoulders and sighed. "When did you get so wise?"

"I had to." Gwyn squeezed me back before letting her arms fall beside her. "It was either that or die."

CHAPTER FIFTY

The melancholic singing from the grove kept me from sleep. I laid there until the moon was high in the cloudy skies before I decided to forgo sleep altogether. I rose and walked along the branches to one of the farther groves.

The peaceful roll of the lake beckoned me closer as my mind whirled with every interaction that I had ever had with Riven and Killian. It seemed so clear now. Where Riven had gone to that night in Cereliath while I was dancing with the prince. I had been so shocked that Killian would press a kiss to my neck but it had been Riven the entire time.

Someone moved behind me and the cool breeze carried the scent of parchment and fire. I flung a rock across the lake. "Go away, Killian." I winced. I hadn't meant to be mean.

A flash of violet light and the air was filled with the scent of dew and birchwood.

I turned on Riven as his shadows coiled around my feet. "You think now is the time for jokes?"

"I'll likely die tomorrow." Riven shrugged. "It would be nice to hear you laugh one more time."

The casualness of Riven's words tore at me. I hadn't considered that he would be there for the final seal. But I knew the truth now. Riven needn't pretend. He could fight as the prince, without the distraction of the pain.

"Though I'm glad to know that I will be buried with my true face."

I let the last rock drop from my hand. "Is that why you keep switching to this form even though it causes you so much pain? You think it more worthy than the one with the crown on its head?"

My words drove through Riven's chest. His violet eyes hardened. "It is the form I prefer. And the one that I wanted you to know."

I shook my head and kicked the stone into the water. It sent a flock of glowing flies into the air from the ripples. "Don't start telling half-truths again."

Riven's brows furrowed. "How is that not true?"

"I've been thinking about all the times I've spoken with Killian." I crossed my arms. "Each one is like the scene of a play, recast over and over again in my mind. But I think I have sorted you and Vrail amongst the dozens of encounters. But there's still something that does not make any sense to me."

"What?" Riven's question was part fearful and part daring. The shadows curled higher up my legs and his brow twitched in pain. He could barely keep them leashed.

"If you were so desperate for me to love Riven and not the prince. Why dance with me in Cereliath? Why share those parts of yourself that you hate so much at all? Why kiss me *twice*." I coated that last word with all the venom I could muster.

Riven's brow peaked and his gaze trailed along my chest. "You're angry because I flirted with you?" Riven asked hotly. There was an explosion of light and he stood in front of me as Killian once more. "Or because *I* flirted with you?"

"See, it's all just a game to you." I shook my head and started walking back down the path to Myrelinth. "I'm done playing games."

Riven grabbed my arm, still in his Killian form. "I wasn't playing a game, *diizra*."

"Don't." I turned on him like a viper. My skin sizzled as I walked across the sand. "You've been flirting with me since Cereliath. It's like you needed me to fall for the Fae *and* the prince."

Riven didn't bother to deny it.

I clenched my jaw and his Mortal cheeks went red. "You wanted me to *want* you? Like this." I gestured to his Mortal form. "If the secret meant so much to you, why toy with me at all?"

A feral hunger I had never seen on Killian's face tugged at his lips. Somewhere in the heat of his jade stare I could recognize Riven within it. "You think I *meant* to flirt with you as openly as I did at that ball?" Riven stalked toward me, still in his Mortal form, but somehow just as commanding of the shadows around us. "That Harvest was meant to be a reprieve *from* you. I couldn't help the way my Fae body reacted to your presence. I couldn't stop the bond making my magic call out to you even when I despised our alliance. I went *weeks* without shifting back, without a moment of relief from the pain, only to find that this body yearns for you all the same because *I* yearn for you."

Another violet flash and Riven stood only inches from me cloaked in shadows. I took a step back and found myself pressed against a tree trunk. "You asked me once if we would be together if it weren't for our magic." Riven pressed a hard, scraping kiss to my throat, it sent a shiver down my spine, so powerful I couldn't push him away. I wasn't sure I wanted to. "If we weren't *miiskwithir*." His teeth tugged on my ear. "But I crave *nothing* except the taste of you, Keera. In this form"—a flash of violet light—"or this one."

I was engulfed by the scent of parchment and ink as Riven's hands tangled into the hair at the base of my neck and pulled. My eyes fluttered open and I was met with soft jade eyes wrapped in amber. My pulse quickened, but I didn't look away. For so long those eyes only reminded me of everything I had lost. My childhood, my first love, myself. All the pieces I had to carve out of my soul and offer up to the Crown. But now, I stared into the eyes I'd known so long as Killian's and found a chance to reclaim some of what I'd lost.

"Prove it," I whispered in a hard voice.

Riven raised a blond brow. "What are you asking me?"

I ran my finger across Riven's mouth, feeling how much thinner and firmer his lips were in his Mortal form. "You crave me just as much as a prince?"

Riven nodded his head against my thumb.

"Then show me."

A grin grew along his thin Mortal lips before Riven grabbed the back of my head and kissed me. He tugged the hair at the nape of my neck until I gasped against his lips. He scraped his teeth down my throat and squeezed my thigh, bringing it to his waist.

His kisses were desperate and harder in this form, knowing that he could not hurt me in his Mortal body. There were no shadows pulling at his focus, no distraction in his touch. His hands gripped the neck of my tunic and ripped it down the middle. I could see it in the feral way he looked at me that his entire world ended at my skin.

"I have missed this." He groaned as his mouth found my breast. I gasped in shock as he pulled at my nipple with his teeth and swirled his tongue around the tip. My head fell back against the tree as he did it again, this time on the other side.

He made quick work of my trousers, only letting go of me long enough to pull them off entirely. Then he grabbed one leg and licked up from my knee, pressing a kiss along the inside of my thigh, and then another, and then another, lifting my leg each time until it was bent over his shoulder. Then he nipped at the softness where my leg ended and looked up at me.

"Are you sure you want this, *diizra*?" he whispered against my skin. That nickname should have sounded wrong coming from Killian's lips but it didn't. The melody of it was still the same, the hunger, the love, the need, it was all there in whatever voice Riven used.

When I didn't answer his question, Riven's hand trailed up my torso. It carved a path between my breasts until he reached my throat. His fingers wrapped around the base of it and he pulled my jaw down to look at him.

Jade eyes stared up at me; they swam with desire but something else too. Patience and worry. I knew that if I told Riven to stop he would without question. But seeing him on his knees, his mouth so close to where I needed him, was too much to turn away.

"Yes," I rasped, my head scratching against the tree as I angled my hips toward him.

His teeth scraped along the top of my mound, a gentle tease followed by firm kisses. My leg shook with the need for him.

"Please," I whispered, his hand still wrapped around my throat.

His tongue parted me, slowly at first, like an itch being scratched. But then his nails trailed down my body from my neck, scraping at my skin just as his other hand slipped inside me. Riven captured that swell of need on his tongue and did not relent until I was sure he had split me in two.

I fell back thinking Riven was done but he didn't stop. He pumped his fingers into me without pause, matching the tempo of my moans as he reignited the wave of heat that had exploded through my core. He stared up at me, his eyes narrowing as my chest shook at every touch.

That warmth spread through my body once again, more intense than the first time. My head lolled to the side and I felt the thrashing power of my magic unleash. The lake bubbled and tiny droplets of water floated from the surface and coated my skin, but it did not do enough to cool me.

Riven didn't stop, though his eyes tracked the movement of my water magic through the trees. He added a third finger and caressed that inner part of me that felt so good it bordered on pain. My hand dropped to his hair, pinning him against me so he knew not to stop. My hips bucked against his face but Riven only groaned, enjoying every second of it.

He kept me on that edge with water droplets floating in the air all across the small grove we were in. "I want to see you come undone," he ordered from beneath me. His tongue circled that tiny spot until I gave him what he wanted.

The waves of pleasure were still pulsing through me as I pulled him to my face and claimed his mouth with mine. Riven pushed against me until there no space left between our bodies, so tightly pressed we could have become part of the tree.

Riven unlaced the top of his pants and I turned around so my chest was pressed against the smooth bark. Riven paused for only the slightest moment and I knew he was looking at the scars along my back. His hand trembled as he touched them in this form for the first time, a form that looked so much like the one who made them.

"*Diizra*." Riven kissed my shoulder blades. "You can face me if that is more comfortable."

There was no judgment in his tone, only deep concern. It made my heart flutter, but I had known what I was doing when I turned around. "No." There were no secrets between us now. I wasn't going to let what Damien had done to me wedge itself between us, no matter what form Riven took. I reached back and pulled him closer to me by his hip.

Riven nipped at my ear and slowly pushed that hardness against me. He pulled back so I could feel the length of him. Even in this body, Riven could reach parts of me only he had touched.

"Keera," he groaned as our bodies joined together. His arm wrapping around my shoulders, arching my back toward him as he slid in and out of me. He kissed the nape of my neck and then the top of my large scar. I gasped but he kept going, leaving gentle, loving kisses along the ragged parts of me while his hands dimpled my thighs, pulling me against him in primal thrusts.

"*Diizra*." His breath was hot on my ear and sent a wave of pleasure down my spine. "I want to look at you when I finish."

I groaned, pressing into him one more time before he stepped back from the tree. I turned and stared at him in the pale moonlight. This form was so different from his Fae one. His frame was slimmer, but still as toned as any soldier's. He lifted his fingers to my belly and I could feel the callouses on his hands—some from swordplay, but most from flipping through books and pressing quills to parchment.

I stepped toward him, licking my lips as every muscle in his body tensed with anticipation. I dragged one finger up his chest, starting at his thigh and then circling over his hip. Riven's jaw pulsed but he did not move an inch, relishing the pleasure of my touch. I kissed him deeply, letting his hands roam over my skin with abandon. Then I caught his bottom lip with my teeth.

He stilled. The amber rings around his jade eyes seemed to deepen as he watched his own lip snap back from my mouth. I ran my thumb across it, noticing how much more swollen his Mortal lips had become. Then I pressed a single finger to his chin and made him fall to his knees.

Riven licked his lips, ready to feast on me again. I shook my head and shoved him back with my foot along his chest. He fell back onto the sand with wide eyes that narrowed as I stood over him.

I smirked at the hunger in his face as I lowered myself on top of him. Our bodies reunited without protest. Riven groaned, fisting the flesh along my hips as they bucked. His neck stretched back and I leaned down to drag my fangs across his beating pulse just as he had done to me. Goosebumps covered his skin and his breath hitched as my grinding became more intense.

He nipped at my breast with his teeth and moaned my name into the night. I fell over that edge of ecstasy with him, my body collapsing on top of his until the only sound was our joined and ragged breaths.

I sat up and lifted my leg, but Riven held me by the hips. "I'm not close to finished with you." He pulled me by my neck and kissed me with just as much vigor as before.

I peered down at his sweaty chest. His Mortal body was covered in red patches and he could barely catch his breath. "You're spent." I chuckled, caressing his nose with mine and stroking his blond hair.

"This form might be." Riven flipped me over in the sand and there was a flash of light. My body tensed, taking in the new length that pierced me. "But this form is quite rested, I assure you."

Black shadows burst from Riven in all directions. I wrapped my legs around him and pulled him into a kiss. The first light of dawn was only a few short hours away and I would have Riven in as many ways and as many forms as he would give me.

"I love you, Riven," I whispered, pressing my lips to his jaw.

He stilled above me. A wet drop fell on my chest and his head hung loose between his shoulder blades. He cleared his throat and buried his face in my neck. "I will love you to whatever end, my *diizra*." He kissed me with the desperate passion of a lover who did not know if this embrace would be the last. I held him to me, memorizing every part of him in case it was.

CHAPTER FIFTY-ONE

We reached the Pool of Elvera just after dawn. The lake shone in the morning sun and the mountainous tree at the center of the island made it appear deceptively close. Even without Damien's soldiers to contend with, the journey across the lake would take some time.

Our group was small but well equipped to the task. Feron stood at the front with me and Riven in his Mortal form. Syrra flanked one end with Nikolai and Vrail, while Gerarda and Elaran stood behind Myrrah on the other.

I recognized Kairn's black cloak waving in the wind of one of the many ships Damien had sent to defend the last seal. They circled the entire island, though the fleet tripled in depth along the southernmost point.

Damien had gleaned even more from Volcar.

I turned back toward the group. "We move as planned. Their presence does not change anything. Break their lines, draw them out, and I will break the seal."

The two lines nodded in unison. I turned to Nikolai and tried not to cringe at his puffy, red eyes and blank stare. He grabbed four vials from his hands and stepped into the lake. The vials were not filled with flower petals or elixir, but intricate little ships the size of a fly. Nikolai placed each one in the water, pacing four times before he dropped the second and then the third.

Gold swirls encased the glass until it dissolved like sugar. Then they wrapped around the tiny ships and spun. The wood creaked as the water underneath continued to spiral and thrash. Within seconds we were staring at four small boats with even tinier sails attached to the front.

A horn sounded across the lake and the first line of ships armed their archers. With the favorable breeze, we were just within range.

"On the ready!" Gerarda called, looking at me.

I nodded and waited for her arm to fall. I heard the *snap* of a hundred drawstrings behind me but did not turn. I waited until Gerarda gave the signal and channeled a gust fierce enough to blow the arrows into the lake. They fell across the calm water like raindrops.

My shoulders eased and I turned back to the group only to see furrowed brows across everyone's faces.

Purple vapor began to waft from the drowned bolts. Out of the corner of my eye, I saw Kairn launch an arrow of his own, this one coated in dancing tendrils of flame.

"Fall back!" I yelled as the vapor ignited the air. A flash of violet flame cooked the space above our heads and heated my back beyond the point of comfort. I looked up and saw a billowing cloud of violet flame suspended in the air. It slowly rose, inch by inch, but not nearly quickly enough.

In one move, Kairn had clipped my wings. I couldn't fly to the island without risking the range of their arrows. Exactly as he'd planned.

Fyrel broke from the line and headed to the boats. She stepped into the water and screamed. She folded under the pain, crashing into the water only for her scream to transform into an animal-like shriek.

Feron raised his hand and the lake floor bubbled underneath her, pushing her out of the water on a platform made of mud. Elaran and Gerarda ran to her, careful not to step into the lake, and cut the leg of her trousers. It was burnt and bubbled.

"They've poisoned the lake," Elaran said in disgust.

I knelt at Fyrel's side, calling my healing gift forward and letting it flow through her. She sighed and went still in Gerarda's arms.

I checked Fyrel's skin. "Get Rheih to put mudkilp paste on that when we return." She nodded shyly. I turned to Gerarda. "We need to break their lines."

I let the coldness creep up my spine just like I had in Volcar. I cast my arm over the lake shore and froze the water into a solid slab around our ships.

Riven took a cautious step. When he didn't yelp in pain, the others ran onto the ice to load into the hulls. Syrra and Elaran lifted Myrrah into her special seat at the back of the largest ship. Riven embarked on the ship beside me and gave me a tight nod.

I returned it and let the whirlwind in my chest out in four large streams. I knotted them together and let them push us free of the ice.

Kairn whipped his cloak around him and pointed at the island, leaving the sellswords to protect the waters on their own. The troops along the island shore began to drum.

"Archers, take your posts!" Gerarda called to the group. Everyone but me, Myrrah, and Feron nocked an arrow where they sat in the boat. "Release!"

A barrage of arrows flew through the air. I called a light breeze to propel them farther along the lake but the soldiers pulled large shields over their heads, blocking the sharp points from piercing a single one.

"Nock!" Gerarda yelled through clenched teeth. The soldiers only tightened their cover.

I turned to Riven. "They can't use their shields if they're ash and ember." I let the whirlwind build in my chest and focused on the hot air above one of the boats. I made it spin in circles, tighter and faster each time, growing taller until it connected with the cloud of violet flame overhead.

The flames didn't need any coaxing. They traveled down the whirlwind and devoured the shields as well as the men holding them. Their screams rang out over the lake as I burned three more boats.

Another horn sounded and the third flank of boats fell back toward the island shore. I smirked across the horizon at the tiny black cloak waving in the wind. Kairn would be much more careful facing me than his comrades were.

"Nock!" Gerarda called again. "Aim for their bellies!"

The arrows flew through the air once more, straight and low just as Gerarda had commanded. Five men fell over the edge of their boat and burned screaming for someone to save them.

By the time our hulls passed through that part of the lake, the men were floating facedown in the water.

"Feron, can you see if the water is still toxic that far back?" I pointed at one of the ships clambering for the shore.

Feron's purple eyes glowed as he nodded. He turned toward the black sail and plucked one of the men from the ship with a weed from the lake bottom. The man screamed in agony the moment his flesh touched the water.

"Excellent." I grinned, allowing the thrashing sensation to build in my stomach. I raised my arms, relishing in the power coursing through them until a wall of water stood between us and the soldiers wanting us dead.

Fyrel and Elaran gasped up at the sheer size of it. I let it grow into the flaming cloud and then I released it.

The shrieks were muffled as the swirling wall dropped onto the remaining ships. The current of the wave propelled the closest boats to shore carrying nothing but survivors.

Chaos erupted on the beach as the soldiers loaded rocks into tiny catapults they had set up along shore and their archers devised a line across the beach. The risk of disembarking in their range was too high.

"Stop the boats!" I called when we neared too close to shore. I unraveled my gusts and our sails went limp. A chill ran down my spine and the waters around the boat froze, almost to the shore but not quite.

The Shades moved without the need for a command, helping others out of the boat and Myrrah back into her chair. I unsheathed my sword and Riven did the same. He no longer carried his broad sword behind his back, but a thinner long blade that suited his Mortal form.

Syrra had her curved blades in her hands and looked out onto the beach with a fury I had never seen. Even Nikolai beside her stalked toward the men with a blade in each fist, determined to hurt Damien in all the ways he had hurt him.

"Charge!" I commanded and our line erupted into a run.

Elaran ran behind Myrrah, her chair slipping on the flat ice.

"Feron!" I shouted as we neared the shore. The barrage of arrows plummeting to our heads was easy enough for me to deal with. But the catapults and the large mechanical bows were something better dealt with by a master earth wielder.

I turned to see Feron standing on the ice behind us. His eyes glowed violet and there was a loud, thunderous crack. But the fiery sky did not flash with light. The sand along the beach began to move, drifting downward into a chasm Feron had split across the island.

The men shouted, running away from the sinkhole, but many were caught in the flow of falling sand. When their catapults had fallen underneath the surface of the beach another loud crack sounded as Feron moved the earth back together again.

Their archers shot again and I lifted their arrows into the violet flames still burning above our heads. But the skies above the island were clear and then we would be able to fight at our full force. I let out that chilly power once more, fusing the ice completely to the shore as we stormed the beach.

"Keera, go!" Gerarda shouted, taking three soldiers down in one twist through the air.

I nodded and transformed into my winged form. I soared above, searching for the seal over the south end of the island. The glamour shattered and I saw the interwoven pattern glowing along the beach. It was as if the seal had been made of sunlight, glowing brightly under the smoke-covered sky.

Kairn was running toward it. I dove without a second thought.

I hooked my talons through his shoulders and dropped him to the ground before transforming midair and bringing my blade to his head. But Kairn was quick footed for such a mountain of a man. He rolled away from my blade and turned with a sharp sword of his own.

We circled each other as his men shouted in the distance. From the corner of my eye, I saw that Feron had reached the shore. He'd built a platform and wall to protect Myrrah from the soldiers but not the soldiers from her well-aimed bow. He had called thick roots from the earth and they wrapped around his legs like one of Riven's shadows, keeping him straight as he walked across the beach as a giant tree. He kicked his legs as he walked, knocking through the battle lines and leaving soldiers in his wake.

Kairn snarled at me. His black eye didn't move in his head like his gray one. Instead the amber iris flared until there was nothing left of the darkness. Kairn's back straightened and his limbs went limp at his side.

"Hello, Keera," he cooed in his thick rasp of a voice, but somehow I knew it wasn't him speaking at all.

My lip curled over my fangs. "It's over, Damien." I lifted my blade. "You have lost."

"Have I?" A cruel grin grew across Kairn's face in an identical match to Damien's. He pulled out a thin blade from his belt. It dripped with thick, black liquid.

I swallowed waiting for him to attack, but he didn't. Instead Kairn plunged the blade into the seal. There was a flash of light and he yelped in pain as the seal blew him backward onto the beach. Soldiers turned to protect their captain, but my friends would take good care of them.

I needed to end this.

I pulled out the red dagger from my waist and plunged it into the ground. The pressure of the seal elicited a gasp from my chest as every bit of power was pulled into the earth. It felt like the chasm of sand Feron had created, a one-way drain too powerful for me to stop.

I clenched my jaw and traced the outline of the seal. Every inch was hard fought and sweat already poured down my face. When I was finished with the outer circle, the ground shook beneath my feet, but I didn't look up to see what Feron was doing.

Only when I cut through the first intersecting line did I realize it wasn't Feron's gifts at all, but the island itself. Water rushed back into the lake as the entire chunk of land began to rise into the air. Gerarda and Nikolai ran to my side with their swords in front of them, ready for an attack.

I kept cutting even as the amber blood dripped from my mouth and onto the sand. I screamed as the pressure on my arm moved up my chest until it felt like I was being squeezed underneath the island. There was a crash of steel as the soldiers circled around us. I heard Syrra's swift swipes of her blades and the sound of bodies crashing to the ground.

I was barely moving now and still so much of the seal was left. I didn't know if I would be able to undo it before the rest of my energy was claimed.

Riven appeared by my side. There was a flash of light and his Fae back arched in pain, but he did not transform back into his Mortal form. Instead he grabbed my hand. "Let me help you, *diizra*."

I shook my head as Riven let the flow of his magic pour into me from our bond. It was cold and prickly, but my arm moved easier across the sand.

Riven's arm spasmed with pain as we started the last line. His violet eyes were almost red from where blood vessels had blown and his lower face was coated in his own blood. "Riven, it's killing you," I wheezed.

"We must see this through. Together." He somehow found the strength to caress my cheek, not caring that it was caked with dirt and blood. "It has been an honor to love you, *diizra*." Riven yanked our hands through the middle of the seal just as the words *I love you* fell from my lips.

Our connection went cold and Riven's shadows faded to nothing. His entire body seized in a fit of pain and then he fell, rolling off the seal in front of me.

Tears flowed down my face, but there was nothing I could do for him now. There was nothing I could do to save myself from that pain, except plunge my dagger through the last seal. The pressure on my arm lifted as the silver liquid turned to gold underneath me. The red blade flashed in the sunlight as it plummeted into the center of the seal and the entire beach exploded into waves of light and shadow.

CHAPTER FIFTY-TWO

I OPENED MY EYES and felt more power than I had ever thought possible. My gusts flowed beneath me, carrying me into the air as I waved my arms over the violet flames. They went out with barely an impact to the surge of power the seal had given me.

Black tendrils oozed from the seal. They took the shape of tiny snapping creatures before disappearing on the wind. There was something familiar in their faces as they roared, but I didn't have time to study them.

I set my sights along the beach and blew tiny streams around each soldier's throat. Their eyes bulged as they fought against the ropes they could not see, but could feel tightening around their necks. One by one they dropped.

"Nikolai!" Vrail shouted, running toward the wood.

Nikolai was kicking and thrashing, but it was no use against Kairn's strong frame. I dropped to the ground and tried to find a way to stop them without risking injury to Nikolai. The moment cost us all as Kairn pulled a vial of black berries from his pocket and threw them in between the twisted root of the mountainous tree at the mouth of the waterfall that now poured from the center of the island.

They disappeared inside the water and Syrra screamed, falling to her knees.

"We can go after them!" I shouted, running toward the portal but Gerarda yanked me back.

Vrail's face was coated in tears. "That portal can bring you anywhere in Elverath. We have no way of knowing where they went."

My stomach lurched as I saw the golden light between the roots fade away and with it our hopes of bringing Nikolai back with us.

There was a cough behind me and I turned, my focus narrowing onto the black-clothed body behind me. Riven's chest heaved with a gasping breath and I fell to my knees.

Streams of tears flowed down my face as I crawled to Riven, nestling his head in my lap. I gasped as he opened his eyes to see me.

He was still in his Fae form. Long black hair and olive brown skin, but the eyes that stared up at me were not violet but jade green ringed in amber. "The pain," Riven huffed a laugh in disbelief. "It's gone."

"Can you feel your magic at all?" I asked, already knowing the answer.

Riven shook his head, but he held no disappointment. His new eyes flashed with hope as he realized what he had become. No longer Mortal and Fae living two split lives, but one whole Halfling. The smile that stretched across his face was one of unimpeded joy.

My chest heaved and I collapsed on top of him, not caring that I didn't understand what had happened.

I turned to the others, relieved to see that apart from Nikolai, everyone else was standing unharmed. Syrra's jaw dropped as she looked at me and she fell to her knees.

"*Niinokwenira*," she whispered with a bow of her head.

I furrowed my brow and glanced at Gerarda and Elaran, but they were staring at me like I was a sea creature walking across land. "It's not possible," Gerarda whispered to herself.

I shook my head and leaned back. "What are you talking about?"

"Keera." Gerarda took a tentative step toward me. "Your eyes."

I grabbed a silver blade from my belt, wondering if the seal had changed my powers too. But I still felt them coursing through my veins as strong as ever, with a hint of something new in the mix of it. I held the small blade up to the bridge of my nose and gasped at the unfocused reflection. There was no denying that my eyes had changed colors just as Riven's had.

But mine were not green.

They were gold.

ACKNOWLEDGMENTS

This was the book I was waiting to write ever since I first penned Keera's name on a pad of paper. I've imagined so many of these scenes since the very beginning, giggling to myself about how readers would react. This book has been the most delicious and exciting of my career so far and it would never have been possible without the amazing people who helped along the way.

Firstly, thank you to Laura, my wonderful editor for helping put the puzzle pieces together and pushing me to include a certain love scene that I was nervous to type out. You were right, it made the story so much better.

Emma, while you didn't get to read this book in draft, you were there every time my imposter syndrome creeped too close and I convinced myself I had made a huge mistake and should give up writing altogether. I could never say miigwetch enough. I am so grateful to have such a supportive sister, and since I am currently writing this before you've read the book, I hope you like it and that you aren't *too* mad at me.

My dear friend Marissa, thank you for answering every excited, anxious, angry, frustrated, or pessimistic FaceTime call. I wouldn't have been able to get through finishing the first draft of this without you there each day. Miigwetch a thousand times over.

Chi-miigwetch to my mom and dad for encouraging me when I said that I was going to quit my job and write full time. Your trust and open ears meant so much.

Thank you, Jenny and Dan, for working hard to promote and market this book and the rest of Keera's story. So many readers have found her because of all you do.

I'd also like to say thank you to the friends I've made because of this story and the app that launched it all. Thank you to Bri and El for your endless excitement and belief in Keera and in me. I hope we have many more late-night calls talking about writing and books and stories to come. Miigwetch to Alex for loving Keera like I do and stacking my bookshelves with so many books that have changed my perspective as a writer and a human. Thank you to Gracie, Tori, Cait, Deeqy, and Amivi for posting clues and launching the title of this book. And to all of Scooby Gang, I'm so glad to have met such an amazing group of curious, kind, insightful minds. May the soupdom always reign.

There are too many to name, but I would like to thank every reader of this series. Whether you care for Keera or not, you have changed my life and helped me achieve my dream so early in life. And to the ones who have taken the time to send emails, DMs, letters, voice notes, comments, and one curious image I think was meant to be a telegram, I can never express how much your kind words mean to me and how much they keep me centered when my mind starts playing tricks on me. I am forever grateful for every single one of you.

TURN THE PAGE FOR A SPECIAL BONUS CHAPTER FROM DYNARA'S PERSPECTIVE . . .

DYNARA

I DIDN'T KNOW if it was a fitting end or a bad omen that the room where I'd almost died was softly lit from within, glowing down at me from the hill. I opened the fabric-covered door of the carriage before the coachman could reach it. The House of Harvest stood tall over Cereliath—keeping the western block in its shadow, where the pleasures of night were always available at Mistress Augustine's windowless theatre.

It stood across the alley, the hum of music and drunken laughter oozing out into the streets even though the second sun had yet to set. Mistress Augustine was one of the most respected madames in the city and she had made it a foundational part of her business to provide only the most beautiful and talented of women.

Women. Not Halflings.

A Mortal like Mistress Augustine would never tangle with such creatures. She left that to the royal courtesan houses, where men were free to feast on their more *exotic* appetites. Mistress Augustine was a private connoisseur of the finest experiences.

No amber blood allowed.

But I had been a courtesan long enough to know that the girls at Augustine's weren't all they seemed to be. And Mistress Augustine had connections and power within the House of Harvest that I would need to utilize to see my plan through.

The coachman offered his arm and I lowered myself to the ground, finally stepping into the city I had not returned to since my escape. There was a bite to the air, but I was not chilled by any fear.

I was the monster creeping in the alley at night. And the power was mine to take.

The healed brand on my wrist ached but I ignored it, pulling my lace glove over the skin. The black silk emphasized the intricate gold band of my glamoured ring that I wore outside of the glove. It kept my true face concealed and served as a symbol of wealth for whoever opened that door.

"Are you certain you want me to leave you here, miss?" The gangly young coachman's eyes trailed up the stone dwelling to the cast iron sign hanging above the door. It told no name, only had a lock surrounded by three keys of varying sizes. Bile coated my tongue. Somehow the subtlety made it all worse.

But this was the house I needed to take.

"Leave me." I lifted my chin in the same calm but dangerous way as the Mortal women who found me in bed with their husbands. At least the ones who hadn't realized I was a Halfling.

He nodded without another word and I heard the door click shut behind me. I waited until the jostling of wooden wheels softened in the distance before I knocked.

Muffled shouts erupted behind the thick wood. I took a deep breath and held my satchel with both hands. Every Harvest Lady did so on their strolls.

"Jalisse I told you, never answer the door!" A voice bellowed from the other side before the door slowly opened. A tall woman stood there. She had thick waves of nightshade that billowed past her waist. They were loose apart from the intricate crown of braids that pulled them between her shoulders to show off her proud, beautiful face.

A face that had captured an entire city.

Crison Clairbelle. The most sought-after courtesan at Mistress Augustine's theater, and therefore the most sought-after courtesan in the city. I kept my surprise hidden. I didn't expect the crown jewel to be answering the door.

Her full pout and feline eyes were so familiar to me already. She had never seen my face before, distorted as it was from my other glamour, but I had been watching her and eavesdropping on the gossip. Word was that Mistress Augustine no longer supplied girls younger than sixteen. After three decades, she seemed to have had a change of heart that just so happened to coincide with Crison's arrival in Cereliath.

An apparent new beauty in the quarter, but who was said to bear a striking resemblance to another famed courtesan from Volcar who had been bought by a foreign lord and taken across the sea to be his lady wife. A remarkable story for any romantic. A remarkably false tale to any courtesan's ear.

It had been enough to pique my interest. But it was the soft bump along the ridge of her ear that made me sure. Her healer had been meticulous. Concealing the scar to grow like a Mortal's ear.

I didn't smile. A Lady of the Harvest would not be excited about coming around this house. "I'm here to speak with Mistress Augustine."

Crison's jaw pulsed. "I'm afraid she's not in."

"No?" I raised a brow and glanced over to the lit window to the left. "Is that not her study?"

The little girl beside Crison pulled at her skirt to speak. "Yes, she's in there tallying the books."

Crison shot Jalisse a warning look. "She is not expecting visitors."

I pulled out a small but heavy coin purse. I placed it in her hand. "I'm not a visitor." I raised my chin once more. "I'm a client."

Crison crossed her arms. I liked the defiant edge to her stance. It was an undesirable trait in a courtesan, but exactly the trait that was required to see this plan through. "We do not see clients at the house," she stated plainly.

I pulled another, fatter, pouch out of my belt purse. "I think you can make an exception."

Crison pushed the money back, handing me both bags. "It's house policy."

A cool breeze blew between us as I studied her hard, gray eyes. I had been trained to see the deepest desires in people, to use them to serve my own mistress's ends, but now I served my own.

"I think you will make the exception." I looked down at Jalisse's perfectly round ears before making a point to linger on Crison's stitched one. "My husband has *unique* tastes that I would like to discuss with Mistress Augustine ahead of time."

Crison pulled the small girl behind her like a bear protecting her cub. "We do not entertain such *tastes* here."

I smiled through the bile in my throat. "Which is precisely why I have chosen to come to this establishment." I pulled out the small letter I had Killian help me forge. "I have a letter from Prince Damien himself."

Crison stared at the royal seal until her neck tensed. "Of course." She opened the door wide and stood to the right. "I will call the mistress for you, Miss . . ."

"Call me Dynara, dear." I didn't have to worry about Augustine knowing my name.

Crison's eyes widened at the Elvish-sounding name before she ushered Jalisse up the stairs. The young girl slowly walked up the wooden steps, looking back at me through the balusters as she stomped to her room. An older girl, though not by much, followed after her without a word.

"She will see you now," Crison said, stepping out of Mistress Augustine's study. She held the large oak door open before closing it with us both inside.

Mistress Augustine wasn't as old as Mortals could be, but she had spent decades building her business on the trade of young women—and apparently Halflings when it suited her. Her gray hair was pulled back into an elaborate bun. Her dress was plain black, but exquisite. I recognized the lace as Wilden's. She stood with a cane, but I knew from whispers on the street that it was one she used to hide a blade, not to aid her steps.

"Good evening." Mistress Augustine pointed to the chair in front of her desk. It had tiny blooms carved into the wood, rimmed in the thinnest coating of dust. "I was not expecting a visitor so late in the day."

"Apologies." I drew my arms under my skirts before I sat and crossed my ankles. It disturbed me how automatic it felt to act as I had been instructed after so many years outside of the kingdom. "His Highness implored me to make this one of my first stops when my husband and I moved into the house." I glanced westward as if I could see the House of Harvest through the stone and wood.

Mistress Augustine licked her lips as she eyed my ring. "Always a pleasure to make acquaintances, especially ones who come so well recommended." She lifted the royal seal on her desk. She hadn't even opened the letter to read my forgery.

“That reminds me.” I feigned a jump of surprise and reached for my bag. I pulled out a bottle of Elvish wine with a small bow of ribbon tied to the top. “His Highness pulled this out of the royal stores himself. For all your trouble.”

Mistress Augustine’s spotted hands gripped the neck of the bottle with surprising strength. “A drink to be split between new friends.” She stepped back around her desk and fished a corkscrew from the drawer.

She pointed at the cabinet behind her and Crison fetched three glasses.

Mistress Augustine poured the first two cups, but I placed my hand over the third. “I don’t think His Highness expected such fine wine to be shared with the *help*. I wouldn’t want to get anyone into trouble.” I glanced at Crison and her exposed ears. She folded her arms and shrugged, stepping back from the desk, but not leaving the room.

Mistress Augustine lowered her goblet. Her brown eyes suddenly sharp and watchful. She sat back down in her chair and took a small sip of the wine. “And what kind of trouble are *you* looking for?”

I watched as the mistress took another sip. “My husband’s tastes are more *exotic*, but for a man of his new status, it is prudent that we work only with someone discreet.”

Mistress Augustine’s eyes narrowed. I fought the urge to hold my breath under her scrutiny. I was the client. I held the purse. If Augustine was evaluating me, it was only to assess how deep my pockets were and nothing more.

I hoped.

She took another small sip. “I have the ability to serve such tastes and with enough discretion no one will breathe a word of it.”

“Excellent.” I raised my glass and feigned a sip as Mistress Augustine took a swig of the wine.

"Delicious," she said with a smile. But then her eyes widened. Her hand shook as it lifted to her throat. Her eyes turned red, threatening to burst. "What did you do?" she rasped as bloody bubbles fizzed from her throat.

Her head banged against the solid wood of her desk. She was dead.

It was painful, but quick. I reckoned she deserved worse.

Crison did not react at all. She merely stepped in front of her dead mistress to face me. "Did you want anything else?" Crison's brow lifted with her chin, nothing but pure defiance carved into her jaw. "Apart from killing my mistress?"

I stooped down to where Augustine lay face down on the desk, unmoving, and snapped her pendant from her neck. I pulled it off its thin gold chain and restrung the pendant onto a chain of my own. A chain imbued with Feron's magic.

"Whatever do you mean? Mistress Augustine is alive and well." I handed Crison the white bone pendant. "As long as you wear her face."

Crison blinked at the pendant in her palm. A thin line slowly appeared between her brows as she looked up at me. "You came from the Faeland."

I nodded.

Crison's fingers wrapped around the pendant. "But why?"

"Because I need access to the House of Harvest. And to get it I need Mistress Augustine's"—I waved my hands widely over Crison—"endorsement."

A hint of a smile tugged at Crison's lips. I knew I had picked the right one. "Access to what end?"

"To kill every lord in this city that has ever purchased a courtesan."

Crison's eye glanced toward the door. I knew she was thinking of the young girl who had climbed up the stairs with her pretty, red cheeks. "Halflings are not the only courtesans in Cereliath."

I stood and placed the glamour around Crison's neck, for a moment she transformed into the late Mistress Augustine before the glamor shattered for only me. "I said *courtesan*, and I meant it. When we are done, each one will have their freedom, Halfling and Mortal alike."

She let out a disbelieving breath. "Would they even know what to do with freedom?"

I raised a brow. "What would *you* do?"

Crison did not need a moment's thought. Her lips curved into a feline smirk, the perfect blend of beauty and danger. "Burn this godsforsaken city to the ground."